"Readers will relish this ~~n~~ ...
ger. . . . The unexpected is the norm in this urban fantasy."
                                        —Alternative Worlds

"Thurman has broken new ground, expanding the mythology of her world in new and ingenious ways, while offering new challenges to her heroes. . . . The finale of the story is perhaps the most emotionally moving bit of writing I've read this year . . . *Roadkill* is a great addition to the series and will delight Thurman's growing legions of fans."   —SFRevu

"A never-ending thrill-ride. . . . The characters are kick-ass, especially Cal, but there were certainly parts that had me tearing up. The plot was a blast to read, and I will definitely be reading the previous and future books featuring the Leandros brothers."   —Night Owl Reviews

"Thurman is a master at delivering raw emotion and uncompromising danger spiced with just the right touch of sarcastic humor. Unforgettable!"   —*Romantic Times*

"The Leandros brothers series is fully realized and highly detailed, *Roadkill* most of all (at least so far). Each successive book shows growth not just of the characters, but of the author. Her skills keep getting better. The stories keep getting better. You do yourself a disservice if you're not reading her. This is as good as an urban fantasy series can be. Buy it. Read it. I defy you not to love it."   —Horror-Web

Deathwish

"Fans of street-level urban fantasy will enjoy this new novel. . . . Thurman continues to deliver strong tales of dark urban fantasy."   —SFRevu

"The action is fast-paced and fascinating, and the plot twists are delicious."   —Errant Dreams Reviews

continued . . .

"A subtly warped world compellingly built by Thurman . . . This book has an absolutely marvelous voice in Cal's first-person narrative. The combination of Chandler-esque detective dialogue and a lyrically noir style of description are stunningly original. The reader's attention is captured and held from page one."   —Green Man Review

THE TRICKSTER NOVELS

Trick of the Light

"Rob Thurman's new series has all the great elements I've come to expect from this writer: an engaging protagonist, fast-paced adventure, a touch of sensuality, and a surprise twist that'll make you blink."
          —*New York Times* bestselling author Charlaine Harris

"A beautiful, wild ride, a story with tremendous heart. A must-read."
          —*New York Times* bestselling author Marjorie M. Liu

"A terrific premise. It's got Vegas, angels, demons, and a hunt for a mysterious artifact that by comparison makes Indiana Jones look like he was grubbing in the dirt for Precious Moments kitsch. If I had only three words to describe this book? They'd be: Best. Twist. Ever."
          —*New York Times* bestselling author Lynn Viehl

"Thurman weaves an amazingly suspenseful tale that will have readers so thoroughly enthralled from the first page that they'll be unwilling to set it down. *Trick of the Light* is meticulously plotted, completely fresh, and one of the best books I've had the pleasure of reading. Readers are in for a wonderful treat!"   —Darque Reviews

"[An] inventive new series . . . Trixa comes off as a strong-willed heroine with a long-standing ax to grind, yet that is only one facet of her character. The plot is suitably complex with enough clue-dropping along the way to point attentive readers toward Trixa's true nature while still packing plenty of surprises."   —Monsters and Critics

Blackout

A Cal Leandros Novel

Rob Thurman

A ROC BOOK

ROC

Published by New American Library, a division of
Penguin Group (USA) Inc., 375 Hudson Street,
New York, New York 10014, USA
Penguin Group (Canada), 90 Eglinton Avenue East, Suite 700, Toronto,
Ontario M4P 2Y3, Canada (a division of Pearson Penguin Canada Inc.)
Penguin Books Ltd., 80 Strand, London WC2R 0RL, England
Penguin Ireland, 25 St. Stephen's Green, Dublin 2,
Ireland (a division of Penguin Books Ltd.)
Penguin Group (Australia), 250 Camberwell Road, Camberwell, Victoria 3124,
Australia (a division of Pearson Australia Group Pty. Ltd.)
Penguin Books India Pvt. Ltd., 11 Community Centre, Panchsheel Park,
New Delhi - 110 017, India
Penguin Group (NZ), 67 Apollo Drive, Rosedale, North Shore 0632,
New Zealand (a division of Pearson New Zealand Ltd.)
Penguin Books (South Africa) (Pty.) Ltd., 24 Sturdee Avenue,
Rosebank, Johannesburg 2196, South Africa

Penguin Books Ltd., Registered Offices:
80 Strand, London WC2R 0RL, England

First published by Roc, an imprint of New American Library,
a division of Penguin Group (USA) Inc.

First Printing, March 2011
10 9 8 7 6 5 4 3 2 1

To Dakota: my own werewolf superhero.

Where the sun always shines, the grass is always green,
and the rabbits are always slow. . . .

Wait for me there.

ACKNOWLEDGMENTS

Heartfelt appreciation to my mom for being my unpaid indentured assistant since her retirement. Thanks to J. F. Lewis for letting me borrow Fang, the flesh-eating convertible Mustang. Where can I get one?? Thanks to Kaysha and Jesse for all the computer/art assistance they provided a technologically inept writer. You earned your requested mention in this book, although it's not often someone requests being killed by Cal. As always, a nod to my guy in the FBI, Jeff Thurman (no relation unfortunately). Kudos to my best friend, Shannon, for keeping me sane, fed, and led to the correct locations at conventions. To Linda and Richard for being invaluable medical and friendship resources. Continued good wishes to Michael and Sara, Ariel (just for being generally wonderful), all my fans (also doing their best to keep me fed), my editor, Anne Sowards, agent, Lucienne Diver, and the infallible, unbelievably efficient, incredibly hardworking Kat Sherbo. Without her, I would be lost—lost and pretty damn cranky.

"In silent unspeakable memories."
—George Eliot (1859)

"Truth is beautiful, without doubt; but so are lies."
—Ralph Waldo Emerson (1835)

And finally:
"Two roads diverged in a wood, and I—
I took the one less traveled by . . . "
—Robert Frost (1916)

". . . and it's been a bitch and a half."
—Caliban Leandros (current day)

1

I was a killer. I woke up knowing that before I knew anything else.

There was a moment between sleeping and waking where I swung lazily. The dark was my hammock, moving back and forth. One way was a deeper darkness, a longer sleep. But there was more than darkness there. There were trees past the black, hundreds and thousands of trees.

And an ocean blue as a crayon fresh from a brandnew box. A ship rode on its waves with sails as white as a seagull's wings and flying a flag as black as the seabird's eyes.

There were fierce dark-eyed princesses named after lilies.

Waterfalls that fell forever.

Flying.

Tree houses.

It was a place where no one could find you. A safe place. Of all of it, vibrant and amazing, the one thing I wanted to sink my fingers into and hang on to for my life was that last—a safe place.

Sanctuary.

But all that disappeared when I swung the other

way, where there were sibilant whispers, an unpleasant clicking, insectile and ominous, and a cold, bone
deep and embedded in every part of me. If I'd had a
choice, I would've gone with sleep, safe in the trees. Who
wouldn't? But I didn't have that warm and comforting
option. Instead, I was slapped in the face with icy water.
That did the trick of swinging me hard in the wrong direction and keeping me there. I opened my eyes, blinked
several times, and licked the taste of salt from my lips. It
was still dark, but not nearly as dark as when my eyes
had been shut. There was a scattering of stars overhead
and a bright full moon. The white light reflected as shattered shards in the water washing up over my legs and
up to my chest. It looked like splinters of ice. It felt cold
enough to be. There was the smell of seaweed and dead
fish in the air. More seaweed was tangled around my
hand when I lifted it, the same hand that held a gun—a
big gun.

A priest, a rabbi, and a killer walk into a bar. . . .

A killer woke up on that beach, and that killer was
me. How did I know that? It wasn't difficult. I slowly
propped myself up on my elbows, my hand refusing to
drop the gun it held, and took a look around to see a
stretch of water and sand littered with bodies—bodies
with bullet holes in them. The gun in my hand was
lighter than it should've been. That meant an empty
clip. It didn't take an Einstein to work out that calcula-
tion. The fact that the bodies weren't my first concern—
pissing and food actually were, in that order—helped
too. Killers have different priorities.

I could piss here. I wasn't a frigging Rodeo Drive
princess. There were only the night, the ocean, and me.
I could whip it out and let fly. But food? Where would I
get the food? Where was the nearest restaurant or take-
out place? Where was I? Because this wasn't right. This

wasn't home. I dragged my feet up through the wet sand, bent my knees, and pushed up to stagger to my feet to get my bearings. I might be lost. I *felt* lost, but I needed only to look closer, to recognize some landmarks, and I'd be fine. But I didn't. I didn't recognize shit. I had no idea where I was and I was not fine.

I was the farthest from fine as those bodies on the sand were.

That was when the killer realized something: I knew *what* I was all right, but I didn't have a goddamn idea who.

I reached for me and I wasn't there. I took a step into my own head and fell. There was nothing there to hold me up. There was no home and there was no me. Nothing to grab or ground me—no memories, only one big gaping hole filled with a cliché. And that—being a cliché? It bothered me more than the killer part. That part I took so much in stride that I'd automatically used my free hand to start dragging the bodies farther out into the water where they'd be carried away—out of sight, out of mind. The killer in me needed no direction. It knew it wasn't Joe Average, law-abiding citizen. It knew it couldn't be caught with bodies—and definitely not these bodies.

They weren't human.

There were monsters in the world, and that didn't surprise the killer or the cliché in me one damn bit either. They both knew why I carried that gun. Monsters weren't very fucking nice.

I looked down at the one I was currently dragging through the surf. It looked like an ape crossed with a spider—not a good look for anyone. It weighed a ton, was hairy with several eyes on a flattened skull, and a thick tangle of legs sprouting below—six to eight at least. The mouth was simian, but there were no teeth.

Instead, there were two sets of mandibles, upper and lower. Both were dripping with something other than water, something thicker. At the sight, the base of my neck began to throb with red spikes of pain flaring behind my eyelids each time I blinked. I released Harry—Hairy, Harry, close enough—into the waist-deep water I'd pulled it into and swiped my hand at the nape of my neck. I felt two puncture marks about three inches apart, then held my hand up to the moon. There was blood, not much, and a clear viscous fluid on my palm. It looked like good old dead Harry had gotten one in me before I'd gotten one in him.

The venom couldn't be too poisonous. I was alive and, aside from my neck hurting and a massive headache from Hell, I wasn't too impaired. I went on to prove it by wiping my hand on my jeans and going back for Harry's friends. Larry, Barry, and Gary—monsters I took in stride as much as I did the moon up in the sky. They were just part of the world. I'd forgotten myself, but the world didn't go that easily. The world I did know, it seemed, so I kept doing what kept you alive in this particular world. I towed all the bodies out into the freezing water—Christ, it couldn't have been more than fifty degrees—and sent them on their way. So long, farewell, auf Wiedersehen . . .

Good-bye.

I didn't wave.

When it was done, I slogged back to the beach and stood, shivering hard from the cold. I watched as the last body disappeared past the distant moon-spangled waves—they were nice, those waves. Scenic, too much so for monsters. After they were gone, I spun around slowly, taking in every foot, every inch of the beach, and the empty dunes behind me with suspicion. Seeing nothing moving besides me, I holstered the gun . . . in a shoulder holster my hand knew very well was there. As I did, my skin brushed more metal. I pulled my jacket open wide to see three knives strapped to the inside, right and left, six total. I felt an itch and weight around my ankle, but I didn't bother to check for what kind of death-dealing device it was.

A priest, a rabbi, and a killer walk into a bar. . . . No.

Four monsters and a killer walk into a bar. . . . That wasn't right either.

A killer wakes up on a beach. . . . The monsters don't wake up at all.

I was wearing a leather jacket, sodden and ruined. Something was weighing down the right pocket more heavily than the left. I put my hand in and closed it around something oval shaped. I was vaguely hoping it was a wayward clam that had climbed in while I was snoozing in the tide. That hope choked and fell, dead as the floating monsters. In the moonlight, I'd opened my fingers to see a grenade resting against my palm. There was a cheerful yellow smiley face on the side. The hand-painted, slightly sloppy circle smirked at me.

Have a nice day!

I looked up at the sky, the beaming moon, and said my first words, the first words I could remember anyway. Baby's first words in his brand-new life.

"What the *fuck*?"

A killer walked into a motel. Okay, that was getting old fast. *I* walked into the motel, still damp, but at least I wasn't sloshing with every step anymore. It had been a twenty-minute walk from that beach. There had been houses that were closer, but they weren't vacation houses abandoned in cold weather. People were living in them, which meant I couldn't break in, my first instinct, and squat long enough to get dry and—shit—get dry. I wasn't ready to think beyond that point right now. There were other things that needed to be done. Important things, and while they gnawed at me with tiny sharp teeth to do them, they weren't willing to say what exactly they were. Do. Go. Run. Hide. Tell. But there was no "what" for the "do," no "where" for the "go" or the "run," and no "who" for the "tell."

It was a thousand itches that couldn't be scratched. Annoying didn't begin to cover a fraction of how it felt. It did cover the no-tell motel clerk, however. Annoying covered him hunky-frigging-dory. Wide nose, big ears, enough acne to say puberty was going to last through his nineties, and frizzy blond hair that wanted to be long but ended up being wide instead. He was reading a porn mag with a hand covering his mouth and a finger jammed halfway up one nostril. That wasn't where your hand should be when looking at porn, but whatever. How he got his rocks off was the least of my concerns.

"Room," I said, slapping down four ten-dollar bills on the countertop. Fresh from a wet wallet, which was equally fresh from my wet jeans, the money quickly made a puddle around itself.

The finger descended from its perch and idly poked at the bills. "They're wet."

True that and not requiring a comment. "Room," I repeated. "Now."

He looked past me at the door. "I didn't hear you come in. How come I didn't hear you come in? We got a bell."

Correction—they had a bell. Bells made noise and noise wasn't good. Any cat sneaking around in the shadows would tell you that. It'd probably also tell you talking to a booger-picking brick wall was pointless. I reached past the clerk and grabbed a key hanging on the wall. Lucky number thirteen. I turned and walked back toward the door.

"ID," the guy called after me. "Hey, dude, I need some ID."

I gave him an extra ten. It was all the ID he needed. Zit cream is pretty cheap at any local drugstore, and he forgot about the ID. But it was the first thing on my mind when I opened the warped wooden door to room thirteen, walked through chips of peeling paint that had fallen on the cracked asphalt of the small parking lot, and went into my new home. Hell, it was the only home I'd known as of this moment as far as my brain cells were concerned. I pulled the blinds shut, flipped the light on the table beside the bed, and opened the wallet. The clerk might not need it, but ID would be helpful as shit to me right now. Let's see what we had.

No, not we. There was no we.... I had to see what I had. Because it was me, only me. And I didn't know my life was any different from that. The clerk hadn't considered me too social, and I didn't feel especially social, friendly, or full of love for my fellow fucking man. I had a sliver of feeling that it wasn't entirely due to my current situation. If you forgot who you were, were you still who you were? I didn't know, but I thought it might be safe to say that I usually didn't have an entourage of partying friends in tow.

Other than the monsters, the abominations, from the beach.

So ... time to see who exactly the nonexistent entourage wasn't swarming around.

I pulled out the driver's license from the worn black wallet and scanned it. New York City. 355 Aviles Street. I was ... Well, shit, I didn't know what year it was exactly, so I didn't know how old I was, but the picture that I checked against my reflection in the cracked mir-

ror on the bureau across the room looked right. Early
twenties probably. Black hair, gray eyes, flatly opaque
expression—it would've been a mug shot through and
through if there hadn't been the tiniest curl to his . . . my
mouth. One that said, *I have a boot and I'm just looking
for an ass to put it up.* Okay, social was out the window.
I focused on the important thing—my name, clearly and
boldly printed beside the picture. My identity. Me.

"Calvin F. Krueger," I said aloud. "Fuck me."

Calvin? A monster-killing, walking goddamn armory
with an attitude so bad, even the DMV captured it on
film, and my name was *Calvin*?

Maybe the middle initial led to something more ac-
ceptable. F. Frank, Fred, Ferdi-fucking-nand. Shit. I laid
the license aside and went back to the wallet. There
was nothing. Yeah, a big wad of soaking cash, but no
credit card, no ATM card, no video card. Nothing. I had
the minimum ID required by law and that was it. That
smelled as fishy as I did. I was going to have to get out
of these clothes soon and wash them in the bathtub, or
the reek of low tide would never come out of them. And
right now they were the only clothes I had.

After spreading out the cash on the nightstand to dry,
I tried to wring out the wallet. It was worn and cracked,
on its last legs anyway, and I kicked those last legs out
from under it. It split along the side seam and out spilled
two more licenses. I picked them up from the frayed carpet to see the same picture, same address, and two different names. Calvert M. Myers and Calhoun J. Voorhees.
That I had aliases didn't bother me—I killed monsters,
so what was a fake name?—but the aliases themselves
did. How much did I hate myself?

Calvin F. Krueger, Calvert M. Myers, Calhoun J.
Voorhees. Seriously, *Calhoun*?

Then it hit me. F. Krueger, M. Myers, J. Voorhees.

Freddy Krueger, Michael Myers, and Jason Voorhees. Three monster-movie villains, and I, a monster killer, was carting around their names on my ID. Didn't I have one helluva sense of humor? I thought about the grenade I'd tossed into the ocean, that cheerful yellow smile on a potentially lethal explosion. A dark sense of humor, I amended to myself, but, hey, wasn't that better than none at all?

The rank smell hovering around me and my clothes was getting worse. The stink was incredible. Good sense of humor, good sense of smell, and neither one was doing anything productive for me right now. I left the ID and the money on the table and went to the bathroom. I toed off black leather boots that were scarred and worn, like the wallet. They'd been used hard. Well-worn, they would've been comfortable if they weren't wet and full of sand. How they'd gotten worn, what crap they'd stomped through, I didn't know. I dumped them in the tub that had once been white but was now a dull, aged yellow. It had been used hard too. I related. I felt that way myself—used hard and put up wet. I threw in my jeans, T-shirt, underwear, and even the leather jacket once I removed the knives.

As I did, a small bubble of panic began to rise. I couldn't remember. I couldn't remember a goddamn thing about myself. I didn't remember putting those weapons in my jacket, although I knew exactly what they were for. Knives and guns and monsters; they were the things I was certain of, but when it came to me, I was certain of absolutely nothing.

Shit. *Shit*. Okay, I obviously knew how to stay alive; those monsters on the beach didn't just kill themselves. People who knew how to stay alive also knew not to panic and I was *not* panicking. By God, I wasn't. I was sucking it up and moving on. I was surviving. With or without my memory, at least I seemed to be good at that. Calvin the survivor; watch me in action. I was alive to mock my fake names, and I planned on staying that way.

Turning on the shower, I waited until the water was lukewarm and I stood on top of the clothes. There were two small bottles of shampoo and an equally small bar of soap. I used them all, letting the lather run off me onto the cotton and leather around and under my feet.

I learned something about myself while scrubbing up. I killed monsters, and they tried to kill me back with a great deal of enthusiasm, but not just them. I had a scar from a bullet on my chest, another from what was probably a knife on my abdomen, and a fist-sized doozy on the other side of my chest. It looked as if something had taken a bite out of me and had been motivated when doing it. Man and monster; apparently they both disliked me or I them—could be a mutual feeling. It was just one more thing I didn't know. I moved on to something I did know. Besides the scars, I was a little pale, but that could be from near hypothermia or I could be anemic. Maybe iron supplements were the answer to all my questions—iron and bigger, badder guns.

I had a tattoo around my upper arm, a band of black and red with something written in Latin woven in it. Funny how I knew it was Latin, but I didn't know what it said. Yeah, funny, I thought, despite the lurch of loss in my stomach. There was my sense of humor again.

The rest of me was standard issue. I wasn't a porn star, too bad, but I had proof of a Y chromosome. That was all a guy needed. That and some memories. Were a dick and a mind too much to ask for? That was something every guy had to ask himself at some point, even if I couldn't remember the first time I'd asked it. This time the question bounced back and forth inside my skull, hitting nothing on its way. I guessed that proved it was too much . . . at least for now.

My head still hurt and trying to remember made it worse. I gave up, closed my eyes, and scrubbed at my hair. I shook from the lingering cold of the ocean, but the warm water helped. It didn't do the same for my damn hair, though. It had been in a ponytail, shoulder length. I'd pulled the tie free, but there was something in it . . . sticky and stubborn as gum or tar. It could be the blood of one of those supernatural spider monkeys from Hell. It could actually be gum. Maybe I fought bubble-gum-smacking preteens from Hell too. I didn't know and it didn't matter. You didn't have to know the question to be the solution.

The answer ended up being one of those knives I'd taken out of the jacket. The shit wouldn't come out of my hair for love or money, and I finally stood naked in front of the cloudy bathroom mirror, took a handful of my hair, and sawed through it. I let the clump, matted together with a green-gray crap, fall into the sink. The remaining wet hair fell raggedly about two inches past my jaw. I didn't try to even it up with the blade, slender and sharp as it was. I could have, some at least, but . . .

I turned away from the mirror.

Looking at my picture was okay; not recognizing myself less okay; studying myself in the mirror, not okay at all. I didn't like it. I didn't know why, but I didn't. A quick glance was fine, a long look was a trip someplace and, from the acid sloshing around my stomach, that place wasn't Wonderland. I had guns and knives, scars, and dead things; maybe I wasn't a nice guy. If I didn't like looking in the mirror, it could be I didn't like what I saw. Pictures were only echoes. The guy in the mirror was real.

But it didn't matter why I didn't like it, because I

didn't have to look. Problem solved. I spent the next fifteen minutes drying off and doing my best to hand-wash the funk out of my clothes before draping them over the shower rod to dry. By then I was weaving, had the next best thing to double-vision, and a wet towel in my hand that I used to cover up the bureau mirror. I didn't ask myself why. I was only half conscious and barely made it to the bed anyway. So to hell with whys. I pulled the stale, musty-smelling covers over me with one hand and slapped the lamp off the table to crash to the floor. I was too clumsy with exhaustion to switch it off. This worked the same. The bulb shattered with a pop and it was lights-out.

I didn't think about it then, but the next day I did, when I had more than pain and drowsiness rolling around in my head. I'd woken up with monsters. I was alone, and I was lost. I didn't know where I was; I didn't know who I was. It doesn't get more lost than that. Wouldn't you leave a light on? Knowing what I knew and not knowing anything else at all, why would I want the darkness where monsters hide?

Because killers hide there too.

2

Phone.

That was my first thought when I woke up. The second was that I was glad I was in a bed and not sleeping, too damn literally, with the fishes. The third, nope, still no clue who I was. Fourth ... Fourth was a situation a lot of guys faced in the morning. I dealt with it, which, considering I couldn't remember the faces or details of any woman I knew personally from my past, was pretty noteworthy. Unless I was on speaking terms with Angelina Jolie and then that was more than noteworthy. Either way, I worked with what I had.

Nothing keeps a good man down, but you can get him down for a while if you work at it.

Afterward I stared at the ceiling, as yellowed and cracked as the tub, and went back to my first thought. Where was my phone? I had ID, even if it was fake. I had money. I should've had a phone. Hell, three-year-olds had cell phones these days—whatever days these were. There was a bright spot. I was a little fuzzy on the year, absolutely blank on me, but everything else appeared to be in place in my gray matter. Sun in the sky, bacon in the skillet, and a cell phone for everyone past the first stage of mitosis.

So . . . where the hell was my phone? That could tell me a whole damn sight more than fake licenses. The names were fake, the address was fake . . . common sense. You didn't put a real address on a falsified ID. But a phone would have the numbers of people I'd called. Or, on the other hand, it might just have numbers of AA, Guns-R-Us, and a dating service, because where do you find the time to meet women when you're gutting the spawn of evil for profit or simply as one rocking hobby?

I needed that damn phone.

Rolling out of bed, I padded into the bathroom, hoping I'd overlooked it when I'd been stripping my clothes of six knives, two guns, and something that resembled brass knuckles without finger holes but with spikes—a Tekko. It was Japanese and old, but it worked just fine despite its age. My own name I didn't know, but that I knew. There were extra clips of ammunition and all six knives were different types with different names and functions. I knew those too. Good old Calvin F. Krueger knew that, but fuck all about himself.

Frustrating.

I poked through the clothes, now dry except for the jacket. The lining was still damp, but they all smelled like soap and not dead squid. Score one for amnesia boy. But nowhere in the clothes or the pile of weapons was there a phone. Take one away from amnesia boy. I must've lost it at the beach and, just as the tide had taken the spider creatures, it had no doubt taken the phone as well. Nature, what a bitch.

Okay. I'd do this the hard way, although, considering where I'd ended up and with what, the easy way didn't seem my style. I fingered the puncture wounds on my neck. They'd scabbed over nicely and my headache was gone. That was something. I dressed in the wrinkled long-sleeve black T-shirt. I noticed only now that it said

EAT ME in dark red letters on the front, and, below that, in parentheses, *before i eat you*. A stash of weapons a gang-banger would drool over, monsters trying to kill me, and a shirt that advertised my dickitude to the world. I was turning out to be one subtle guy.

I finished dressing, down to the roach-stomping boots that didn't fit quite the same after their double-dipping. I dumped the jacket on the one wobbly chair, shoved the destroyed lamp under the bed to mope with the dust bunnies, and sat while I studied the phone book from the drawer of the bedside table. It was about as thick as a comic book. Wherever I was, it wasn't anyplace big enough that I could disappear into an anonymous mass of people. In places this small, anyone who lived here would know you didn't belong. And if anyone came looking for you, they'd be quick to point you out.

Nobody trusted a *gadje*, I thought absently as I scanned the cover. Ocean waves, a lighthouse, and a breezy script that read *Nevah's Landing, South Carolina*. Good for Nevah, whoever she was. She had her own landing. Now let's see if she had anything else to offer.

Crocodile. They had a crocodile, ticking like a time bomb.

An albino one, pale as a dead soul, with a voice of broken glass and red eyes that saw you, no matter how deep the water.

And it knew my name.

I blinked and dropped the phone book back in the drawer. I didn't know my name and I was pretty sure a sun-loving, tourist-eating lizard didn't either. Amnesia was one thing. Small bursts of psychosis were another. I didn't even know if there were crocodiles or alligators in South Carolina. I suspected that wasn't amnesia, but more like ignorance. I didn't mind. I'd take ignorance over the first any day. The ignorant can learn . . . theoretically. I wasn't sure there was anything I could do to get my memories back or why they were gone in the first place. My head had been killing me last night, but I hadn't found any bumps or contusions—only the remnants of a bloody nose. I didn't think I'd hit my head, although a spider might've smacked me a good one in the face. As for being bitten, why would that give you amnesia? Kill you or paralyze you, that I could see. Again, nature is a bitch and an efficient one. Paralyzing your enemy is good stuff. Making him forget who he is will only freak him out all the more and possibly make him run even faster, if he's the running type. What else could cause amnesia? There was emotional trauma. . . .

I tilted my head down and read my T-shirt slogan again. It was likely I dished out more emotional trauma than I took in. As a matter of fact . . . I took off the shirt, turned it inside out, and put it back on. If I had to mingle with the locals—and I didn't see much way around it, since someone had to know me or have seen me come into town—then I'd better be on my best behavior. Which meant instead of carrying arms, I'd have to make do with charm. Places this small had little law enforcement, but what they did have tended to be bored law enforcement. I didn't need a retired city cop working as sheriff in his spare time taking one look at me and knowing I was carrying just by the way my jacket fit.

That meant I ended up hiding all the weapons under the mattress. The day this roach motel flipped those suckers, I wouldn't have to worry about being found out. I'd be eating snow cones in Hell with Satan. It made sense. It also made sense if I could handle what I had on the beach last night, I could deal with any normal townie. I was human like them, not a spider knit from shadows and death, but I was also a human who had the

skills to use knives in addition to guns. Chances were I
had enough of a different set of skills to take someone
down unarmed as well or use what was at hand. I could
impale a nosy son of a bitch on a Norman Rockwell
picket fence if I had to. MacGyver had nothing on me.

Not that I would impale a person. A monster spider
from Hell, yes—a person, no. I had faith that a spirited
debate between my foot and their ass would get the job
done for most people. I was a killer, but I wasn't that
kind of killer.

Was I?

No. I wasn't. I hadn't been as sure of that last night,
but I was pretty sure now.

Although . . . I frowned down at the letters I could no
longer see—EAT ME. Thoughts of impaling and kicking
ass before I even left the motel room—I hoped anyone
I ran across got my particular sense of humor, because it
might be an acquired taste.

Leaving the room was harder than I thought it'd be.
I knew browsing through the phone book wasn't going to help me. I had to get out of the yellow pages and
into Nevah's Landing for real if I hoped to accomplish
anything. But the room was the only haven I had; the
only port in a memory-gobbling sea. That had me duck-
ing my head as I walked out into the gray morning. The
desire to twitch came from leaving the weapons. I didn't
want to. No matter what my brain said, my gut said it
was wrong in all the ways there were to be wrong. From
the fit my stomach was pitching, there were a whole lot
of fucking ways.

I went with my head. As far as I knew, there were
only people out there, not monsters. Be smart. Be smart
and then you'd have less cause to be psychotically homicidal or rashly suicidal. It was good advice, and damn
firmly ingrained, so I followed it. And if I twitched once

or twice, I told myself it was low blood sugar and let's get some food already. More good advice, and I was on my way to follow it when I encountered the first local. I'd left the motel, set among scrubby grass and a cracked asphalt parking lot, and started down the street. Begonia Avenue. There were two stores past the motel, an antique store and a junk store masquerading as an antique store. Both were closed. Across the street with the occasional car parked on it was a drugstore, closed, and a clothing store with lots of fancy sweaters in the window, also closed. All that meant that it was Sunday morning in a town so small that if it had ten streets, I would kiss . . . someone's ass. Whoever's. Right now the only person I knew was the porn-loving, walking zit party of a motel clerk.

I wasn't kissing that ass. If the town had ten streets, I'd be surprised. I was currently being unsurprised when I turned off Begonia to Magnolia and met the second person of my brand-new, blank-slate life. A black guy was leaning with arms folded in the doorway of the only business I'd seen open so far. It was a barbershop, which was more useful than antiques or sweaters on the Sabbath. People had to look nice when they went to church, neat hair and dress clothes—no sweaters, and the place probably already had all the chairs it needed. No antique ones necessary.

The man shook his head the second he spotted me. He was about forty, with dreads pulled back into a ponytail, a dark green button-down shirt, jeans, and a black barber's smock. "Mmm, damn." He clucked his tongue in disgust. "Boy, you cannot walk around looking like that. Let me even it up for you."

I ran a hand through my DIY haircut and shrugged. "Nah, that's okay. I'm fine with it." It was the one thing I was fine with. When you'd lost most of your mind, you didn't worry about your lack of style offending the local hair-care professional.

"Come on," he said with obvious good nature. You automatically had to suspect anyone that upbeat. It was unnatural. That opinion definitely cemented the conclusion that I didn't live in a small town. "I'll do it for free."

"Free? Why?" I regarded him with even more suspicion, the same level I'd given the deserted beach last night. That seemed to be a current theme for me.

"Because hair is my life, and I don't want to live with you walking around looking like that," he replied, straightening and opening the door to his shop. "You look like something's been gnawing on your head."

It wasn't like I could say for certain that he wasn't right about that. I had the bite on my neck. Who was to say one of those things hadn't tried to swallow my head whole? And if I looked so bad that a guy was willing to give me a free cut, then that meant I would stick out even more than I already did in this four-way-stop, churchgoing, roll-the-sidewalks-up-on-Sunday town. I hesitated for another second before going on into the shop. I'd wanted to find out if anyone knew me anyway. If anyone had seen me come into town before the beach. If I'd said anything to anyone. This wasn't home; I'd known that before ... not from memory, but from the fact that it wasn't a good place to hide. Hiding was important. Always. That was a "sky is blue" fact. The memory of why was gone, but the tendencies it caused weren't. It was an instinct as basic as you're hungry, you eat; you're tired, you sleep; you're out in the open, you run. You hide.

But I was also thinking about ghost white crocodiles. I reminded myself to take it all with a big grain of salt to go with the little bit of crazy.

It was in my best interest to accept the offer, I reminded myself, and I cautiously followed him into the shop. I sat in the one chair he had. There was a tile floor gleaming and empty of a single hair and one big-ass utilitarian rectangular mirror on the wall. I avoided its clear-water shimmer and waited while the smock was shaken over me and tied around my neck. I needed a good question to ask. *So . . . you know me?* wasn't the most subtle. *You know you have, okay,* had *a monster epidemic on your beach?* wasn't any better, and I already knew the answer to that.

He didn't know. I knew, yeah, but I knew it in a way you knew a secret—one that was dark and wrong. When that kind of secret lived in you, then you could just look at someone and know if they were part of the club or not. This guy wasn't. His nights were just nights. The glitter of lights outside his window were only fireflies in the dark, not the greedy eyes of a predator. He'd never know how lucky he was. Hopefully. I wouldn't tell him. He was giving me a free haircut. I wasn't going to ruin his life with the truth. That was no kind of tip.

"Um . . . ," I started. Shockingly articulate, but still without a viable question, I was prepared to wing it. It turned out I didn't have to.

"I'm Llewellyn." Fingers tunneled ruthlessly through my hair. "Jumped-up Jesus, look at this mess. Sorry, Lord, but take a look down this way and you'll forgive the blasphemy." A squirt bottle was snagged and it was as if a cloud dumped its contents on my hair, soaking it in five efficient pumps. "I know, Llewellyn. It's Welsh. Do I look Welsh to you? Black Irish maybe." He grinned as scissors began flashing past my ears with startling speed, making it a damn good thing on my part I'd left my weapons back in the room or instinct would've left me with more uneven hair and a dead barber on the floor.

Unaware of my inner defensive instinct, he kept talking. "Most people around here call me Lew. But you're not from around here. We don't get much in the way of tourists in the off-season. It's as cold and miserable here as most places in February. We ain't Miami. But as pasty as you are—and sorry, man, but you're like Cool Whip— you're no sun lover. So I guess any time on the beach is a good time for you. And, like our tourist bureau would tell you, cold water, wet sand, and all the sweaters you can fit in a suitcase. Nevah's Landing's got it all. Live it up."

The scissors kept snipping and I kept trying not to flinch when he laid his first question on me. "So, what's your name? Where you from? Besides someplace where people don't give a shit about their hair."

Since he had answered my one unspoken question, *Do you know me, have you seen me around before?* I owed him . . . nothing—not a damn thing. This was my life. I couldn't afford a misstep. But it didn't matter, because what I gave him was nothing anyway. "Cal . . . ," I said, glumly starting to supply one of my fake names, but I became stuck on which was the least offensive, the least god-awful. And I was stumped. Calvin, Calvert, Calhoun—what a trifecta of bad choices.

It didn't come to that. Lew, the friendly barber, made the choice for me. "Good to meet you, Cal." A hand shoved my head forward and there was more metallic clicking. "What brings you to the Landing?"

Cal was better than the full version of any of my fake names and it might not have been a coincidence that they all began with Cal. If you were going to choose fake names, how much better would it be if you could genuinely answer to a fake name because part of it was true?

"Just roaming around," I answered easily. "I was taking care of my grandma, but she died last month. She

raised me." I shifted my shoulders in the most minute
of shrugs. I didn't want those scissors spearing me in the
scalp or neck. "She always told me I should travel when
she went. Find who I was besides her, hell, nurse, I guess.
See where I fit in. Not that she dragged me down. She
never did. She took me in when I had no one else and
made the best damn double-chocolate-chip cookies in
the world. But she wanted me to travel, and I'm traveling, looking for that place I fit in. It would've made her
happy."

It was the biggest load of bullshit ever, and I had
no problem spinning it as naturally—more naturally
than if it were true. And so much talking at one time
almost made my throat sore, but not only was it a massive amount of bullshit I'd so easily shoveled up, it was
absolutely perfect bullshit. Dead granny, all alone in the
world, I was practically a lost puppy. It covered a number of sins, such as looking ratty and homeless or being
a smart-ass. Poor widdle guy lost all the family he had
in the world. He's hurt, wounded, sad. Pat pat. Give him
a Milk-Bone. Monster killer, liar—I was beefing up my
résumé fast. I wondered if it was wrong to be proud of
talents like those.

Probably.

"And you think the Landing might be where you fit
in?" Lew asked dubiously. "That wouldn't have been my
first guess."

"Why?" I shot back. "Am I not good enough for your
sweater-loving town?"

He snorted. "Seriously, Cal, my friend, are you kidding? There's a shitload of crazy in little towns. Big cit-
ies can't hold a candle to us. And that's what I'd have
pegged you for—big city all the way." Lew and I agreed
there. "Dressing all in black. And your hair, again, Lord,
I'm sorry, but Jesus Christ himself lived two thousand

some years ago and he had a better conditioner than you. With hair that bad, you probably come from someplace where no one knows your name or cares enough to tell you to get thine ass to a barber. That smells like big city to me."

He didn't give me a chance to reply, to say I'd cut it myself, or to ask what the hell conditioner was. He towel-dried my hair vigorously, combed it again, and said, "There you go. Minimum fuss. I figure you're a minimum-fuss guy. Wash it, comb it, and you're done."

This time I risked the mirror to see hair that was now an inch above my jaw. No more ponytails for me. I dropped my gaze. Mirrors—I was never going to like them. As I moved my head, my hair flopped in my face like a frigging Labradoodle. No, they were curly, weren't they? Like a sheepdog, then. A pissed-off sheepdog. Damn annoying either way. "I'm glad you don't want money for this," I bitched.

"You look like a damn rock star." I could hear the wide grin in his voice without needing to see it. When I grunted, less than impressed, he added, "Okay, at least you don't look like a goth bum anymore. That's something." He whisked the cape off me. "By the way, if you want to try out small-town life, for your granny's sake, I know the diner is hiring. Tell them Lew sent you. Can't get a better reference there, and if you stick around and get paid on a regular basis, maybe you'll come back. I can always use the business, plus it'll do my soul good to know you're not walking around looking like a deranged mop. Do your granny up on high good to see it too."

I got up and the last thing I expected came out of my mouth. "The diner, huh?" Despite the inner need to move, to run, I had to look at this logically. Monster killing was either my job or my hobby or both. Whichever it was or not, without my memories, I didn't have a client list to go by.

It was a ridiculous thought. Getting paid to kill monsters. What crappy career fair steered you in that direction? Bottom line, the money I had wasn't going to last forever. If "Cal" didn't have a job, I'd soon be as homeless as my hair had labeled me. And this was where I'd woken up without most of my mind; this was the best place I could think of to look for it. My license's fake address was in New York City. Good luck walking the streets there and randomly running into a clue to my identity. Going against my visceral fight-or-flight reaction was my best option. I had to have gotten here somehow. Maybe I'd find my car. Maybe it would contain some real ID or would trigger my memories. Then again, maybe my badass monster-slaying self rode into town on a fucking scooter. Sticking around was the best thing to do, no matter how wrong it felt.

Brain over guts. Brain over guts. Unnatural, but that was what I was going to do.

Besides, no matter what my guts were clamoring about, there was something about the Landing. I couldn't put my finger on it and I definitely didn't belong, but there was something.... I sensed that it was waiting right around the corner, if only I could find the right corner. Something waiting. Something ... interesting.

Crazy thoughts for a crazy guy.

It turned out that the diner was two blocks away on Oleander. Besides loving their sweaters, they loved their flowers here too. Campy tourist Southern. The diner was the same on the outside. Flowers were painted on the plate-glass window.... Maybe they were oleanders— what did I know about flowers? Red-and-white awning, a welcome mat that actually said WELCOME, Y'ALL! No joke ... WELCOME, Y'ALL! I didn't step on it as I went through the door. It scared me worse than the dead monsters from the beach.

Inside it was the same. Red vinyl booths, desserts in a rotating pie case, little cow salt and pepper shakers on the table. It was homey and quaint, and anyone, with or without memories, could see this was not my kind of place. I started backing out the door before I was all the way through, but there was no escape.

"Lord, there you are. It's two blocks. Did you get yourself lost on the way?" She was either Llewellyn's older sister or aunt. She had the same face, same eyes, but not the same grin. She had no kind of smile showing, big or little. She was also about three times his size, but if you thought anything except "just more to love," I didn't think you'd live to regret it.

Moving over to me, she shook her head at my appearance. "I should've never answered the phone. That Lew and his damn strays. Three dogs, five cats, and now you."

"I'm not a stray," I objected immediately, although, technically, I was.

"Whatever you say," she replied dismissively, obviously not believing me and as obviously too busy to bother coddling my self-image. "I'm down to one employee. That trash waitress of mine ran off with the principal at the school, if you can believe that. And him married with three kids. Trash, trash, trash." She looked me up and down. "Lew said your name is Cal. He didn't say you'd be dressed like some sort of undertaker or vampire. Suppose that'll have all those silly girls hanging around—see if you sprout a fang. Like they never saw a real man before. Denzel, Clooney, now those are men. Mmm mmm." She shook her head again, this time probably wishing I was one of those real men. "Well, hardly matters. Might up the business some. All right, Cal, tell me, can you cook? And I mean really cook.

Sling it, dice it, and throw it on a plate, looking *and* tasting pretty?"

The question had me automatically checking for the nearest fire extinguisher. It could drive you nuts, your body remembering what your brain couldn't. But whoever was doing the telling, it let me know that me and a griddle went together like Frankenstein's monster and fire. "Not so much," I said.

"Fine. Then you can replace that home-wrecking waitress of mine." She pushed up against the counter, reached over, and returned with a red-and-white checkered apron that matched the napkins and the awning outside. That kind of pattern had a name, something that began with a *G*, but I couldn't remember it. I doubted it was amnesia, though, and figured it was more of a guy thing that was causing that particular failure. "Now put that on and be the best damn waitress you can be. Don't let Lew down."

Taking the apron with two reluctant fingers, I asked, "Don't you mean waiter? I'm a guy. Guys are waiters."

"Not in a diner, honey. We only have waitresses. That's part of our charm." She gave my arm a light pinch. "Now hustle, Vlad, and stop with the scowl. Smile. This is a happy dining establishment. Happy sells."

"You're telling me to wear this"—I held up the apron—"*and* smile?"

"No, sugar, I *know* you'll wear it and smile or you won't get one tip. And with what I pay, you're going to need those tips." She swatted my ass. "You can call me ma'am or Miss Terrwyn. I had the same crazy-ass parents as Lew, but, unlike him, I'm going to respect their wishes when it comes to my name. Now get that apron on and hustle. The church crowd will be here soon. And there isn't nothing like a good churching-up to give you an appetite." When I hesitated, she gave me another pinch. "Go! Hustle!"

I went.

I took off my jacket, put that apron on, and hoped that when I did get my memories back, I'd lose this one in the process. But I hustled, as told, and found out I wasn't a half-bad server—there wasn't any way I was going to say or think "waitress." I wouldn't win any contests, but I dropped only two plates and threw only one guy through the window, all while wearing a red-and-white apron with a goddamn ruffle on the bottom. All in all, I considered that pretty successful.

Or so I thought almost seven hours later as I stood watching the son of a bitch I'd tossed through the glass roll around in the short shrubs outside the window, moaning for an ambulance. Now that ... *that* had a smile on my face. He had it coming. He'd been leering at some teenage girls who were eating a whole lot of pie and giggling whenever I refilled their Cokes, which were actually Sprites, but I'd soon picked up that any kind of soda here was called Coke. It could be a Barney the Dinosaur–purple Grape Crush and it was still called a Coke. It was kind of intriguing, far more so than spider monsters, and that made me think Lew and my intuition were right. Either I'd been born a big-city guy or had lived long enough in a big city to have forgotten that backwater factoid. It also made me think what the hell kind of life did I lead that I found the Coke issue more interesting and exotic than monsters?

"You threw Luther Van Johnson through my window?" Miss Terrwyn's voice said at my shoulder; she wasn't much taller than that. "You threw that boy through my window? On your very first day?"

That boy weighed two-thirty easy, with the thirty being his gut. He was also at least forty. He'd been a full-grown man and full-grown pervert for a long time now.

I put the smile away and tried to look contrite. But since I barely knew what the word contrite meant and I in no way was feeling it, pulling that off wasn't easy. "He had it coming?" I tried, saying aloud the same excuse I'd given myself internally when I'd first considered tossing Luther's ass like a ball for a golden retriever. Of course I hadn't been at all difficult to convince, so that excuse might have been somewhat lacking. "Ma'am," I added hastily.

The high school girls, however, were quick to back me up. "He was looking at us and making these pervy gestures." One of the girls demonstrated, and it was indeed damn fucking pervy with two fingers and a tongue.

Miss Terrwyn had passed me to lean and look out what was left of the window at good old Luther, who'd stopped flopping around. "Good Lord, I can smell the whiskey on him from here. And, Rachel Kaysha Marie, you could've described that. You didn't have to show us. You girls should be home now anyway. Not sitting around eating pie and mooning over the help. He could be as perverted as Luther out there for all you know. Now get on home."

The girls went as ordered. One of them had red hair, curly, a cloud of it, bright as fire. I watched her until the door shut behind her. She looked almost familiar, but I couldn't pin the feeling down, so I let it go as I moved my eyes back to those of my new boss. "You aren't, are you?" she demanded. "A pervert? With lust in your heart and nothing in your soul but wicked desire, because I have a butcher's knife behind the counter that'll do just the trick if you are. We don't serve that kind of sausage here, no sir. Well? Are you?"

Pervert, lust, wicked desire. None of that rang a

bell . . . Eh, maybe lust. But appropriate lust for the appropriate age group. "No, ma'am," I replied, and began to bus the table of the pie plates and glasses the girls had left behind. "No butcher knife needed, ma'am."

"Good. You keep it that way. I have no tolerance for the wicked. Like Luther. If I hadn't been in back making sure Joseph didn't set all the food afire, I never would've let that man sit down in my diner." She took another look at him and sighed. "I have to say, it needed doing. But the door is only about fifteen feet away and windows cost."

That made sense. Windows did cost, but throwing someone out a door just didn't have the same bang for your buck. But she was my boss and I wanted to fit in here temporarily to find out where I actually fit in when it came to the world. Keeping my boss happy would help me out. I dropped my towel on the table, moved to Luther's former booth, and stepped over that metal frame that had held the glass. Landing in the bushes with my victim, I took Luther's wallet out of his pocket and stripped it of money.

"He still alive?" Miss Terrwyn demanded.

"Yeah. I mean, yes, ma'am. You want me to change that for you?" I wasn't serious—entirely.

"You have a mouth on you, don't you? I was thinking you were the quiet sort, but maybe I was only thinking you *should* be the quiet sort," she warned.

I handed her the money. "Here. That should cover the window. And I'll take it under advisement, ma'am."

"You do that. Now get back inside while I call the sheriff. We'll say perverted old Luther there was so drunk, and on the Lord's day too, the heathen, that he fell through the window. He's so liquored up, he won't remember if it's the truth or not. Maybe this time they'll lock him up for a while like he deserves."

She stashed the money away in her own red-and-white apron, then clapped her hands. "Well, come on. We've got to close the place up for the night and board up the window. You playing Superman doesn't change that. Hurry. Hurry."

That was the beginning of the end of my first day working at the Oleander Diner, the Ole Diner, as everyone who came in called it. I'd worked my ass off, was paid a little better than nothing plus tips, and not one person had recognized me. Or if they had, they hadn't mentioned it to me.

I had seen one guy walk by outside. I just caught a glimpse of ginger hair and a rangy male frame through the window before he disappeared from sight. He seemed familiar, but not the kind of familiar where you think you know a person. It was more the kind of familiar of recognizing one snake as being poisonous and one as being not. If he was a snake, I'd say he was dead-on poisonous. But that was a weird, freaky thought, so I shrugged and did what I was starting to get good at—I let it go.

Miss Terrwyn caught me watching. "Pshhh. Jesse. Ignore that one. He slinks into town once a week to buy raw meat. He must have some mighty big, hungry dogs, but he's like Luther. He doesn't smell righteous."

I wasn't surprised she could smell righteous. I wouldn't have been surprised at anything Miss Terrwyn could do. Before I left for the day, I filled out my paperwork for the job using the Calvin fake ID, and promised Miss Terrwyn I'd be back bright and early. Her bright and early turned out to be different from my bright and early, and there was nothing but a storm of bitching and swats to the back of my head when I did show up at nine a.m. The bitching and swatting was strangely comforting in a way. Maybe I was a monster killer and a masochist, and out there somewhere was a person with a leash and spiked collar with my name on it.

I hadn't spent the time before nine sleeping, although my body would've preferred it. My body would've preferred I slept until noon from the way it and my brain complained when I rolled out of bed at seven. I showered, dressed in the same clothes that I'd washed again in more soap the housekeeper had left—I desperately needed to buy more clothes—and spent an hour and a half roaming the streets of the Landing looking for a car that seemed familiar. I'd lost my keys on the beach as well as my phone. Whatever I'd driven into town was a mystery. There was no key to give me a clue to make or model. I walked the town proper's twelve streets—two more streets than I'd guessed the day before. I owed someone's ass a kissing. There were only a few cars parked on the streets and none looked familiar or had a New York tag or anything but the standard South Carolina one.

When I reached the diner, I sat on the freshly painted green bench in front and let my hands dangle between my knees as I stared at the Victorian/plantation/some kind of big-ass old Southern house across the street. I wasn't actually looking at it; it just happened to be in the way of my "What the hell do I do now?" gaze. The house, I didn't really notice, and the house had the good manners not to notice me either. But the dog on the wraparound porch? It noticed me right off the bat.

As I heard the growl, I blinked and stopped my thoughts running through my brain in the panicked what? where? who? that was my life now. The dog was a German shepherd, big and mostly black with some russet on its legs and the same russet-colored eyes. It'd been curled up by a rocker, but now it was looking at me, its head up and lip peeled back to show its teeth. As far as I knew, I didn't have anything against dogs. Why would I? Man's best friend. "Woof," I said, low and friendly.

The shepherd disagreed with me on the friendly part. It was up in a split second, hitting the large dog flap in the front door to disappear from sight. It left behind a trail of yellow urine on the white board porch. I could see it, just barely, but I could smell it, strong and acrid as if the dog had pissed on my shoe. I might not have a problem with dogs, but this one had a problem with me. I didn't know who I was, what I was doing here, where I lived, what I did outside the monster thing, and other than keep hoping someone would volunteer that, sure, they'd seen me drive into town in a black 1964 Mustang convertible affectionately known as Fang, license plate XYZ-123, which was parked at the Old Goddamn Mill, I didn't have any way of finding out. I didn't know a damn thing about anything—oh yeah, except that the dog across the street didn't like strangers.

Things were looking bleak, my investigative skills even bleaker, and my dog-whispering skills nonexistent. For one brief second I thought about going to the cops and admitting I didn't know who I was. They could plaster my face on their database to see if anyone was missing me. But there was the arsenal under my mattress, the fact I knew about monsters, and that I knew that the people living their lives in Nevah's Landing were cocooned in ignorant bliss. I didn't belong here. I knew that, but in a world full of houses, dogs, diner food, department stores, condos, sushi, cars, trains, subways, ordinary people doing ordinary things, could I belong anywhere? Or was I like a rat, sticking to the shadows; part of the world, but outside it too?

Did rats have friends? Colleagues? Competitors? Were you born into the rat business or did you just fall into it?

Did anyone give a shit I was gone?

I did. A big one. I felt . . . a lack, to use a better word. There was a gaping hole in my life and it wasn't only my memory. Every time I looked over my shoulder, I expected someone or something to be there. It never was, and until I found out who I was, I wouldn't find out who or what I thought . . . I *knew* should be there. And I wouldn't feel right until it was there.

Of course my brain was scrambled and good, so what the hell did I know?

A hand slapped me briskly on the back of my head, and Miss Terrwyn snapped, "Are you deaf, boy, or mentally challenged? Did you not hear me say be back bright and early?"

I rubbed the back of my head and quickly pushed down the knee-jerk growl. "It is bright and early."

"Lord help me, a lazy one. Bright and early was three hours ago. Get up and get in there and start slinging the hash. And don't you have anything but black to wear? You look like the Grim Reaper himself moping around. You think anyone wants Death serving him up pancakes? No, for a fact they don't."

I was through the still-swinging doors as she kept dressing me down from behind. She could bitch like there was no tomorrow. I didn't have to take it, even though, as I'd thought earlier, it was in a bizarre way comforting. I could turn around, walk out of here, and get a bus ticket to New York City—land of my fake IDs. But my brain twisted in a knot trying to avoid that reasoning. There was still no way to find out anything there; it was too goddamn big, and there was no denying there was something about this place. There was something about the Landing that gripped me, a hand around my wrist. I couldn't deny something was here for me—a clue to who I was. A feeling of safety. A feeling of responsibility. A feeling of belonging, even though I knew there was no way that I did. It didn't fill that hole in me, but it knew me, somehow, even if I didn't know it.

The confusion didn't clear, but it did get shoved to the back of my mind at a particularly hard pinch over my ribs, and my day at the diner began all over again. It wasn't bad. I didn't get breakfast as I was late and too busy serving it, but I did get lunch. Joe, a big bald guy working the grill, made me a cheeseburger almost too big to fit on the plate. I had a separate plate for the thick-cut fries and a big glass of tea. That was another thing I learned about the South. The tea came already sweet, the kind of sweet where they tossed a tea bag in a pitcher of sugar and there you go. They called it sweet tea—a nice innocent name for something I would've called a glass of diabetic death. But it was good and the food was great. The grease was thick, the cheese hot and melting, the meat pink in the middle, and those were apparently things I liked quite a bit. I wiped at my chin with a napkin, gave Joe a thumbs-up, and he grunted.

The same happened at supper—hot chili with a huge wedge of cheddar. A thumbs-up and a grunt. Four days later I was sitting at a table in the corner. It was Reuben-and-fries day, and I was trying to eat without getting it on the blue shirt Miss Terrwyn had given me, saying she couldn't look at my silly vampire-wannabe white-boy self anymore. She must've gotten it from her brother, Lew. It was the same button-down look and it was patriotic as hell with the red-and-white checkered apron.

Joy.

But I wore it, because my boss wasn't that bad. She had a soft spot for strays like her brother, whether she'd admit it or not. She'd acted as if the shirt were nothing, but she'd pushed my hands aside to button up the last three buttons for me and spun me around for a look

to make sure I was all tucked in—like I were a kid off
to his first day of school. She also hadn't threatened to
cut my dick off since that first day with Luther of the
sinful desire, which meant her sharp eyes had seen no
wickedness in my soul. That meant something. When all
you know is that you have snarky tastes in T-shirts and
you're a killer of monsters and you pass Miss Terrwyn's
good-character test, you had to think maybe you weren't
too bad. If I'd killed monsters, then I'd saved innocent
people. I defended the honor of teen girls from per-
verts, even if I overreacted somewhat. I wasn't such a
bad guy. When you had amnesia, finding out something
that seemed simple was actually pretty damn huge. Cal
Whoever-the-hell wasn't a bad guy.

Not a bad guy. Not a bad guy.

That I repeated it silently to myself almost hourly
was a little weird, but I didn't hold it against myself.
Shit, what hadn't been weird since I'd woken up on that
beach, except for working at the diner? I didn't mind it.
It was peaceful in a way. The customers were all regu-
lars and not one of them was ever in a hurry. Although I
didn't smile as much as Miss Terrwyn told me I should,
they still tipped big for the effort, which was good because Miss Terrwyn hadn't been lying about the pay being for crap. And everyone in town passed through here.
None of them had mentioned knowing me, not yet. But
it had only been a few days. I hadn't come across everyone in the Landing yet, but I would. There wasn't any
hurry to take off.

There was one big goddamn hurry.

I didn't stop eating at the internal shout. I had them
frequently, every day, but countering them was the inescapable, annoying feeling I was here for a reason. I
tended to take the middle path and ignore both bicker-
ing sides of my brain. It wasn't as if either side was reli-

able. All I could do was all I could do, and right now that happened to be dipping a French fry bigger around than my thumb into ketchup. The door of the diner opened. I didn't hear it open, but I saw the light change on the tile floor. I saw someone's shadow—someone very quiet because that door creaked like a weather vane in a high wind. I'd noted that the first time I walked through it. I'd also noticed there wasn't any place where I didn't instantly determine the back way out or notice who was coming through the front way in.

This guy, the quiet one, was tall, dark blond hair pulled back in either a ponytail or a braid, olive skin. He was dressed in a black shirt, black pants, and a long gray duster that moved in the way my jacket had moved when I'd been armed. Everyone else who walked through that door was a happy and harmless goldfish, splashing obliviously along. This one was a shark, a dorsal fin slicing smoothly through the water with not a sound to give him away. My silverware—fork, steak knife, and spoon—had been wrapped in a napkin when I'd sat down to eat. The napkin was wadded up beside the plate. In a split second the steak knife was in my hand under the table; a second later I was back to slathering the fry with ketchup. This guy didn't belong here, and he didn't belong here in exactly the same way I didn't.

Wasn't that a coincidence?

I was chewing my French fry when a fist slammed down on the table, rattling my plate. "Where in the unholy *hell* have you been?" a voice demanded, sounding furious. There were other emotions behind the fury, but as that was the one most relevant when you were armed with diner silverware, that was the one I concentrated on.

"Who wants to know?" I countered placidly, dipping another fry and tightening my grip on the knife. I wasn't a bad guy, I'd figured that out, but I didn't know the same about him.

"Who?" The anger was overridden by another emotion, one that made me doubt that the fury had been completely real. This one was, though, as real as they came and easy to read: dread. "Your brother, Cal. I'm your brother."

Well, fuck me running.

I hadn't seen that coming.

3

I deserted the rest of my food and walked out of the diner, with more than my arm up my sleeve. I waved an "I'll be back" at Miss Terrwyn, then ducked her scowl before hitting the door. She had a soft spot all right, but no tolerance for slackers. Outside, I considered standing but decided, whatever this guy had to say, I'd prefer to hear it sitting down. And with a knife, I thought, I could hurt someone standing or sitting. Was I that confident? I took stock in myself and four dead spider monsters and decided that, yeah, I was. This guy could be as quiet and armed as he wanted. I was armed too, and had a T-shirt whose EAT ME message no one had yet been able to take me up on. I might not be a bad guy, but nobody had said I couldn't take care of myself.

While I might have the haircut of a sheepdog, I was one badass motherfucking sheepdog.

I sat on the bench and leaned back as if this sort of thing happened to me every day and twice on Christmas. "You're my brother," I echoed him. I started out very skeptically, but his darker skin to my pale, his blond hair to my black, all meant nothing when I looked into eyes the same color gray as mine. All right, we were related, but that didn't mean brothers, and being related didn't mean there was love, warmth, family bonding, and all that shit either. Cain and Abel. *The Godfather* movies. These were some of the things I hadn't forgotten. I had to play it safe. I wasn't a bad guy, but I wasn't a stupid one either. If my brother was so worried about me, where had he been when I'd taken on four giant spider monkeys from Hell by myself?

"Are you waiting for a brotherly man hug?" I drawled. "Yeah, keep waiting, buddy."

He crouched down in front of me to be eye to eye. I could feel my knees pop in outraged sympathy at the fluid movement. "You don't remember, do you?" For a moment he looked lost beyond an innate confidence he wore the same as he wore his skin. That lost expression was the same lost I'd been feeling for days. "Damn. We were afraid that might be it."

"You found him? More lost than Atlantis ever claimed to be and there he is. Grab him and tag his *poutanas yie* ass before he wanders away again."

I spared the quickest of glances toward a brown-haired man about thirty feet down the sidewalk and moving toward us fast before I had the knife at the blond guy's throat the second I faced him again. "No one is grabbing or tagging any part of me. Period. We clear?" No, I wasn't stupid, and I didn't like the looks of this one damn bit. I hadn't killed Luther the perv when I tossed him through the window, and I had no real desire to kill anybody, because I was *not* a bad guy. This guy, though, wasn't your average anybody. He was like me. He moved like me, carried weapons, was a killer. I'd seen that in one quick look. But what I couldn't see was what kind of killer he was. I killed monsters. I didn't know where he drew the line or if he had a line at all.

"Goodfellow, stay back." The eyes that so oddly mirrored mine stayed calm. "Cal, I'm going to take the knife. Don't be alarmed."

Don't be alarmed. He had balls, I had to give him that. He could fight me for the knife and, from the way he moved, he might give me a run for my money, shark to shark, but to tell me up front that he was going to disarm me and think that I was just going to let that happen. He could kiss my . . .

Holy shit.

The knife was gone and my hand was empty. I was unarmed and facing someone very dangerous. This was serious, but more than that, it was flat-out embarrassing. I flexed my fingers and dropped my hand as casually as if I'd been swiping a fly instead of holding a blade at someone's throat. He was like me all right, only better, and that added proof to having the same color eyes. "Cal," I said, disgruntled. "You called me Cal. So which is it? Calvin, Calvert, or Calhoun?"

Brother. I might have a brother. I'd wrapped my mind around a lot of crazy-ass shit these past few days, but I could have hit a wall on this one. A brother . . . holy hell. When I looked over my shoulder at that empty spot, was he the one I was looking for? This guy? Tired, he looked tired—at least he did to me, with the skin under his eyes a deeper olive than the rest of his face, but his lips still quirked up slightly at the edges at my belligerent question. "Caliban. It's short for Caliban."

"Like the monster, the one from Shakespeare." Jesus. I was all about that, from the beach to my fake IDs to the real deal. I flashed monster cred as if it were a goddamn gold card. I was a wannabe like Miss Terrwyn had said. Again, embarrassing. Could you roll your eyes at your own idiotic ego?

My remark about Shakespeare had the almost-smile fading from his lips. "No, not like the monster."

"Where have you been? Have you been here all this time? The days and days we searched without sleep, with barely a hope to keep us going, and, Zeus, what are you wearing? Is that gingham? Tell me that's not a gingham apron. I'm not sure I care to go on in this vale of tears knowing that you are actually wearing a gingham apron. *Why* are you wearing a gingham apron?" The other one, the brown-haired guy down the sidewalk, had stayed back for all of two seconds before he was at our side, his green eyes pained as if it hurt to look at me.

"Because I can't cook," I answered absently. It was happening. Right now. I hadn't found my past, but it had found me and hauling family with it. I'd thought maybe associates in the same business. I'd thought maybe, wild chance, a friend or two. But a brother? I didn't know if I was prepared for a brother. Worse yet, I didn't know if a brother was prepared for me. Then again, I worked hard at the diner, and slaying monsters. I wanted to mouth off once or twice or twenty times, but I didn't, because it wasn't smart, careful, or safe. I'd been nothing but those three things since I'd woken up in the Landing, with the minor exception of throwing Luther through the window. Maybe I wasn't giving myself credit. I wasn't a bad guy, right? So maybe I was a good deal in the brother department too. On sale and barely used.

As for his being a killer, if I was his brother and one he missed enough to come looking for, he couldn't be that bad either. No worse than I was, or I wouldn't have had anything to do with him. I knew right from wrong. I knew people from monsters.

One, like Luther, you disciplined. One, like the spiders, you destroyed.

"You're wearing an apron *with* ruffles because you can't cook. Ah. That makes perfect sense. You've no idea how I appreciate your clearing that up for me," the other guy, the fashion critic, said. "You're wearing blue as well? Bright, frighteningly neon blue? I've never seen you wear anything but black and gray. And your hair, what by all that is unholy . . . Actually I approve of the hair. If less were hanging in your face, that would be better, but overall—I approve." He sat on the bench beside me with a weary "Whoosh," stretched his legs, and wrapped an arm around my shoulders to give me a slight shake, then a rough squeeze. "You scared us, kid. Scared the Hades out of us."

I dropped my eyes to his hand on my shoulder. The man, the self-proclaimed brother who had disarmed me as if I were a kitten with a ball of yarn, smiled. "There's that brotherly man hug you're so intent on avoiding."

"He's my brother too?" I asked, mildly panicked.

Mr. Touchy-feely answered for himself. "No, you're not that fortunate. You're not as endowed, not as fashion conscious, not as rakishly charming, not as . . . *Malaka!*" he yelped as I stabbed him in the leg with the fork I'd had up my other sleeve. I had two sleeves. I wasn't only arming one of them. I'd slipped a knife up one and a fork up the other before I left my table in the diner.

"I'm not as crazy about being touched either." I stood up, pulling the fork out of his leg as I did, to face "my brother." All that smart, careful, and safe I'd been so smug about a moment ago had disappeared. That was interesting. As for the not-a-bad-guy thing . . . I knew I shouldn't kill people, but I didn't think good guys stabbed people with forks either. These two were bringing out the worst in me or they were bringing out the *me* in me. I hoped it was the first. "If you think I'm going to swallow whatever crap you two are throwing at me without some questions, lots of goddamn questions, and without some proof, then brother or not, you don't know me at fucking all."

But maybe it wasn't them at all. Maybe it was just him doing it, the one I'd stabbed, because I smelled it now. I smelled him.

Three drops of blood fell from the tines of the fork to make a trinity of scarlet on the sidewalk. The smell grew even stronger. My subconscious had known what my conscious hadn't. I should've smelled the difference, noticed the difference sooner. If they were telling the truth, though, they knew me and I knew them, which meant I was used to them, used to the green-eyed one's smell. He wasn't human. He didn't smell like Lew or Terrwyn or anyone else in this town. He smelled of grass and trees, the musk of bucks in rut, the dew on a meadow blanketed by a morning mist. He also smelled of a fox in the henhouse.

Sneaky.

"You're one of them." I changed my grip on the fork, a less respect-my-space hold and more of one suited to puncturing a carotid artery. Thank God I hadn't grabbed a spork. "You're a monster."

Why I could smell that and no one else could was something I didn't have time to think about. I had to decide whether to take out a monster in broad daylight in front of the diner patrons watching through the window and the sheriff who'd be showing up soon. Or should I back away from this all? Let these two explain themselves. Do the sensible thing like I had since I'd washed up here.

Fuck that.

He was a *monster*.

Abomination.

I slashed at his throat with the fork; then something happened. I had no idea what. It was that abrupt, as if I were watching a movie and the power went out. No people. No light. Nothing at all. When I woke up in the backseat of a car, "the something that had happened" was driving and I could see the hair was in a braid, not a ponytail. Not that it mattered, but it was always nice to get things cleared up. I sat up slowly and rubbed my forehead with the heel of my hand. It hurt—my head not my hand. Not much, but there was a definite mild ache.

I'd dreamed when I'd been out. I'd been in a car, old and junky, looking through the back window at the road unspooling behind. With every beat of my heart I'd thought they were coming. They were coming. They would always be coming. I'd been young in the dream; too damn young to know what to do. A kid, early teens maybe. That was all I could remember of it. That and that there was someone with me. He was the only hope I had that whatever was coming might not find me, and he had blond hair—the same color as the guy driving this car.

Not that that meant anything. Dreams were dreams. I had reality to deal with now.

"You. Blond guy. What did you do to me?" I asked, hoarse enough to know it had been several hours for my throat to be that dry. Without slow-motion replay in my brain, as I didn't remember seeing one damn thing before the darkness had sucked me down, I was genuinely curious to hear the answer. He was the one who had taken me down, that I knew. The other one had been in front of me when I attacked. The monster, the one who'd said he was my brother, had been behind me. Lesson learned: Don't turn your back on anyone, not even your brother.

"I hit you," he said matter-of-factly, eyes still on the road. "But it was for your own good."

Isn't that what they all say? And I hadn't seen him move, not even a flicker out of the corner of my eye.

Either he was that incredibly fast or I was that utterly focused on bleeding a monster dry. Maybe both. "That's not very brotherly of you." Neither were the handcuffs I was wearing. I rattled the links. "You going to sell me overseas into the sex trade?"

"Like we could give your ungrateful, utensil-waving, frenzied fork-stabbing self away. We'd have to pay them, give them frequent-flier miles, not to mention a ten-year free warranty, and then change our addresses," continued the familiar fox-in-the-henhouse complaining. "I'm Robin Goodfellow, by the way. In case you were curious who you attacked besides a good and faithful friend who has spent days worrying about you and watching your brother worry as well. His name, as you haven't asked, is Niko, and he should've hit you harder."

That one, Goodfellow, was in the passenger's seat. Despite the fact that I had stabbed him with a fork and had then tried to kill him with the same, he didn't appear as pissed off as I would've been. Then again, aside from being a monster, he was also mouthy enough that probably everyone he met tried to kill him with the first thing that came to hand. Fork, keys, chair, Pomeranian—whatever they had.

"I didn't know monsters had names." I studied the glass of the the back window as he muttered more about my ingratitude and general lack of anything desirable in a sentient being. I could kick out the glass, but I couldn't kick it out and escape before Niko stopped me. He was apparently some sort of ninja/samurai frigging Jedi Knight who probably didn't bend the fucking grass he walked on, and he didn't need a T-shirt saying EAT ME to reassure himself about his general badassness. I was suddenly glad I was wearing my new blue shirt that didn't label me as something I hadn't been able to back up. Miss Terrwyn had given me that reprieve with plain blue cotton. She was gone now, though. I was gone too—in the wind. In a week I'd be only a memory to her, her brother, and everyone else who'd met me at the diner.

I was going to miss them. It was stupid. I hadn't been there even a week, but there you go. They'd given me a free haircut, shirt, and the stamp of approval on my soul. Cal-the-not-so-bad-guy. I was guessing from the handcuffs that my brother and his monster partner had spun some tale of escaped convict . . . wanted by the feds . . . blah blah. And now Cal-the-not-so-bad-guy was Cal, a guy bad enough he had to be dragged out of town unconscious by some mysterious authorities. That sucked. My good reputation, all four days of it, was shot. It shouldn't have mattered that much, but it did. They'd given me more than I'd given them, although I had cleared up their monster problem. That was something.

I saw a sign as I looked out the window and squinted quickly to read it as it receded in the distance. It said nothing about Nevah's Landing. Yeah, I was long in the wind. "Where's the Landing? My weapons are there."

My apron was gone too but that wasn't the important thing. There was something in the Landing for me besides slinging hash and winning the approval of the locals. There was something that I hadn't gotten around to yet. Something that needed doing. Something that felt more familiar than these two guys. Something that only I . . . No. No.

I turned away. I was looking for my past and it was here in the car with me. I didn't need the Landing anymore, despite the lingering feeling of a hooked finger that tugged in my gut, a whisper that said, *Come back. Come play.* I didn't even know why I'd been there to begin with. Maybe my past and present knew.

"You . . . um . . . Niko. You're supposed to be my

brother. Why was I in Nevah's Landing fighting monsters?" I settled back against the seat and began scanning the floorboards for something to pick the handcuff lock.

"I am not supposed to be your brother. I am your brother. Although there could be a certain sense of destiny to it." He pulled off the exit we'd been approaching and into the parking lot of a motel almost exactly like the one I had stayed in, where my weapons still were. I was going to miss them, not that I remembered using them. But their cold metal in my hands was comforting. It beat a teddy bear hands down. "I am your brother. I was supposed to be your brother since before either of us was born. Karmic debt. It appears I was Vlad the Impaler or Genghis Khan in a past life." He parked the car. "As for Nevah's Landing, you were there because of Peter Pan."

I'd been about to comment on all that mystical destiny crap, but I choked on it instead, coughing out, "Peter Pan? You're shitting me, right?"

"I cannot shit you," solemn as a proverbial judge, "it is not in my nature."

Uh huh. It hadn't been long since he'd kidnapped me, but I already knew better than that.

Goodfellow, ignoring the exchange, said, "I do not want to hear how a tale that appropriated the name of a member of my mighty race led Cal to wearing a girly apron in a diner in the quaint and culturally deprived town of Nevah's Landing. I'll check us in." He opened the door and climbed out with only a small limp. I should've stabbed deeper. A monster in human form was still a monster. And monsters were wrong, evil, alien, unclean. Abominations. I knew that. Oceans were made of water, forest fires were made of a thousand flickering flames, and monsters were made of murder. I knew it.

But I didn't know about Peter Pan and Nevah's Landing. I shifted my attention from picturing a target on Goodfellow's back as he limped away to Niko, now turned to face me. "You were seven years old and I was eleven when we passed through Nevah's Landing," he started, holding out the handcuff key to me. I took it after a brief hesitation and didn't take my eyes off him as I unlocked the cuffs. He was faster than I was and better than I was. That didn't make me at all comfortable, whether he was my brother or not.

"We stayed about a week. Our mother, Sophia, did some fortune-telling, tarot readings, and other things." He glossed over "other things" so quickly I almost didn't catch it. Whatever those other things had been, he wasn't going to make that part of the story. "It was cold, like it is now, too cold for swimming. You were bored." I didn't know how he did it, but with the tiniest movement of an eyebrow he made me feel as if at seven I had been bored frequently and not afraid to nag an older brother about it. "So I told you the story of Peter Pan and Never Land. Nevah's Landing. Never Land. It wasn't that much of a stretch. The real Nevah of Nevah's Landing was actually the matriarch of a family who settled . . ."

I groaned and let my head flop back against the seat. My two captors weren't familiar, but this feeling—a frustrated weight of boring knowledge I didn't need or want—was surprisingly so. "At least you remember something," Niko observed, looking pleased with himself, even though the emotion wasn't plastered across his face. Pleased and relieved, and while I couldn't point out specific physical clues to that, I knew it all the same. "Very well. Historical education aside, I told you the story of Peter Pan. I even took you to the library there so you could look at the pictures in the book. You always were about the pictures. You called Nevah's Landing Never Land for months after we left. I think you saw it as it was in the book, a sanctuary for lost boys."

I ignored the jab at my not being well read unless the books came with lots of pictures and big print—hey, I'd known Shakespeare, hadn't I? Instead, I concentrated on the first moments that I could remember. When I'd woken up on the beach, the second before as I'd drifted in and out of consciousness, what had I seen in the darkness?

Pirate ships. Princesses. Waterfalls. Tree houses. A safe place. You couldn't get there if you couldn't fly, and the pirates were ridiculously easy to defeat. The crocodile, though, that white crocodile—it whispered to me, with an unbelievably wide stretch of toothy smile and jack-o'-lantern eyes. They were only whispers, but it could do other things if it wanted. What those things were a seven-year-old boy couldn't imagine, and it told me things; things I didn't remember. But it also said it was my friend. Who's going to tell a phantom crocodile no when he tells you that? No seven-year-old I could think of. That was one scary damn thing to put in a kid's book, that ghost of a crocodile.

"My own personal safe place. That's why I, what? Trucked in some eight-legged monsters so I could fight in a place that was comfy-cozy? Or I went there for another reason and happened to find giant spiders splashing around in the surf without their water wings? No one knew me there. I hadn't been staying there. Did I track the monsters there and decide because I had so much fun in Never Land as a kid I'd give them a free exterminator job?" Although I didn't mind the thought of killing monsters for free—a community service—I had a damn lot of weapons, and those cost. I couldn't have bought them on diner tips. "And what about the amnesia? Care to explain that one? Did I catch a cliché virus and just kept killing because deep down I wanted to be monster killer of the month?" My lips flattened. "Peter fucking Pan doesn't answer a single one of those questions." I could see Goodfellow on his way back to the car. "And what about him? He's not human. If you're my brother, if you know about the monsters, why are you hanging out with him?"

"Because, as he said, he's a friend and a good one."

I grunted, "He's a monster. Not only is he a monster, but he's one that never shuts up. What's good about that?"

"He grows on you."

"Like a fungus?" I snorted.

"More like a sexually transmitted disease." He opened the door and swung a leg out. "Now, let's get in the room, eat, and I'll tell you the rest of the story, amnesia and all. You'll get your memory back, Cal. This isn't permanent. You'll remember. I promise." Strangely, it didn't sound like a promise he was one hundred percent sure about. Maybe it was only hope. Hope and monsters, what a mix.

The room was practically a carbon copy of the one I'd had back in the Landing, except this one had two beds instead of the one, but two still weren't enough. "I'm not sleeping in a bed with either of you." I folded my arms. "I don't care if we were all Siamese triplets separated at birth. It's not happening."

"Conjoined, not Siamese, you politically incorrect Neanderthal." Goodfellow sat at the table and rubbed at his leg while giving me a pointed glare. "And, when you're returned to your normal state of mind—not that I ever considered it normal until now—you owe me twelve hundred dollars for these pants. Tine puncture marks don't go well with fine couture." I had some thoughts on his "couture," but he chose that moment to pull a sword out of his long brown coat, rotate it with a deceptively lazy speed, and slap it across the table. "Also, I don't accept checks or plastic, especially not yours, as I faked most of them myself."

That was a big sword, and he handled it as if it weighed nothing. He moved with the same lethal grace the Niko guy did. I wasn't quite the hot shit I thought I was, the killer born on a South Carolina beach. Not in this company. At the very least I had some competition. "Jesus, were you born with that in your hand?" I asked with reluctant admiration.

He grinned wickedly. "Kid, you don't want to know what I was holding when I was born."

"We need only two beds, because Robin and I will take turns keeping watch. Besides, you didn't mind sleeping with me when you were four and were afraid of the neighbor's dachshund," Niko said as he stripped off his own coat.

"Keep watch? You afraid I'll try and run or . . . I was not!" I said with automatic outrage when I caught up to the important part of the conversation.

"I think her name was Princess Poochika. She was brown with short legs. She looked like a Ho-Ho with a pink rhinestone collar. You thought she was the reincarnation of Cujo." He sat on the bed and dropped his head in his hands to rub his eyes with the heels of his hands. He was more than tired. He was exhausted—because of me. Because he'd been looking for me. I'd wondered every day in Nevah's Landing if anyone had given a shit I was gone. Now I had my answer.

"You can be forgiven. She was a little temperamental. Nipping little kids' ankles was her favorite activity." He raised his head. "Come here, Cal."

I unfolded my arms just so I could fold them again stubbornly. "Why?"

He exhaled. "Just come here."

"Why?" I repeated.

"Cal." One patient word. My name . . . my real name. Caliban. He'd told me that. If I owed anyone, it was him. It was too bad for us all that I didn't have the trust in me to owe anyone anything. Whether the color of our eyes said we were related, even brothers, I, this version of me, had been born on that beach—my first emotion had been a general "What the fuck?" My second one of suspicion. You could be a not-so-bad guy and be suspicious too, in certain situations. In the past few days suspicion had worked well for me. I was sticking with it.

I cocked my head with attitude and skepticism. "If there's no why, there's no Cal."

Niko rubbed his face again and said for what would be the last time, "Cal, I need you to come here." He didn't sound irritated. He only sounded more tired. I almost felt bad for the guy, almost. Shit, I *did* feel bad for the guy, but I was still beach Cal, and beach Cal didn't trust anyone without proof—especially when that anyone knocked you out and kidnapped you. That was what I thought, but my body had opinions of its own. Without any orders from my brain, I took the few steps between us.

Stopping, I asked warily, "So, what do you want?"

His hand moved toward me, and I flinched, but it was too late. He cupped the back of my head and turned it to one side. He was looking at my neck, the healing bites. "You were bitten by one of the Nepenthe spiders. That's why you have amnesia." It was good information, if utterly meaningless, to have. But before I could move, Niko pulled me down in one quick motion to rest my forehead on the top of his blond head. "Missed you, little brother." That I didn't immediately pull away was a thought I did think and then promptly tried but failed to unthink.

Moving back, I asked, trying for some control of the situation, "What the fuck is a Nepenthe spider?"

Niko removed his shoes, moved up farther in the bed, and closed his eyes. "Your turn, Goodfellow," he murmured, before falling asleep between that breath and the next. He hadn't gotten under the covers or beat the pillow at least once to soften it up. He was just here and then gone. It was sort of . . . Zen, I guess. I am awake; now I am asleep. I'll chant later. Now that—all that—felt vaguely familiar too. This Niko—my brother, shit, denial was beginning to fail me—was as ninja/samurai on the inside as well as the out. How'd you become one of those these days? Climb a mountain and live in a cave for ten years? Take a class in an online school of dubious accreditation? Who knew?

Goodfellow had taken his foot and scooted a chair over so he could prop his legs up, ankles crossed. "I need to keep the weight off it," he explained. "There was no doubt some sort of mustard-spawned Ebola on that fork you stabbed me with." I stared back at him, wholly unimpressed. "Which," he continued, "might have a civilized being slobbering heartfelt apologies in my direction." The sly green eyes fixed on me in anticipation. When nothing was forthcoming, he tapped his chest. "If you're confused, this is my direction. You don't need a compass, kid."

"You're a monster," I pointed out, as he seemed to keep forgetting.

"I'm a monster? That's rather . . . interesting." The interest wasn't the amusing kind as the cocky smile faded and the eyes darkened. "How about we agree that I'm not human, but not necessarily a monster either." He folded his hands across his stomach. "Oh, and before I forget, I do have to tell you that no matter how incredibly hot you find me, I am in a monogamous relationship."

That overrode any monster issues instantly. "Dude!"

He grinned. "It's simply my standard disclaimer. In the past you have never tried to 'get with this,' as they say. Although you have seen me naked. You couldn't look me in the eye for days."

"Dude!"

"I can't be held responsible for your shame at your own shortcomings or your puritanical sexual mores." The grin was wider, definitely wider and considerably more evil. "Now, do you want to order pizza or Chinese?"

I decided I wanted to go to bed. The hell with the food. The hell with the Nep . . . Nef . . . whatever fucking kind of amnesia spider it was. I'd find all that out from Niko or from them both when Niko was awake. Goodfellow made the monsters from the beach seem like one tiny ladybug I'd crushed under my boot. They didn't scare me. He did. My curiosity could wait and so could my hunger. It was only as I'd kicked off my own boots and crawled under the covers of the other bed, fully clothed—very fully clothed—that I realized I'd never gotten an answer as to why one of them was keeping watch. Was it to make sure I didn't take off, or something else? Considering how easily Niko had taken me down, I had the uneasy suspicion it was not my sneaking off they were worried about.

4

"I don't want to go back to New York," I repeated, spearing a sausage patty with my fork. A patty to go with my petty, and I was feeling petty.

Goodfellow had one eye on that very same fork, smart of him, and one on the waitress with more breasts than she, God, and her bra knew what to do with. "I am sorry," he told her, "but despite your wealth of exquisite mammary tissue, I am in a monogamous relationship. Disappointing for you, I know, but I have faith that after a grieving process, you'll learn to live again."

"I heard you the first time," Niko snapped at me before going after Goodfellow, "and, Robin, let the woman refill your orange juice and get on with her day, as bereaved as she is over your unavailable status, all right?" He began to whip his granola and yogurt into more of a froth than was called for. The Zen Niko was having issues. I was one of those issues. "Why, Cal, do you not want to go home?"

I chewed the sausage and swallowed, using some of my own orange juice to chase it down. "I was attacked by giant spiders, I've lost my memory, I carried more weapons than the Deathstar, and I woke up on a beach a few minutes before I would've drowned. If that's what I do in New York, why would I want to go back? I worked four days at a diner and no one tried to kill me once. The money wasn't great, but, again, no one tried to kill me. If I'm some kind of monster exterminator, I have to think there's a better way to make money. And you still haven't explained why I was fighting the spiders, who for, did I get paid, and what was I doing in South Carolina if I live in New York." I took a bite of my waffles and said, muffled, around the mouthful, "Or if you're keeping watch at night for me or for something else. Don't think I forgot about that because you sicced Mr. Monogamy on me."

Niko put his spoon down with a sigh. "We, not just you, are working for a coalition of the preternatural in New York. Something is sending the Nepenthe spiders to kidnap werewolves, vampires, revenants, lamia, succubi, incubi, on and on—anything nonhuman. Sometimes their bodies are found, sometimes not, but none are ever seen alive again. We were hired to stop the creature behind this."

"God, not creature. Well, goddess. Ammut," Robin said cheerfully, slicing his ham to small pieces. "She's supposedly an Egyptian goddess, which, of course, *I*, personally, figured out from the Nepenthe spiders. I was in Egypt hanging at the court of Ramses for a while. That obelisk he built, let's just say I personally might be the reason he was obsessed with large phallic objects. But I digress. The spiders are from Egypt, originally birthed before the time of the pyramids. Their venom, greatly diluted, can bring forgetfulness to the sorrowful. It was called the nepenthe elixir—psychotherapy for the pharaohs. It was all the rage for the royalty who could afford to lose several servants to catch one of the spiders. However, a direct bite will make an animal or human forget how to run, to stand, to move, to think, to breathe even, making them easy prey. Snap, snap and all the baby spiders have dinner that night. Very efficient."

Goddess? We were after a *goddess*?

The next bite of waffle on my fork slowly slid off to splat in a pool of syrup on the plate. "What ... the ... fuck?" I said with what I classified as extraordinary calm before throwing that calm out the window and trying to stab Goodfellow with the fork—again.

Niko dragged me backward out of the diner, which was across the street from the motel, with his arm in a chokehold around my neck. Goodfellow followed, though, with enough lag that I was guessing he paid the check. I stumbled purposely as he came through the doors, felt the hold on my throat ease slightly—brotherly love turned out to be a great weakness—flipped Niko over my shoulder, and went after Goodfellow again. Who needed guns and knives—forks were my new weapon of choice.

As I hit Goodfellow, he twisted in a move I'd swear no one, unless they had Silly Putty for bones, could accomplish, and I somersaulted over his hip to land flat on my back. My head bounced on the asphalt in a manner I didn't at all enjoy. Hissing in pain, I blinked against the double vision to bring into focus the two faces peering down at me. One was concerned and one puzzled.

"Was it something I said?" Goodfellow questioned, all innocence. He tilted his head toward Niko. "It could've been you. Vampires, werewolves, revenants, yadda yadda. Perhaps you blew a circuit in his view of a two-monster world: spiders and the magnificence that are pucks in all our glory."

Right then I hated them both equally enough that Goodfellow had a good argument in the blame department. No, not Goodfellow. Puck. He was a puck. He didn't deserve a name, the annoying shit. "You." I pointed at Niko with the fork. At least, I attempted to point at him. Things were still a little blurry. As much as I wanted to hold the two of them responsible for that, I knew better. This was my fault. I'd let myself forget one basic fact, the very first fact I knew about myself—the one that nobody, not even Miss Terrwyn, had to tell me. "We have a last name? Same last name? Fuck it. Who cares? What's your last name?"

"Leandros of the Vayash Clan. Our last name is Leandros." He reached down, slid his hands under my shoulders, and sat me up.

"Whatever." I closed my eyes and let the world stop whirling. "You, puck. Go back and get my food. I'm still starving." I wasn't, not anymore, but it was a matter of principle. "Leandros, get me back to the motel so I can throw up."

"Are you dizzy? Nauseated? You could have a concussion." The last possibility sounded accusatory, and Goodfellow countered in the same tone.

"He tried to stab me with a fork, Niko. For the third time, I might add. He is as my own family, and I'm willing to take one for the team, but taking syrup-coated metal like a spear through my throat is a lot to ask for." I felt a hand gingerly pat the top of my head. "I'm sorry, kid. I'd have steered you toward the waitress's bountiful bosom if she'd been out here. Oh, here she comes now ... with the manager ... who's calling the police. *Skata*, it's always something. Take him back to the room, Niko, and I'll clear this up here."

Just that quickly I was on my feet and across the road before I was able to get my eyes open. Then we were in the room, and I was sitting on one of the beds. Vampires, werewolves, other crap, gods. *Gods*. Goodfellow was on the money. I wanted the world back where and when I thought spiders and pucks were all I knew. Although

I had known when I'd woken up in the Landing that the world was full of monsters, not only spiders, I simply didn't have names to put to them and proof that I was right. I'd let myself think in those four normal days that I might just be a little crazy, because crazy was better than a world made of nightmares.

"Are you all right?"

I stopped rubbing the small lump on the back of my head and looked up at Niko. No. Leandros. Leandros was easier right now. There was too much to absorb and I needed some distance to do that. I needed to be able to breathe and to think. "I just found out that the world is one big frigging horror movie. I might need at least thirty seconds to process that, okay?"

"I can understand that," he said slowly. "But you do need to know that being a vampire or a Wolf,"—as werewolves apparently preferred to be called. Good for them—"or a puck or a peri or any other number of things, doesn't necessarily mean they are monsters. The majority are like people. Some are good; some are not. And some . . ." He let the rest of the sentence trail away.

"And some are?" I prompted.

He exhaled and sat beside me. "And some *are* monsters with no thought other than killing and no more soul than lies in the bullet of a gun. That doesn't make the world a horror movie. It merely makes it like it already is, only with a few more layers that ordinary people will never see."

"Just lucky ones like us," I said grimly. "Whoopee."

The puck came through the door then with my food in a Styrofoam container. "I paid off the manager, but I'd advise we leave as soon as possible. You, Junior, now owe me an extra three hundred on top of the damage to my pants."

"Okay, I have to hurl." Not from the bill or his obsession with his pants, but from the smell of the food. It looked as though I'd bought myself a slight concussion after all. I made it to the bathroom, slammed the door behind me, and vomited into the toilet. It wasn't much. I'd had but half of my lunch, no supper yesterday, and not much of breakfast today before having my world—and my stomach—turned inside out.

I had straightened and grabbed the towel to wipe my mouth when the window about five feet up the wall exploded. It was frosted glass for privacy and fair sized, about two feet by two feet. It was the perfect size for the Nepenthe spider that came barging in. Double pincers in simian jaws were opening and closing rapidly, eight black legs were supporting it on the wall and reaching for me, six eyes were fixed on me as its bulbous body finished sliding through the window. It was the size of a big dog, exactly the same size as the German shepherd across from the Oleander Diner that had fled at the sight of me, leaving piss in its wake. The spider's eyes were the same color as that piss, bright, cheer, middle-of-the-daisy yellow.

I jammed the waffle fork that I still had in my hand right in the middle of all six of those eyes. "Hello, Sunshine."

Here was the fact I'd let myself forget across the street minutes ago—what I was. I hadn't been completely serious with my attack on Goodfellow. I was serious now. I kept my arm up and barely out of reach of the pincers as the spider thrashed and screamed. I didn't know spiders could scream, but this kind was doing a damn good job of it. I pushed the fork in farther until the heel of my hand hit eye and flesh before I rotated the metal, scrambling whatever it was using for a brain. Behind me the door flew open as the spider screeched one last time, twitched violently, and then went seventy-five pounds of dead on the floor. I let go of the remaining five inches of metal and wiped eye goo off my hand and onto my jeans.

"You . . . You killed a Nepenthe spider with a *fork*?" Goodfellow said in a strangled croak over my shoulder.

"Yeah." I snorted and returned to flushing the toilet. I wanted to be a tidy killer for the maid's sake. "Now imagine what I could've done to you at breakfast if I'd really tried." I gave him a dark grin and added, "Sunshine."

Goodfellow was less talkative—say "Hallelujah"—as we once again climbed into the car and headed north. Despite what I said about not wanting to go back to New York, I didn't see I had much choice with spiders either following the two of them or following me. I was guessing me. I'd racked up five to my name so far, and if that didn't make me the most popular target for the eight-legged crowd, I didn't know what did. I could try to bail anytime I wanted before we reached the city, but I'd have to start carrying forks by the bucketful if I did.

Speaking of which, I watched as the puck picked up from the floor a clear plastic Baggie containing a plastic fork and knife typical of fast-food "silverware" and then cracked open the car window enough to shove it out.

"That's called littering," I commented with the smirk of a mean-spirited ten-year-old bully, which was very close to how I felt. Not pretty, but honest. I wasn't a bad guy, repeat-repeat, if a damn good monster killer, but I had a headache. I'd been kidnapped—sort of. I was finding out about a weird and creepy world, and I had a job that no one with an ounce of self-preservation would want, where the customers were as freaky as your targets, and you could bet your ass no one tipped—or gave you a free shirt. Being an okay guy was different from being a hero. How long did monster-fighting heroes live in this shadowed world?

"Littering or self-survival," Leandros added. "Cal, behave and tell Robin you won't kill him with a fork if he drops his guard."

Behave? Leandros could claim to be my older brother all he wanted, but I didn't ever see a moment in the future where his telling me to behave would have any impact on what I did. If that was the brother I had been before, well, best plant a cross in the dirt, because that brother was dead and dust. I was my own man. "No," I replied, amiably enough. There was no need to be too rotten. I'd already proved my point with the spider. They'd scooped me up like a toddler out of a playpen at Nevah's Landing, but I knew what I was dealing with now. So did they.

"No?"

"You sound like the Grand Canyon. Every time I say something you don't want to hear, you repeat it right back. It's rather unninja of you. Do you get a ninja silence-in-crisis merit badge taken away for that? Do they slice it off with a shuriken from a hundred feet away?" I was wearing one of Leandros's shirts, black—which led to all the ninja bashing. "And that's right. I said no. I will collect as many forks as I can and the puckster here will never know when one is headed for his monogamy-loving ass. I don't *know* you. Either of you, and all the talk in the world isn't going to change that." I leaned back against the seat to watch the scenery pass. "Since I don't know you, I don't know what you might do. And since I don't know that, I don't know how I'll react. That's just honesty. I'm good with forks, but I'm not psychic."

There was an immediate stinging flick to my ear, not to my head, which was sporting an asphalt headache. He was that considerate at least. "Ow! Shit." I cupped the ear that burned like fire. He was as bad as Miss Terrwyn had been with a swat.

"Now you know what I, personally, will do if you don't show respect for your elders." This time I had seen him move, but he was quick, this brother of mine—cheetah double take quick. "As for Robin, he may just forget about his newly found monogamy and show you a rerun of what you've forgotten. He comes by his reputation honestly, from what you told me."

Jesus. An event I couldn't remember, but I was doomed to hear about it on a daily basis. "You play dirty." I sulked, dropping my hand.

"Yes, I do. You taught me how." Leandros kept driving, seemingly unperturbed at the thought of any reprisal from me. "Since you don't know us, we'll tell you anything and everything you want until your memory comes back."

"Great," I interrupted before he could say anything further. "I have a shitload of questions for you." Now that I'd found out about the number of nasties in the world, a list so long, the rain forest would have to be entirely razed to make the paper for it, I could focus on more personal questions. "The puck said one of those spider bites would make someone forget everything, forget how to move, how to fucking breathe." Jesus. "Even if none of them was left alive to eat me, why didn't I suffocate on that beach?"

Goodfellow answered that one without thinking twice, which meant he had thought twice or more than twice. The henhouse, I reminded myself. Always remember the henhouse and the fox with a mouthful of feathers. "The only thing I can think is the spider bit something or someone else before you. Like a rattlesnake, it didn't have a full dose of venom—you received enough that you lost part of your memory, but you kept everything else. You managed to get the ancient pharaoh Prozac, only double or triple the amount. You didn't forget a recent sorrow. You forgot your entire life. But it does wear off. Have faith." It was a very smooth explanation, but before I had a chance to comment on how smooth, he'd already changed subjects. "Also, have faith that if you do kill me with a fork, someone will avenge me. Someone with wings, a sword, and a temper to drown the world in fire instead of water."

"Robin," Leandros warned.

"What? I'm simply saying. He wanted information. I want to make sure he has the entire picture," the puck defended himself. He went on to give me more information, not waiting for me to ask for it. Niko and I were brothers. Niko was full Rom with a handful of centuries-old North Greek thrown in, which explained the blond hair. I was half Rom, half *gadje*—a combination frowned on by the gypsy clans, but not by our mother who had taken off on her own when she was a teenager. She had no prejudices when it came to bed partners, gypsy or non. He put that very carefully. He did not say Sophia didn't care whom she screwed, but as he went on to say that Niko and I had no other family, that neither of us knew who our father was, it was easy to connect the dots. Mom got around—and around and around and around. That was a good reason that Niko wasn't telling me this himself. Who would want to tell his brother that his mom was a slut?

Mom was also dead. She'd died in a fire, the result of bad trailer wiring. I waited to feel something on hearing that. Fine, she never met a mattress she didn't like, but she'd been my mom. She could've had good qualities. She could've made cupcakes for my birthday or played with me on a beach that wasn't freezing. There are worse things than liking to screw around. I had to feel something knowing she was dead, knowing she'd burned to death. Goodfellow hadn't said that; she could've died of smoke inhalation, but I knew better. I didn't remember, but I knew.

She'd burned.

But I felt . . . nothing. There was nothing but a bitter taste in the back of my throat. I gave up. Why would I want to remember something that horrible if I didn't have to? I shrugged for Goodfellow to go on. He did, winding it up quickly. She'd died, leaving Niko and me on our own when we were in our teens. We traveled a lot before and after her death, ran into some monsters eventually, and had our eyes opened in a big way. We ended up in New York, met Goodfellow, started a business, and here we were.

For someone who didn't know how to shut up, he was succinct as a one-line fortune cookie when he wanted to be. "That's it?" I demanded. "I grew up, ran around, saw some monsters, came to New York, and am now part of the Leandros Brothers and Monogamy Boy Monster Killers Incorporated?"

"And you work at a bar part-time," he added. "Oh, you were sexing it up with a Wolf, Delilah, for a while, but she tried to kill a friend of yours, thought about killing you, and things haven't been the same since. The usual drama that goes along with sex. She's now the first female pack leader in the Kin—that would be the werewolf Mafia to you—as she managed to get her Alpha and entire pack killed. It was quite clever, how she did that, clever in an inexcusably evil way. of course." He coughed—a fake cough, I thought, to cover up his jealousy of just how clever she'd been. Pucks, I was learning or slowly remembering, were tricksters through and through.

After clearing his throat—uh huh—he continued. "It's an all-female pack she started too, another first in the Kin. They've been kicking furry ass and pissing on names for several months now. It's quite impressive. She might one day rule the entire leg-humping enchilada. Which is only fair—equal rights for all, regardless of gender." He tossed a candy bar back to me. "As for monogamy boy, I've never been a boy." His grin gave me crocodile flashbacks. "I was born a man, *more* than a man. Do you want to hear a little about my history? It's far more entertaining than yours, I promise you."

I ripped at the candy bar wrapper carelessly, tossing pieces of it onto the seat around me. "Jesus Christ, no. I don't want to hear about your history, not a single second of it. Wait a minute. I was dating a werewolf?"

"No, you were screwing a werewolf. Wolves don't have relationships outside their own kind. Wolf is for Wolf. You two were simply fornicating, fucking, whatever you wish to call it, although you certainly seemed to enjoy it. Your mood improved enormously. Your complexion cleared up, and the hair on the palms of your hands fell off. Naturally you owe all that to me as I was the one to help you lose your virginity. There wouldn't have been any furry fornication for you if I hadn't shown you the way, so to speak." His smirk was as evil as mine had ever hoped to be when I'd commented on his newly found fork phobia. "Do you want to hear *that* story? I've told it to every single creature I know and sent it in to *Penthouse Forum*. I may as well tell it to the person it actually happened to."

If we hadn't been on the interstate, I would've thrown myself out of the car. I didn't think it, I knew it. If this car weren't so old, Leandros would've hit the child safety locks the minute the puck had ever opened his mouth. Instead, he'd reached back and slammed the lock down with his hand. I'd lost my memory, but he hadn't lost his.

"Goodfellow, if he doesn't kill you with a fork, I may. Stop taunting him. He's been through enough." Finally, Leandros cut in, looking out for little brother. I could see the upside to having a brother—for as long as I was trapped in a car with the puck anyway. "It was with a nymph, Cal. Your first time was with a meadow nymph in Central Park. I think you said her name was Charm. As for Delilah, yes, she's a Wolf, and off-limits now, considering that she did try to kill a friend and would've killed you in his place if it would've gotten her what she wanted. I myself have an arrangement with a vampire named Promise. I told you, nonhuman does not mean monster. It only means be careful."

I'd been doing a werewolf. My brother had an "arrangement" with a vampire. The puck was monogamous with something with wings and a sword and had been nonmonogamous with anything that moved in the past. "Thanks, guys. Way to go with putting my whole monsters-are-evil thing in perspective. Mom's dead. I don't have a father because getting a guy's name when you screw him is so boring. And I did her great example one better by sleeping with someone who wanted to kill me or use me in some bizarre furry Mafia power play. Life is less a horror movie and more of a goth soap opera. Again, thanks so much for saving me from that god-awful normal life I had working in the diner back in Nevah's Landing. You're real pals." I shifted my ass to a corner between seat and door, ate my candy bar, and tried to ignore them. They didn't make it easy.

Goodfellow explained how there'd been a rumor of an Ammut priestess doing some very bad things for her goddess down in South Carolina, but it was barely a hint of supernatural gossip. We'd known it would most likely end up as nothing, so I'd gone alone. I'd called and said there was no priestess but a nest of spiders—nothing I couldn't handle, especially with the grenade I'd taken with me. Apparently I'd never had the chance to use it. They didn't know what had happened—whether the spiders had gotten the jump on me or I'd had a bad day when I took them on—but I hadn't called back. They hadn't been able to track me down with the GPS of my phone, the one I'd lost in the water. I hadn't even been supposed to be in the Landing. I'd been several towns over when I'd called. How had I ended up there? Other than a childhood longing for Never Land, it was a mystery.

I grunted and kept working on the candy bar.

Leandros said they hadn't found my car, borrowed from Goodfellow's used-car lot. He was a used-car salesman—didn't that figure? The puck could probably sell vibrating panties to nuns. The two of them hadn't known whether the spiders had chased me to the Landing or I had chased them. They'd been depending on me to fill them in once they found me, because not finding me had never been an option. Leandros was very clear about that. He'd let Goodfellow do most of the talking, ninety-nine point nine percent of the never-ending talking, but of this he personally wanted to make absolutely sure I knew I hadn't been deserted. I was his brother. He was finding me and bringing me back. Nothing and no one would stop him. He'd hunt until he found me or dropped dead of old age still in search of my bleached bones. It was all very Inigo Montoya of him. My identity was buried in black clouds, but movies I knew. Stupid goddamn spider.

"You're loyal and faithful, like ... um ... a basset hound," I offered Leandros in reply as I swallowed the last bite of chocolate. It was lame, no doubt about it, but I had to say something. His knuckles were whitening on the steering wheel. He wanted or needed some sort of acknowledgment. I tried again. "That's good to know, especially in the monster-killing business." There. I'd done my duty. On to other things. "Are there more candy bars?"

"You're my only family, Cal." He sounded more determined, if possible, to get his point across. "I will not let you down. Ever." I was half afraid he'd pull over to write that vow in blood. He appeared impassive to the casual eye, but there was a mass of emotion under that outer stoicism. Look at me with the big words. Being impressed with my mental literary skills was a good distraction from admitting to myself that I knew what Leandros was hiding on the inside.

Too fast, all this was too damn fast. It was like meeting a woman's parents on the first date. It was too much, too soon, and the cherry on top of all the strange and weird I'd woken up to less than a week ago.

"Yeah, that's great." I went for casual. There was nothing wrong with casual. "We're close. Work together. You don't let your vampire chick eat me. I'm grateful. About those candy bars . . ."

Goodfellow interrupted me and this time the smug, salacious, mocking voice was anything but. "Do not. Do not joke about this. Niko won't say or do anything about it, but I will. You respect this and you respect that you are the luckiest man living to have the family you do, to have the brother you have."

Just like that, casual was gone and I felt a complete and utter dick. I'd been so damn appreciative of what the people of the Landing had done for me, a haircut and a job, and here Leandros was telling me he practically would've spent the rest of his *life* hunting for me if that was what it took. What did I do? Asked for more candy bars. Called him a basset hound—not that there was anything wrong with basset hounds, but this was my brother. I didn't remember it yet, but he was, and I was an idiot if I didn't count myself lucky to have any family at all, much less family that refused to give up on me. Granted, he had kidnapped me, but, technically, it was for my own good. I'd wondered that first day in the Landing if I had friends, and I was all but spitting on a brother.

"Leandros, Christ, I'm sorry about the loyal and faithful thing. I'm sure you're a better brother than a basset hound." I grimaced. As apologies went, that was a concoction of frigging beauty. "Sorry about being a shit." I could've said more, but, let's face it, if he was my brother—the kind that evidently swore blood oaths and would battle armies single-handedly to make sure I got regular dental care or a yearly flu shot—then he knew what was under my outer candy-coated shell too.

The tense lines of his shoulders relaxed a fraction. "You don't have to say that. In fact, it could start a precedent that would have you apologizing every minute of every day, and your time-management skills aren't that impressive to begin with. Only know that you're not alone. That's enough."

I was off the hook for being an ass, but more than that, I knew I wasn't alone in the world. Not too many people could say that. It was humbling to know someone always had your back. It honestly was. I sat and "humbled" for a while before asking one more time. "I hate to bring it up again, but after cutting up that spider and flushing the pieces down the toilet, I didn't get a chance to finish my breakf—"

A candy bar hit me in the forehead. Not particularly offended, I ate it and then napped. Concussions, evil Egyptian spiders, a brother whose code of honor was so deep he'd consider the Knights of the Round Table drunken and corrupt frat boys; it'd been an eventful day. Amnesia-man needed his rest.

When I woke up, we were in New York City, and Leandros and Goodfellow had switched positions. I straightened for a better look. Cars were bumper-to-bumper on all sides, a mighty herd of rush-hour bison headed for the cliff's edge, too tightly packed to know their fate. I looked past them at the people on the sidewalks. People rushed along, streams of them, crabby and impatient cockroaches muttering and pushing. Late, late, for a very important date. Rude and obnoxious and everywhere.

This was a good place to hide—if you had to.

The Landing would always have a part of me for some indefinable reason, but this—*this* was home. I knew this city. I knew its heart and its whole, if not the details. I knew Central Park and the subway. I knew the rich places and the less than; the places you could walk alone and the places you shouldn't. I knew graffiti and garbage-filled stairwells. I didn't know any specific club or bagel shop, but I highly doubted I ate bagels anyway. I was hot dogs and relish down to my bones. It didn't matter that I didn't know where to go to get that hot dog yet. I took it all in.

"Home."

I couldn't stop myself from agreeing with Leandros on that one. "Yeah, it is."

Finally we reached a smaller street and Goodfellow pulled the car halfway up on the curb. "Welcome to the Lower East Side, if you don't recall, a very exclusive part."

Leandros was already out of the car as I opened my door. "What's so exclusive about it?" It wasn't as nice as some of the other streets we'd gone down. The buildings here were more "old garage" than nice converted apartments.

He nodded for me to get out as well. He didn't touch me, which was considerate of him. I was trying to go with the flow, but having space to think and time to do it in helped. "The privacy element," he answered for the puck. "Promise has a deceased husband or two. . . ."

"Five," Goodfellow corrected in a manner he didn't try to pass off as remotely helpful.

"Regardless of the number," said Leandros, able to grind his teeth with the best of them, "one owned a good deal of real estate. We moved from our last place a few months ago when it became difficult to smuggle out the bodies and more difficult to explain why the "thieves" that kept breaking into our apartment through the window did it by scaling four stories. Here it's considerably easier to go about the business of our business, and Promise keeps the rent reasonable."

Goodfellow opened his mouth, noted Leandros's blanker-than-blank face, then addressed me instead. "See you soon, kid," he called through the open window. "I'd slap you on the shoulder and say something witty and movingly eloquent, but as you'd only stab me with a fork, I'll save it for another time." He raised a hand and the car bounced off the curb and back into the street almost before Leandros finished closing the trunk after retrieving his duffel bag. The shirt I was wearing had come out of that bag. From the heft and clank of it, that shirt was the only nonlethal thing in there.

"I live here?" I asked. The building we stood by had a definite old-garage feel. There were flyers on the metal advertising a hundred different things. There were no garbage-filled stairwells or a homeless guy pissing on a potted bush, but that was probably because there was no potted bush. It was inside living, though, which meant monster killing paid, because I knew that no part-time bartender could afford anything but a cardboard box with wall-to-wall scrap carpeting.

There was some graffiti on the sidewalk, less graffiti maybe than long scratches scraped with something hard like metal. It read, *Where are your brothers and sisters?* A religious nut had been by recently, it appeared, as the scratches looked fresh. It was along the same line as "Am I not my brother's keeper?" only more gender friendly. Gotta watch out for the sisters too.

"You live here," Leandros confirmed. I walked across the letters to the door that had been placed off center into the corrugated metal that fronted the building. Battleship gray, the door opened without a key. You didn't need a key when someone had taken a crowbar to the lock sometime in the past.

"Okay, that's not right. I don't need a memory to know that," I said. "Great. I get amnesia, attacked by a spider in the john, and robbed. It just keeps getting better and better."

"Hmm. It happens. It is New York." Niko went in first and I followed, seeing that I had no neighbors. The entire building was one big space with the metal ceiling two stories high. There were windows up there to see the daylight beginning to dim. To the right was an area devoted to living. I noted a coffee table that looked cheap but brand-new, a couch that was about fifteen years past its prime with only prayer and duct tape holding it together, and beside it a small kitchen area with a bar separating the two spaces. You could eat there too and still swivel to see the TV hanging on the wall . . . and it was a great TV—big and flat with what I knew had to be one frigging amazing picture. I was in love with that TV.

So I hadn't been robbed. No one would've left that TV. More and more weird.

The other half of the room was devoted to living in another way—keeping yourself alive. There were weights, a punching bag, mats on the floor, and untouched targets on the walls. Fresh paper, black silhouettes of human bodies intact. I liked that too. If you plan on surviving giant spiders, it's nice to have a home gym to train in. Only one thing was off.

It was pristine, despite the couch carcass. Immaculate with a place for everything and everything in its place. The new targets were the worst, like hotels that fold your toilet paper into a neat point. Who wants their toilet paper practically folded into an airplane? I didn't know me, not all of me, only five going on six days of me if you wanted to count, but I compared the condition of my motel room on my last day in the Landing with this. "This isn't right," I said, walking to the coffee table and nudging the remote control out of its perfectly parallel alignment with the table's edge. Leandros reached past me and nudged it right back, then started to give me a similar nudge toward a six-foot-long hall. Whoever had converted this place had put up a wall that stopped about nine feet up. You had the open space above you, but you had privacy as well. The hall was dead center of that wall. This time Niko moved past me to lead the way and open the door on the right. I followed him and peered into the room.

There was no floor; only piles of clothes. Chances were that Einstein in his day could've theorized there was a floor under all that dirty laundry, but I wouldn't bet a Nobel Prize on it. The bed was unmade with dark blue sheets and a cover so tangled they were almost one giant complex knot, the kind kids who go to Boy Scout camp learn to make. One pillow was at the head of the bed and one at the foot with a petrified piece of pizza resting on it. The wall you would face while you were in that bed was scarred with hundreds of slashes. The knife that had made them was still embedded in the plasterboard. A black marker had been used to connect all the marks to spell out *Screw you*. Under the bed I could see the gleam of metal and lots of it. If the bogey-man showed up under there, good luck finding a place to wedge itself amidst that arsenal. It was a disaster area. You could get federal funds to airlift people out of this biohazard nightmare.

I grinned. I didn't mean to, but this was right. This was the room of a guy who didn't know what the word pristine meant. "Now this I get."

Leandros snorted, and the guy had plenty of nose to snort with. "There are some places men aren't meant to go. This room is five steps above the Bermuda Triangle on that list. I pretend it doesn't exist and you do what you can to confine your chaos here lest it escape the apartment and gobble up the neighbors. That is the bathroom." He pointed to the closed door across from my room and then indicated the last room, the one at the end of the hall. "And that is my room."

His room. *His* room? "We live together?" Hell, no. Family, brothers, sacred oaths sealed with a bar of chocolate smacking you in the face; I was doing all I could to accept that. But living together? "What if you want to bring your vamp over and do . . . I don't know . . . whatever you do? Bite each other, talk about how sexy losing a pint of blood is, and how iron deficiency is so hot? Do you leave a blood bank brochure taped to the door to warn me? What did I do when I brought over Lassie? Hang a chew toy on the doorknob? Aren't we a little old to be bunking together as if this were sleep-away camp?"

He could've given me reasons. It took two to pay the rent, especially on a place this huge, even with a good

deal on that rent. It was also convenient if your room-
mate was in the same business as you so you didn't have
to explain the spider guts on your clothes and the knives
in the dishwasher—the kind of knives you aren't using
on toast unless you planned to gut and field-dress it. The
stalest toast didn't deserve that treatment.

But there were things on his mind other than explaining our living arrangement. "Do you know how
very hard I'm trying not to smack your thick skull right
now?" He pinched the bridge of his nose. "Open the
bathroom door."

I didn't see how that was going to affect his wanting
to inflict bodily injury due to my runaway mouth and
a weariness that still deepened the creases beside his
mouth. Four and a half days searching while not knowing if your brother was dead or alive, I'd have wanted
to pop me and my smart-ass self one too. "Is there as-
pirin in there? You look like you could use it." I put my
hand out and turned the knob. "I think we need to get
the landlord over here. It smells like the toilet's been
backed up for a month or you have a body decomposing
in the bathtub."

Holy shit.

There *was* a decomposing body, and more surprising
than that was how fast it moved. I'd have thought the
death and putrefaction would've slowed it down some,
but nope. It was hell on wheels, a graveyard on wheels,
whatever you wanted to call it. It snarled in my direction, showing me yellow teeth stained with fluids I didn't
want to think about. The eyes were white and clouded,
but it could see. They were fixed on me with unmistak-
able greed as its mottled tongue swiped at the dead gray
of its lips. The slime of its flesh wasn't nearly covered up
enough by the shabby clothes of a bum, and there was
nothing at all that could cover up the stench of it out

in the open. It saw me, it wanted me, but it didn't have a chance to reach for me. Its head had already landed on the floor with the sound of a rotten melon splitting apart.

Niko's sword wasn't like Goodfellow's. While Goodfellow went for a more traditional broadsword, Leandros carried a katana he'd pulled from a sheath strapped to his back and hidden by his coat. What had been a fan of silver slicing through the air was now held before him, as ready as it had been before chopping through the zombie's neck.

"What the fuck? What's with you people?" I demanded, "First giant spiders, now zombies. Can't you take a piss without running into a monster? Just goddamn once?"

It did explain the broken lock, though. As zombies were always wanting to eat brains, they couldn't have enough of their own left to pick a lock. It had smashed it instead.

"Don't be so dramatic. I wanted you to see how you need to always be prepared, even when you're home, especially when you're home. Revenants have always hated us and they work for the Kin, who aren't particularly fond of us either. And this is not a zombie. There are no such things as zombies."

The torso on the floor twitched, convulsed, and for a gruesome and nearly pants-wetting moment, I was positive it was going to get to its feet and keep going, decapitated or not. Head? Who needed that? I was damn grateful Goodfellow wasn't here to answer that question for me.

"No zombies. Thanks for clearing that up for me. With it rotting and smelling like roadkill, I let myself jump to conclusions." Dramatic, my ass. I stepped over its splayed arm and worked further on the urine-suppression issue when a hand with thick twisted nails grabbed my ankle. Even badass monster killers had freaked-out moments and this was one of them.

"Always cut their head off, and even then it takes a minute of two for them to die," Leandros advised. "Don't bother with their arms or legs. They'll only pick them up and do their best to bludgeon you to death with them."

"The head. No arms or legs. I'll write it down. Just let me get my notebook." I kicked the hand off my ankle and went into my room, then immediately under the bed. When I returned, I had two things with me I didn't need memories to know that I loved with all the passion of an alcoholic for his next drink. In one hand I had a matte black Desert Eagle .50 and in the other, a knife, also matte black. She was a Ka-Bar serrated combat knife, and if she was good enough for the United States Marine Corps, she might let me survive taking a leak in peace. It wasn't that peculiar that I could remember things like that, weapons down to the last detail, but I couldn't remember a brother. That could be blamed on the fact that he and my whole life up until a week ago would take up a much bigger chunk of my gray matter than the best weapons to use to clear a path to the toilet paper.

"Cover me," I said, stepping over the body this time . . . after giving it a solid kick in the ribs. He wanted me to be prepared, he'd said. I was prepared, but no one was going to pass up pausing to sightsee at what he thought was a zombie. "I'm going in. I'll flush twice if I need reinforcements."

It'd been a long drive and all the new information—new to me at any rate—in the world couldn't change one of life's most basic facts: When you gotta go, you gotta go.

killer, protector of the weak, kicker of the alcoholic and
perverted ass. Why wouldn't I deserve family?

"Who are you?" He distracted me from my inner pep
talk/argument with myself. "As in you are Caliban Leandros of the Vayash Clan? That you work in this bar that
cannot serve one drink in three years that hasn't had at
least one feather in it? That you hunt monsters if they
warrant it?" Resigned to the feather issue, he sipped the
milk before finishing. "Or who are you, starting from
birth until now? Then there's that most basically raw
level, the psychological one. Goodfellow would probably rather tell you that—if you want to be on a ledge
without the will to live within five minutes. He drove
Freud into a phallic-obsessed psychosis. He could drive
you into an early grave. He's that persuasive." He fished
out another feather. "Besides, we need to return to work
on finding Ammut. Her killing won't have stopped while
we were gone looking for you."

I took a swallow of my own drink. Beer. I deserved it
after what Leandros had inflicted on me since eight a.m.
We'd run. For no reason. That was the baffling part. No
one was chasing us; yet we'd run miles and miles. I'd discovered I goddamn hated running or anything remotely
exercise related . . . even if it was, again, "for my own
good." That kind of epic discovery merited a beer. That
we routinely ran every single day, rain or shine, called
for a pitcher of beer, but I stuck with the bottle. If we
ran again later, it would mean less to puke up. The lunch
we'd had a few hours ago had made its own attempt
without any alcoholic help. Leandros's favorite place
had turned out not to be vegetarian, but vegan, which
was for people who preferred their suicide slow. Starving yourself to death via bean curd took commitment.

"Huh. That's the most I've heard you say since I met
you. It's been only two days, but damn. I didn't know you

had it in you," I said. "And considering how well we've apparently not done against Ammut so far, maybe we should leave her spider-loving ass alone."

"At least you aren't saying kidnapped any longer, and you're the one who does most of the talking. My role is usually trying to keep you from talking as it tends to annoy our clients and our enemies. You do like your"—he searched for the right word—"hobby. And your hobby involves irritating nearly everyone you can. As for Ammut, we can handle her. We've handled worse."

I had a hobby, one I was probably born with, but still it was another piece of me confirmed. I grinned and took another swallow. "Who doesn't love sarcasm?"

"Anything you've killed. I've actually seen you hesitate on a deathblow so you could deliver some sort of action movie tagline first." He shook his head, giving me the same look he'd given the feather in his milk.

"Then I'm a sarcastic idiot?" I grinned again. Brotherly resignation——that was fun too.

The eyes that were my mirror suddenly weren't anymore. They lightened and I saw amusement in the gray. Did I ever look like that? Content? At peace? The way I semi-avoided my own reflection, who knew? "Yes, you're a sarcastic idiot, but you're easier to keep alive than a fichus and you look good in the corner of the apartment."

"And I can water myself. Handy." The bar where we were drinking, the Ninth Circle, was where I was a part-time bartender. It was also a "peri" bar. Peris, Leandros had told me, were rumored to be half angel, half demon, but they were simply supernatural creatures with wings and the source of most angel myths. Then he added that all myths were wrong in one way or the other and to never depend on them, assuming I remembered them. I should depend on him instead.

For someone who *had* kidnapped me—no matter how he phrased it, claimed me as his brother, and made me run this morning until I'd hoped I'd cough up my lungs so I could die and end it all, he made me want to believe him. He had this air about him. If this were a movie, and it seemed more like it all the time, he'd be dead in the first fifteen minutes; it was just that kind of aura of too damn good and noble for this world. A Goose in a world full of Mavericks.

On the other hand, he chopped the head off a revenant as if he were dicing a carrot for a salad. Honorable but deadly. I was lucky to be related to him and that he liked me. If he didn't, it might've been my head bouncing down the hall. I frowned slightly at the thought. "You like me, right? I mean, you swore to find me to the ends of the earth with all sorts of angst in your great big noble basset hound heart, but that's duty. That's an obligation. Do you actually like me?" Okay, that didn't make me sound like a girl at all. "Do you not hate me, I mean. Am I an okay coworker? Do a good job with the monster killing? Not cause too much trouble? Remember to get you a Christmas present, like extra hefty garbage bags for tossing out nonzombie bodies? Am I a not-too-crappy brother?" Oh shit, forgetting Christmas seemed like something I would do, considering the condition of my room. My brain was probably in the same condition—a crazed mess where not one dutiful holiday responsibility could be found until a month too late. "Fuck. Am I a *bad* brother?"

Under all of that verbal diarrhea was the same thing I'd kept repeating in Nevah's Landing—I'm not such a bad guy. Tell me I'm not a bad guy. Only this time, here was someone who actually knew for sure.

This was stupid. It wasn't as though he'd want to waste his time on someone who wasn't halfway decent.

His standards were high—up-in-the-atmosphere high. I could tell—anyone who was around him longer than two minutes could tell. That meant I couldn't see him putting up with someone who wasn't worth it. I didn't know why I wanted the Leandros brothers' seal of approval anyway. I was who I was. I'd worn a gingham apron without killing anyone over it. Really, how bad could I be?

He studied me so intently that I instantly wished I'd kept my mouth shut. Unless I was eight years old and had a Barbie Diary, this wasn't the kind of conversation I should be having. I was a guy. Guys were stoic and macho and we had three emotions: bored, angry, and horny. If there were more, they'd have sent around a memo. I slid down in my seat and concentrated on my beer. God knew I couldn't fake a piss break. Godzilla himself would probably pop out of the goddamn toilet with the luck I'd been having in bathrooms.

Leandros reached across to tap his soy milk glass against my beer bottle. "Aside from a rather excessive enthusiasm for your work, you are a good brother, yes. You're certainly not a bad one." He smiled. Though all his smiles seemed barely a reflection of a dictionary-defined one, this one was genuine. "You might have some impulse and sarcasm issues, but other than that, not a bad brother or a bad person. I'm proud to call you my brother."

That was something. When you didn't know who you were other than you woke up in a nest of dead spiders and carried a large number of things that could kill an equally large number of people, to hear that from someone who *did* know you . . . It was . . . Damn. I went on the defensive. I had to. I had the reputation of my gonads to protect. "If it weren't for the sword you carry, I'd tell you what a wuss you are. I'm embarrassed for you, Leandros, seriously."

"Love you too, little brother." He kicked me under the table with meticulous precision, hitting some sort of nerve that made my ankle and foot go instantly numb. It wasn't the first time either. How did he do that? "There's Ishiah. I'll be back."

He left the table and had one of the peris, a big blond one—light blond hair and skin compared to Niko's darker version—up against a wall and was talking with him as I cursed and rubbed my ankle. When I looked closer, it wasn't so much of a talk as Niko telling the peri something—forcefully. He didn't have a finger planted in the guy's chest, not physically anyway, but he was laying down the law somehow. As he did, the peri's wings appeared.

They came out of nowhere in a shimmer of light, a flash of brightness as if the sun had exploded. Not there, then there. It was like a magic trick. I felt as if I should applaud and send his feathered ass to Vegas for a new career. With gold-barred white feathers, he did look like an angel, a muscular, anger-me-not, scarred angel, but an angel all the same. I could see where the myths had come from. If this guy came after me with a flaming sword, I'd get my ass to temple quick. Cross a desert. Free a cheap source of labor. Whatever. Just say the word.

Minutes later they were both back at the table. "Cal," Leandros said in introduction, "this is your employer, Ishiah. He owns the bar. You're the only nonperi to work here, so you can expect the patrons to give you somewhat of a hard time. When you come back to work, that is, which won't be until this Ammut mess is cleared up."

I stood, trying not to favor the still-throbbing ankle. "You're the boss, huh?" I didn't offer to shake hands. That would be too surreal in this world, and I didn't have an instinct to stick out a hand unless it had a weapon in it. A shaker I was not, it seemed. I went with the assumption that Niko had explained about my memory problem. "I made a pretty decent server at a diner. I think I'll do okay as a bartender. Oh yeah, if I try to kill you, I'm sorry. Just a reflex. I'm having trouble getting it through my head that monsters ... er ... nonhumans aren't always evil."

The peri switched focus from me to Leandros. "Robin told me, but I didn't completely understand. This ..." His wings spread to a span nearly twelve feet wide. Then they tucked back in before spreading wide again. If he'd been a hawk, I would've said he was unsettled. "Never mind. Take as long as you need." He turned his attention back to me for the last part. "Take as much vacation time as you require until your memory returns. The Ninth Circle isn't what you would call a tame drinking establishment. We tend to lose at least one customer weekly. I want you at your best when you come back."

"My old self. Gotcha."

The peri gripped my shoulder and somewhat harder than an employer-employee chat called for. "Let us just say whenever you're ready." Then he was gone with one last long look at Leandros before he was behind the bar with another peri, this one with dark hair.

"You are a bunch of touchy-type people, I gotta tell you." There was a trail of feathers from in front of me all the way back to the bar. As with the indecisive wings, that didn't strike me as a good sign. Didn't birds lose feathers when stressed? If I were a bird, I would. "Is he molting? Does he have some sort of giant-bird disease?"

"Only if Goodfellow gave it to him." Pointing back at my chair, he added, "You may as well settle in. We've a long meeting ahead of us. Promise, Robin ..."

He went on some more, but I blanked it out as I realized that my part-time boss, who looked like an angel and shed like a dog with mange, was the other half of the monogamy special that the puck bragged about. I hoped Goodfellow hadn't told him about the fork incidents. I'd hate for him to get pissed at me and have to put Polly-Want-a-Cracker down. I only killed bad monsters—I was coming to terms with that—and he didn't seem bad.

All monsters are. You know that. You're born a monster, you die a monster, and there is nothing but slaughter between.

"Cal? Are you listening?" Leandros's hand pushed me into the chair. "Obviously not. I suppose it's good to know some things don't change, amnesia or not."

I was listening, but to myself, not to my newly discovered brother. There was no denying whose voice was in my head. It was mine and, although people lied to themselves all the time, I didn't sound unsure on this. No tent-revival hellfire preacher was more absolute. I didn't get it. The puck wasn't human and he'd helped Leandros find me. The peri wasn't human and he didn't come across as a bad guy except for a little get-thee-sinning-asses-out-of-Eden grimness to him. Two nonhumans who were good enough not to try to kill me should balance the spiders and that revenant creature that had. It should prove what Leandros had told me. You took it on a case-by-case basis, because not all monsters were like people. Some were good and some were bad. They weren't all evil. They all didn't need to die.

All monsters. All.

I pushed it all aside for the moment. I had amnesia. Let's face it: Who knew what else was screwed up in my skull? A half hour later and my scrambled brain had much more to distract it.

The Wolves—there was no real reason to get side-tracked by the Wolves. So said Leandros. The fact that they smelled like a hundred and one wet dogs, I over-looked. I brought it up, don't get me wrong, but Leandros said, whereas some people were born artists or musi-cians, I was born with a nose that could smell a meatball sub five miles away. I was talented. Stop complaining about it and stop asking Samyel, the peri bartender, to take them to the nearest groomer for a shampoo and toenail painting. Let them drink and play pool in peace without any "go fetch" jokes. The fact that they all stared at me—at length, every last one, with unblinking eyes, after sniffing in my direction—and then whispered and growled among themselves, I took to mean that I wasn't their favorite server at the bar. A human—how disgust-ing. They'd probably hoped when I'd disappeared that it was for good. Whatever.

As I said, I overlooked them . . . eventually. Then there was the cat. It was Goodfellow's cat or Goodfel-low was the cat's puck. Probably Goodfellow being the cat's puck was the right choice. It was bald, it had teeth that made a grizzly bear look like a still-nursing baby rabbit, and it was dead. Deader than dead. Mummified. Glowing empty eye sockets. That didn't stop it from batting pretzels around the table or stalking one of the Wolves to the back alley. She, the cat Salome, was the only one to return from the alley, but that wasn't my business. What the dead cat wanted, the dead cat could have. In my opinion, it was one less Wolf stinking up the place.

And, let me repeat: walking, purring dead cat. Dead cat with attitude.

Dead fucking cat. Holy shit.

Following the cat in a general "tie my sanity to the tracks and let the train run over it" was Leandros's . . . girlfriend? Lady friend? Vamp friend? Vamp tramp? No, I'd had enough sense not to say any of them or think that last one for more than a second. She didn't look like a tramp anyway. She wasn't pretty, beautiful, or hot. She was more of a marble statue under a cascade of moonlight, smelling like flowers and ivy—the glory of a weeping graveyard angel. She was solemn and silk and as much of a promise as her name.

I expected not to like her. I was doing better at restraining the nonhuman twitch and all the Wolves, not to mention other things in the bar, had nearly overloaded it. You could only twitch so much before you either went into convulsions or acclimated. I was doing my best to avoid seizures, which meant acclimation it was. But I'd already made up my mind about this in particular in advance. Whether she was monster or only nonhuman, evil or not, she wasn't good enough for my brother. It didn't matter if I remembered his being my brother or not. The puck had said Wolves were for Wolves; humans weren't good enough. I was all set to have the same opinion about humans and vamps. Keep to your own kind.

First, while Wolves and vampires were born, not made, so sayeth that brother I was worried about, she still was a few hundred years older than he, which made her a cougar. Second, sooner or later she'd leave him when he got older, and he would. All humans did. If he was only screwing her, maybe it would be different, but he was a six-foot-tall ball of commitment. After only two days, I could see that. He would hurt. If I was lucky enough to have family, I didn't want them hurt. Third, he had told me vampires didn't drink blood anymore. They didn't kill anymore—the majority of them. But how many people had she killed before modern vampire technology came up with a good old vitamin-B-for-blood shot, those secret vampire underground supplements you can't buy online? They were on the wagon now, the vamps, and she could be remorseful as they came for what she'd done to survive in ye olden days. It didn't matter.

And why would a vamp want to be with a human anyway? What they used to eat? That was like getting horny for your hamburger. Farmer John cozying up to Bessie the cow. It was weird. Fuck not the food, that was my opinion. I couldn't help it. I didn't like the idea of it, and I wasn't going to.

That was that.

Then came the moment she entered the bar, sat down, took off her cloak of violet wool, and extended her pale hand toward me with a concerned "Caliban, how are you feeling?"

There she sat, with striped dark brown and pale blond hair pulled up in a twist that only women can manage. Simple yet somehow complex. I could've braided a lariat and taught myself how to rope a steer before coming up with that knot. She wore a dress that covered up too much to be sexy while still being snug enough to catch the eye, with knee-high boots to take the prim-and-proper down a notch but still look like a lady—a rich one. Her eyes, violet as her cloak, and her smooth face were as concerned as her tone. She looked nice. She sounded nice. It didn't stop the twitch.

You're born a monster, you die a monster, and there's nothing but murder in between.

The same refrain as before and it felt as true as before, but I felt something else. She was sad, this vampire— damn sad and with good reason to be, although I had no idea what that reason was.

There's no such thing as the best. There's good enough, though. Sometimes. She makes you happy, Nik. A happy brother's not such a bad thing.

My voice again, but this time it was a flash of memory crawling out of the past, my first real one. I didn't remember when or why I'd said it, but it sounded as if I'd meant it.

I looked at her hand. "Yeah . . . I'm sorry. I'm trying to be good, I am, but it's probably best I don't touch you just yet." I might be forgiven for accidentally attacking my boss, but Leandros might not be so forgiving if I did the same to his girlfriend.

She withdrew her hand, her ivory mouth, as pale as the rest of her, losing that reassuring smile she'd been giving me. "I don't understand."

Goodfellow almost choked as he laughed around the last swallow of his drink and waved his hand at a peri for another bottle of scotch. Yes, not a glass—a bottle. The puck had some serious tolerance. "He's telling the truth. He *is* trying to be good, difficult as that is to believe. And polite. What a change a few days down south can make. He's become a Southern gentleman. It's almost as amusing as when Venus became too fat to float on that shell. That's what you get for eating nothing but honey cakes and mead." He took the new bottle of scotch and poured himself a glass. "To be fair, however, anything the kid does that doesn't involve him stabbing me with a fork goes in my entertaining column these days."

Her eyes glanced at the puck skeptically, then back at me. "You tried to stab Robin with a fork?"

I held up three fingers. "Sorry to say I don't regret a one of them. Okay, strictly not true. I sort of regret the two that didn't connect."

Niko intervened when Goodfellow began to look less amused. "Cal has some . . . difficulties, let's say, with non-humans. All nonhumans. He's having trouble discerning between the good and the bad."

I shrugged. "Monsters are monsters, and monsters are bad, but I'm working on it."

Like Ishiah, the guy with the feathers, she said nearly

the same thing: "You told me on the phone, but I hadn't comprehended he'd be quite like . . . this." The fingers touched the back of Leandros's hand in what appeared to be support as the ocean of heather concentrated on me. "You'll be yourself soon enough, Caliban. I can wait until then to touch your hand or kiss your cheek."

I couldn't help it. I wasn't expecting her to say that, and monsters' mouths were made to eat you, maul you, tear you; there was no damn silverware on the table, but there were knives. I had knives. My hand was already going for one inside my jacket when Leandros's hand clamped down on my wrist, not enough to hurt, but enough to shake me out of it.

"Could you please," he requested in a mild tone and with an unbreakable grip, "not attempt to stab Promise with one of your knives."

"Or a fork," Goodfellow interjected.

"Or a fork," Leandros repeated with a patience that had to make him double as a saint. "Promise, if you could avoid startling Cal until he remembers that you do care for him and he for you, we might all survive this," he said, and added with a wry tinge to the words, "He startles easily now."

I could say I did not startle easily, but it was hard to back up when I'd wanted to stab someone for threatening to kiss me on the damn cheek. I decided to ignore the entire thing. It had never happened. Pride saved. "So"—I shook off the hand and rested my own on the table— "let's talk goddesses and what the fuck you do about them except pray at their altars or run far far away."

Hours later Goodfellow was close to being buzzed, the bar had run out of scotch, and I knew Ammut, the Eater of Hearts, had been born of the Egyptian Nile; she was as old as Goodfellow, which was so old he couldn't remember; and she wasn't a goddess in truth.

Relieved? Yeah, a little bit.

"Everyone back then who could get more than two humans to worship them was claiming to be a god or a goddess. And why not? Free food. Vestal virgins . . . vestal horny virgins. Fertility rites. Good times. Very good times. If you could pass as one, why not claim it?" Goodfellow had said. While I marveled that there was nothing in his view of history that couldn't be directly linked to some sort of orgy, he went on with the rest of it. Ammut thought hearts were a nice snack, but she really liked souls much better. Except nonhumans didn't call them souls, because they weren't souls. It was a creature's life force she drained and consumed.

Ammut, in Egyptian legend, ate the heart of a dead person if they were found unworthy of passing on to the afterlife. If you did bad things, it weighted down your heart, much like fried pork chops weighted it down with cholesterol. Sin and fried pork chops—two of the best things in the world, and all they got you was an early death and acting as the dinner for a greedy Egyptian fake goddess.

We'd gone through this all before, but I'd forgotten it. I didn't think it would be that long before I started remembering things on my own again. Last night lying on a bed surrounded by enough rumpled clothes to stock a Salvation Army store, seeing the city lights through the windows high above, it had felt the way it should. Right. True. As if I recognized it with my body if not my mind. It was the same when I woke up this morning when Leandros had kicked lightly at the bottom of my mattress. I hadn't thought about shooting him with the gun under my pillow once. I'd been tempted. . . . It was eight a.m. for Christ's sake . . . but I hadn't actually put any real thought into it. It had felt right too. Then there were the shadows and bits of thoughts I couldn't connect to any solid memory, but that hadn't stopped them from popping up today.

"When she sucks out their life force, they die." I started to take a pretzel out of the bowl, when the dead cat gave me a look. I let her have the pretzel. She didn't eat it, but she wanted it and that was good enough for me. I feared no giant spider, but her . . . I was on the fence. "Are there souls? What if she did eat them? Does that mean no afterlife for the unlucky bastard? Is there an afterlife?" The cat didn't count. She was still moving. She wasn't so much after life as predeath. Halfway between.

Goodfellow looked up at the ceiling and scratched the bald head of his pet. "That's far too encompassing a topic for now. Philosophy can wait. Let's focus on the part of her devouring their life force and they die. That's enough to get the job done."

"On that note, I've got a job to get done. Be right back." I got up and searched out the bathroom. Dick in hand, I was reading the graffiti, a lot of which was about me, go figure, and not in a "for a good time" kind of way, when I heard the door swing and smelled the Wolf. It was an accomplishment. The entire place smelled of the furry bastards. I'd be smelling Wolf for a week. Then came the growl, the breath reeking of rotting meat—not much on flossing—and the mangled words, "You are *weak* now." He moved closer. "I smell it on you." Closer still. "You are weak like a sheep."

Mother*fucker.*

Could a guy literally not take a leak in this messed-up world without fighting for the goddamn privilege?

I had no illusions about what normal wolves did to normal sheep, what Wolves did to human sheep, or what this Wolf wanted to do to me. I kept pissing and raised my other hand that held the Desert Eagle to ram the

muzzle between his eyes as he started to snap his jaws at
my throat. Yeah, I'd learned my lesson the past few days.
I now held my dick in one hand and my gun in the other
when nature called. Guns worked better than forks.

I dug the muzzle harder into his flesh, the metal grat-
ing on the bone of his overhanging brow. He was one
freaky-looking Wolf—not in entirely wolf or human
form, like a cut-rate Halloween werewolf costume. Not
a good look. He looked like a guy overdosing on steroids, Rogaine, and with teeth. . . . Okay, the teeth definitely couldn't pass for human. "You're not that bright,
Rover. I don't know or care why you think the rest of
me is weak, but my trigger finger is Arnold-fucking-
Schwarzenegger. Now back the fuck off or I'll blow your
empty skull apart and finish pissing on your body like a
fire hydrant." I grinned. "You won't get a more appropriate memorial than that."

His skull wasn't as empty as it seemed. He had at
least one brain cell and he used it to back away and out
of the bathroom. Puppies.

Weak? I thought I'd proven I was anything but and
had Nepenthe spiders to testify on that—if they weren't
dead, but maybe he smelled the amnesia on me and
thought without memories I couldn't kick furry tail and
take ID and rabies tags while I did it. Who knew? A few
minutes later I was back at the table with Goodfellow
picking up the Ammut snooze blah blah right where he
left off the second I sat down.

"And the more powerful the nonhuman, the better
Ammut likes it. She isn't wasting much time sending her
spiders after the revenants. They're not worth her time,
but the vampires, Wolves, boggles—they've been more
to her taste, which is why the Kin has said they would
cooperate until this is all over. We have yet to find her or
her nest of spiders. Before you left for South Carolina,

we were going to check Central Park and see if Mama Boggle and her brood were there or if Ammut had gotten to them yet."

Leandros braved an undead paw and put a pretzel in front of me. He did it automatically. I could see a lifetime of feeding the "little brother" behind it. It was so automatic, in fact, I guessed there'd been times we'd gone hungry as kids. Or Leandros had anyway. All his pretzels on hungry days, I'd bet, had gone to me. It was things like that that had made me believe his and Goodfellow's story more than the words. "We can go there tonight. If I had a choice, I'd leave you here with Ishiah and Samyel, but I think you would be safer with the three of us. Too many old enemies know you work here."

"You're worried about me?" I picked up the pretzel and saluted him with it. "I killed an eighty-pound spider with a fork—even if I missed Goodfellow twice. It looks like killing doesn't require a memory." A lesson I'd just taught Rover. "You can put away the diaper and bottle."

I proved that, again, when we stepped outside the bar into a seven o'clock gloom to head to Central Park. I took four steps, pulled the Desert Eagle, pointed it upward, and pulled the trigger. Then I took another step, this time back, as the body hit the pavement at my feet. It was a Wolf, female, and more wolf than human. Another half-and-half. All Wolf. The jaw was twisted and wide-open for my throat, the fangs bared. Her hands were more like elongated paws, her eyes open and staring pure gold. There wasn't any blood to speak of, only a hole in her forehead. Shattered bone and burned flesh. The dead don't bleed. She'd jumped from three stories up; that and the bad lighting made it a good shot. And that was all I felt—the satisfaction of a job well-done.

At first.

I was a not-so-bad brother. I saved people. And I was

a killer. I didn't feel bad about the last item. I only killed monsters, I killed only to save those who needed it. I counted myself on that list. If you were going to try to kill me—try hard. I could guarantee I was going to try my best to do the same back to you. If you were a werewolf perched three stories up, you shouldn't make any noise when you jump, because any would be too much. It can seal your fate and it had hers. "A Wolf." I didn't mention the one in the bathroom. He was more braindamaged mutt than Wolf, drunk, and with delusions of fuzzy grandeur. If he was in the Kin, he probably was their equivalent of a janitor. He hadn't had the intelligence for more.

I chambered another round in the Eagle. "Not to mention the revenant-thing in the apartment. I thought you said the Furry Mafia was on our side on this one."

"Except for Delilah. Every pack but hers agreed. The Lupa pack didn't bother to send a reply." Niko was resheathing his sword. He was the big killer looking out for the little killer. "Although I think this may be that response."

My ex's pack, the Lupa, was named for the wolf that suckled the founders of ancient Rome. Leandros liked shoving those little factoids in your ear at every opportunity. He'd told me too that Wolves weren't actually werewolves; they were were-people. They'd started out as wolves and evolved to being able to switch back and forth between wolf and human. Some Wolves wanted to go back to what they'd been before that Jurassic mutation. The cult of All Wolf. That had led to inbreeding and damn odd-looking people with pointed ears or jaws, stuck in between human and wolf, unable to be completely one or the other.

My reaction to that lecture? *Tell* me I hadn't been doing a chick with a hairy back. Dear God, tell me she hadn't had a hairy back. I'd been relieved to find out that Delilah looked all human when she was human and all wolf when she was Wolf. Not like this one lying at my feet.

The gold eyes were fogging over. They'd belonged in the forest, peering through the underbrush, not dead on a sidewalk outside a bar. Suddenly I wasn't as proud of my perfect shot anymore. When killers had the eyes of an animal whose predatory temperament was nature and nature wasn't meant to be the subject of punishment, it was harder to feel a hero. That was how I'd thought of it. I was a cop or a soldier on the front line between the innocent and the nightmares. But I saw it for what it was now. Take pride in whom you're saving, but don't take it in the killing. It was necessary, but it wasn't something to glory in—especially when the creature you killed had thoughts and emotions the same as you, the only difference being a wild and free soul living as born instinct had taught her.

Be good at your job, but don't think your job is good. The road to Hell . . .

I squatted down beside the dead Wolf and touched her hair. It was thick and black, like mine, but long. "We can't leave her just lying here." Killer or not, person or creature of the wild, asphalt was not a peaceful place for any body to find its rest.

"Ishiah will take care of her. This street is nonhuman. It'll be handled." Niko's hand landed on my back and grabbed a handful of my jacket to urge me up. "She's playing with you. Delilah. She knows one of hers couldn't take you, much less all of us. If Delilah wanted you dead, she would've come herself."

Delilah didn't think a pack member could take me, but she thought she could. Since she had gotten her Alpha and pack killed off to the last Wolf, she might be right. I sure knew how to pick them. "If this is a game, I don't want to play." I stood up. "I'm a killer, but I don't think I want to be if this is how it is. Protecting is one thing. Playing, using killing as a damn pastime, that's wrong."

I remembered, in that moment, wings flapping behind my eyes. I was young, little—I had no idea how little, but enough that I remembered being surprised and shocked when a blackbird flew into a window at a house we were living in. I didn't recall the house itself, but I thought it was grubby, dirty, old. I was sitting in grass and weeds, playing with a plastic truck that had three wheels. I was happy, content, until the sound of a stick breaking, but softer, more muffled. The bird had hit the window, and I looked up in time to see it fall to the ground without a single flutter of a feather. A blond boy was there. Six or seven, he was older than me. He picked up the bird gently, then carried it off to a deeper patch of weeds and laid it down. It was swallowed up by green and yellow. I asked why.

Why, Nik? Why won't it fly away?

Because it's dead, Cal. It broke its neck.

But that wasn't right. It wasn't the bird's fault some stupid person had built a house in its way. It wasn't right that birds died, because if birds died, then maybe everything died.

They do, the other boy explained gravely. *It's the way things are, Cal.*

"It shouldn't be," I murmured to myself. "Blackbirds shouldn't die and neither should Wolves or people. Not like this. Not for goddamn sport." I put my gun away. It wasn't reassuring anymore or to be drooled over the size of the hole it could put through something—or someone's head. It was a necessary evil.

"You remember?" Leandros asked. His hand hadn't

released my jacket and he gave me a light shake. "You remember that?"

"I remember the blackbird. That's all. But it's enough to know that if I like what I do [an excessive enthusiasm for my work Leandros had said], then maybe I'm a dick." I looked away from the Wolf and all that had roamed untamed and free in her. Wolves were wolves. They killed. I got that. They had evolved that way. You should stop them, but you shouldn't blame them. If it runs, you chase it. If you catch it, you kill it. If you kill it, you eat it. That sounded familiar too, but if you'd ever seen a lion eating a zebra on the Discovery Channel, you knew that.

Facts of life. Zebras didn't die of old age as much as a little boy and a dead blackbird wished they did.

I exhaled and let it all go. It was coming back, faster and faster now. Soon enough who I was now would be who I was then, and it'd all be the same as it ever was. There was no point in thinking about that. There were other things to do. "The park," I said. "Someone said Central Park and boggles. Boggles, huh? I guess you're not talking that game old people play."

6

Boggle was not the game old people played, because wouldn't that have been too easy?

What it turned out to be was a nine-foot-tall mud-encrusted, humanoid lizard that weighed about five hundred pounds, had pumpkin orange eyes full of fury, and about six cute little kiddies to make the whole thing a party.

"You said she was a mom," I hissed at Leandros from behind a tree. The boggle, Ms. Boggle, whatever name she went by, had just tossed another tree, a complete tree from roots to top that she pulled up out of the ground with no effort whatsoever, at us. She'd missed by inches. In this situation, as in all situations, inches mattered; they could embarrass you and they could make or break you. I was leaning toward embarrassment as the better choice.

Leandros was unperturbed by the trees sailing through the air—another day at the office with staplers, copy machines, bad coffee, and trees almost crushing you. No big deal. That was nice for him. "She is a mother. See behind her? The boglets? Those are her children."

Her children. Her cute bundles of joy. The kiddies were only seven feet tall with grinning jaws, lashing tails, and teeth that curved inward shark-fashion. Yeah, they were so sweet and adorable that I wanted to tie ribbons around their necks and put them on the cover of a Humane Society calendar. "You said she liked us. If she likes us, why is she throwing maple trees at us?"

"Oak. That's an inexcusable mistake, whether it's nighttime or not. Didn't you see the shape of the dead leaves? The root pattern?" He gave up when I picked up a small rock and winged it at him. He dodged easily behind his shelter of another tree. "Never mind. I didn't say she liked us. I said she didn't necessarily hate us, depending on the present we brought her."

I heard the rustle of leaves above me and looked up to see eyes that spread their own lambent pumpkin-colored light, letting me see the teeth, the scales, and claws of black that were about the size of your average butcher's knife. "Then give her the damn present," I said, pointing the Eagle up at Junior. I'd taken down a Wolf, but I wasn't sure what a round would do against those layers of muddy scales, besides extremely pissing off their owner. "Before I ruin this boggle's dream of making the basketball team at his junior high."

"Now that we've seen they're all accounted for and thriving, which means they haven't fallen victim to Ammut's spiders, it would be a waste to give her what we might need to bribe her with at a later date."

It had been two, going on three days now since Leandros had appeared in his brotherly glory. Two and a half days combined with a couple of hazy memories that I couldn't depend on. Was it any doubt I would think I hallucinated half of what the guy said? His actions made me trust him. His words often made me want to beat him with a two-by-four.

"Later date? You mean from-beyond-the-grave later date? Because I have better plans for my afterlife than tossing rhinestones at a white-trash monster living in pigsty heaven instead of a double-wide. They're going to kill us. They won't bother to eat you as you're made up of bean curd and soy, but I'm pure pizza, fried chicken, and burgers. They will eat my *ass*. Give her the damn bling."

"You and common sense. I'm not sure I can get used to that combination. I suppose I may as well ask her if she's heard anything." He put a hand in his coat pocket and then tossed out a handful of pearls. They landed in the mud pit that Mama Boggle had climbed out of and where she now crouched on the edge. In a small clearing in the trees of Central Park, you didn't need a moon to see. The sky was as orange as the eyes of the boggles. New York was a city so big that it sucked the darkness out of the night itself.

Some of the pearls stuck in wet mud while some rolled on the surface of more dry pieces. Whatever color they were in the daylight, they were all orange here. That didn't stop the big boggle—Boggle with a capital *B*—from pulling her enormous dark claws out of yet another tree and squatting on muscled legs and rolling them around with a talon tip. "From the world of water. Fresh. Untouched by any human's grubby baby paws but yours." Her voice was so deep and loud, an auditory avalanche, I expected the ground to shake under our feet.

Leandros stepped out from behind his tree as I used the Eagle to swat the talons reaching for my head. If mommy was in a better mood, I didn't want to change that by shooting her kid. That and it *was* a kid, a juvenile mega-alligator with a brain hanging up in that tree. If you walked into the Everglades and got your leg bitten off by a leftover prehistoric lizard, you had no one to blame but yourself. That was their territory, not yours, and this part of the park was the same as far as boggles were concerned.

"They eat muggers and sometimes joggers who stray from the common paths. Don't feel too bad for them," my companion suggested.

I ignored my brother. Goodfellow and the vampire had dropped us off in the limo at the park's south entrance, and now I saw why. While they were sipping champagne and headed to an after-hours party, I was again smacking the claws of the boglet above me. "No. Bad boy. Bad. Behave or you'll get a time-out." They ate muggers and joggers. I didn't have a problem with that. Muggers were rotten people and joggers who came this far out in the name of exercise had to be insane. Getting eaten was the best thing for them. It had to save a fortune in psych meds. As for the all-monsters-are-evil twitch, I told myself that it didn't apply to baby monsters, and it grumbled but shut up. I was a softy for kids. Who knew?

"Boggle." Leandros had walked forward, his sword in hand. "Ammut has come to the city. Do you know of Ammut?"

"No. No Ammut. I care not for strangers or the city. I care for home only," she said, holding up one particularly large pearl before a large harvest moon eye, "and for my trinkets." There was a rough, chain saw buzz in the air. She was purring . . . if boggles purred.

"Then you haven't been attacked by Nepenthe spiders in the past two weeks."

I turned my head to watch the exchange and felt a tongue lick the top of my head. "I am not kidding," I warned the boglet, without taking my eyes from Leandros and Boggle. "Don't make me shoot off the end of your tail. The other kids will make fun of you."

"Spiders," she said, the purr disappearing. "Disgusting pests. Boring vermin." Letting the pearl fall back to lie with the others, she rammed her hand down into the mud up to her elbow joint. Pulling back, she yanked free a black articulated leg more than three feet long. I recognized it, from the beach and from a motel bathroom. It was the leg of a Nepenthe spider. "Many came, all died, but they are not good for eating. They smell unclean." She threw the leg over her hulking shoulder. "They scuttled, full of poison. We did what you do with such things."

"You squashed them," I said.

Her grin, twice the size and voraciousness of her offspring, gleamed. "It was good hunting practice for my children. They could not eat them, but they could kill them. Yes, we squashed them and will do the same to any more that come here."

"And Ammut?" Leandros asked.

"I do not know Ammut." It was the same as she'd said before, which made her finished with our conversation. As she played with her pearls, the other boglets moved closer to us. They were up for another practice hunt if we didn't move it.

"Where is it?" asked the boglet above me, its rumble a lighter reflection of its mother's. "The Auphe in you, it is all but gone. You taste weak." Again with the weak. Did I need to start pumping iron?

Leandros's hand was on my arm. "We are done here. Let's go before they try to store our limbs in the mud with that of the spiders."

I let myself be moved along. "What did it say? Where did my 'off' go? My 'off-fey?' What—" My mouth shut abruptly, my teeth snapping together and barely missing the tip of my tongue, as Leandros gave me a particularly brisk yank that had me running to keep up. It was a good idea since the boglets had decided they might be in the mood after all whether we moved our asses or not. I put the gun away and drew one of my knives. Little monsters. Little seven-foot-tall monsters. Underage monsters then. It didn't matter how big they were, only that killing them would be the equivalent of doing in a 'tween, which would be wrong, no matter how annoying they were—baby monsters and 'tweens.

One boglet raced up beside me as we hit another clearing. They could walk upright or go on all fours, and their speed setting was on all fours. I'd watched some TV last night while trying to readjust or remember home. Nothing good had been on—there was no porn channel—but I had caught some animal special. It would've been difficult to not catch as Leandros had tripped me when I'd tried to walk away—the several times that I'd tried to walk away. He had a move for everything. That meant that against my will, and I had a feeling it wasn't the first thing he'd made me do against my will, I'd watched a show about Komodo dragons.

A Komodo could run a man to the ground in seconds. *Seconds.* These guys must've used that special as an exercise tape.

I saw the tooth-crammed grin, the light of the eyes, and the claws of one large hand slashing out to gut me. I dropped flat instantly. That boglet tried to stop, dirt and dead grass flying as he dug in, and the one behind me ran over the top of me and kept going. He was a dog chasing a ball that his master had only pretended to throw. He was the slow one in his class, but he seemed happy. Let him run to China and back if it kept him that way.

The one who'd made a try for me did manage to stop, flip head for tail, and lunge back at me where I lay on my stomach. I was up in a fraction of a second and his stopping skills improved as the surface of his luminous eye came to rest against the point of my knife. I could feel the slight give under the tip. A sixteenth of an inch and it would puncture, and that wouldn't make his mama proud of his hunting skills at all.

"Weak?" I leaned in until my own grin made a clinking sound as it touched his. Teeth to teeth. Hunter to hunter. "I taste weak?" I heard hisses and growls from behind me. I reminded myself—baby monsters, emphasis on baby. No matter what my hand wanted to do, it was going to listen to me. "Kids. You're so cute. I don't have to want to kill you. To kill you I only have to be better than you." The fetid breath mixed with mine, but his eyes were gleaming now, from pained moisture. "Junior, I'm better than you. Go home to Mommy."

He thumped his tail against the ground. I was concentrating on his eyes and the intent smoldering there, but I heard the sound. It was a signal. The rapacious snapping and rumbling from behind went silent. "You are not weak. We will go." He gave a cautiously sinuous step back away from my blade and I let him. The scaly lids blinked to take away the pain. As tough as they were, if I'd scratched his cornea I'd have been surprised. I'd been careful, but I'd been ready. If I'd had to jam the blade through his eye into his brain, I would have, but teenagers do stupid shit all the time. Giving him the chance to think it out and make the smart choice was the right thing to do. When he was a full-grown monster, then I'd hold him accountable for his decision-making skills and take him out without a second thought. Until that happened, I'd make like a social worker.

Slithering past me, he and his brothers and sisters ran, disappearing into the trees. I turned my attention to Leandros, who had a boglet on the ground, one foot on the grass, one on the muddy throat, and his sword embedded a few inches into flesh over where I guessed a boggle might carry its heart. "Jesus, Leandros, you're not going to kill it, are you? It probably has a date for monster homecoming later. Cut it some slack."

"I hadn't planned on killing it as that would annoy Mama Boggle. She's fond of her children. I was merely keeping it from killing me while I kept an eye on you." He stepped back, removing his foot and his sword. The boglet gave a growl before following the rest of its litter, exhibiting a definitely dejected slink to his lope. "Killing a boglet would bring Boggle and the rest of them on us. That we might not be able to handle. Boggle on her own is more deadly than all her children combined."

"Good point," I granted. "She looked badass, but I didn't know she was that badass."

"I told you on the way over. . . . Never mind. Why do I try?" He turned his eyes up to the sky, searching for the answer or peace. I looked up too. I didn't see either one. "Amnesia or not," he started again, sheathing his sword, "your attention span hasn't changed. If you didn't kill your boglet because of the mother, then why didn't you?"

I started walking beside him when he began moving. "It was a kid. Killing a kid, even a monster kid, you shouldn't do that." Because death was forever and blackbirds fell from the sky. If you had an opportunity to spare one, if only for a little while, you should.

"That's true, although you normally would've taunted the boglet more. You do enjoy a good insult."

"I insulted," I protested, my breath a frozen fog as a mix of fallen leaves and dead grass crunched under my feet. "I didn't spend all night doing it, but I'm freezing my ass off out here. And what did that thing mean when it was talking about my being weak? About off? My being off or not having off. Something. What was he talking about?"

"Face it, little brother," he answered, walking faster,

despite not having complained about the cold once. "Even to boggles, your humor has always been a little off."

We didn't go home after Central Park and, when I asked where we were going, Leandros answered to do something worse than play hide-and-seek with mud-loving homicidal alligators.

"What could be worse? Saddling them up and riding them like broncos in some bizarre supernatural rodeo? I'm sure Goodfellow has a few assless chaps he could lend us."

"Smart-ass." Leandros snorted as we reached the edge of the park and he hailed a taxi. "That certainly didn't disappear with your memory."

"Worse things than being a smart-ass," I grumbled.

"Far worse," he agreed. "So be prepared, because we're going to see one of those far worse things."

"Which is?" I asked.

"Our annoyed clients."

The building was close to Central Park but on the opposite side, making me glad for the taxi. I'd run enough today. The limo was long gone. Promise and Goodfellow had better things to do. Lucky them. I'd asked Leandros if he wasn't worried about Promise becoming an Ammut snack—Goodfellow had someone else to bunk with; I wasn't sure Moses would approve, but not my business. Regarding Promise, Leandros had said she was staying with several vampires; there was safety in numbers. Normally she would've stayed with us or vice versa, but he was afraid I'd have a glitch of die-monster-die and try to stab her with a kitchen knife if she reached past me for a breakfast bagel.

Inside, we made the grade past the doorman, just barely, considering all the mud we were streaked with, and not exactly fragrant mud either. We stank. The security desk had our names and had us sign in. Leandros signed Sun Tzu. I didn't ask. I was learning to bob and weave those lectures. I signed Captain Hook. Unlike me, he did ask.

I'd turned toward the elevators and got a lecture anyway. You should never take an elevator. Elevators were death traps—metal boxes that turned into untelevised caged death matches when something slithered in there with you and tried to tear you apart. And if you survived, you still had to walk out wearing monster guts from head to toe. It was not a good look from security's point of view. Leandros all but smacked my hand as if I were a two-year-old reaching for a hot stove when I aimed a finger for the UP button.

On the stairs Leandros asked, "Why Captain Hook? It's not one of your usual fake names. Did you forget?"

Nope, I did remember those from my fake IDs in South Carolina. *Nightmare on Elm Street*, *Friday the Thirteenth*, and *Halloween*. Movie villains R us or R me. I started climbing. "No, I remember those. I was thinking about Nevah's Landing. You said you told me the story *Peter Pan* there when I was a kid, right? I was kind of picturing my memories chasing me like that albino crocodile with the ticking clock chased Hook." I remembered it as well as the blackbird, if not more. Creepy damn thing.

"Albino?"

We passed the third floor. "Yeah, the one that ate Hook's hand. Albino. Big white crocodile with red eyes. It would sneak up and whisper in your ear. Spooky as hell. That's a damn scary story to be telling a kid by the way, Leandros. But it is like that. My memories are whispering with that blackbird memory," my inner self with its rampant monster prejudice was whispering more, "but I just can't make them out. And what floor did you say this meeting is on?"

"Sixteenth," he answered, but there was a distracted tone in his voice. Maybe the albino croc had scared him as a kid too and he'd forgotten it. Although I doubt anyone or anything had scared Niko Leandros, no matter what his age.

Christ. I would rather take the death trap. Sixteen floors. Forget death trap. I'd rather take a real crocodile gnawing off my leg. "If we haven't found anything yet on . . ." Crap, what was it again? "Ammut," I said triumphantly. "If we haven't found anything on that life-force-sucking, spider-loving Egyptian bitch to report, why are we here?"

"To tell why we have nothing to show, hope they don't attempt to kill us for the delay, and to find out how many more of her victims have gone missing or been found dead."

"Dead. Kill. Say them like bad words," someone scoffed.

The voice was striking, as was the Wolf's surprising plunge out of nowhere to the fourth-floor landing, hitting the tile barely a foot from me. She was all that made a Wolf, predatory in her speed, there was no doubt, but she was all female too, that being almost more dangerous than the Wolf in her. She crouched on all fours, silver blond hair like a bridal veil over her face. Through the winter strands I could see tilted amber eyes the same color as the skin that showed between the white leather shirt and black jeans. Her arms were bare. Her throat and her lower abdomen were the same except for a tattooed choker around the first and wicked slashes of scar tissue across the last. She smiled, teeth bright against her darker skin, as she tossed her hair back to show her face. I wanted to say she was beautiful. She *was* beautiful, but it wasn't a human kind of beauty. Hers was the beauty of a mountain so high, so fierce, so deadly, it would suck the oxygen from your lungs and take your life in a heartbeat for the crime of wanting to see that beauty up close.

Remaining on all fours, she said, "Where have you been, pretty boy? You leave, who is here to play games?" Beauty like hers took; it never gave. And if it pretended that it did, it was only to soften you up to make your fall that much harder.

The same kind of hard fall that Wolf I'd shot in the head had taken. "Delilah." I didn't remember her face or her body or her unique lupine smell, but Niko and Goodfellow had said the Alpha of the Lupa pack liked to play games. And as my ex, she especially liked to play them with me.

Also, the first night we'd been in the city, while I slept, Leandros had made index cards. Memory joggers. Who was who. Who could be trusted and who could not. The guy was brilliant in everything he did. The way he fought the boggle, when he sparred, all the books he had—each one weighing twenty pounds minimum—the precise way he made his tea, the equally precise way he disarmed me when I thought I was a hotshot back in South Carolina. Not even a week and some of those days were cloudy, but I saw what I saw: Niko was an expert in everything he did, mental or physical. He was the kind of man the world saw only every few centuries. Born to rule and gifted by nature beyond all others.

But nature does hate perfection. The guy couldn't draw his ass out of a wet paper bag. I'd thumbed through my stack of cards on the subway to the Ninth Circle. The first had been a stick figure with circles for breasts, long blond hair indicated by two swoopy lines, a fluffy dog tail, and a fang-filled smile. *Delilah (bad)* was written in machine-perfect calligraphy at the top of the card.

There'd been stick men with angel wings, *Ishiah (good) Samyel (good)*, a stick woman with vampire fangs, *Promise (good)*, a round thing with Mickey Mouse ears and a skinny tail marked *Mickey (debatable)*. Then there'd been one stick figure with curly hair and three legs. I didn't need the *Robin Goodfellow (Run for your life)* to ball it up and throw it at Leandros, which I had.

"I thought the Lupa pack wasn't committing to this fight," Niko said at my shoulder.

She stood and shrugged as more Lupa rained down around her. "I can change my mind—did change my mind. Spiders took four of my pack. What the Kin is learning, what the vampires know, I want this bitch to *feel*. We Lupa are untouchable. To kill Lupa is to take your last breath." The Wolves around her smiled in a lightning-swift shadow of hers. They smelled her arousal. I smelled it. "Except for you, pretty boy." The muzzle of my Desert Eagle was pressed against her forehead as her fingers ran along my jaw. My brain might stay out to lunch forever, but my body always knew what it was doing.

"Any present I give to you, you are free. Do as you wish. Play, kill, eat." She laughed, the gun not existing in her reality at all. She slapped me in the face, playfully to another Wolf maybe, but it was a damn hard smack to a human. She laughed again. "Stop with the silly puck cologne. Who do you hide from in this city? Yourself?"

I didn't have a chance to wonder why she'd think I was into cologne, much less *Goodfellow's* cologne when she was under my gun, feinting, and leaping over me, a diver into water far below. That it wasn't water, only more stairs, didn't matter. She landed on her feet and kept running. Her pack moved around us. I felt the swipe of claws and pulled a combat knife with my other hand to slap back hands and paws and several elongated jaws with fangs ready for one tiny opening. Play to them, following their Alpha's lead. Except for Delilah, they all were obviously All Wolf—stuck in between. Wolf eyes, human face. Wolf face, human eyes and hands. Some used hooded jackets to hide and some needed nothing; they simply were exotic-looking women. But if you knew . . .

"Delilah is Alpha, but the whole pack is that All Wolf cult?" I asked, rubbing my burning jaw as I watched them all disappear down the stairs in the blink of an eye, wolves on a rabbit. Run, run, run.

"Her vocal cords." He answered the question I hadn't asked. "That's not an accent. Delilah's All Wolf is hidden inside her, but she's All Wolf, and more than that, she's Kin; make no mistake." He tapped my arm and pointed. "Kin."

There were bloody fingerprints, footprints, and paw prints on the stairs. Kin were killers, I'd been told—every last one of them. I touched my jaw where Delilah's fingers had been. There was a smudge of blood there too. "You think Delilah is now our only client?"

"I think she may be," he said as he started running up the rest of the stairs.

But the boardroom he charged into was empty except for a card with neatly written letters, *Fourth Alternate Location*, resting in the middle of the table. The blood was from a dead security guard at the end of the hall. He wasn't human. He looked human . . . until I lifted his upper lip to see small fangs, right before they slid out of sight, the gums sealing over them. Nature—keeping the vamp's secret for them. I checked his vitals just in case, although I wasn't precisely sure what made a vampire dead. "No heartbeat," I was informed. Born, not made—live, not undead. They were the same as humans that way with the same vital signs or lack of them after a she-Wolf Alpha took one down. And they even bled red like humans. Made sense. They used to drain humans. You wouldn't eat what you couldn't digest. I hadn't seen a scratch on Delilah, and Leandros said vamps were fast and strong—very fast, very strong. She was something all right.

"They must've suspected the Lupa were coming for them," Leandros said, tapping the card against his palm. "They took precautions and moved the meet."

Precautions. In other words, you did not fuck with the Lupa, but, damn, they would fuck with you if they felt like it. If you wanted to be noticed you had to make a big bang—such as taking out an unprecedented council of the supernatural joined to fight Ammut. Delilah was ambitious *and* hot. She was also a matter-of-fact killer, but we couldn't all be perfect.

"So . . . ," I said casually as I straightened, "that was Delilah, huh?"

Leandros already knew where this was going. I could tell by the twitch of his jaw. "Yes, that was Delilah as the conversation on the stairs and the index card I gave you made perfectly clear."

"And I nailed that?"

The roll of his eyes indicated I was beyond immature. I gave a smug grin. "Damn, I'm good."

We ended up at not the first, second, or even third, but the fourth alternate location, which had to be Leandros's idea. Who else would have four? Two days and I'd seen enough of his ways to know that. I was surprised he could stand up without a chair sticking to his ass, the gravitational pull of his anal-retentive nature too strong to be overcome by mere furniture.

We'd taken another cab up until about a twenty-minute walk away. Leandros wanted either to determine if the Lupa were following us or to simply kill my tired ass, one of the two. I missed the Landing with its twelve streets where everyone walked slow and in a hurry meant not stopping to sit on your neighbor's porch to "chat a spell." All right, an exaggeration about the porch thing, but I damn sure missed the twelve streets.

"And the fourth alternate location would be?" I asked as I hunched in my jacket, tired of the cold, the endless walking and running, and not too happy with the smell.

"Brooklyn. Gowanus Canal."

"I liked the Central Park place better," I grunted. "It didn't stink." I didn't know if the water stank to him, but it did to me—like a chemical-coated rotting body. "And there were hot Wolf chicks."

There weren't many . . . Correction, there weren't any people I could see hanging around, ready to jump in for a swim as we moved through several rusted-through tanks to a scrap metal yard. As for Gowanus Canal, an up-close look said they should've called it Gowanus Ditch. Encased in concrete forever as far as I could tell from the lights reflecting off the dank, fetid black water, it wasn't close to being a tourist attraction. You weren't going to see any gondolas with singing guys in striped shirts around here. If they fell in, they'd crawl out a mutated creature with superpowers that involved killing you with a massive wave of stench.

"Up here."

I turned away from the canal and followed Leandros up some broken concrete stairs to a squat corrugated metal building. There were no windows, only a light showing under and around the door. Weatherproofing was not their primary issue. He knocked once, said, "Leandros," and opened the door. Our clients were waiting for us, all of them.

Also dead, every damn one.

This time it wasn't the Lupa. This time I saw what I'd only heard about in my briefing at the bar to catch me up to preamnesiac speed. At a much less fancy table than at the conference room, they were gathered around what must have been a rickety poker table. Vampire, Wolf, succubus, incu . . . incub . . . the male version of succubus, and something I had no idea about, other than he was as dead as the rest now lying scattered around the large shack. All of them except one were curled into dried husks. Their eyes were sunken so far back into the sockets, only withered raisins remained. What skin I could see that showed outside their clothes was almost transparent and veined with dark blue and cancer-clot purple.

Leandros knelt beside the one client who hadn't had his life force sucked out by Ammut. She'd done him in the more popular modern way—ripped him to pieces. He'd been halfway to turning, patches here and there of black fur, now slowly receding back under the skin, his dead eyes yellow but clouding to a human-appearing dull brown, and teeth still bared in a frozen snarl. She'd disemboweled him and used his blood to write on the back metal wall.

Give them to me. The letters were large; the medium used to write them sincere. You're not screwing around when you make your demands painted with someone's death.

"Give them to me?" I read out loud, confused. "Isn't she doing a bang-up job of getting her victims herself? Not like she needs our help."

Shaking his head, Leandros admitted, "I have no idea." He stood and nudged the dead Wolf with his boot. "Vukasin. The Kin Alpha liaison. Not that high up in the order of things. The Kin wouldn't show us that much respect." The nudge turned his body over to show this side had no face. A few scraps of muscle and skin clinging to scored bone. Life force and just life, both brutally taken—Ammut didn't limit herself to one way of killing. "Not Delilah's work, but she would've been capable of it and I have little doubt she'll claim it. The Kin will believe her and think taking out this Alpha a very bold move, despite her All Wolf cult breeding. I'm beginning to think we were right. Delilah may well end up running the entire Kin before long."

He left Vukasin to study the other bodies and then headed toward the door. "Not that that's our concern now. Ammut's path of destruction is getting worse. To take out the council who hired us. That is true disdain and an escalation of feeding. We have to stop her before they form a council on dealing with inept subcontractors such as ourselves."

I followed him. "We're just going to leave them here? I know about monsters." The sky is blue, what goes up must come down, and here there be monsters. "I remember knowing about them even if I don't remember much else, but I also remember hardly anyone else knows. How do we keep that from happening?"

"We take care of our own bodies, and we leave the bigger messes for the Vigil. This is a bigger mess."

Outside in the cold air, I asked, "Who's the Vigil?"

"They keep humans from finding out about the supernatural. If that happened, there would be worldwide war. Their calling is to prevent that, which means they make things such as this disappear. You know how at night the garbage piles up and the street sweepers come through so in the morning, it's all clean as if it were never there?"

I shut the door behind us, to hide the bodies from plain view in case this Vigil was slow on the uptake.

"I guess that depends on your definition of clean, but yeah."

"The Vigil are the street sweepers, and, on occasion when too noticeable, people like us can be considered garbage to be disposed of as well. So try to keep a low profile," he said, starting along the canal at a faster pace. How the Vigil found out about these messes was a mystery he didn't bother to explain, and I didn't bother to ask. I had more than enough freaky shit on my plate as it was. That one could wait. "Ammut could still be here somewhere in the scrap yard. If you can smell her, we should search."

If I couldn't smell her, the place was too big to search, but we were out of luck. I took a few steps closer to the canal and hooked a thumb toward it. "Over that? I can't smell anything over that god-awful . . ."

I didn't get to finish the sentence as a loop of wet muscle thicker than a man's waist erupted out of the water and wrapped around my chest and one arm to yank me into and under the water. It was unbelievably fast and the light bad. I hadn't seen if it was scaled or not—if it was a giant snake or a tentacle, but it didn't matter. Whatever it was, it was crushing the air out of my chest, what little air I'd had to begin with after the first tight squeeze expelled it from my lungs. It dragged me deeper into the water, moving almost as quickly through the water as outside of it, which meant even if Leandros could've helped me, we were leaving him behind.

I had the one arm free and I used it to fumble for my gun. I went by feel. I was afraid if I opened my eyes the chemicals in the water would blind me. Finding it instantly—true love couldn't bring anything together as fast as my hand and the grip of my Eagle—I fired in the direction I was being dragged. I emptied the clip and the one I carried in the pipe to grow on. Nothing. I was losing my remaining air, my chest aching with oxygen loss and the pressure squeezing me until I felt as if I'd break in half. I went for my Glock next, but I was slow and clumsy, a pounding in my ears—I knew I wasn't going to make it and if I did, why would it do any more good than the Eagle?

But that didn't mean I wasn't going to try. I let the Eagle go with the fuzzy, blood-drenched thought that all monsters were bad and why had I let anyone tell me different, and I went for the Glock with a hand now too weak to grasp anything, but trying . . . goddamn it, still trying. I expected to fail with my last semicoherent thought and I did. I expected to die, but I didn't. Not thanks to Ammut or the first or second mouthful of water I finally couldn't help but inhale and choke on. Nope, that was not how I went.

Instead, the world blew up.

Blue skies, pirate ships, flying children; they were there again as I woke up, soaked in freezing cold water—almost drowning brought them back every time. Only this time I didn't think I'd almost drowned. "Almost" was kicked out of that sentence. There was a hand on my forehead tilting my head back, a mouth pressed hard against mine, air blown in inflating my chest, and I didn't know what it meant—not quite. I couldn't breathe—so wasn't I dead? Hazy, sluggish thoughts, but logical. Dead and logical, that took talent.

There went another pirate ship sailing overhead, backlit by stars where there were no stars.

And didn't I hear a waterfall?

"Cal, you son of a bitch. I've had enough this week. Do you hear me? Goddamn *enough*."

More air was blown into my lungs, but they didn't have any idea what to do with it. Lazy damn lungs. The ship disappeared, the sound of the cascading water faded away and panic set in. Jesus, I couldn't breathe; I couldn't move; I couldn't goddamn *breathe*....

It did turn out that I could vomit. And I did so profusely, all over the front of the shadowed figure I saw bending over me as I opened my eyes. Efficient hands rolled me on my side where I kept emptying my stomach and lungs of canal water. It went on for what seemed a year or so—and not the best of years, although it couldn't have been more than a few minutes. As oxygen took the place of water, I dragged in breaths between the heaving and began to think a little more clearly. As in, what the fuck happened?

Was that CPR?

Was that *Goodfellow* giving me CPR? Please God no. It'd been a rough day already. Mouth to mouth from the puck would never be lived down.

The same hands were slapping my back firmly, only making me barf more. I appreciated the effort. Puking wasn't great, but I didn't want any of that putrid, tainted water left in me, not a damn drop of it. I didn't know how chemicals could taste like death, but they did. I doubled up, knees to chest, and went from vomiting to coughing, which hurt worse.

"Cal? Can you hear me? Damn it, little brother, can you hear me?"

Actually, I could barely hear the words. The pounding in my ears underwater had gone to a ringing so loud that I was surprised I heard anything at all. I kept coughing and slanted my eyes up to see a blurry Leandros kneeling over me, hands keeping me on my side. On his shirt, coat, and braid, he was wearing the chili dog I'd eaten at the bar since he'd starved me at his tofu diner, and I was dimly pleased I'd found the time to sneak it in.

"What?" I coughed again, vomited again, then glared at him. "What . . . you . . . do?"

He held up something I recognized—a grenade with a smirking smiley face on it. This one was red with devil horns. Have a not so nice day! That would explain the ringing in my ears. "I borrowed a few from you. Inelegant but effective." It disappeared and a hand wiped at my mouth as I kept coughing. Good for him. I was too weak to do it myself and he deserved more puke. "She had you. Ammut. I could see the wake where she was pulling you through the water, too fast for me to stop her. I threw a grenade in front of her. It was the only thing left to do." He sounded apologetic, despite the fact I'd driven him to more cursing. The man didn't swear much, I'd noticed, even in situations when he should've been whipping them out nonstop. Swearing or not, he should sound sorry. Damn, *damn* sorry. Boggles, homicidal Wolves, dead clients, Ammut nearly drowning me, and my brother blowing me up to finish the job. As workdays went, not a good beginning.

"I almost lost you. Again." He was blurry, yeah, and his voice faint, but I heard. He meant what he said. The blame was as solid as the concrete beneath me and as dark as the water he'd pulled me from—and it was aimed in one direction. "Ammut. This fucking bitch is going to be sorry the universe ever spit her into existence."

The f-bomb. Now we were cooking. Forget the other cursing, this was serious language from an equally seriously upset, vengeance-bound brother . . . who *had* almost lost me twice in a week. He did deserve more than barf. Any brother who'd gone through that would. I was getting back the finer movements of my arms and legs, and I managed to lift my hand to snag it in his coat. "Leandros . . ." I coughed spastically, grabbed what air I could, then tried for the most annoyed, pissy little-brother-worthy expression I could manage. As I didn't remember what that looked like, I hoped I got it right.

7

"What do I do for fun?"

This time it was me waking Leandros up too damn early in the morning. Not that I hadn't already woken him up walking into his room in socked feet. I didn't hear any noise of my own making, but while I'd heard a killer she-Wolf above, I was learning my brother heard almost everything. If a squirrel burped in Central Park, this guy heard it half a city away. He was sleeping on his stomach, one arm hidden under the covers.

My well-intentioned last puke by the canal hadn't distracted him from thoughts of lost brothers as much as I'd hoped. He'd had a long night, what with checking on me every hour to make sure I didn't die of secondary drowning. I'd asked what that was and he told me if I did die of it, then he'd tell me. Until then it wasn't pertinent knowledge for me and might interfere with my sleep. Considering we'd run—I'd staggered—to get away before the cops arrived to investigate an explosion and it had been the longest day of my life, I did need the sleep. Unfortunately, the grenade hadn't injured Ammut as we didn't spot any unrecognizable chunks of whatever she looked like floating in the water. If we had, I'd have slept a lot sounder.

Good thing I hadn't.

"Betcha have a sword under your mattress and you sleep holding on to the hilt." I grinned as an eye slitted at me, fully aware. "That's what I would do if I were a sword guy." But a pillow and a gun were what helped me sleep at night. Warm milk didn't cut it in this business.

"You're extremely observant of people's behavior and the general area around you or you're remembering more." He sat up and laid the sword on the bed as he swung his legs to the ground. He wore black cotton pajama pants but was bare chested. He had a scar there that wasn't as deep and ugly as mine. It was plenty odd, though—a round circle of silvery scar tissue as big as a dinner plate as if someone had drawn a giant *O* on his chest. I guessed they had, only they'd used a knife instead of a crayon to do it. "How are you feeling? Any more coughing?"

"No more coughing and no more remembering, but things are more . . . eh . . . déjà vu-ish." His room was as clean, feng shui-ed out the ass, painted in a calm, serene silver green with not a single dust mote daring to rear its fuzzy head. Same as yesterday and the day before. He had a low bed and an equally low and discreet dresser. No mirror, though. There was one mirror in the place—in the bathroom, and it was a small one with a towel rolled up and propped on top of it. The towel was to wipe off the mirror if the shower steamed it up or to cover up the mirror for no good reason at all, which I did before I went to bed last night after showering twice to sluice the canal taint off me.

Leandros hadn't mentioned the mirror; I followed right along in his nonverbal footsteps. I didn't like monsters and I wasn't that fond of mirrors. I'd work on the monster thing first. I imagined the mirror thing, if I brought it up, would only embarrass me or make me look like a phobia-ridden nut job—maybe both. All humiliation in its own time.

"You didn't answer my question," I pointed out. "What do I do for fun?"

"Why are you up so early?" he countered. "One of the primary extracurricular activities of your life is sleeping, not to mention running, fighting boggles, Wolves, and doing your best to die yesterday. I'd expect you to sleep extra late today."

Oh, as if it were my fault, almost dying. That made me enjoy what was coming next all the more.

"Eh, there was this thing."

Yeah, there had been this thing all right, and it was getting more and more annoying.

"And I was hungry anyway. Ate some cereal. Knew we had some shit to do early and then I thought, hey, what's a guy like me—when I don't have amnesia—do for fun? I'm curious," I said, then added, "Wouldn't you be?"

He took the ponytail holder out of his hair, then pulled it back again, straightening the sleep fuzz. "I work as a TA teaching history at NYU part-time and part-time at a dojo as an instructor. I train you so that you can fight off a toddler should one escape the local preschool. I meditate. Read. Research. Spend time with Promise."

That was all fascinating. The life of Niko Leandros, multitasking modern samurai. He was stalling. If this guy valued perfection, and he did, he valued it in all things, including excruciatingly accurate (and long) answers to easy questions. That made me wonder why he'd stall at all, much less over such a simple question. "But I'm not you," I said, boosting myself up to sit on one end of the dresser. "What do I do?" Slouching, elbow on knee and chin resting in hand, I waited for the answer.

He watched the impatient swing of my foot, or the dirty bottom thereof invading his oasis of sterile tranquility. "You like to . . . hmm . . . watch TV." He paused. "You enjoy browsing gun shops, although of course we obtain our weapons in a less legal fashion. You like your job at the bar." There was a longer pause before he said triumphantly, "Ah, sometimes you like to read."

He grabbed on to that one as if it were a life preserver. Brothers who worked together, lived together, weren't at each other's throat, but that didn't necessarily mean we were close. Then again, there was that lie-down-and-die-for-me attitude he'd been spouting on the drive from South Carolina. Willing to spend his life looking for me, willing to die for me, but as for knowing what I did in my spare time, he was drawing a blank. Lots of people needed their personal space? Right? That was normal, especially as we did work *and* live together. He could not have a clue as to what I got up to on my own time.

Yeah. I wasn't buying it.

"I read. What? Porn?" I was a guy. Sue me if the important literary works rose to the top.

"Mostly, but the occasional book that has a paragraph or two to give the porn context isn't completely out of the question." The end of his katana smacked against my foot smartly. It stung, but it was a baby tap compared to what the weapon could've done and I stopped swinging the clearly irritating foot. "You like to shoot."

As if the world's largest weapon store shoved under my bed hadn't told me that much. That and how very quick I'd been to kill the Wolf outside the bar last night. I wasn't quite right with that yet, and I didn't know when I would be.

I could've shot to wound—why didn't I? A good guy would have, but it was a surprise, quick, and over before my thoughts caught up to my trigger finger. If I'd had

time to think, I would've shot to hurt, not kill. I knew it.
Good guys don't kill if they don't have to ... now that I
was slowly accepting monsters as people, sort of.

*Lies. You're lying to yourself. You know what mon-
sters are.*

I returned to the conversation, leaving uncomfortable
thoughts behind. "Shooting. Gotcha. One-track-mind
me. Porn. Guns. Sleeping with chicks who want to kill
me. Nothing else? No, I don't know, movies? Bars and
not just to work in, but to do more interesting things,
such as get laid by someone who doesn't want to kill
me? Sports? Parties?"

Leandros jumped on the last item quickly enough
that it smacked of desperation. "Parties. Yes. You went
to a ... You like parties." He stood, moved to the dresser,
and opened the bottom drawer farthest from me and my
unclean, heathen foot. "Here." He handed me a photo,
computer printed but on glossy paper, the extra white
neatly trimmed away. It was headed for framing one day.
Awww, wasn't that sweet?

I stared at it and raised my eyebrows at him. "A
party? What kind of party?"

"Halloween. Ishiah hosted it at the Ninth Circle.
Whatever you must say about the preternatural, they do
like their celebrations. Pagan creatures did invent them,
after all."

Looking back at the picture again, I saw Leandros,
dressed in, as I'd only seen since he found me, black and
gray, including his weapon-concealing duster. Promise
was made up as something fancy from the days when
men wore tights and enjoyed it. It was a wonder there
was a nonovercooked sperm in those days. I had no idea
how the human race had survived. Ishiah was dressed
normally as Niko had been, but with his wings out.
Goodfellow stood behind the bar. I could see him only

from the waist up. He was bare chested. "What's the puck dressed up as?"

There was a sigh and the sound of the drawer shutting. "He thought it would be entertaining to have his costume complement Ishiah's. Ishiah went as an angel and Goodfellow went as"—you can't hear eyes roll, but you can imagine that you can—"the Baby Jesus."

I grimaced. "That means he's wearing a diaper. . . ." I didn't get to finish.

"Preswaddled."

Preswaddled. That meant he was naked behind that bar. Holy shit, why did he ever bitch about me ruining his clothes when from his talk and the illustrations to go with them he rarely fucking wore any? I moved my eyes quickly to the last one left: me. I was wearing a T-shirt, jeans, two guns in a dual shoulder holster, and had a black apron tied around my waist. I was working, not partying. And my costume? The T-shirt said it all: *This is my costume. Now fuck off.*

That, as festive as my EAT ME T-shirt had been, didn't tell the whole story. My hair, half of which was now gone, was in a shoulder-length ponytail, and my expression—it wasn't an expression. It was a lack of one. It was the same as the expression on the panthers you see in the zoo. They weren't hungry. And they didn't give one good goddamn shit about you one way or the other, but if you stuck your arm between the bars, they would rip it off in a second. Why? That was what panthers did, hungry or not. My eyes . . . They were not the eyes of a not-so-bad guy or a good brother. I'd say they belonged to a very motherfucking bad guy indeed. I'd semi-avoided mirrors since I'd woken up on the beach, but I knew I hadn't seen that face or those eyes since I'd been spitting salt water.

I'd thought I was badass.

Mama Boggle knew she was badass.

I didn't think either one of us wanted to meet that guy in the picture.

I tried not to assume. It could've been a bad day. A Wolf could've marked my sneakers as his territory... while I was wearing them. That werewolf chick Delilah could've jumped me, put a collar and leash on me, and tied me to the nearest fire hydrant. Goodfellow might've trapped me in a corner and told me more stories that *Hustler* itself wouldn't touch with a ten-foot pole, which I'm positive he'd claim to be hauling around in his pants—when he wore any. There were tons of reasons I could've been in a bad mood—so catastrophically pissed that the black ice behind my eyes alone would have serial killers writing *me* love letters from prison instead of vice versa.

Or there was the truth: This guy shot Wolves in the head and didn't once consider only wounding them.

"Yeah, I'm the life of the party all right. I'm surprised balloons don't pop out of my ass and streamers fall wherever I go." I shoved the photo back at him, then thought belatedly about asking what his costume was. I didn't bother. I knew. Lived with that guy in the picture. Worked with him. Willing to sacrifice his life to find him. Martyr-in-the-making—that was his costume and his reality.

"This is really me? This is the guy you're waiting to wake up in a few days? He...I...We look like a nuclear bomb with a timer clicking over zero and fast into the negative numbers. And you want him back?" Look at him.... Look at me, I finished silently. If I saw him in a well-lit alley, I'd run like hell. If I saw him in a dark alley, I'd piss myself.

"You are him. Sometimes you have a bad day, but we have a shared history. You have a reason for an occasional bad day, and I have a reason to miss you with your memories. You know me just as I know you." I could understand that.

Context, he'd said before. I gave him context to his world. I knew that because nothing gave me context to mine right now. "I am who I am because of you," he added. "You were the making of me and that's a good thing. I miss you knowing that, knowing what I know, our whole life, good and bad." He accepted the picture and laid it carefully on top of the dresser.

"Leandros . . . *Niko*, you might want to take a closer look at that picture and buy a cattle prod for when I'm all the way back, because that guy is *not* happy and that guy is not right. I don't want to be that guy. I really don't. But, hey, just my opinion . . . of myself. Since you told me our mom didn't remember him, maybe my dad was Ted Bundy. Charles Manson on a furlough. Genetics and memories are weird stuff. Take what you want from it all and think hard about getting that cattle prod."

I didn't look for his reaction, because I didn't want to see it. Truth is truth, but sometimes it hurts. Realistically, most of the time it hurt. Instead, I moved on. I had other business, and I preferred not thinking about what I might be under the amnesia, who the real me was.

But how could I not be the real me, amnesia or not? With the same personality formed by genetics and memories, "weird stuff" that they were. I didn't recall those memories, but they'd already molded my brain and personality. Losing them wouldn't make me someone else. I couldn't be that different from the me in the picture, right?

How do *monster genetics work?* This time that inner voice sounded amused. This was a voice that had no problem with monsters.

Who knew? Who cared? I was human, and that was

the only genetics that concerned me now. The picture—it was a bad day, bad day, he—me, the both of us, were just having a bad day. Had to be. Why would these people, even my own brother, want me back if that weren't true?

I felt somewhat reassured by that train of thought. "Before we start the big Ammut scavenger hunt of the day," I said, heading out his door, "there's a spider in my room. Put it in the Dumpster or cut it up and flush it down the toilet again. I don't mind clogging a motel toilet, but I don't want to sit down tonight and feel something biting my ass because we didn't flush hard enough."

The dead spider was a small one—barely the size of a beagle. Leandros sent it, wrapped in two garbage bags, boxed, then taped securely, by an express-delivery service to the puck. When I asked him why, he asked if I wanted to see the Halloween picture of Robin again. It was a good point. The puck had it coming. But then he went on to say Goodfellow knew a forest nymph who subcontracted for a CSI lab, all about the bugs and leaves, and might be able to find any clues as to where this particular spider had been in the past twenty-four hours. When he finished that, he went out for an hour to get a better lock to replace the spare he'd installed last night. Yep, we kept spare locks, and, yep, we were running low. That didn't make you think twice, no, not at all.

That he didn't make me go along did make me think. The boggle and Wolf had shown I could take care of myself, but you rarely saw just one bug. Then there was Ammut, but maybe she stuck to the canal or was recuperating from the explosion. Could be Leandros had a black market secret lock guy who would deal with no one but Leandros. Who knew?

Then again, he was pissed. Or disturbed, annoyed—

something in the pissed-off area. With Leandros it was hard to tell simply by looking at him, but he was feeling something all right. That I could tell from the moment he'd walked into the diner. I guessed it was a brother thing. It could've been that he hadn't woken up when I'd killed the spider. He'd been making hourly checks, heard my socked feet, the Central Park squirrel burp, but a killer arachnid he missed? To be fair, it dropped down from the metal ceiling on a silken chain as thick as my finger. Soundless. I hadn't heard it either. But I'd smelled it. Sour venom, silk that had a sticky sweet scent for wrapping up prey. I'd let it get close enough to see the chitin shine of its legs in the city light through the dirt-coated high windows and impaled it on a sword I'd found under my bed with everything else. I was a gun person, but I kept around a sword or two just in case. I also had a flamethrower.

Of all the things I'd found out so far . . . I think I liked that about myself the most. Gotta love a flamethrower.

I took a shower while Niko was off FedExing Charlotte's asocial big brother. When I was done, I wiped the mist from the mirror and took a long look—the longest since I'd come to on that beach. I exhaled in relief and covered the mirror back up. It wasn't me. The Cal in the picture had had his worst day ever when that picture had been taken because that wasn't me. Eyes, face—it was as if a shadowy film had been peeled away. I still had a mild thing for wanting to kill monsters and a fondness for forks in all their destructive power, but I'd let a bad photo make me think I was something a helluva lot darker than I was.

I'd also told Leandros his brother sucked, which could have been another reason his mouth was a tight slash of irritation when he came back. It didn't matter if that brother was the same one making with the insults.

I shouldn't have said it. I'd been wrong, and, worse, I'd told him the brother he would die for was a freak. I'd compared him to a bomb, one in mid-explosion.

Not the behavior of a good brother, and *I* was a good brother. Leandros said so. The mirror said so. I fucking said so.

Good brother. Not-so-bad guy. I repeated it in my head like a . . . mantra, yeah. Mantra. Niko was bound to know about those since he said he meditated for fun. Who meditates for fun? For your blood pressure, okay, but for fun? It must kick-start his soy-and-yogurt morning. Meditation and soy all in one day; he was such a daredevil.

By the time he was back with the lock, I was dressed, armed, and ready to kick some ass. I regretted the Wolf, but I didn't regret the spider. Some are wild, some are bad, and some are evil meant to die. Fighting the boggles I'd enjoyed, because it hadn't involved killing, but it did have a whole lot of running and fighting and kicking scaly butt. That I liked. I wouldn't have minded doing some more of that. I'd been wrong on the trip back from South Carolina. This did beat serving up hash and waffles . . . except the drowning part, but other than that—I *liked* this shit. Look at me, the adrenaline junkie. Another brick slid into place to help rebuild the old me. "Where to?"

Leandros's mood hadn't improved. He could hold a grudge. I wouldn't have thought that about him. It wasn't very karmic. Next time I'd throw the spider, still living, over the wall at him, and I wouldn't insult the me I couldn't remember. Lesson learned.

"Wahanket," he replied. "He made Salome, and he's a mummy himself." And why wouldn't he be? Keep dishing out the insanity. At least I wasn't bored. "If he knows how to infuse a dead cat with some form of life force," he continued, "then he and Ammut may have crossed paths. Plus, they're both ancient and of Egyptian origin." He was in the kitchen washing a bowl and spoon I'd used to eat the Lucky Charms I'd found in the cabinet. I'd left the dishes there on purpose. Cleaning was one hobby he hadn't mentioned, but come on. Except for my room, you could operate in here. Hopefully, scrubbing in the sink would distract him from the high levels of grimness he was radiating. Being a good brother and being lazy could go hand in hand, I was pleased to discover.

"Maybe they dated," I offered. "Two wild and crazy kids who both liked screwing around with life forces. Can't get a match that good online."

"Of it all, the sarcasm was one thing you couldn't forget." He scrubbed harder.

I grinned. "That's amnesia-proof." Not to mention, the thicker I laid it on, the easier it was to convince him and the others and myself that I wasn't as lost as I'd been—and I wasn't. Some things were slightly familiar, the little things that squatted on one brain cell, the people-only dreams—the two genuine memories of which I'd caught the barest fragment. I didn't have myself or my life back yet. I had found one or two bread crumbs, but the forest was thick and the path turned out of sight.

Lost, but trying my best to get back home, and trying not to let it show how being lost felt—like falling and falling and seeing glimpses as you went. All the stories Leandros and Goodfellow told me . . . I couldn't connect with them. The flashes of memory I'd had, that I felt. I knew them—knew they were real. What people were telling me, though, didn't trigger any further memories as I'd hoped. The stories seemed as if they were missing something. They were off or wrong, or maybe I was the one who was off, but when I heard them, they didn't feel like anything other than something that had happened to someone else. Not to me.

"Maybe your mummy can tell me why the spiders like me so much," I offered. "That one was number six. Pretty good for someone not in the exterminating business, especially if you count them by pounds."

"You did kill a nest of four of them. The fifth could've been part of the nest and followed you." He put the bowl and spoon away, slamming the drawer. The washing and drying hadn't been enough to let him swim out of that mood yet. I should've eaten five more bowls. "This spider no doubt wanted payback. It's a frequent complication. Those who have killed anything that crosses their path can become inconveniently vengeful when something kills one of their own." Much like Leandros himself did.

"They don't get that occupational hazard deal?"

"No, they do not. Irksome, I know." He moved from the kitchen and tossed me my jacket from the couch. "And this is neither a closet nor a coatrack, nor has it ever been."

"I have amnesia. Cut me some slack," I protested as I slipped the jacket on, feeling the comfortable weight of metal fall into place. I'd scrubbed the leather down when we'd gotten home to get rid of the canal smell. It didn't hurt it any. The leather had been plenty distressed long before that wipe down.

"Laziness and sarcasm—now two things Nepenthe venom cannot affect." He was already wearing his own weapon-concealing long coat. "Zip up your jacket. It's a fair trip to the museum."

I groaned. Brain damaged or not, I knew I didn't want to see some dusty old relics or equally dusty and evil-minded mummies who hung about the place. Nonetheless, see them both, I did. The fact that the mummy ended up set on fire . . .

Completely not my fault.

Someone Leandros knew managed to sneak us past security at the New York Metropolitan Museum of Art by the devious and cunning method of having someone walk us through the metal detectors and snap her fingers at the guard who moved toward us when the beep beep beep filled the air. Snap. Point. Bad dog. Go. Sit. Her name was Sangrida Odins-something. She was big, blond, and, had she been wearing a metal bra, she could've taken out a tank. She also was a monst— She wasn't human. If I'd been pushed to the wall on it, I would've guessed Valkyrie. She looked like Thor from the comic books, only with breasts . . . and maybe more muscle.

She aimed an annoyed flap of her hand at the detectors, explaining it was for an ancient gemstone and jewelry traveling exhibit. I understood her lack of enthusiasm for jewelry. She'd probably much rather have a nice gut-stabbing spear than a bracelet.

Leandros introduced her as the director of the museum. I nodded and kept my eyes off her as much as possible while he asked in low tones as we walked if she'd had any trouble from Ammut or the spiders. If she caught any of what she considered inappropriate looks from me, I knew—in my bones I *knew*—she'd stomp me to death with her size-twelve sensible-heel shoe. And there was no way it would take more than one stomp.

Sangrida said they had had no trouble at the museum nor had she had any at home, but she would alert us if she did. As she unlocked a door to the basement, she also stated she wanted to thank us again for handling the museum's small difficulty before. I waited until the door shut behind us and Leandros and I had started down the stairs before I asked, "What kind of small difficulty did Wonder Woman there have that she couldn't handle by herself?"

"A cannibalistic serial killer with a body count of near seven hundred. He rose from his own fifteenth-century ashes to eat whomever he could find and hang dead bodies in trees," he replied, as offhandedly as if we'd simply dropped by one time to shoo a homeless person out of the souvenir shop.

"You do that on purpose, don't you? You and that puck," I accused with a growl. "You love screwing with my head and trying to scare the shit out of me." I was tempted to give that blond braid of his a hard pull to let him know my leg was feeling just as pulled. "Making things sound worse than they are. Like Goodfellow freaking me out with that gods and goddesses thing when Ammut is just another monster. And you wonder why I tried to stab him with a fork. Now you're doing the same damn thing."

"No. Goodfellow enjoys that, but as for me?" There was a glimmer of his serious gaze over his shoulder as he went down several more steps, pulling ahead of me. Longer legs, the bastard. "The truth is enough. I'm sure you've noticed the bite on your chest."

The bite? Holy shit. That enormous scar that looked like someone with a big mouth and a bigger appetite had tried to make me lunch? "That was him? He did that? He tried to turn me into a buffet?" I gritted my teeth. "*Before* he killed me? He couldn't kill me first and then eat me? That's just fucking rude. Tell me he's dead and tell me he cried like a goddamn baby when he went."

"He's dead. Permanently this time." He took another step. "Very permanently."

"Good. I hope we got paid a shitload for that one.

Because, you know, being eaten and all, I think we deserved a fat paycheck for that."

"Could we change the subject?" The demand was abrupt and sharply edged.

Curious, I took the steps faster to keep up with him. "Why? What happened to that shared-past stuff? You know me, I know you. History. I thought we were bonded through blood, family, fighting side by side. All that. Follow me to the ends of the earth, hairy bare feet, ring, volcano. Mordor, here we come. Epic bromance."

He stopped, but he didn't turn to look at me. He simply . . . stopped. After a few seconds I thought again about tugging on the braid. Ding-dong. Anyone home? But before I could, he said, "Blood doesn't always mean family. Sometimes it only means blood. As in how much you lost, how you nearly died, and how it was by the barest chance we found a way to save you."

And we didn't talk about that—watching a brother almost die on you. He'd nearly seen it again last night. Leandros was my brother before he was anything else in this world. If you knew where to look, you could see it in his pelting me with a candy bar and stealing pretzels for me from the dead cat. Or searching for me days without sleep because a brother did not lose a brother. Ever. If you had to go to Hell itself to bring him back, then that was what you would do. Memory or observation, either way, it was true about Leandros. Talking about it made him relive it and reliving it—that was obviously bad, and the canal thing last night couldn't have helped. It hadn't done me any good, I knew that. But another rule in the *Good Brother Handbook*—you don't hurt your brother. Not sincerely. Not outside atomic wedgie range.

"So . . . Wahanket's a mummy, huh?"

The stiff spine unlocked, the shoulders relaxed, and we were moving again. "A mummy, yes, but a mummy of a human? No, I don't think so. And Robin won't tell us, which means he doesn't know either. He can keep a secret if he wants to, but—"

"He never wants to?" I snorted.

"Precisely." The glance over the shoulder this time was more amused. "Sangrida would probably pay us to evict him from the museum basement, but the destruction wouldn't be worth the payoff. Now, watch out for the cats. Salome might be the pick of the litter, but she wasn't the only one in it."

Great. More dead cats. Salome's compadres. If I had to take one of those out, assuming I could take one of those out, would the puck's cat want revenge as the spider had? Damn. It was too bad Ms. Thor couldn't have gotten me *and* a flamethrower past security.

Past the basement there was another basement. Subbasement. Basement squared. Whatever you wanted to call it, it meant a lot of goddamn stairs. "I don't like exercise," I grumbled.

"I know."

We were wending our way through stacks and boxes and glass cases so dusty you couldn't see what they held. Treasure? Gold? Something sharp like an ancient dagger? That last thought had me stopping to rub at the grime to take a look. I didn't like exercise, but I did like weapons. "It's boring," I went on, disappointed. Tiny carven bits of rock. No daggers.

"So you've said many times. Many, many, many times."

Many, many times. Ninja-know-it-all. "Have I ever said," I asked casually, "there's a dead koala bear on the ceiling that's about to bite your head off?"

His head whipped back as he looked up, his sword out and ready, but I'd already nailed it in the chest as it plummeted down. The shot knocked it ahead of us into the shadows of boxes stacked eighteen feet high. "Winnie was gunning for your ass." I chambered another round. I knew better than to think I'd killed it with one shot. It was already dead. Predead. Undead. Whatever. I'd most likely just pissed it off. "You should always look up. Even while you're bitching at me. The worst things come from there, and people never fucking look."

Wolves, spiders, furry mummies—that was nothing. Bad things, worse things—the absolute fucking worst came from above; it didn't matter if I couldn't put a name or a memory to them right now. I still knew. You didn't stick your hand into a fire, and you always looked up.

Or be the one looking down.

Living with one whispering voice in my head was bad enough, but two was getting to be too damn much.

I shook my head, a sliver of worry spiking through me. "And you're not just 'people.' You should know better." He should. He did, but he was distracted—by me. That had to stop.

"Whoops, here he comes again." I aimed at the form lunging out of the darkness, sputtering candlelight eyes, tawny fur here and there in lonely tufts peeking through its tightly bandaged frame. The ears, nose, and mouth full of non–koala bear fangs weren't bandaged, though. "It's kind of cute." Except for the barracuda teeth implanted in its jaws. I lowered the Desert Eagle. "I'll feel bad if we kill it. Piglet, Christopher Robin, they'd never get over it."

Niko skewered it with his katana in midleap. It hissed, snapped, and tried to pull itself closer using its much longer than average talons to grasp the metal and heave. What was it about mummification that made everything remotely lethal on the thing get so damn much bigger?

I glanced down at the front of my jeans and considered. Nah. There were bound to be complications.

"Except for incinerating it, I doubt we could kill it even if we wanted to." He raised his voice. "Wahanket, we have business with you. Call off your pet before I dice it into a hundred pieces. They can bounce about all they want then, but I don't think they'll accomplish much."

"Pooh hater," I muttered under my breath.

"Winnie-the-Pooh was not a koala—why am I even arguing about this with you?" He pointed the blade at me as the impaled mummified guard bear continued to thrash and hiss. "This creature could kill you as easily as one of those spiders. Keep that in mind."

"You mean the six spiders *I* killed? Really. That easy, huh?" I grinned. "You're pissed because you missed it, hanging up there. Big bad ninja missed it. Hey, do we keep tabs on things like this? Is that a brother thing? As in it's my six spiders and one rabid undead Pooh to your . . . um . . . nothing? Nothing, right? Did I miscount?"

I couldn't see the exact color of them down here, the lights were dim—the bare minimum, but I could see the tug-of-war behind his eyes. One side was, best guess, hit your brother with the mummified killer koala bear. The other side, which I'd have laid money on pulling ahead, wasn't nearly as forgiving as that.

"Sooo . . . we don't keep count?" I concluded.

"Wahanket!"

Damn, Leandros could get the volume up there when he wanted. Where had all that Zen gone?

There was a long sigh, a hot breeze over distant sands, and finally, "I am here."

"Here" was two narrow corridors over and five rows down. There a space was cleared for what looked like a wooden Egyptian reclining couch—as far as I could tell. It had a King Tut look to it. That was what I apparently used to classify old Egyptian things, and I had no problem with that. It was a good system in my book, especially as it didn't involve reading actual books about what ancient Egyptians used for furniture before IKEA came along. There was also a computer, a television nicer than the one we had, several mounds of smaller electronics scattered about, a fucking Wii, if you could believe that, and a metal table littered with sharp instruments and blood—old.

But once it had been new.

It was hideous. I could picture . . . I could remember . . . cats. Dead cats. Completely dead and being cut up. Couldn't mummify without cutting, could you? The smell of it. The smell of fear and spilled urine and guts . . . Monsters kill, monsters murder, and, given the chance, some monsters do a great deal worse.

Wahanket was a monster, no waivers for good behavior, and I hated him. The feeling was sharp and cold, and I knew it was right.

Righteous. Both voices were a choir on that one.

The growl in my chest rose up in my savage smile as I saw the claws of a great lizard where one hand should've been. "I did that, didn't I? You pissed me off. You fucked with me, and I didn't much like it." The specifics I didn't have yet, only the taste of the memory, but the fact was solid and true. Sometimes you didn't have to remember to simply *know*. I took a step closer. I'd done that, and I wouldn't mind doing it again. I took another step.

No, I wouldn't mind at all.

A hand landed on my shoulder and held me back. "Wait, Cal. If he has information, we need it."

Wahanket wasn't the mummy of a human being, but I couldn't have told the difference, except for the scales and claws of his replaced hand. Resin-stained bandages cracked with his every movement. His nose was a dark cavity, his teeth stripped of gums and blackened, a scrap of leather revealed to be his tongue when those teeth parted. A mummy so disgusting and unnatural that Salome and the bear in comparison could be plucked off a toy store shelf. They all did share the same eyes, a wavering, undying glow.

"Why do you come here?" He didn't bother with my talk of his hand or how I'd been responsible. With his other hand he gestured, joints creaking, and the bear wriggled off Niko's blade to land on the table where it had been made, turning to hiss and keep us in view. At least it had been long dead before Wahanket had gotten at it, not like the cats, dug up from some old boxed exhibit down here. One stuffed koala bear meant for educational purposes turned into a killer Teddy with no interest in eucalyptus leaves whatsoever. "And with nothing to offer in trade?"

"One of the last times we traded, you tried to shoot my brother with his own gun. That covers our tab indefinitely, I've decided." A hand swatted the back of my head, a daily event, I was learning. No wonder it had felt familiar when Miss Terrwyn had done the same, as it had its roots here. "As for you, little brother, trading guns to homicidal mummies for information is not a good idea. An obvious statement, but one that escaped you at the time."

As I rubbed the back of my head with one hand, my other was in my jacket searching for something appropriate for the situation—that situation making Wahanket unavailable for all future trading activities. He was a monster even among other monsters—strike one; Niko said he'd tried to shoot me sometime in the fuzzy past—strike two; and I didn't like him in so many goddamn ways—strike three. Plenty of reasons, although the "not liking him" one was more than enough for me.

The swat I'd gotten on the head was doubled to be felt through the leather of my jacket covering the back of my shoulder. I growled again but let my hand drop. Niko wanted information. I could wait. Once he had it, then I could kill Wahanket, and we'd both be happy. Win-win. I didn't need the warning tickling the back of my skull.

Monstermonstermonster.

Blackened teeth snapped together, but Wahanket gave in without argument while laying a soothing claw on the back of the hissing Disney reject. "Very well. I can be generous when I wish. What is it you want to know?"

"Of Ammut, and don't claim you know nothing, you desiccated depravity. If anything, you are one and the same kind, only you are far weaker than she is. She is a god and you're nothing more than a killer of cats hiding in a basement, the lowest of cockroaches fearing the light." If this was Niko buttering up an informant, I wished I'd washed my own cereal bowl that morning.

Wahanket . . . Hadn't I once called him Hank? There'd been a stupid cowboy hat he'd worn. He'd seemed harmless then. He'd . . . I blinked and whatever I'd been thinking was gone. It slithered away into the corner of my mind, out of sight but waiting. It was coming back. The cats. The hand. Slowly and playing hide-and-seek, but it was all coming back, the memories. Me.

"A god? She is no god. She can but steal life. I can give"—his claws stilled on the back of the ragged beast of his creation—"as well as take." The light disappeared in the eye sockets of the bear and it fell stiffly onto his side. It was the same as it was before he had done his work on it—dead. Defaced and definitely less educational, but dead.

"If you're her equal, why aren't you aboveground killing vampires, Wolves, lamia, and whatever else she can gather with her spiders?" Niko asked. I saw the yellow eyes of a cat crouched on the crates behind him, but Salome's brother or sister in undeath was content to watch. Maybe it didn't want to end up like the bear. Or maybe it liked Salome more than the mummy that had killed it before raising it from the dead.

"I have spent more years than you can imagine taking and giving lives. I am older than the pharaohs, older than Egypt or any pyramid. I knew the Nile when it was only a trickle of water and I have existed long enough to know there is no thrill to be had any longer, none that I haven't tasted. Save one." The tendons of his neck stretched and split as he turned his head to take in the computer.

"If you wish to know of Ammut, now she cares for higher nests as opposed to warm dens. She likes to view her kingdom, but I have my window into endless kingdoms. I do not need what she needs. I can sustain myself without feeding. I am beyond that. If she were as powerful as I, then she could do the same. If she does not feed, she will starve within a month. Pathetic. I have heard of deaths that could be caused by her, but if she is here, I cannot say for sure. We come from the same place, but we are not the same kind. We are not connected. We are not"—the claws of one hand curled tight—"sociable creatures, either of us." It was funny how "sociable" could sound as if he'd like to skin her alive and reupholster his King Tut sofa. "She would not come here to me. I know not where in this world that she now perches."

"She likes to perch while you like to hide from your shadow like Punxsutawney Phil. Is that right?" I asked with a sneer that had a mind of its own.

The distant glimmer in his skull switched its regard from the computer to me. The glow, hepatitis yellow, brightened. Sometimes bright means cheerful; sometimes it means a heightened interest—either good or bad; and sometimes it's the blaze of sheer fury. His head jerked forward toward me with the same quick action of a striking snake. "What have you done?" His eyes were so bright, it was as painful to look at as staring into the sun. "What have you become? How have you let someone else steal what should be mine?" His teeth snapped and parted to let through a sound like nothing I'd ever heard. It damn sure put the hissing of a dead bear to shame. "I have bided my time, waiting for you to ripen, and now you are barely half of what you were, barely worth taking at all. What have you *done*?"

Mummies could move faster than any spider when they wanted, faster than a half-grown boggle. Wahanket was a hurricane-force wind and I was the palm tree that went down before it. Long, thin fingers and a lizard's talons wrapped around my neck, cutting off my air instantly. "It was mine, and you lost it, you worthless sack of skin. It was mine. Itwasmine. Itwasmine. Mineminemine."

It was getting dark fast and I didn't think that had anything to do with the natural gloom down here. You didn't have to choke someone for minutes, unless you were an amateur. Less than fifteen seconds of pressure on the carotid arteries would have your victim out cold. Out cold and on a dissection table. Of all the memories I'd lost, that couldn't have been one of them. Of course not.

The blackness spread and I couldn't see Wahanket anymore, but I didn't need to see to get a hand inside my jacket. My thoughts were getting hazy, but I didn't need them to choose the right weapon. I only needed instinct, and instinct was all over this.

Monster.

Cat killer.

Motherfucking mummified *asshole*.

Instinct chose one of my backup Desert Eagles, the one having been lost in the canal. Instinct pulled the trigger. It was a few seconds later when blood made its way back to my brain and I could see again that I found out instinct had been cock-blocked. The round that should've shattered Wahanket's skull had hit nothing. Niko must have kicked him off me, because the mummy was on his back several feet away with a katana skewering him to the floor. But to judge from his thrashing, strong for a pile of bones and jerky, the blade wasn't going to hold Wahanket forever. The man who'd turned him into a temporary shish kebab didn't strike me as that concerned. His hand disappeared inside his duster and reappeared with a can of lighter fluid. I hadn't asked about it when we'd stopped and bought it on the way. If I asked about everything I didn't know or understand right now, I would never shut up. I was going with a mostly wait-and-see policy until I was back to normal.

I had to say, I liked what I was seeing.

Niko sprayed the mummy from head to toe and with one flick of his thumb set him on fire. The flailing redoubled and the cursing started. I sat up. "What about your sword?"

There was a dismissive shrug. "It's not one of my favorites. I came prepared. You never know when Wahanket will have useful information or not, the same as you never know if he'll go from mildly cooperative to wildly homicidal." He held down a hand to me and pulled me to my feet.

A lot of people seemed to be taking my amnesia personally—the Wolves, the boggles, and now this piece of shit. "What was he talking about? That I'm only half of what I was?" I rubbed at my throat, but it was in one piece other than the scabbed spider bite. I owed that to

Leandros, who was as fast as he'd been when disarming me in Nevah's Landing—as fast as I had the strong feeling that he always was.

"He can take life forces like Ammut, even if they're not the same. Perhaps a meal for these kinds of predators includes it all: your life, your memories, your skills, your emotions. And you most definitely do not care for Wahanket, the same as he does not care for you." That was fairly obvious, I thought as Niko went on. "He might have been waiting for your . . . dislike of him to peak before he tried to drain you."

"The cherry on the top of a Cal sundae, huh?" Niko appeared to have no problem accepting that guess, and Wahanket was one of a kind—puzzling over it would probably be pointless, although it still didn't explain the Wolves and boggles. I was about to bring that up when I was distracted by Wahanket—not by what he was doing, but by what he wasn't doing.

The mummy's cursing was indecipherable, a language I didn't know—if he was as old as he claimed, then one that no one knew. "Shouldn't he be screaming? If you set me on fire, don't think less of my manliness—*muy macho* and all, but I'd scream like a banshee." He was burning fast and furiously without a hint of smoke. Too bad, if you were going to eat old meat, it was better smoked.

"I doubt it hurts much. His body is dead. No living nerve endings to register pain. This is more of a temper tantrum and hopefully, once burned to a crisp, he'll be less physically capable of attacking us in the future—the near future at least. There's no need to kill him, if we actually could kill him. And we do need informants. He's no more homicidal than the rest—as long as you show some sense and don't come alone."

Being set on fire would only slow him down and not

even permanently? Well, damn, let's see if we could slow his ass down a little more that that. "I'll be back."

"Good idea," Niko commented. "Find a fire extinguisher. We don't want this to spread. Watch out for the cats." I had every intention, but I still thought the cats were more on our side than Wahanket's.

When I came back, I tossed him the extinguisher, which had actually been his thought and not mine, with one hand and hoisted the fire axe with the other. I hadn't forgotten my prechoking opinions. Tried to shoot me once and strangle me this time. Monster. Cat killer. Wannabe murderer of me. Motherfucking asshole.

Oh yeah . . . the last one.

I just didn't like him. Best reason of all.

He was more sizzling than flaming now. I barely felt the heat as I chopped off his arms and legs. Niko hadn't mentioned it when reading me his mental list of what entertained baby brother Cal—reading, parties, yeah . . . lame. No, this—*this* was what I did for fun. And, *goddamn*, it was fun.

On the beach when I'd woken up, I'd known I was a killer, but I'd convinced myself along the way that I was a good killer. A noble Boy Scout of killers. But there were no good killers. There were only killers . . . period, and this bullshit about do the job but don't enjoy the kill? The road to Hell . . . The slippery slope; why had I been embracing those idiotic clichés days ago?

What's worse than killing for a living? Being bored killing for a living. Hell, yes, enjoy your job. *Love* your damn job. I was on the side of good, right? I killed monsters, kept people safe and all that crap. Why shouldn't I enjoy it?

"A happy monster killer is an efficient monster killer," I told Wahanket with the last chop as the yellow eyes continued to glare at me from a blackened, burned skull. He'd gone quiet, the cursing done, but that stare told me I was on his list—forever and top of. Numero uno. That was fair. He was certainly on mine.

"We wouldn't want me to lose my edge, would we, pal? Practice makes perfect." I pushed his arm a few feet from his torso. "As for thinking I'm not all I was, I'm catching up and quick. Good thoughts for you to think about while you put yourself back together. By the time you do that, I'll be myself again and won't we have some good times then?" I kicked his other arm even farther away. "Hope you have some superglue around, shit-head." I dropped the axe beside him and smiled. It felt good, that smile. Satisfied. So much so that I considered picking the axe back up and turning the mummy into some even smaller pieces. Yep, very, very satisfied.

Niko, oddly, looked anything but.

"Fun and games with Wahanket over already?" Robin, who was sitting on our apartment couch when we arrived home, checked his watch. "That was quick, quicker than Ammut trying to have Cal swimming with the fishes like mobsters of old, and, as 'quick' so very often means, I'm guessing you came away unsatisfied."

"He has a key?" I jammed an elbow in Niko's ribs. "You have to be kidding me. And you just installed the new lock this morning."

"Kid, I was picking locks before the human race invented them . . . or reinvented them. Blatant patent infringement, stealing from our kind." He stretched and propped his feet on the coffee table. "Well? Wahanket?"

"You're wrong there. I came away very satisfied." I grinned—it felt a little dark and a little nasty, but that was okay. Things were coming back. Feelings, no full-on memories yet, but the apartment seemed more familiar—I felt like a driver who had missed the curve but was driving over the median and seconds away from getting back on the right path. No, not the right path— the correct path.

My path.

"He cooperated then?"

"Nope, not worth a damn, which made it massively more entertaining." I went to the refrigerator and got a beer. There was only one and as it wasn't made of soy, I was assuming it was mine.

"Mmm. That's unfortunate, but Wahanket is who he is. We've always known that. We've always accepted that. It would be a mistake to think he could change or should change." When I turned back, I saw the fox's eyes settled not on me, but on Leandros, and there was an odd emphasis not on Wahanket's name but on the word "change."

I shrugged. "Then you'd be wrong. He has changed. He's now a scorched Wahanket puzzle made of six pieces. Not a complicated puzzle, but one I'm not putting back together." I took a drink. "Especially as I spent the time taking him apart."

"Mmm," Robin repeated, running a hand down the front of his silk shirt. I'd noticed him do that before and was now having a déjà vu shimmer that it was a habit of his. I checked my weapons; he checked his clothes. "Spiders and mummies. None are spared your wrath. Tell me you didn't do it with a fork."

Shaking my head, I took another swallow and flopped on the couch next to him. "Better. Axe. And I've been thinking about that Wolf at the bar. I have no idea why I'd felt bad about that. She'd tried to kill me. What was I supposed to do? Pet her furry little head and tell her home? Home, girl! Drag her out to a pet cemetery and have her cremated with a shiny brass urn, bow, and framed dog treat? Jesus. My first and last ever sentimental moment." She'd been a killer—through and through. Who cared how she'd gotten that way? Born wild, born to hunt, you still made your choices and suffered the consequences. Evolution was no free ride.

But is there anything wrong with free rides?

Things were going great, working out, and I had no time for more voices whispering in my head, especially when the two already there kept contradicting each other. I ignored them. Basically, as they were my voice times two, I was ignoring myself. That was fine by me. I finished my beer. "Maybe I could try a shift at the bar. I'm getting some stuff back up here." I tapped my temple. "It might be . . . fun." A different type of amusement than I would've considered this morning when I'd asked Leandros what I did for that sort of thing, but fun all the same. "Mummy fun."

Wahanket, the boggles, Wolves; I could protect myself against them all, but I could also do more whether I had to or not. I didn't have to kill. I could . . . play. Make them sorry. Didn't they deserve it? Didn't every one of them who'd scorned me or tried to kill me deserve a little of their own back?

Scorned me—why had they scorned me? Did it matter? For being human. For kicking their asses? For keeping monsters in line.

The one voice laughed. *Monsters? There are no such things as monsters. Not to you.*

It didn't make any difference, none of it—the whys, the reasons, the schizophrenic confusion. It didn't matter, because I was on my way. I was coming back all right.

Coming home . . .

I was on the path and turning that last curve in the woods, almost in sight of home. A dark path, but I liked the dark. I controlled the dark. Then there were times that it controlled me.

Fair is fair. Share and share alike.

I felt a sudden spasm in my stomach. Shit. My hand resting on my knee was shadowed where a shadow shouldn't be—like that dark film covering my face in the Halloween picture. Leandros and Goodfellow didn't say anything. They didn't see it; they couldn't see it. If they had, they would've said something—something like *Wake up, Cal. You're having a nightmare.* But it wasn't a dream and it wasn't a nightmare. Nightmares never are nightmares when you want them to be.

I held my hand out under the brightest light by the couch and it was still there, that murky film. The Cal of the worst day ever . . . pathetic, lame excuse. The Cal of the Halloween picture with ice in his eyes and a flat expression that said killing was nothing but a hobby. You—in the sights of my gun? Sorry—you're nothing but a pastime. You didn't come close to ranking as personal. Hope you had a littermate who cared you died, because the only thing I cared about was making sure your blood stayed off my new sneakers. Your blood? That was easy to come by. But good shoes? Much harder.

Shit. Shitshitshit. It hurt. Why the hell did it hurt? "My head . . ." It wasn't my head, but I couldn't say where exactly it was. I knew what it was, though, not that it made any sense.

It was my soul; my damn soul hurt.

"I feel wrong. Something bad is coming." They were stupid, overly dramatic words I couldn't stop myself from saying. I hid my shadowed hand under my leg, sandwiched by the couch cushion. They couldn't see it, but I could. Why had I said that? Something bad is coming? What the hell did that mean?

Something bad is coming.

No, something gooooood.

"Wrong?" Niko echoed, the corners of his mouth tilting downward.

"Sick. I meant sick. Not right. Just a headache." With my other hand I took the dish towel my brother handed me and wiped my suddenly sweaty face with it. It was a cold sweat, like beads of ice frozen to my skin. "Why did I do that to the mummy?" Because he deserved it and I'd liked it. I'd slipped my leash and *let* myself like it. I shouldn't have, but I did. I'd chopped him up and I'd enjoyed every second of it. Whether it killed him or not, how could that be right?

How could it be wrong?

Jesus. If you were going to have voices, your own voices, screwing with your head, they ought to have the fucking decency to agree with each other at least once. I wiped my face again. "Why didn't I just leave him like he was? Why'd I go that far?" I asked it aloud, to myself but not to the others.

"You see?" Leandros said to Goodfellow quietly.

Before I could ask what he was meant to see, Goodfellow stood suddenly. "If you're sick, then I had best be off. I can't afford to come down with some ancient, dusty disease you picked up in that equally ancient and dusty basement. I have places to go, things to do, peris to puck." He put on his coat. "I don't suppose you had a chance to tell Wahanket about my monogamous ways before you roasted and chopped him into Mongolian barbecue? Don't bother with excuses. My condition is everyone's concern." He tossed a handful of business cards on the table. They were green with bronze-colored lettering. Trying to cover up my confusion, reaching for casual, I picked one up with a hand that wanted to shake. I didn't let it, and read the lettering aloud. "'Robin Goodfellow, Monogamite, established 2010.'" Beneath that was a phone number.

"What's the—"

"Suicide Hotline," Robin answered before I had a chance to finish. "I've heard their call volume has increased tenfold." He bowed his head in a solemn tilt. "I do what I can." Then he was heading for the door. "Niko, I left you a few things as you've not been eating much while we looked for your wayward, apron-wearing brother. Enjoy. I'll see the two of you later. I just have time to surprise Ishiah before he heads to work." He paused as he opened the door, his eyebrows rising as he smirked. "Forget mice and men. The best-laid plans of *vice* and *sin* never go astray."

He added more seriously, "But other things often do, well intentioned or not. Something to keep in mind."

As the door slammed, I said, "There's a lot I didn't understand with that whole conversation and a lot I wish I hadn't understood. Maybe I'll skip the Ninth Circle." There was no way I was going to the bar. Halloween Cal waited at the bar. I wasn't ready to be Halloween Cal. At that moment I wasn't ready to be any kind of Cal. "You don't think Goodfellow and my boss have done it on the bar, do you? Where I serve drinks? Gah. I think I need a nap to wash my brain." That was good. That sounded offhand, not on the edge of losing it at all . . . Never mind the sweat still soaking the back of my neck, the pain, the sickness so sharp I'd have left my own body to escape it if I could.

Leandros was already in the kitchen area, investigating the bags Goodfellow had left behind. He pulled out containers of yogurt, soy cheese, and various other inedibles, but then he tossed me a boxed tube of toothpaste. Minty fresh. Chocolate minty fresh. "You took your own with you to South Carolina and judging from the sounds of gagging coming from the bathroom last night, mine doesn't meet your approval."

"Seaweed is apparently not my dental care of choice. Hard to believe, I know." I pushed up off the couch, steadying myself while he watched from the corner of his eye.

"Are you all right?" He tried to sound casual too, but he didn't pull it off well. Not with me. Leandros . . . No . . . Niko. Niko—he'd always hated lying, all the lying we'd had to do as kids when we had run from . . . from . . .

The pain sharpened, leaving only thoughts of bed and collapse. "Just a headache, that's all," I repeated, my lie not much better than his. I avoided his face and a concern as sharp as the sickness in me and headed back for my bedroom. I didn't stop by the bathroom . . . until Niko spoke up as I passed it.

"Chili cheese dog with extra onions." That would've been the vendor five blocks from the museum. "I'm surprised your breath alone didn't do to Wahanket what lighter fluid and a lighter did. Brush."

I was barely on my feet, but I didn't argue. That would only lead to more time wasted before I made it to my bed. I also knew bitching about it would result in an educational beat-down on the sparring mats or toothpaste squirted into an unsuspecting body orifice. I chose to brush my teeth. I wasn't afraid of my brother, but I was aware of his limits—none that I knew of.

None that I remembered.

Memories, feelings, pain, fear—fast, coming so damn fast. I was close—God, I was right there, as if it all were on the tip of my tongue. It was, surprisingly, not the best taste in the world. Not sweet, almost bitter with a copper hint of blood. Should coming home taste of blood? I brushed quickly, but extra hard. Chocolate and mint had it all over seaweed, even if the mint had a helluva tingle. If that didn't erase onion breath and the metallic taste of a brand-new penny, nothing would. Then I made it across the hall to my bed. I didn't stagger, but it was close. I could feel my brain bunched like a fist, one that was getting ready to relax into an open hand. I had every expectation that a little sleep would finally reset my brain and when I woke up, it would be back.

All of it.

And fighting it was senseless. There'd be no more wondering who I was. No wondering if I was Halloween Cal. I was thinking bad things, wrong things, because all the knots unraveling in my brain were confusing me; that was all. I wasn't wasting any more time on the imaginary right and wrong of them. I'd spent only days in this life. How the hell could I know right from wrong in this bizarre world in just days? When I woke up, I would be who I was meant to be. No more doubts, no more freaky voices or hallucinations of shadows that didn't exist. I'd had enough, and I didn't mind telling myself or my brain so. I yanked the covers up and rolled over as the afternoon light spilled down from above. I closed my eyes and yawned. The pain, wherever it was, head or heart, was suddenly fading, slipping away like sand between my fingers—Egyptian sand. The sickness and pain disappeared along with the last grain to fall. God, that was better.

I was coming home, all the way this time, I thought, foggy and dim.

For better or worse? I didn't know. I'd find out soon enough.

The next time I opened my eyes, I'd know.

The next time I opened my eyes . . .

8

I opened my eyes and had no fucking clue where I was.

There were twilight shadows spilling around me. They came from windows almost two stories up. Damn. Too high. Dropping my gaze, I faced a wall full of holes where *Screw you* was spelled out, connect-the-dot style. There was a flash of pain behind my eyes and I grunted, sucking in a breath. Don't panic. Think it out. Okay, okay, what was all this? What . . . Leandros. I exhaled harshly in relief. That was right. Leandros, my brother. He'd found me at the diner in Nevah's Landing and had brought me back. I was in his apartment. My apartment too, he'd said. We'd gotten here yesterday, or had it been the day before, two days before? I wasn't sure. Goddamn it, I couldn't remember. Shit, keep it together. Let it go and concentrate on something you are sure of.

Monsters.

There'd been monsters, a shitload of monsters. We fought monsters for a living. Giant lizards in Central Park, a Wolf who'd jumped me from the top of a building—a beautiful predator and gone now. Hopefully to a place that welcomed the wild when they died. Then there'd been a mummy. It was mostly clearing up until the mummy part—that memory cut out almost instantly to the smallest of bits and pieces. There'd been someone choking me, a fire, and an axe. That was all mixed up. Fuzzy and distant.

I was leaving it that way. Whatever memory I was not having, I was completely happy to not be having it. It felt wrong, as if something best locked in a box and shoved under the bed. The smell of burning frankincense, myrrh, and wine—I could forget that too, because I didn't know what frankincense and myrrh smelled like, did I? How would I know that?

Oh. The cat. The damn dead mummy cat from the bar. She'd smelled like the world's most expensive deodorizer. Leandros had used her as a tool to bore me with a lesson in how mummies were made and what ingredients were used in the process. He'd said it was the fourth time he'd told me and I could blame only one of those times on amnesia.

The mummy in the basement and the mummy cat smelled the same—if you took away the smell of burned flesh, which I did. Or tried and failed. All right then, the smell I couldn't forget, but everything else I could. We'd been in a museum basement. There was a talking mummy and somewhere along the way a fire. I could've tried to push past that, but I didn't want to. If I didn't want to, then I probably had a good reason.

"Cal, are you feeling better?"

My hand started automatically for the gun under the pillow. I managed to stop it halfway. It was Leandros. Niko. My brother. At the diner, he'd disarmed me. I stabbed a guy with a fork.... Goodfellow; all monsters weren't bad; NYC; peris; vamps; Wolves—it all ran through my head. It was faded, not nearly as sharp as I thought it should've been, but it was all there—a little muddled, but not gone. I moved my hand back from the gun, although I knew the shadowed figure standing in

my doorway had seen the movement. I ran the gun hand
through my hair instead. It flopped into my eyes, making me feel like a predator peering through the grass on
the plains waiting for its next meal to pass by. Or I could
be an ill-groomed Shetland pony. I was going to get that
barber one day.

"Cal?"

I tried again with the hair and this time succeeded in
actual sight. "Not bad. Why?"

"You said you felt sick before you went to bed and
slept through the afternoon and all night. Are you running a fever?" The figure formed from shadows into my
brother, braid and sparring sweats, as he stepped into
my room. I didn't know if he was going to go for the
mom's-hand-on-the-forehead TV commercial, whip out
a thermometer, or wave a hand around me to judge the
ambient temperature of the air in my immediate area.
All sounded as if they would kick me several slots down
the list of most macho badasses in the city.

I slid out of bed on the other side, keeping it between
us. "No, no fever. I'm not sick." I barely remembered going to bed. Only a bad feeling . . . dread—good old hokey
Edgar Allan Poe type of black houses, withered graveyard trees, ravens-at-your-door dread, and pain. Hadn't
there been pain? I couldn't remember. There had been
the darkness of sleep, and now I was up and I felt okay.
Not fantastic, but all right. "I think," I said, hesitating,
but he was my brother. If anyone had a right to know,
he did—my primary babysitter. A babysitter. Jesus, how
embarrassing. "I think I might've had some kind of relapse with the spider venom. When I woke up, things
were foggy. They cleared up for the most part. I remember you finding me in South Carolina, bringing me back.
I remember this place and going to a bar where a Wolf
tried to kill me. I remember nearly everything trying to

kill me, including Ammut. And then I remember the museum and that there was a talking mummy, but that's about it. Once I hit the mummy, things are gone. I don't remember much of any of that or after that. There are a lot of gaps. I don't remember what the mummy said. I don't remember leaving the museum. I remember getting back here . . . a little. I think Goodfellow was here." I shook my head. "And then I went to bed."

Because it had all been coming back. Coming in your sleep. The best place to keep hidden treasures.

The best place to lock up the worst nightmares.

I was within seconds of grabbing the gun and smacking my own head with the butt. Amnesia was enough. I was tired unto death of dealing with squabbling inner voices too, especially when it was literally my own voice I was hearing. I was actually beginning to hate the sound of my voice. Enough was enough.

"Come here." A hand reached over my bed to pull me around it and across the hall into the bathroom. "Sit."

I put the toilet lid down and sat. That, at least, ruled out one less-manly place to get my temperature taken. Niko's hand pushed my head with care to one side as he examined the puncture with gloved fingers. Whoa. "Um . . . Where'd the surgical gloves come from?"

"Goodfellow. He's a proctologist on the weekends." Before I could comment on how wrong that was, how very, very wrong, he continued. "Amnesia and gullibility, I didn't know they went hand in hand. We have gloves because we have many medical supplies as our on-the-job injuries are frequently the kind the hospitals rarely see, which would lead to questions we can't answer. We make do with our own medical skills." Now there was the cool feel of ointment being rubbed on the bite, as casually as he'd done it a thousand times before. The question he asked was less casual. It should've sounded casual. . . . It was only hair, but that wasn't the vibe I was getting. "Why did you cut your hair?"

Could they come more out of the blue than that one? "To get the Goodfellow seal of approval?" I snorted. I already knew there was something wrong with my haircut if the puck liked it. "It's just hair. What's the big deal?"

"Our clan, the Vayash, some intermingled a time or two with the Northern Greek centuries ago. We picked up a custom of theirs—when someone dies, you cut your hair to mourn their passing." That . . . That was yet less casual than before. But before when? When no answer was forthcoming in my memories, I let it go.

I could see his point, why it was important to him and not casual at all. In a way someone had died when I'd first woken up—me. But that person would be back. Resurrected, although it was taking longer than three days. I ran a hand over the mop of jaw-length hair. "I had spider goop stuck in it. I couldn't get it out for anything. That stuff is worse than superglue. I had to chop it off. Nobody died but a bunch of spiders, and I think those bastards had it coming.

"That they did." Discussion over. I couldn't tell for sure if he was relieved or not at my answer, but I thought he was. No, I knew he was. Leandros had a labyrinth of a brain, no getting past that, but I was getting better at navigating it. "The bite isn't infected," he said. "I would say your immune system is still fighting off venom, but even at whatever reduced dose you received, it's a challenge. As with any other allergic reaction or flu, you'll get better, get worse, and get better again." He taped a square of gauze over it. "As you remember the important things such as where you keep your guns and how to use them, this is nothing but an inconvenience."

I plucked at the bottom of my T-shirt and held it out to better see the lettering. It must've been the one I'd worn to the museum, because I didn't remember changing when I fell into bed last night. *King of the fucking universe*. That was above and beyond the one I'd been wearing on the beach, which I wouldn't have thought possible. "I'd say being an inconvenience is something I'm good at."

"Ah . . ." Leandros stalled while pulling off the glove and throwing it away, but when he was caught by my expectant stare, he gave in. "Yes, you live to exasperate, irritate, piss off, and at times enrage others, but only those you think deserve it. You were a born smart-ass, Cal. Trust me, I was there when it happened, and that will never change."

Something had changed, though. My brain had hopped a bus and gone bye-bye again, at least for yesterday. I remembered Ammut trying to drown me. I also remembered something else. It had come back instantly when Leandros had asked about my hair. Cutting and mourning—it hadn't made me remember anything the night had stolen, but it had brought out one emotion, a gut feeling that couldn't be denied any more than the rising or setting of the sun.

Leandros wasn't a man who said he was my brother. He was my brother. Le . . . Niko was my brother and he'd lost me days ago, almost lost me the night before, and lost more of me again last night. He could stall all he wanted, but he was floundering and badly and I knew it. My memory didn't have to tell me that; my gut did.

"We need to go out and check with Mickey, our other informant. He might know more than Wahanket. Take a shower and get dressed. Oh, and where Mickey lives, dress down, although considering what you normally wear, I'm not sure that's possible. And for Buddha's sake, brush your teeth. I'm beginning to think a boggle lives in your mouth at night when you sleep."

Yeah, ignoring my relapse was a time-honored way to cover up what he actually felt, but he wasn't getting away with it. Memories were hard to come by, but now I did have one thing and I wasn't letting go of it. I had a brother, and I was going to show Niko that he still did too.

"Sure," I said agreeably. "I just need to do one thing first."

One small thing.

Hours later I was still doing it.

"What are you looking for?"

He'd asked once before and I could tell he thought he was being extremely patient when he asked again. And he was. Just as he was being patient dragging me out of a kill shed before some mysterious organization called the Vigil (how lame was that name?) showed up and sanitized our asses; or when he made me cards so I wouldn't kill the wrong person or jump the bones of someone who'd kill me and use *my* bones for jewelry. He'd been patient when I'd stabbed the puck with a fork and tried to a few more times. He'd been patient when I'd been mildly appalled that we lived together—no wild bachelor freedom for either of us. Those memories I still had in a somewhat faded fashion. The other I was less able to recall, but I grabbed hold of it, stifled by shadows as it was.

He'd been as patient as was possible when he'd shown me a picture of him and me and some other people standing around. I didn't remember exactly why I hadn't liked the picture or whom I'd insulted in it, but I knew I had. I'd said something harsh and nasty, and he'd been patient with that as well.

That was one thing I wasn't looking for—that picture.

It had disappeared into one of yesterday's memory gaps and it could stay there. I didn't want to know why it had freaked me out. Or why it had made me say things I didn't remember, but I knew those things weren't too nice. Not fucking nice at all. But it didn't matter, because if I accidentally stumbled across it, I'd toss it over my shoulder without a single look and keep going.

What I *was* looking for took two hours to find as I tore through the garage apartment like a tornado, which was appropriate, considering the midnight black morning sky outside with crashing peals of thunder and flashes of lightning. I didn't pay it any attention as I kept moving, leaving weapons, food, furniture, clothes, anything I could lift, in my wake. What I was looking for, well, was pretty simple—I was looking for a break. Yeah, two hours, but I finally got it. I finally got that break.

I broke Niko Leandros.

I was beginning to paw through an Oriental lacquered chest against one wall in the living room when a hand grabbed my shirt and lifted me up to my toes. With his face in mine, he was looking much less stoic than he had since I'd first seen him. Met him. Seen him again after losing my memory and missing for days. Whatever.

"What . . . are . . . you . . . looking . . . for?" He enunciated each word with an angry pause between each one. The patience was all gone, which meant we might get somewhere. His darker skin was reddened, his eyes were slits, and he smelled how I imagined a charging rhino would smell. Rage—sheer out-of-its-cage fury.

Why had I been looking for this? One pissy super-ninja who could kill you with a pickle, resuscitate you, make you eat it, and then kill you again? Because Leandros was off his game. He was off his game because he'd lost his brother, and when you fight monsters, you can't be off your game. Period. I didn't know how I knew he wasn't himself, but it was the same as with the other things I knew without any past associations to back them up. How my brain managed to work around my missing life to spit it out was a secret to me, but it wasn't wrong and Leandros wasn't right.

He was quiet. He'd been the quiet kind since he'd shown up to get me, I did recall that—not the mummy in the basement, but the quiet I did remember. He'd gotten quieter since Ammut and the canal and since I'd said what I had, whatever it had been about that picture, which made this quiet a different one. Uncomfortable, not Zen. We'd had Zen on tap on the trip from South Carolina, and then we'd had this non–Kwai Chang Caine version since this morning . . . since he'd asked about my hair, as if he thought I really had cut it to mourn my own death. *His* brother's death. Although he'd come across to me as reassured as best as I could tell, it hadn't changed his mood. He'd gone from right to wrong, but with the past few days and my near death. I didn't blame him, because the man blamed himself more than I ever could. I was hoping that, as with lots of things in this world, I could fix him with one good swift kick—and two hours of destroying his obsessively clean world was just that. Now here was hoping he reacted like most appliances when you smacked 'em.

Presto—toaster, thou art healed. Make with the English muffin.

"Me? I'm looking for a map." I grinned before saying more somberly, "I need a map. But what are you looking for, Leandros? What do you need?"

He looked at me as if he didn't know himself, before giving in. "My brother." He let go of my shirt, dropping me back on my heels, and turned his back to me. "Goddamn it, I need my brother."

"And I'm not him?" He already regretted what he'd

said. I saw the rise and fall of his shoulders, his head bow, and a spine stiff enough I was surprised it didn't shatter like brittle ice. But it didn't as he walked over to one of the cabinets next to the refrigerator and brought back a neatly folded map of New York City.

"You could be, but, no. You're not." I *could* be, but I wasn't? Unless my memory came back and then I would be. Or would I? He said I wasn't his brother with as much belief and conviction as if that brother truly was dead and buried, his coming back an impossibility. That was confusing and then some, especially after he'd spent so much time on the drive back from South Carolina convincing me he was my brother. He all but stopped at a drugstore to see if they had a Whozurbrudder box next to the Whozurdaddy paternity test. I'm your brother. I swear I'm your brother. Hand to Buddha, I am your brother. On and on.

The mummy I couldn't or didn't want to remember, but that endless debate I couldn't forget. Figured.

But, now, wait—this guy suddenly thinks, maybe I'm not his brother after all? The "What the fuck?" thought bubble over my head was implied, because, seriously, What the fuck?

I sat down on the workout mats and he sat opposite me. He pulled apart his braid with impatient fingers. Callused hands, hair long and from another time, eyes the color of an iron sword. If it weren't for the darker skin, I'd expect him to be leading a charge of Vikings, swinging an axe, and taking the head of everyone who passed his way. Born too late, he was meant to be a warlord or a general or a god to both, with blood-soaked altars and every first son named for him.

But this wasn't then and he'd shown himself to be a man of control, because if he wasn't, what might he do with what nature had given him? His mind knew that, but his body belonged to the past. Warlord, general, god. All three sounded damn lonely things to be. You couldn't be friends with someone who might die that day or the next. If you did, you'd pay. For every friend or comrade, you'd pay. Those days were ancient history, but we were living a reflection of them now. When you fought for your life, wouldn't you need someone—just one person—who would always be there? Who was good enough to win those fights? Wouldn't you need to know you wouldn't end up a sole survivor? Alone in a world where the monsters never stopped coming? Wouldn't you need that to not go out of your damn mind?

Fuck, yes, you would.

I spread out the map. "So I'm not your brother . . . yet. But I will be. Stop tiptoeing around me. Smack my head when I deserve it. It'll remind me." I'd seen aborted twitches several times before he managed to pull back in time before he swatted me. "I had a setback last night. Big deal. The venom can't last forever. I forgot part of one day. I'll remember it all soon enough. Then it'll be the good old days again."

He didn't comment as he unfolded the map on his side. All that former optimism had disappeared, when he or Goodfellow was telling me every other minute on the trip back from South Carolina that I'd get it all back. Wait and see. I'd get it back. No time at all. She was coming round the mountain, riding six white horses and pulling my memory like a U-Haul. Now we were playing no comment on the subject.

With the map laid out, he did find something to say. "I said something idiotic. I'm sorry. You are my brother, only without certain . . . memories." Memories hadn't been his first choice of words, but I didn't know what he had almost said instead. "I think you're happier as you are now," he went on, weighting down his two cor-

ners of the map with two of his steel bead mala brace-
lets. I remembered those when he'd grabbed me to stop
me from stabbing the puck with a fork. "Our childhood
wasn't the best, and there's no escaping it made us who
we are. If you can't remember those things and you're
more content this way, perhaps it's better if you stay like
this. Maybe I'm being selfish to want you to be who you
were before."

Ah, that was it. Guilt. Throwing himself under the
bus. He certainly seemed the type from the bits and
pieces floating around inside my skull. But, Jesus, how
bad had our childhood been anyway? Slutty mom—I'd
picked up on that, but to think I'd be better not remembering any of it? At all? That sounded much worse than
a mom who screwed around a lot and liked to stay on
the move. Goodfellow had said that, not Leandros. A
puck, a trickster, but oddly more truthful than my own
brother seemed now.

I looked up from the map and raised my eyebrows
at him. "Are you happier? The way I am now, you don't
know for sure anymore that I'm your brother. That's
what you said, idiotic or not." Despite the conversation,
he frowned at associating himself with that particular
word although he'd been the one to first say it. That
cracked me up. He was vain about his intellect. That I
would have to remember, no matter what. It was mocking material too good to pass up. "I have amnesia, but I
can still hear. Tell me, are you happier if I stay like this?"

His forehead furrowed as if he weren't used to me
backing him in a corner. That was the great thing about
control. You rarely lose a little. You usually lose it all. I
smacked the side of his head just as he caught my wrist
a fraction of a second too late. With his speed, "too late"
meant a definite loss of control. I'd kicked the hell out
of his toaster all right. "I didn't think so," I said, answer-

ing my own question. "I'm your brother all right, and
one of us doesn't get to be happy and one of us miserable. Now, get me a Magic Marker and I'll make you
glad your obviously not-that-bright other version of me
isn't totally back yet. I've got an idea while he'd probably be out hunting for offensive shirts. Take advantage
of my usefulness. Soon I'll be back scouring the city for
the dirtiest T-shirt in existence."

He let go of my wrist, rubbed the side of his head, but
got up and returned with a marker. Sitting back down,
control already back in place, for the most part anyway,
he flipped the marker like a knife, flipped it again, and at
last got around to asking, "Do you think you could call
me Niko? Or Nik? Leandros, every time you say it . . ."
He handed me the marker without the rest of the words.
But I still got them.

It was like a kick in the gut for him, every time I said
his name as if he were a stranger. I should've figured
that out sooner. "Niko. Gotcha. Any nicknames? With
your nose, I have to give you some sort of hell over
that. Pinocchio? Never mind. I'll figure something out.
Now, show me where all the bodies were found or went
missing."

That was another memory that unfortunately hadn't
disappeared this morning—all the details on Ammut
and how we were going to find Ammut—and Ammut
the goddess, but not a goddess, but she could suck your
life force anyway. Between Leandr . . . Niko and Goodfellow, they somehow managed to make simple life-
threatening killer monsters boring.

"You know, pissing me off to force me to release a
little tension, that is very much my brother all over. And
you, too often, call me Cyrano." *Too often.* That was
what he said, but that wasn't what he meant. I'd been
right. Niko wasn't a good liar, not when I was the one

doing the listening. Another observation to push me a little closer to the old me.

Too bad you don't remember the mummy. Too bad for the mummy he did remember the old you.

I didn't bother to twitch at that one. The voices could kiss my ass. I was done with them. They were nothing but Muzak. "Cyrano. Ain't I the educated one?" I snorted and kept my eyes on the map. In Nevah's Landing, I thought a brother was something I could never get used to, but now I was more used to it than the brother himself. Those first few days in the Landing when I'd been lost and alone, I'd kept looking back over my shoulder. I hadn't known for what . . . or for whom. Now I did. "Genetics and memories aren't everything, you know," I said, directly contradicting what I'd thought barely a few days ago. "Think of me as Sven, your adopted foreign exchange cousin, if it makes you feel better. Now, enough with the therapy. Pretend we hugged. Now, dead bodies. Go."

I'd gotten the rundown before last night's relapse on the body count, but it didn't hurt to double-check when at a moment's notice I might forget how to wipe my own ass. The count stood at twenty vamps, Wolves, incubi, succubi, all found dead or reported missing by their pack or loved one . . . er . . . creature; their significant supernatural other. The dead bodies were found as little more than husks, autumn leaves ready to fly away on a fall breeze. They were dried up and drained of all life, still recognizable, but what had animated their body was gone. Creatures, supernatural or not, were basically batteries. It was that biological energy that got Ammut's engines revving.

Where they were found I marked with a circle with *X*s for eyes and a frown with a tongue hanging out. "Okay, what about the missing ones?" For those I put

question marks. We ended up with eight dead bodies
and twelve missing ones. "Goodfellow said the spider's
venom would make whatever it bit forget everything,
including how to breathe." I'd gotten a reduced dose,
he'd said. It bit something before me or I'd be dead now.
"How does Ammut get life force out of dead things?"

"That's only with humans, which is why Ammut
doesn't eat humans," Niko answered. "Their life force
isn't half as powerful as that of the supernatural. If the
spiders bite the supernatural creatures, it paralyzes
them, but they're still alive to be wrapped up in cocoons
and brought back to Ammut."

I turned the map from one side to the other and then
upside down, Niko's prayer beads tumbling to the mat.
First, the dead, then the missing, and then over again.
It was plain as day. "Huh. Look at that. Damn, we were
five kinds of stupid." I gave a small smile, thinking about
how Miss Terrwyn said that at least ten times a day at
the diner. Down-to-earth and smarter by a mile than we
badass monster killers were. I was glad I hadn't forgotten her when I woke up this morning. "Yeah, we were
five kinds of stupid all right."

Niko frowned as if he'd never heard that particular
insult aimed at him before. Intellectual vanity again.
"What do you mean?"

"Forget Ammut being at the canal. She was only
there to wipe out the council. That was personal. Look
at everything else." I pointed at eight different spots.
"I have amnesia, but I can read a map and I know if
you live around Central Park, you're rich. Ammut took
those victims herself. Walked into some fancy building
with fancy security, went right upstairs, and ate herself
some dinner." Next I pointed at the question marks.
"And I know that these places aren't near parks, aren't
fancy, and that last one is near a waste treatment plant."

As I said, I could read a damn map. "Why does Ammut need her spiders when she can go where most people could never get in? Think about it. Why send them there when she can go anywhere?" I smirked, full of myself that I'd seen what everyone else had missed. I was hot shit all right. Amnesia boy takes the lead. "Because she's a *snob*."

Niko grabbed the map and scrutinized it. "But if that's true, then that means—"

"It means she doesn't want to get her Manolo what-chamacallits dirty. It means she probably gets her hair and nails done at whatever expensive champagne-swilling place your vampire lady friend does. She can look human when she wants, same as most of your . . . our friends out there. Hell, Promise and she might even know each other." Ammut wasn't some lion-headed, alligator-jawed, hippopotamus-assed Egyptian goddess she'd been in the picture Goodfellow had drawn on a bar napkin. She was a rich Park Avenue bitch who could afford a personal trainer to make sure her ass stayed well below hippo size.

And occasionally she turned into a giant slithery snake creature in a canal, but we all had bad hair days. At least chicks did, right? I hadn't been that upset with my hair even with spider goop in it.

"We thought she sent the spiders to the easier loca-tions because they're not particularly intelligent and that she kept the more difficult locations for herself," Niko murmured, shaking his head in self-recrimination.

"Nope. Stuck-up bitch." I'd seen one or two come through the diner in the Landing when I'd been there. Passing through to Charleston and damn near horrified that the diner was the only place to eat in town. Here I might not get up close and personal with those kinds of people, and Niko's friend Promise didn't rub her wealth in anyone's face. Those at the diner, though, were bitches through and through. They'd sent the silverware back four times, the tea twice, the food once—not that they ate more than a bite of the second serving, and left a dollar tip. I heard one say as she left with her party that she could feel the grease in the air clogging up her fucking immaculate pores. It'd made my day that I'd washed in the toilet the last two forks I'd given them. I hoped they'd tasted Comet all the way to Charleston.

That made me think. The relapse definitely only went back a day, because those things were perfectly clear. A small relapse, which was good. It meant Niko would get back what he needed, and I'd get back who I was.

"With this, we don't need to visit Mickey, and that is a huge plus as he lives in a garbage dump." Niko began to fold the map up with a brisk decisive emotion. "Cal, that's something. I'm proud of you."

"What? Was I that stupid when I had all of my memory?" I demanded, folding my arms and trying to look offended, but I couldn't lose the grin. Hell, I was proud of myself, and who didn't like feeling smug? If they said they didn't, they were big, fat liars.

"No, You've always been smart. However, when it comes to laziness, you're a genius, Nobel league. You prefer to wait for Goodfellow or me to do the boring research. Then you turn off the cartoons and shoot at whatever we find," he said dryly.

I had no desire to clean up my room, so, nope, the laziness hadn't changed. I was about to point that out when Niko whipped his head around and looked up.

Like he hadn't last time . . . in the mummy's lair. Sheep being sheep. But even sheep can learn.

"Get your weapons. *Now.*"

He was good. I could barely see the motion in the shadows where the outer wall met the ceiling two stories up when I knew to look for it. But I could smell them now that I knew they were there and bothered to take a whiff. "Seriously?" I groaned. "Again? Christ, the goddamn Hatfields and McCoys didn't hold grudges this long."

But apparently spiders did.

9

It was storming outside and had been all morning, at least the two hours of it that it had taken me to drive Niko nuts; otherwise they probably would've waited until night. Ammut didn't want the neighbors calling 911 and every exterminator in the city on her pets. The spiders scuttled down the walls; all of them were bigger than the beagle-sized one from the previous night. I grabbed for my holster I'd hung on the wall in the training area. Yanking the Eagle from one side and the Glock from the other, I fired as one jumped from the wall to the breakfast bar. Flung to the floor, it spasmed, legs curling in, flailing out, and then curling back in as greenish black slime pooled around it. That part of it didn't look much different from what I'd seen Niko drink yesterday for supper. "If they keep coming after me to avenge their spider buddies, then I have to keep killing more of them, and if I kill more of them, then even fucking more will come. I'll have every goddamn spider in the world after my ass."

I shot another one that bounded from the wall to the top of the refrigerator and then down to the floor, twenty feet closer to us in less than two seconds. Along with the muffled clap from the gun's silencer, the spider flipped onto its back, leaking blood by the gallons and squirting web silk by whatever you used to measure web silk. Bundles? Haystacks? A whole shitload of it. If you took every one of Spider-Man's wet dreams, added them together, then multiplied by ten, that was what you'd get. Not that I wanted anything to do with Spider-Man's wet dreams, but for measurement purposes, that was about right.

Niko moved off to the side in the living area and cut a spider in half with his sword as it leaped through the air. Right in half. Did you want to know what the inside of a Nepenthe spider looked like? Me neither, but I found out. If the Incredible Hulk ate a spaghetti dinner, then puked it up . . .

"I think this may be Ammut, not spider vengeance. Now concentrate," Niko said sharply. "You might've gotten lucky with one bite, but ten will guarantee you won't be that lucky again."

"I am concentrating," I shot back as I ducked one spider that went over my head. Spider vengeance? Did I live in a world where spider vengeance was an actual concept? I had so fucked up in my former life.

"On what?" The next one he impaled, flung it off the blade, and cut the spider chimp's head off by a third.

"The bodily fluids of superheroes, but it's relevant to the situation." I whirled as I felt a tug on my boot. The bastard that had gone over the top of me had snagged me with a line of webbing and yanked me off my feet the moment I turned. This was no beagle or the seventy-five-pound Charlotte from the motel bathroom. This bad boy was huge, a hundred and fifty pounds easy. I wasn't afraid of spiders. When you woke up with four giant dead ones and killed another one with a fork, you'd find out whether or not you had a phobia. All those legs, their impossible speed, fat abdomens full of God knew what; they weren't pretty, but I wasn't arachnophobic. That was before I discovered there was a line between nonphobic and holy-fucking-shit-I-think-I-wet-my-pants—and that line sat firmly on one hundred and fifty pounds of a big black, venom-dripping, six-eyed demon from Hell. And not the biblical Hell either, but some alien, unknowable hell from a distant dimension that would drive you insane with one glimpse.

One hundred and forty-nine pounds and maybe I would've been fine. But one hundred and fifty pounds equaled full-blown arachnophobia right out of nowhere. It filled my guts with a cold worse than the searing burn of dry ice. My brain did its best to curl in on itself, a frightened child seeking the fetal position. All the air was sucked from the room and if I'd tried to say anything, it wouldn't have passed paralyzed vocal cords. In my life, almost six days now, best guess, I'd never been so fucking terrified. If my heart had exploded I wouldn't have been surprised—relieved, but not surprised.

Not, of course, that any of that stopped me from pulling the triggers on both guns and emptying the clips. Fear is fear. It only kills you if you let it. If I felt the need to seek a support group, I'd do it later. Blowing away the motherfucking, disgusting tarantula big enough that you could ride its hairy ass across the plains to settle the West was more pertinent at the moment.

"Cal?"

I waved a gun at Niko, who was behind me, as I put down the other gun to tear at the webbing around my ankle as I kept my eyes on the giant spider riddled with bullet holes lying limp in front of me. "Just throwing up in my mouth. Doing fucking great. No problems here."

"Good. In that case I'm sending you a present."

I snatched a glance over my shoulder to see Niko kick a spider in my direction as he took on three more.

I jammed the muzzle of the Glock into its pulpy underabdomen and blew it away as its legs scrambled for purchase on my arm. You always keep a last one in the chamber. Just in case ... for them or for yourself. The thought swam in and out so quickly, I almost didn't have time to think what a high-class job it was that had that particular rule carved into the neurons so deeply that even amnesia couldn't erase it. College grads everywhere were praying to get an internship here.

I had a new respect for exterminators now. These creepy-crawly bastards did not give up. I knelt, dumped the empty clips, reached into my pocket for a full one, rammed it home, and then did the same for the other. Ever see those movies? The ones where people are running, empty their clips, drop them, toss the guns up in the air, throw new clips out, and the guns flip back down with the downward pull of gravity combined with the upward motion of the clip to meet together in perfect harmony and, damn, you're reloaded in half a second flat.

If I ever found the fucker that came up with that bullshit, I would beat him until he would make week-old roadkill look like an adoptable and perfectly viable pet. It doesn't work that way, and if anyone needs that spelled out to them, then they should find a coupon for a lobotomy, because why carry extra weight if you're not using it?

Put down one gun. Eject the clip in the gun you're holding. Get the new clip from wherever you were hiding it and slam it in. Put that gun down, pick up the other. Shampoo and repeat. It takes a few seconds more, but you don't get hit in the head with a falling gun or trip over the clip you threw in the air that obeyed gravity instead of your dumb-ass wish upon a star. I was back up and ready to go, when I saw Niko had moved again, from the living room to stand between the kitchen area and me. The window above the kitchen was where the spiders were coming from. It wasn't Niko blocking my way to a sandwich or some leftover pizza to save my twenty-some-year-old arteries—how old was I again? No, it was Niko doing the bus thing yet one more time. Hey, here comes an MTA bus and on time too. Pardon me while I throw myself under it.

If he was going to keep this up, I would've been better off convincing him that in that one-second slip of the tongue, he'd been right. I was totally not his brother. Not his family. Not his responsibility. And there was no reason in the world to keep trying to get himself killed in my place. Jesus, it was irritating. There might've been some sort of warm fuzzy feeling, a scrap of belonging, a tiny crumb of appreciation, but mainly it was just goddamn irritating. "Leandros!" I shouted. He didn't turn as he faced ten more spiders coming down the walls. The name thing, right. Not only was he irritating, he was stubborn in the face of hideous death. I wasn't impressed or happy about either quality. "Niko, you fucking kamikaze asshole! Why don't you yell banzai and get it over with?"

That he acknowledged. "'Banzai,' contrary to popular belief, means 'Long life to the emperor' or 'Ten thousand years of life to you.' It wasn't the Japanese version of 'Eat hot lead, you sons of bitches.'"

"And who says that?" I was to one side of him now, taking the heat too, while giving him enough room to swing his katana.

"You do. You talk in your sleep. I assume you picked up that saying in those pulp fiction books with the extremely large-breasted women on the front with a gun pointed at the protagonist." His blade sliced another spider, three pieces this time. Now that did impress me—a horror movie combined with performing sushi chefs at intermission.

"He probably has a gun too," I said. I knew I would. "If you both have guns, it's not attempted homicide. It's love. The kind that ends up with them naked on the second page." Hopefully. That was the way I'd write it. "That's a rare love. Don't mock what you don't understand."

I fired three times and took out two spiders on the wall. The other one fell but dragged itself behind the refrigerator. Wasn't that always the way? Off to the ultimate spider sanctuary. Fifty pounds and you wouldn't think there was any way it would fit, but it proved me wrong. I shot again, at one up by the window nine feet above the cabinets. "Do I really read those kinds of books?" Good question. Then I asked an even better question. "Do I really talk in my sleep?"

"Endlessly on the second. Once or twice a year on the first. We wouldn't want you to strain anything."

There wasn't much I could say about that as I didn't know if it was true or not. But when the amnesia was gone and it turned out not to be true, I was kicking Niko's ass—the very one I saved right then. While the last three spiders came swarming down the walls and simultaneously launched themselves toward us, I ignored them.

Instead, I slammed a boot into Niko's ribs, throwing him off-balance for a second as that evil refrigerator spider popped its bloated body out, leaping as fast, injured or not, as the other spiders. Thanks to my kick, it barely missed Nik except for a furrowing of its claws at the end of one leg across the back of Niko's thigh. I hoped there was no venom there, only repulsive spider cooties. As Niko lifted the katana to chop his attacker in several hundred parts, I shot the last three spiders, thinking that I was concentrating all right, but Niko wasn't, not on what he should've been—himself. Brothers were supposed to watch each other's backs. It sounded like something from that brother handbook I mentioned before. But besides watching his back, you had to watch yourself too or you wouldn't be around to read the rest of the handbook. "Work on your concentration there, Leandros. I might have lost my mind, but the killing part of me works just fine."

"It's Niko, and, yes, that was fortunate, the venom affecting what you use the least," Niko said with not much gratitude. If I found this elusive handbook, I might smack him in the head with it.

I waited cautiously, but there were no more spiders. I relaxed enough to wipe the sweat from my forehead with the back of my hand. It was over, and through it all, the worst thing that could've happened didn't happen. Not one of those bastards touched the TV on the wall— that damn magnificent TV. Now that was luck.

Fifteen minutes later I wasn't feeling as lucky.

Niko was lying on his stomach on his bed. His pants were off, his underwear was . . . you know; let's not go there. Who cares? Underwear is underwear. Boxers versus briefs? Did we need commercials here? No, we did not. Beside him on the bed was our first-aid kit/hospital-in-a-box. "You seriously want me to bandage that?" I asked warily. There hadn't been any venom, but the gash from the claw was four inches across the back of his upper thigh, ragged, not deep, yet a breeding ground for all sorts of killer monster spider germs. What did you put on killer monster spider germs? Hydrogen peroxide? Acid? Cut off the leg?

"It'll be difficult to reach myself." Niko was doing his best to see over his shoulder as there was no mirror in his room to catch the reflection. Because I didn't like

mirrors very much and when he wasn't lunging under
the nearest form of public transportation under the de-
lusion it would save my life, he also kept his room reflection free in deference to my delicate psyche. First there
was Doctors without Borders and now we had Brothers
without Brains. Self-preservation meant nothing to him,
when it came to me at any rate.

My hands were already opening a bottle of Betadine
and a packaged brush. Good for them. If they knew
what to do, I'd sit back and let them drive. "Yeah," I
commented dubiously, "but you're ... you know ... a
guy."

"I'm your *brother*. We discussed this so thoroughly
before the spiders attacked that even my attention span
was challenged," he semi-snapped. At the loss of temper, which some part of me recognized as a sign of a
good deal of pain on his part, I automatically reached
for a bottle of pain pills, prescription strength and ille-
gally obtained—go team. I'd seen both our scars. Tylenol
didn't cover that level of boo-boo.

"True, and brothers are guys," I pointed out. A
thirteen-hour car ride with that horny-ass puck would
spook anyone. If I could've picked the day I forgot, that
one would've been it, but no. Goodfellow said he was
monogamous—yeah, he *said*, but that didn't keep him
from telling tales of the nonmonogamy days. That and
his great love of a challenge—there was no mountain
he couldn't climb and no dick he couldn't get to do the
same. That was when I tried to kick out the back window
of the car. In a perfect world, I would've made it out. No
such luck.

"Buddha, I wish the spider had killed me instead.
Never mind. I'll manage it myself." He started to push
himself up, sounding tired and in pain, with a massive
desire to smack me in the head. He also sounded re-

signed. It wasn't a good mix, not to mention so complicated that I was surprised I could pick up on that many
emotions. Could be I was one of those sensitive guys all
the women wanted. Then I thought about that first T-
shirt, EAT ME (BEFORE I EAT YOU). Nope. That didn't sound
sensitive.

Well, fuck. Whatever I was, sensitive or an ass, he was
family, and it seemed family trumped T-shirts.

"No. Wait. I'll do it. It's what brothers do and that
means I do it." I might not have sounded fully confident,
but he settled back down on the bed after a glance to
see if I meant it.

"It's hardly that big a deal," he said, laying his head
on folded arms. "Especially considering I changed your
diapers when you were a baby."

"Jesus Christ!" I dropped the bottle of pills to roll in a
circular pattern on the floor. "Don't say that! That took
this to the weirdest place ever. What the hell's wrong
with you?" I bent down to pick up the bottle and thought
about winging it at his head to see if that helped his pain
any, but I didn't. I pushed diaper images to the farthest
corner of my mind—weirdest fucking place *ever*—and
did my best to get on with the task at hand.

Eventually pills were passed out; one was accepted
and one sent back. You can't nobly overcome suffering
if you're not suffering to begin with. I didn't see myself
falling in that category. If it had been me, I thought, I'd
have wolfed both down. Inflicted pain was one thing
much better to give than receive. I cleaned the wound
thoroughly with a brush, then peroxide, applied an an-
tibacterial ointment, bandaged it, and gave two shots—
one of Benadryl in case of a mild allergic reaction, with
epinephrine on hand in case of a more severe one, and
an antibiotic shot. I didn't know where that spider claw

had been, but soaking in a footbath full of rose petals was not my first guess.

I did all that. It would've been impressive if my brain had been more involved on the conscious level, but my body and my subconscious weren't waiting for me to catch up. This came from the kind of practice of something you do more than once.

Time and time again.

What a crazy fucking business, but we were in it and, from the number of scars we both had, we had been for a while. Saving the innocent and killing the wicked, the evil, and the big-ass vermin; it was more entertaining than working at the diner, despite what I'd said back then. For supernatural cops, as for normal cops, getting hurt was going to be a possibility—or in our case, a sure thing. We'd survived so far or I wouldn't be standing here still trying not to think about the diaper thing.

Talk about evil—as it turned out, Niko could pull his weight there if he had to. I knew he'd said that on purpose, knowing what my reaction would be. *Knew* it.

I started to give him crap over it, but his noble suffering had turned into sleep. Eh, I'd get him later then. I wasn't about to let him one-up me. Hmm. That must be a brother thing too. I gathered together all the supplies. I took a blanket from the end of his bed, covered him and left his door open. When things were slithering into your home on a regular basis, it was best to hear them coming.

In the kitchen I could see where the spiders had gotten in. There was a circular hole in the top window, about two feet across. It was perfectly cut, as if with a diamond-tipped tool instead of a sharp spider claw. They must have used their web to prevent the glass from falling and then they had their doggy door.

Well, no fixing that tonight, unless there was a two-story ladder hiding under a futon I didn't know about. I double-checked all the spiders to make sure they were dead—deader than dead; the leftovers of an exterminator's worst nightmare. They were. It didn't matter. More could come—or one of these sons of bitches ... or just plain bitches could pop and out could wriggle ten thousand baby spiders. It wasn't quite as bad as the diaper image, but it was enough that I spent the next few hours with all the lights on, fighting the storm's gloom in case I saw a baby eight-legs looking for its bassinet. I watched TV with the sound muted. I scanned the bookcase for those books Niko said I read. They were there. I touched a finger to one and grinned. Big breasts and guns—it was like peanut butter and jelly; green eggs and ham; salt and pepper. They went together.

I found a picture I hadn't noticed before taped to the side of the otherwise-unadorned refrigerator. I almost didn't look. I didn't want to see another picture that could be like the one I'd seen before my relapse. I couldn't remember it, but I knew it was bad news regardless—how? No idea. Isn't brain damage fun? But at the last second I manned up for this one. The photo was of a little kid, maybe four or five, jumping up and down on Santa Claus's nut sack. A cheap picture taken by an elf in a cheap costume; that was the way those things went, and that was me going apeshit on Santa's equipment. The kid had black hair like mine, but that wasn't the giveaway. It was the attitude. I wondered what Santa had done to piss me off so much.

The rest of the day I spent wiping up spider goop and putting those suckers in Hefty trash bags. I was lazy, but I had no desire to live in a place that was going to have spider stink embedded in it for the rest of eternity. It was dirty work but easy enough. The biggest one that had me thinking about carrying extra underwear was no problem either. Once it was dead, no more arachnophobia. Mirrors and monsters were still bad; dead spiders big enough to play in the Super Bowl were no big deal. Did that make me strange?

Compared to what? Against the last six days, the only six days of my life? No, I didn't think it did. And that in itself was far stranger.

After the cleanup and piling the bagged spiders in the workout area, I took another run through the place. I'd done it before. That I did remember. That hadn't fallen into one of the holes that swiss-cheesed yesterday. But as with the other memories I'd kept, some were blurry, such as a fish shimmering under the water, looking twice its true size one second, then half the size the next; others were clear. A refresher course wouldn't hurt me regardless, as long as I stayed away from the picture in Niko's room. I wandered around, peering into drawers and cabinets, and the fridge. The top two shelves were pure sugar and grease, obviously mine. There was a board mounted on the wall by the door that led outside. It was divided in half, the right side labeled *Niko*; the left labeled *Cal*. In dry-erase marker, Niko's side had precise and perfect handwriting spelling out appointments and chores, some of which were labeled in red, more for me than him, I was sure. *Check GPS programming on Cal's phone.* That was curious. GPS was a good thing for keeping track of brothers who were attacked by a nest of spiders and managed to get amnesia; I could see that. But this sounded more specific, as if it weren't something the phone already did.

Keep Cal from starving. I didn't think it would actually come to starvation before I hauled my ass to the grocery store, but the following one was painted a biblical red kick in the ass.

Reassure neighbors the smell of Cal's laundry is not a decomposing body. I snorted. There was more in that general category about sparring and running and making sure I was capable of fighting off a Pomeranian if the need ever arose. On my side of the board, in handwriting so sloppy I should've gone to med school, it read *1) Sit on ass 2) Kill things.* And that was it. That covered my day every day of the week, three hundred and sixty-five a year.

We didn't have a lot of family-type things around. Goodfellow had said something about a fire and Niko had added that our mother had died in a fire. That would tend to wipe out a good deal of when-we-were-little-and-cute mementos. I was surprised the Santa photo had made it. Mementos didn't make a family, though. They made a convincing TV commercial if enough were plastered through a fake house with fake people, but real life wasn't TV.

And didn't I have something more convincing than solid, tangible souvenirs of the past? I had a brother who'd been half dead on his feet from no sleep when he found me after a four-day disappearance. From all the hints I'd gotten, including the horrific diaper one, I gathered that he, rather than our mom, had raised me. His patience was unreal when anyone else would've been looking for a baseball bat to beat me to death. I also had the battle that had happened barely an hour ago. If I was going down, this guy was bound and determined to beat me to the grave by a mile.

What did I do in return? Bagged spiders and told him, no worries, he'd get all of his brother back. He wanted it all too. For all he said I might be happier to be only part of Cal, one that had been born less than a week ago, he wanted me back—the entire package. My past was his past. Before Promise and Goodfellow, it had been him and me alone for a long time. You didn't live with fake IDs and find lying easier than telling the truth if you were surrounded by a caring circle of family and friends. That was easy enough to figure out. It had been him and me, and now he'd lost half of me. If I didn't get the rest back, I wouldn't be whole and neither would Niko.

Oddly enough, I cared more about his being whole than about me.

Softy. Goddamn softy. I didn't even know him. I mean, I knew what he told me and what he showed me and what I felt, what I'd almost remembered....

Because I had almost remembered earlier, and that other picture had been a nudge that had speeded up the boulder already rolling down the hill. The venom had been wearing off. I'd seen the picture and then we'd gone to the museum to talk to that mummy informant and ... shit ... something had happened. I didn't know what, but something had happened—something that, like the picture, I didn't want to remember. At the same time, though, it had felt ... good. It was a bizarre combination of "Don't look, don't see" and the feeling of riding a roller coaster when you're a kid. That adrenaline rush. I'd remembered part of me; I'd been coming home and bringing my past with me. Niko said my past had baggage. That meant his did too. What kind of fucking brother would let some bad memories stop him from being the family his own brother needed him to be?

Not the kind of brother I had. He'd shown me that. He deserved better, and my chickenshit ass was going to give it to him. I was a good guy and good guys didn't leave their brothers twisting in the wind. I was going to start the ball rolling again, no matter how much I didn't want to do the one thing that had started it. It was a picture, for God's sake. I was standing in a mass monster graveyard partially of my making and I didn't want to look at a picture.

Fuck that cowardly shit.

Hours later when Niko woke up, it was six p.m. He came out into the hall, pants on—thank you, God, and just give me a little time on the naked-guy thing—to take in the place. "You cleaned up." It was said as skeptically as if I'd called in a maid service and passed it off as my own work.

"The smell." I shrugged. "Apparently that's the one motivation my laziness can't beat back down. How's the leg?"

"Sore but bearable." He was limping, but not too badly, which was good as we had a lot of dead spider ass to haul. "I'm going to take a shower." There was a towel half in the bathroom and half in the hall. "My keen observational skills tell me you already have. Did you brush your teeth?"

"What are you?" I took another bite of a peanut butter and jelly bagel. We were out of bread. I chewed and propped my elbows on the breakfast bar. "The damn Tooth Fairy? My diaper days are over. Go on already."

He gave me a look, a now easily recognizable "brother look," picked up the towel off the floor, and disappeared into the bathroom, closing the door behind him. I waited until I heard the water running, gave it several seconds, then put the bagel down and went into his room. I hadn't forgotten which drawer the picture was in, but I hesitated before the dresser as if I had. "Suck it up," I muttered under my breath. "It's just a goddamn picture. It's probably of Niko potty-training you. Suck it the hell up." Suck it up I did and opened the drawer with a resolute hand. That same rock-steady hand reached inside and brought the picture out. I stared at it. I saw what I'd seen before. There was no flood of memories or the trickle of a single one, not yet, but I saw. I saw what I'd wanted to deny and never remember and embrace all in one.

I saw everything.

Destiny was easy. Choice was difficult and free will was for the fucked.

I was well and truly fucked.

10

"I am going to make Goodfellow rue the day he ever gave you that gift certificate. His Christmas present to me is years of aggravation from you. Tricksters—no wonder they're the least popular supernatural creature alive," Niko growled. We were at Goodfellow's place to tell him the news about Ammut in person, discuss, plot, and all that shit. Why not just use the phone? Because he wouldn't answer the damn thing or return voice mails. After two hours we gave up and made like Jehovah's Witnesses, knocking on his door.

I blew air upward to clear the hair from my eyes. I could see why I'd had a ponytail. This was on my last nerve and that Goodfellow approved of it meant it was fashionable, and I didn't want to be fashionable. That meant I tried. I didn't want people to think I tried. Cool guys who kick monster ass do not try. Our coolness is inherent, goddamn it.

"It was the only clean thing I had left," I grumbled as I pounded my fist against the puck's apartment door for the third time. "I don't think I like doing laundry." The object of Niko's exasperation was the T-shirt I was wearing under my jacket. It was black. When it came to me, I'd discovered this was the same as saying water is wet. It had cheerful yellow letters across the front: I LIKE PEOPLE! Below that were the words THEY TASTE LIKE CHICKEN!

"You didn't actually say you think you don't like doing laundry, did you? Because if you did, I may have to hurt you in ways the Spanish Inquisition itself couldn't begin to imagine." He was favoring his leg, but short of wrapping a pain pill in tofu in the hopes of shoving it down his throat as you would a cranky cat, there wasn't anything I could do. He was one stubborn bastard.

"I told you to take a pain pill before we left," I said unsympathetically, "or wait until the guy answered his phone instead of coming over here to kick down his door. Don't be getting apocalyptic on my ass. It's not my fault."

"Apocalyptic on your ass?" The aggravation, not that genuine anyway, shifted into a more encouraged echo. The old Cal must snark more than I did. That made me wonder when he/I had time to breathe.

I grinned. It took some effort, but I did it. "Hey, medieval's been done."

Before I got a comeback on that one, the door finally opened and Goodfellow, in all his unclothed glory, snapped, "One knock, wait. Two knocks, leave. Three knocks, and I turn Salome loose on your testicles."

"Oh, fuck me." I covered my eyes as fast as possible with my hand. "No, wait—I didn't mean that. I absolutely did not mean that. Just words. Bad words, very bad. I probably shouldn't curse as much anyway. I blame Leand . . . Niko for not raising me better. Hell, I blame you too. When you answer the door, put on some goddamn clothes."

"I'm a puck with normal puckish needs. You feel I can't walk around in my own home as I please? As a puck and a homeowner, I'm offended."

"As a person with eyes, *I'm* offended," I shot back, offended eyes still shut.

"He's not as secure in his masculinity as he could be," Niko said, his tone indicating that while he was having a good time at my expense, he was also not entirely unfreaked-out himself. "Unfreaked-out" . . . Was that a word? At the moment, did I care? Hell, no. "Although to be fair," he continued, "not many men would be in this position."

"'This position' is why I didn't want to answer the door. I obviously have better things to do." I peered through the crack between two fingers to see Goodfellow wave a cranky hand to invite us in. I edged in, back to the first wall I could find, sealed my fingers again, and waited until I heard a distant bedroom or bathroom door shut. I was about to relax when I felt a touch against my thigh and promptly nearly shot Goodfellow's mummy cat between her firefly yellow eyes.

"Holy shit." I slid down the wall to crouch, gun dangling from my hand as Salome—yeah, that was her name, I was pretty sure—curled herself around my neck and purred in my ear. Of course, purring doesn't often sound like gravel grinding or avalanches crushing hikers beneath them, but we weren't all perfect.

"You'd better find a grip on the situation or Salome may eat your head. She likes fear. Fear is catnip to a mummified feline."

I looked up, growling at Niko's enjoyment of my, yep—I admit it, full-blown terror. We were in a marble foyer. There was a living area, a kitchen that probably came with a chef, through another door, a dining room, and directly across from us a hall that ran to bedrooms and whatever else the orgy king had going on. Rich. Goodfellow was rich. That wasn't worth wasting a thought on. What would be were the two or three gold-barred white feathers I saw here and there down that hall. Ishiah's feathers. "This is so not good for a working relationship with your boss." I groaned. "That guy needs some Rogaine for birds or something. Christ."

"Don't be such an infant." There came the increasingly familiar swat to the back of the head. "It's sex. You're a grown man. You've done it and with an incredibly psychotic Wolf to boot. More times than I could begin to count."

"Then you have no problem with my seeing your vamp Promise parade around our place buck-ass naked?" Actually that was a mental picture I had no problem with. Definitely worth remembering more than a mummy in a museum basement, which was why I guess the visual of her was still spectacularly vivid, practically 3-D. She was pale, but she had all that hair and those clutch-of-violet eyes and probably some spectacular ti . . . The smack was to my forehead this time, banging the back of my head against the wall—a two-for-one special. "Ow. Jesus. What was that for?" I complained, rubbing my forehead, then the back of my head, then my forehead again.

"You know perfectly well what that was for."

Yeah, okay, he did have me there.

By the time Goodfellow came back, leaving whoever left those feathers—yes, I told my mind, I know who, so shut up—hidden in the bedroom, I was sitting on his couch while trying to decide whether to shoot the cat, now humping my leg—I didn't even know cats humped—shoot Niko, whose smirks might be invisible but still detectable, or shoot myself. The puck, wearing a dark green robe, flopped down on the wraparound contour couch and demanded, "Explain, and if this is not very, *very* good, I'll let Salome hump the both of you to death." I stopped trying to shake the cat off and gave

Goodfellow my full attention, which was enough to let me see from his sprawled position what he was wearing under the robe.

Okay. Myself. I was shooting myself. There was no way around it. I pried the cat off my leg and tossed her into Niko's lap. If he was so determined to put himself between me and bodily injury, here was his chance. "I'm hungry. I'm making a sandwich. You two . . . do . . . whatever. Discuss. Maps. Plan. Evil Egyptian snob. Me smart." And I was past the enormous rock crystal coffee table and all but sprinting toward the kitchen.

"Some things never change," Goodfellow commented caustically. "Mice ever cower beneath the shadow of the mighty hawk. Oh, and Cal? Your T-shirt isn't accurate. They don't taste like chicken. People. More like a cross between beef and pork. And don't give me that holier-than-thou judgmental look, Niko. I get that enough in the bedroom. Either I ate with the natives or I joined Captain Cook on the spit. He was a bastard and a half anyway, already practically pickled in his own rum. He didn't as much roast as ignite and explode."

Thoughts of chowing down on a pickled and barbecued captain didn't bother me half as much as a puck who didn't own underwear. I started rooting around in his double-doored, Easter Island statue-sized refrigerator and grabbed whatever looked the least healthy. Luckily Goodfellow wasn't like Niko. He liked his food expensive, but other than that, he didn't give a rat's ass, especially when it came to things like heart disease and diabetes. In that respect, at least, he was just like me. Exactly like me. Equal; I didn't fall short in any way. In any way at all. I scowled as I dug through some drawers, then hovered my hand over a fork before regaining some self-control. I went for the knife and started to chop bread and brisket.

"Speaking of pickled, cut down a gallon or so on your cologne. Delilah said she smelled it all over me after we were at the bar." That must've been before yesterday, because I remembered it fairly clearly. "Not the impression I want to be giving hot lady werewolves." For Niko and my head, which was beginning to throb from all the smacks, I added, "The nonpsychotic, non-Mafia, nonkiller ones I might meet in the future, I mean." I hadn't smelled his cologne on me, but I hadn't tried to either. I damn sure wasn't going to try and smell him now or whatever or whoever else was on him. That thought didn't quite end up in my thumb being the next thing chopped next to the brisket, but it was close.

I was never going to be able to work at that bar again.

"My cologne, that's asking quite a lot of me to give up," the puck said with such polished smoothness and without pause that it meant he was lying.

It also meant he wasn't trying to do a good job of it. Pucks were professional tricksters, born and bred, both Niko and Goodfellow had said. Why he would bother to lie about cologne, I didn't know or care. I wasn't puzzling through his personal life like Sherlock goddamn Holmes. Monsters trying to kill us—now that was worth puzzling over.

Niko filled Robin in as I ate my sandwich with wasabi mayonnaise. He told it all: my relapse into fuzzy memory land. The puck exhaled at that, almost as if he expected it, but he didn't say anything. He only listened to the rest of it. Our dead clients and Ammut trying to carry me upstream to spawn like a salmon, he already knew about. That just left the attack of the spiders, which didn't really need telling. That seemed to be an endless loop playing in my life. And then Niko laid out my logic of Ammut being an uptown girl, living the high life, probably in a penthouse.

Perched . . . Hadn't someone said she liked to perch? Who had said that? The mummy. I lost my appetite but kept eating automatically. That damn mummy . . . Wahanket . . . He was what had happened yesterday. He was what I hadn't wanted to remember. It came into sharper focus—the small spider that had attacked me, Niko boxing it up to send to Goodfellow, the trip to the museum, then slices in the darkness: suffocation, fire, an axe, and a feeling—a feeling of taking my own hand and meeting myself face-to-face. Of finally knowing who I was.

Heeeere's Cal.

Then the relapse. A very conveniently timed relapse combined with a photograph and one basset hound–sized spider led to only one conclusion. It turned out I was Sherlock Holmes after all. But I'd known hours ago when I'd seen the picture for the second time that I had a choice to make. Now I knew how to go about making it.

I'd had one relapse, but if I were a betting man, and, hey, maybe I'd find out I was, I'd lay money down that I wasn't going to have another.

"You?" My thoughts and sandwich both were interrupted. "You figured that out about Ammut? You came up with that? Do you even know how to use a map?" Goodfellow asked with a helping of disbelief as large as the helping of green mayonnaise dripping off my sandwich onto the granite kitchen island.

"Okay. Enough already. What was I before? Someone with the brainpower of a poodle?" I took another bite as I glared at the two of them.

"I wouldn't want to insult the poodle, but . . ." The puck held up his hands. "Jesting. Kidding. All in fun, I swear. No, you're smart enough with or without your memory. Your priorities are simply different." His eyes followed another dollop of mayonnaise to fall. "Not with regard to cleanliness or appetite—those remain the same—but . . . never mind. Fine. Ammut is camouflaged as a socialite or a cougar or one of the wealthy women who gobble boy toys instead of life forces. Between Promise and me, I'm sure one of us has come across her. And was fortunate enough not to be eaten by her."

"Monogamy," Niko said, regarding the bald cat batting at his braid with the caution one would use when trying to give a piranha a surprise proctology exam, "may have saved your life."

"And the rest of the world's sanity." I finished the sandwich and headed back into the fridge for a second raid, not that I'd regained my appetite, but my body was overriding my brain. That was when I heard the sound of movement in one of the back bedrooms. "Shit, gotta go. Arrange something. Society thing maybe. Mix with the rich and the life force–sucking bitch. Kill her then. Good plan. Call us. Later." I was in the living room, grabbing Niko's arm and dragging him out of the condo with the door firmly slammed behind us, by me, before five seconds passed. I didn't feel the slightest bit guilty for throwing out Niko's idea about the society crap without giving him any credit, which was the reason we'd come over to Goodfellow's condo. Add that to the map inspiration and I'd come off a genius.

"You are the biggest coward when it comes to Goodfellow's personal life. I'm almost ashamed to claim you as family."

He was so full of himself, with that tiny flake of mummy cat skin on his black shirt. "You want we should go back in there and have some kind of clothing-optional round-robin Egyptian villain discussion with an underwear-free puck and my boss, the guy with wings and a flaming sword? By the way, we don't know where that flaming sword has been."

"I hate to agree with Robin, but you need therapy. You do. Staying a virgin until you were twenty has obviously done profound damage to your psyche."

"Twenty?" I moaned. *Twenty* years old?

"Or maybe it was twenty-one," he mused.

You didn't tell people that, whether it was true or not. Bastard. I didn't speak to him again until we hit the bar. By then it was eleven at night, but it could've been eleven in the morning. It didn't matter. Sin is open twenty-four hours a day. That was why I liked New York . . . or so I thought. It was a good reason. This bar was considerably different from the peri one. First this was a Kin bar—all Wolves, all the time. There was a fur ball at every table.

By the way, ever had eight breasts bounced in your face at once? I can't recommend it enough. I headed straight for the stage. "Don't they hate us?" I said distractedly, digging for money in my pocket. "Especially after what's-his-name, their liaison with us, was supposedly killed by the Lupa since Delilah is going to hog Ammut's glory?"

"Vukasin. This is his bar. They may hate us, but they honor their word," he said, following me. "And their deal with us. For now."

Vukasin, the dead Wolf. Yeah, the neon *vuk me* in the window should've been a clue, but I'd gone with the breasts. Clues, at that moment, I didn't care about. Who said I didn't have great priorities?

"We may hate the Lupa," the stripper said as she crawled to the edge of the stage and sniffed my hair, "but we honor them now as our pack; Delilah as our Alpha." Wolf hearing was damn good, as she'd demonstrated, but the breasts? Better. The octuplet breasts continued to shake in my face and I was having trouble deciding which set to slide the money between. This bar was much darker than the Ninth Circle, which was dim, but there were enough strobing red lights here to shine in the silver white reflection of wolf eyes and to emphasize those all-important breasts. The patrons didn't bother to give Niko or me a sideways look, except for a sneer for being human . . . a sheep . . . even if a sheep in the know about the supernatural world. They didn't look, but they did sniff. They caught the scent of metal, guns, and knives, then shrugged and continued to ignore us. Sheep, but armed sheep, smart sheep that their Alphas told them to leave alone until Ammut was taken care of, and wouldn't it be easier to have a beer and watch the she-Wolves dance?

I totally agreed. "Row one, two, three, four, or the G-string—can you give me a hint?" I asked the stripper as I waved the bills in my hand.

Niko jerked me down to sit in a chair by the dance stage. "We're looking for Vukasin's Beta or his mate. Is one of them here?"

This Wolf had a full mane of wolf hair, wolf eyes, ears, everything Wolf except the human-sized breasts, ass, and arms and legs that allowed her to swing around the pole upside down. I'd seen that when we'd walked in the door and put it in a mental photo album to revisit in the future. It was weird, it was bizarre, but I wasn't going to judge free porn—furry or not. Now she changed completely to human . . . except for feral yellow eyes. I missed the other six breasts.

She crouched on all fours, stopped sniffing me, and tossed back the wild mane of reddish brown hair that fell down to her hips. All the better to see you with. She was certainly no Wolf in a grandma suit. If she had a grandma suit, she'd left it at home. I searched my pocket for another bill. "Vukasin had no mate, but I was with him. I'm Nashika." She ran a finger along my jaw and then tasted it as if I were cake batter she'd scooped out of a bowl. "I'm one of the few left of my pack. After Delilah killed Vukasin, she moved on to his pack. I was allowed to join the Lupa as I'm she-Wolf, not he-Wolf and not high breed. It is the same reason Vukasin would not make me his mate. I am All Wolf. My disgrace is my salvation." She passed a hand in front of her eyes to demonstrate that. "The high breeds were not so lucky as to be invited." The noninvitation sounded more like not-surviving. Delilah might not have actually been the one to take down Vukasin, but she'd taken down nearly all his pack. She probably owned the bar now too.

"Then you do not especially love Delilah? Or would not be averse to confirming what her nature has her planning regarding Ammut and us?" With a fan of bills appearing in his hand, Niko sat beside me ... in the way I'd noticed he always sat, deceptively relaxed but prepared to leap up at any second. I'd noticed a lot about him and what he did since South Carolina, minus a few gaps from yesterday. He trained ... nonstop. He practiced every spare minute of the day for the job. But what was the real job? I'd seen that already. Keeping little brother safe and sound from the monsters, although I hadn't had any problem taking care of myself so far ... except with regard to Ammut.

I'd asked during my "rescue" why they couldn't leave me working at the diner, destitute but monster free. He hadn't answered.

The Halloween picture was the answer ... and soon enough I'd know the question that made sense of that answer. Why I did this. Why my brother, overprotective to the point of putting me in a bubble, let me live a life that had nothing but short life span written all over it.

And why in a picture revealed by a bright flash, I was the only one who stood in shadows.

Or more important, why I wasn't concentrating more

on the naked breasts in front of me. They were only two now, but they were still spectacular and better things to concentrate on—easier. I kept half my attention on them and half on Niko, who was still talking to the Wolf stripper, the nudity bouncing off him as if he had a force field—or a jealous vamp girlfriend.

"No. I have no love for my new Alpha, but I have respect. I am Kin. I am Wolf. I will not betray her. Betraying her would be betraying myself." She snatched the bills from his hand and then those wrapped around my fingers so quickly I almost lost my index finger to a paper cut. "Telling you the Lupa is waiting for you to find the life drainer so my new Alpha can kill you and claim the credit would not be the Kin way, would it?" She leaned forward, then cocked her head sideways, studying me with eyes curious and wary before kissing me. It was quick and short, but with the definite taste of copper and tongue. She pulled back. "Only a sheep. Clever or not, only a sheep. What did our Alpha Delilah see in you?" Then she was up and prowling from the stage to be replaced by another stripper.

I rolled the taste of blood around in my mouth and didn't find it as bad as I thought. "A trip to a Wolf nudie bar all to find out that this Delilah, my ex who had bad taste in sheep, was going to kill us and steal our thunder?"

Niko was already pushing me toward and out the door. "No. That was a given. This was to let her know we know. As much as Nashika might miss Vukasin, her pretense at wanting revenge by giving us information is just that. Pretense. She is Kin and all Kin are loyal to their Alpha ... unless they can take their Alpha. This little red Wolf wouldn't have a chance against Delilah on her very best day. She'll tell," he explained. "I want Delilah to have second thoughts and perhaps third ones

as well. It is one less thing we could do without, her nipping or ripping quite literally at our heels while we take
on Ammut. Delilah is confident, but we've defeated her
once before. She knows we won't go down as easily as
our clients did."

"And you couldn't have e-mailed her to let her know
we see her coming," I griped, "and saved me about fifty
bucks? You said I needed sex therapy. There was plenty
of therapy there, if anyone was feeling like giving a pity-
hump for a poor sheep, and did I get to touch any of it
except for what was the shortest kiss, I hope, of my life?
No, I didn't." I automatically bent my head to escape
most of the swat.

Poodle brain, my ass. I'd learned that habit of Niko's
early on.

I still was tasting blood from the Wolf's kiss when we
made it home. The tang didn't mix that badly with the
wasabi mayonnaise, but it was still blood and we found
more of the same waiting for us. The window hadn't
been fixed yet. . . . It was so high that getting anyone out
there to do it was going to be a pain in the ass. I saw
learning glass replacement and where to find tall-ass
ladders in NYC in my future.

The blood would've been carried through that break
in the glass . . . and rested in the eight hearts that had
once contained them. I'd smelled it a block away—as little as it was, which was why Nik unlocked the door and
then went through ahead of me with his sword drawn
and an elbow in my gut to keep me back. Never mind he
was limping and I was at my prime, from below the neck
anyway. I thought about shooting him in that forcibly
pointed elbow, but shooting him to try to protect him
from himself might be seen as extreme. Or it might not.

Only one way to find out.

I put aside the fantasies of ninja elbow destruction

for the moment and followed him in, closing the door quietly behind us. The blood smell was stronger, but it wasn't rank. There wasn't much blood. There doesn't tend to be in hearts that are ripped out of chests. The blood tends to stay with the body. And then carrying them over in a bag left behind—from Nordstrom, classy—let more leak out, until you're left with a few tablespoons of blood and the smell of raw meat. That was what was left of eight people—the smell of raw meat. It hadn't been spiders, and they hadn't come through the glass. She—and it had been a she, I could all but taste the perfume—had picked the lock and distributed the hearts around the place. One was even on the kitchen bar in a rectangular Japanese-style glass vase I didn't know we had.

Not that I knew much. Not now . . . not yet.

Soon.

I stared at the heart swimming in the water of the vase. It was small; a child's heart. It was February; one of the first things I'd found out when orienting myself in Nevah's Landing. It was February, but was it a particular holiday? One that featured, among other things, hearts?

Fucking soon, all right. I'd have those memories soon, so I'd know what to do about things like this. Where to put these feelings, because I didn't want to have them. If you lived this life, you had to have a mental box for moments like this, to shut them away. And you needed thick chains to wrap around the box and sink it to the bottom of the ocean. I needed to find that goddamn box.

"Is it Valentine's Day?" I asked. It wasn't my voice and it wasn't the old Cal's voice either, because Leandros gave me an assessing glance—one of those looks that said, "Hang in there, little brother, while I break out the straitjacket."

I ignored it and him. I woke up on a beach with four

giant goddamn spiders that I killed. Me. I'd done that. It had been me and monsters and nothing else. No big brothers to keep reality from me, and I'd survived anyway. In fact, I'd *excelled* for a man with half a brain. I hadn't lost my shit then; I wasn't losing it now. "Hearts and flowers. So where are the flowers?" And where was the Eater of Hearts? Where was Ammut?

On the pale gray counter were letters drawn in what little blood there had been left. For a murderer, she had nice handwriting. Neat. Legible. Written in death, same as in the shed where the dead counsel had lain, but you can't have it all. She'd written four words: Give them to me. Again, the same as in the shed where she'd written it on the wall. At least it wasn't in hieroglyphics. Niko would've had to break out a book or, hell, the guy already knew how to read them.

"Give them to me." Niko had already searched the place. I hadn't bothered. After the revenant-in-the-bathroom test, I made sure I could tell if it was only us or someone else still around. Except for the flower-choking perfume and death she'd left behind, she was long gone. He read the words over my shoulder. "Give them . . . Give her what?" he questioned. "She's already taken and is still taking what she wants. What do we have to give her? Why does she keep repeating this?"

In the Park.

Give them to me.

The trees, the grass, spiders all around.

Give them to me. You know. Only you would now with the true ones past and gone. Where they are? How selfish you are, half-breed. Keeping them all to yourself.

The spiders coming closer, more than four. Twenty at least.

Give them to me.

Maybe it had been Valentine's Day then. It would explain the echo in my head, though not the truly crappy grade school poetry.

Roses are red, violets are blue.

The sound of two guns firing followed by . . .

I'm not giving you a goddamn thing, bitch, so fuck you.

It was so nice when a brand-new voice made room for itself in your head. I had me, two more preamnesia mes with radically different opinions on things, and now this Ammut bitch. The joy and the general party atmosphere of it all were too damn good to be true.

I shot the vase. I didn't hit the heart. I didn't want to. I just wanted the creepy fucking post-Valentine's weirdness gone. The death of a child gone. The letters . . . the words . . . gone. The water didn't wash them away. They were too dried for that, but it made mopping them up with a wad of paper towels easier.

"Cal." He said my name as if he wanted to say that it was all right, but he knew it wasn't all right. He was the big brother, though, and he couldn't not say anything even when there was nothing to say. I didn't look up from scrubbing the letters away, paying attention only to the letters and not to the broken glass. When I cut myself, he found more words to say. "Cal. Stop. Now."

"Why? Because a little of my blood is worse than a bunch of hearts lying around the place?" Eight people—maybe nine if I found one under my pillow—were dead because of us. People. Kids. Fucking kids. All right. I was losing my shit after all—a little. I was entitled. You couldn't ignore that much death when it was your fault.

The short sliver of recall that had flashed through was something I felt even more. "I remembered something." I exhaled, then mumbled as I wiped. "A little. I was in a park. Central Park, I think. There were spiders and I remember a woman's voice telling me to give them to her. Give them to her. I have no idea what she was talking about, what she looked like, or how I managed to get away from twenty-some damn Nepenthe spiders. I'm good, but a Chuck Norris Samuel Jackson fucking parfait of kick-ass isn't that good." I threw the soaked paper towels over the counter into the sink. Shit. The only way I'd know the word parfait was Goodfellow. I'd have to thank him for that later with my foot up his ass. Hopefully he'd be wearing pants by then.

"If I remember that, if that happened, I don't see me surviving it, but since I somehow did, I don't see me not telling you about it before I took off on my priestess-hunting sabbatical down south."

He took another mass of paper towels I'd snatched up but hadn't needed in my scrubbing fest. Folding them into a neat square, he offered them to me. "Your hand is bleeding." I pressed the white to the oozing glass cut and watched it turn red. "And perhaps I thought you were safer on a wild-goose chase in South Carolina after some fictional priestess until we found out what Ammut wanted so badly from you, because you didn't know then either. 'Give them to me' means nothing, to you—to any of us."

"And off I went, but spiders followed me. Turned out I wasn't that safe after all?" The cut didn't hurt. The deep ones never did at first. "I was bitten looking for something that didn't exist, lost my memories, and it still took you four days to find me in Nevah's Landing where I happened to wander because my subconscious remem-bered the good old days when we were kids and Peter Pan was around? And that's me believing I would've even gone to begin with. What about the twenty spiders and an Egyptian fake goddess? How'd I get away from them? Fucking fly?" I let the bloodstained towel fall to the ground. "That's the worst bullshit I have ever heard

and I don't need a memory to know that. It's not even
a lie. Jesus, it's barely half a lie and zero explanation.
Didn't we grow up on the run with our mom moving
from mark to mark? That's what you and Goodfellow
said. Well, you, Leandros, didn't learn a damn thing from
her."

"I can lie." He didn't sound defensive at the accusa-
tion, only at the use of our last name instead of Niko.

"You can lie? Just not to me then." When it was me,
he clearly sucked at it. If you thought about it, that made
him a good brother. I didn't feel like a good anything
right now. "I cleaned up the spiders last night; you can
handle this mess."

I took a last glimpse of the small, pathetic piece of
meat on the counter and for a flicker of time it was much
worse than the death of a blackbird. What is a miracle
inside a person is nothing but a gravestone of flesh on
the outside.

"The bitch gave up her snack just to send us a message." Which we didn't understand. Eight wasted lives to
tell us nothing. "I say it again, you people need to look
into e-mail."

I slammed my bedroom door behind me, lay on my
bed, and started emptying my jacket of knives, throwing them at the wall. It already had "Screw you" spelled
out. I would see if I could add to that. Niko didn't follow me. Wise man—crappy liar, but a wise man. After
a few hours, I decided grown men didn't sulk in their
bedrooms. It was almost two a.m. when I headed out of
our place on my own—because I needed it, to be on my
own. To find not an Egyptian monster, but to find more
of myself as Niko was doing his best to keep the old Cal
buried . . . while mourning him with every halfhearted
swat and god-awful excuse of a lie, every hour of sleep
lost. He wasn't the only one with good hearing. I heard

him up half the night. He was practicing; trying to find a restful mind in an exhausted body—as he was doing now. He was in the gym area in sweats and bare feet. "Use protection" and "Did you brush your teeth?" were his only words in response to my noninvitation when I passed him as he slammed a roundhouse kick into one of the heavy bags.

God, what a fucking bad liar. "Sucked" wasn't close to the word.

It should be a good thing, seeing easily through the man who wanted to be . . . who was my brother. It wasn't. It only made me wonder why he was lying at all. Okay, he thought I was happier this way, and that damn Halloween picture proved him right. I hated to say it, but it was true.

But never mind the picture and my truth; it was the way he was lying. It was weird, as if no lie could explain away our rotten childhood. There were plenty of kids with crappy childhoods. Big deal. Why try so hard to lie and explain something that was almost normal these days?

But no one needed to explain why he followed me when I hit the street. I had a tattoo, the words of which Niko had told me meant "brothers-in-arms" in Latin— could you believe it? I was surprised I wasn't a parasitic twin in a pouch under his armpit that he patted on the head and fed chocolate pudding—we were that close. Let me loose alone on the town by myself, target of spiders and high-class heart-eating bitches? No way would he let that happen. He couldn't lie to me, but he could follow me without my seeing him. Somehow, I still knew he was behind me. I didn't have to see him or smell him. It was pure gut knowledge, no malfunctioning brain cells required.

Always his brother's keeper.

I hesitated two blocks away, deciding where to go, and headed for St. Mark's to catch the six o'clock train while consciously not looking over my shoulder for my brother. Why ruin it for him? Niko didn't have a matching tattoo that I knew of, pussy, but if he had one at all, I was sure it would say Massively Overprotective Brother from Kick-Ass Hell. I doubted they could put that in Latin, but that was what it would say, punctuated with a ninja star or two crossed soybeans, depending on his mood, and announcing his mission to the world.

He had changed my diapers, after all.

That made up my mind for me. No more hesitation. Alcohol—I needed alcohol. Niko could follow me all he wanted and drag my unconscious body home if it came to that. Then he could be the massively overprotective brother who dodged drunken vomit—less martial and heroic when phrased in a tattoo, but I didn't mind.

I went to the Ninth Circle, thanks to three things. I knew how to get there since I'd already been given the tour of my old life and that hadn't fallen into one of the black holes of consciousness that riddled yesterday. I knew someone I wanted to talk to would be there. And, a given, there was a huge amount of alcohol. It wasn't long before I was on what felt like the wrong side of the bar, beer with a whiskey back before me.

"You usually don't drink the more embalming of the alcohols. You most often stay with beer."

Goodfellow, not the one I wanted to talk to, had sat down next to me. I did the shot of whiskey. "And why's that?" I asked.

"Your mother was a raving alcoholic. Raving in most things from what I gather, but alcohol being one of her primary obsessions." His own glass was flanked by two bottles of wine. I'd seen his tolerance. Alcoholism would be a problem for him only if someone started giving him

entire barrels of the stuff. "As a result, you and Niko
rarely drink. Tempting the fate of bad genes isn't always
a good idea." He considered his glass for a moment, then
touched it to mine. "But then sometimes fate is fate and
one learns to live with it if not embrace it. If you don't
remember anything at all in the wilds of your amnesia,
Caliban, remember that. Remember it well."

Now there was the best kind of lie, one that wasn't a
lie at all. He'd told me something, something important,
but I didn't have enough of my past yet to know what
it was. "A raving alcoholic, huh?" He wasn't pulling any
punches.

"Very much so. Verbally abusive, emotionally abusive, especially towards you, which would explain Niko
being as much of a guardian in addition to brother when
it involves you. Sophia had quite the pitching arm as well
when it came to bottles and glasses." He poured himself
a third glass. "She was also a thief, a liar, and a whore—
three qualities I usually favor, but in her case, combined
with the maternal instinct of a wolf spider, she gives the
rest of us liars and thieves a bad name. As for whoring,
I've often been offered money for my brilliant perfor-
mances, but I never took it." He grinned and poured a
second glass. "But it's good to know I have a career to
fall back on if the thieving and lying fail me one day."

"Except . . ." The prompt had a threatening tone.

Goodfellow handed the second glass to Ishiah, who'd
drifted up, no wings or feathers this time. "If it's for
money, it's not cheating. It's a righteous occupation of
long standing. If one dies penniless in a ditch, monogamy becomes difficult . . . or far more easy, depending
on your outlook."

At Ishiah's outlook, a fierce glower, the puck sighed.
"Just remember the Good Samaritan story from that
book you're so very fond of. Picking someone who's been

mugged out of a ditch and carrying them home to *oil* them up? I know they were big on oiling people in those days, feet and all, but when you've been beaten and mugged, oil isn't what you're looking for. Trust me, there's more to that story than anyone knows." Ishiah's glower went to nova-heat proportions. "Fine. Fine. I'll wander off to a table then. Wave when you're done discussing things of great import, and I'll be back with something of far greater import in my pants. Dusty and unused for almost five hours now. Ah, sirens at table six. Perhaps they can sing sad lamentations of a warrior retired from battle."

When he was gone and handing out his monogamy cards to the sirens, beautiful women with a green tint to their skin, Ishiah picked up the wineglass and drained it. After the two swallows that it took, I asked him, "Why? Man to bird, why? Why Goodfellow? Are you that hard up to be laid? How does he ever stop talking long enough to actually screw anyone?"

He instantly fisted my hair and smacked my face against the bar. He was nice enough not to do it hard enough to break my nose, and I was nice enough not to pull the trigger on the gun I had shoved against his throat.

"Show him the respect he deserves. He is your closest friend. He knows you." That had to be true, because Goodfellow wasn't rushing over to break this up. He knew his . . . mmm . . . Wingnificant Other wasn't going to smash my brains out on the bar and that I wasn't going to shoot him for trying. Niko, lurking somewhere outside the bar, hadn't come in either . . . to prevent violence or avenge the fact my beer hadn't been served to me in a baby bottle. Ishiah wasn't a threat—or a monster. He was just my sometimes boss.

I straightened, put my gun away, and pushed the hair back so I could see. If it didn't grow and fast, I was going for a buzz cut. "He knows me. He's my closest friend. Everyone says so, but how do I know for sure?" Now was a time for facts. Considering the decision I'd made based on a brother's need and in spite of a picture I, still to this minute, wish I'd never seen, I wanted facts to go with it. That was why I was here. Ishiah knew Cal . . . and knew me, but as an employer, not a friend. He'd be more likely to tell the truth and not soften the blow.

"What he told you about your mother," the eavesdropper said, "do you think you told him that? All of that? You and Niko are secretive—anyone raised the way you were would be—so despite Robin's being your friend, would you have told him that?"

No. Friend or not . . . no. That kind of past abuse . . . The rest of it was one thing, but to know two kids, kids I didn't remember although I was one of them, had lived through that. I wouldn't be throwing those details around. You shouldn't be ashamed, but you were. You shouldn't feel guilty and tainted, but you did. Niko had carefully edged around that information, blurring it, but Goodfellow had given me the real deal and, although I recalled none of what he'd told me happening to Niko or me, I felt it the same as if he'd kicked me in the stomach. It wasn't a good feeling, which was why Niko hadn't told me . . . and why Goodfellow had. Goodfellow was my friend, but he was Niko's friend too.

Robin knew what Niko was doing to me—for me. After all, he was the supplier, the dealer in the dirty deed, but he also knew what Niko was doing to himself. He wasn't going to choose between us. He gave me a hint about my past self through the truth about my mother, but the rest was up to me. Niko, unlike me, had walked through that past, whole and unshadowed, but how long would he stay that way if he lost his one anchor? If he lost his real brother?

The choice to claim the past and the old Cal that went with it was one Goodfellow was letting me decide for myself. He didn't know I'd already made it.

But I still wanted to know it was the right choice.

"Then how did he know?" I asked as I heard a Wolf pass behind me and laugh. It wasn't a nice laugh, gloating and gleeful with the whisper of sheep behind it. I let it go. It was happening more and more now in the hour I'd been in here. From that, I gathered that pigeons like Ishiah rated above sheep, but Wolves rated above both—in their furry little minds.

"Because it's what he does. He's a trickster that has lived longer than I can remember, and I've lived a very long time." There were the wings, not in disturbance this time, though. Spread and lifted high, they made you think of eagles proudly surveying their domain. "I've seen man take his first step. Robin has been around long enough to have probably stepped on one of man's slippery ancestors crawling from the ooze. He can take the smallest fact and spin an entire tapestry from it. But you gave him that one small fact at some time or another and you never would have if he weren't your friend."

I was getting so much truth now that I was surprised they didn't charge extra for it. Abusive whore of a mother. No wonder Niko had to raise me. A horny puck that never shut up as a best friend, but, considering the T-shirt slogans I picked out, it was a wonder I had a friend at all.

I finished my beer and got another from Samyael. Good old Sammy was quick with the beer. "Can I ask you something, boss?"

"'Boss'?" He took my empty and disposed of it under the bar. He was doing my job tonight. "You usually only call me boss when I have an axe against your neck."

"An axe, huh? I must call in sick a lot." I drank half

of the second beer. As Goodfellow said, fate was fate; genes were genes. I wasn't an alcoholic yet or I'd have gone into DTs in the Landing as I hadn't touched the stuff there. But that didn't change the fact he was trying to tell me something about who I'd been—he simply wouldn't do it outright. Ishiah might. "So can I? Ask you something?" He paused, already looking as if he regretted it, but nodded.

"Is Cal a good guy?" Not me, but Cal, because there was still a difference. I didn't watch his face for the response. I drank some more and waited.

When he finally answered, I accepted the single-word reply with a slight tip of my head in thanks. This time I was the one who had to take a while to think. When I was done, I asked him one more question. "If Niko had to choose between me and a burning orphanage full of big-eyed kids hugging fluffy kittens, which would he choose?" It was facetious as hell, but it got the point across.

Ishiah took the beer from me and drank it himself. "Irish courage . . . in a way. I picked that up from Robin. What it took you barely months to find out about him, it took me thousands of years. I was such a pretentious ass and full of dangerous, even deadly conviction. I judged him. It was only when I judged myself that I saw the truth. Now I won't deny any truth." He replaced my bottle with two more—one for me and one for him.

"Niko's flaw—and it is a fatal one—is that if it came down to saving the world or saving you . . . he would save you."

Fatal to the world and big-eyed orphans, I could see that, but to me it meant one thing:

How could I do anything less?

I didn't know if it was my sheepness that offended the Wolves or my singing. But finally the last sounds that had kept them howling and hiding under their tables wasn't enough to hold one of them back. He was too drunk to care about our Kin agreement or too tone-deaf to appreciate the song. While the rest of the Wolves covered their ears and kicked in agony instead of trying to kill me, this guy had had enough.

One or two or seven or twelve had been giving me the eye—blue, yellow, orange, brown, green, take your pick—and muttering among themselves. The more I drank, the more they muttered and the less their loyalty to the Kin word mattered. Then again, the more I drank, the less putting a bullet in a fuzzy ass bothered me, which made us even. I couldn't say if that bullet would be lethal or not as my double vision was getting worse. I was matching Goodfellow drink for drink, which made me some sort of superhero with a mutant gene for consuming oceans of alcohol. And with mass quantities of alcohol comes singing.

The puck had started and I had followed. From the startled looks the peris gave me, that was not me, but considering this particular me was probably going away, screw it. I'd party while I was here. As for the singing itself, we weren't bad. A karaoke machine would've helped me with the lyrics if not my kick-ass sheep rep, but I had a good voice, go figure, and of course pucks were great at everything, so said Goodfellow.

But while *American Idol* might've thought we could shoot gold records out our asses, the Wolves didn't care for the higher notes of the song and "Danny Boy" was not their thing. I thought their pained howling added to the song, which was sad, or so Goodfellow told me. The peris took it in stride. Ishiah had said he'd given up his judgmental ways. That didn't leave him much room to bitch.

But when the one Wolf broke, there was more than

enough bitching to go around. I was sitting in a chair, singing my lungs out while Robin did his wailing standing on top of our table. Whether he was drunk or not didn't make a difference. I was grateful he'd kept his clothes on. Get a person up on a table and it's a given. Clothes start flying off—the same way the Wolf flew toward me. I saw them—wait, just the one—damn double vision headed toward me like a fur-covered Scud missile. He was young, an All Wolf, a mixture of human teenager and wolf, even when he changed. He lost his clothes, but he still had dark blue human eyes and thickly callused human hands with wolf nails. I knew because I felt them around my throat.

I tipped the chair over, landed on my back, jammed a foot in his fur-covered stomach, and tossed him over my head. Goodfellow dodged him neatly, kept singing, and, yep, the shirt came off. He was whipping it around, dancing some sort of Irish jig, holding a bottle of whiskey in one hand, and the son of a bitch continued singing as if a homicidal Lassie hadn't that second flown by.

It was impressive. I was impressed, no denying it, as I lay on the floor and drank my beer. I'd have been more impressed if he'd put his shirt back on. Well, shit, the Wolf was back. This time he landed on my chest and stomach with enough weight and pressure to have me spewing beer into his face. Coughing, I waved a hand at the Budweiser foam now dripping off his snarling muzzle. "Cujo. Old Yeller." I waved a hand. "Someone give me a gun to put the poor rabid bastard out of his misery. Wait. I have a gun. I think I have two."

I wasn't serious. I'd learned my lesson. You don't bring a gun to a dogfight and you definitely don't bring one to a puppy fight. This guy barely qualified as a puppy. One of those Lupa Wolves would've swallowed him whole. I broke my beer bottle over his shiny black nose. Moist shiny black nose—that meant he was healthy. If he left me alone, he might stay that way.

He didn't—leave me alone or stay that way.

Now the rest of the Wolves were getting caught up in the fight. The growls had tripled and when Old Yeller, who had tumbled backward yelping at the pain in his nose, started back toward me again, he had a friend. This guy was not young; he was twice the size and five times the Wolf. He had scars running thick and gray through his black fur, fangs that were made for tearing flesh, half of one ear missing, and from the abrupt silence of howls in the bar, he was one badass son of a bitch.

Goodfellow hadn't stopped singing, although the Wolves had, but the choice of songs was too close to home now. This one—he could've been mistaken for a small black bear in the woods but with the temper of a grizzly. He was a fighter, a killer, and he knew what he was doing.

Him, I shot. Teen Wolf, eh, not worth it. I pepper-sprayed him. Mailmen and monster killers of the world, unite. The black Wolf I put a round in didn't make a sound. He went down, crawled a few feet away to settle in a pool of his own blood and watched me with enraged eyes. Wolves healed fast. He was biding his time. The kid, the Wolf version of Benji, had changed back to curl naked on the floor, his swelled-shut eyes flowing with tears, and his nose pouring snot. But they were both alive . . . and it didn't have to be that way. Neither one looked the least bit grateful, though. Bastards. Someone else wasn't grateful for my restraint either.

Leandros came through the front door, walked through the quiet Wolves muttering in confusion, the sirens who were applauding Goodfellow's talent, before grabbing my shirtfront to drag me up off the floor and out of the bar.

"Hey," I protested, "don't take it out on me if your ass froze out here for two hours. I didn't ask you to follow me. And the Wolves started the bar fight. It was hardly a bar fight anyway. Barely counted. I didn't kill anybody, did I?"

He did wait until I managed to get my feet under me before continuing to drag me, this time not as silently. "Maybe you should have. Maicoh, the one you shot, holds grudges. Or instead of killing him, perhaps you should have tried thinking instead. If you are intoxicated, especially this intoxicated, which you've had the sense to never be in the past, you run the risk of someone better than Maicoh killing you. Someone besides me. And pepper spray? Are you suicidal? You are *not* a mailman." I was about to say that was what I'd been thinking, except more pro-mailman, when he gave me a not-so-gentle shake—ninja punctuation to equal my vomit punctuation from last night. "And why were you singing? You don't sing."

"It's a wake, and 'Danny Boy' is what you sing when someone dies. It turns out I cut my hair for the right reason after all."

He stopped again. "Who died?"

"No one you know." This time I was the one moving him. I shoved him or he allowed himself to be shoved. I saved my ego and didn't guess. "Look. A tattoo place. Ishiah said it opened yesterday. Run by some ancient Mayan guy. Acat. Another one of those, 'Yeah, I'm a god, okay, maybe not, but I live forever' things. Good for business. Keeping the street monster-eclectic and human free."

"Are you feeling the victim of discrimination?" He had immediately stopped yet one more time the moment I'd said tattoo, balancing with ease on the curb. It looked effortless, and apparently it was, because when I shoved harder, he was concrete—a mountain.

"Nah, I have sheep solidarity with you. At least I can say there are two humans in the city. Good to know." He tensed under my hand as I said that, but I was too drunk to know why and too drunk to care that I didn't know why. And too drunk to care that I didn't care. It was a very Zen thought process. Good for me. Good for drunk-off-his-ass me. "And, Niko, you're getting a tattoo. I have one." I waved the arm it was on. I was proud that I didn't stagger. I was a mountain too. Look at me. "Brothers-in-arms, right? It's a brother thing. In the fucking handbook, I know it—if I could ever find the fucking handbook. Now it's your turn."

So he'd understand.

When the time came, I wanted him to understand. The tattoo would tell him then what I couldn't tell him now.

"And what tattoo am I getting?" The mountain was shifting, minutely, under my hands.

"Bros before Hos." I got him off the curb and across the street, where he stopped for the last time.

"My body is a temple. I may let you deface it with graffiti if it means that much to you that I reciprocate your brotherly brand, but *that* phrase is not an option." Ah, there was a limit to all that family do-or-die after all.

"It's not that exactly. Christ. It's just sort of the same sentiment, but without the hos and with the same sort of rhyming. . . . Just shut up and get the goddamn tattoo, would you?"

He did. In the tiny shop that was spotlessly clean, he did it because I asked, maybe to get more of the brotherhood back that a spider had stolen. Or maybe he was just too damn tired to fight about it. Mourning one brother, adopting a new one—because Cal and I weren't the same, as much as Niko was trying to tell himself that we were. Trying to tell himself I was the old Cal, only with a creamy icing of happy-go-lucky contentment on top.

It was hard work, adoption and lying to yourself. It would make anyone tired, this superninja included. I handed the wrinkled napkin to a red guy with earlobes down to his shoulders and four arms—or that might've been that annoying double vision. Niko, in the chair with his shirt off and his upper arm bared for the needle, frowned at the writing on the stained paper. "What is that? I don't recognize it."

"Aramaic." I sat down on the one small plastic chair provided for those who wanted to wait. Yawning, I finished the thought. "Ishiah wrote it for me. Figured it was the one language you probably didn't know." And wouldn't be able to read until he was ready to hear it and I was ready to tell it.

"There are many dialects incorporated through other languages, regions, time periods. . . ."

I dozed off, and I couldn't blame the alcohol. Faced with death by boredom, my brain took the only other way out—unconsciousness. When I woke up, it was morning and I was in my bedroom at home. I wasn't in bed, though, and my knife-practicing wall no longer said *Screw you.*

It said something worse.

Something that was getting damn familiar.

11

AbominationAbominationAbominationAbomination-
AbominationAbominationAbomination.

I wobbled for a second as I woke up or realized I was
awake. It wasn't that easy to tell the difference between
the two. I was in bare feet, sweatpants, and a T-shirt. It
was cold. We needed to get that window fixed. I hated
the cold worse than I hated Niko's tofu. The wall in front
of me, the knife wall, was covered with that scarlet word,
from as far up as I could reach down to the floor. My
hand was cramping and I lifted it up to see the pen I was
holding. The red was ink, not blood; that was something.

"You've been at it for three hours. I gave up trying to
wake you up after the first hour. This, naturally, means
you will never drink again."

Sleepwriting; it was better than sleepwalking, I
guessed. I dropped the pen as I turned. Niko was lying
on my bed, which was neatly made with fresh sheets and
a blanket—a pillow too. Fancy schmancy. "How'd we get
home?"

"Cab. You were upright, technically, but not especially coherent. You went to sleep on the sidewalk while
I unlocked the door and then woke up, only to pass out
again here on your floor, which, lucky for you, was as

always padded with your dirty clothes. I thought it might be a good idea for one of us to be conscious in case the spiders returned. I made your bed and have been here since." He sat up, indicating the gauze wrapped around his biceps. It showed about half an inch, the rest covered by his own T-shirt sleeve. Removing the tape and bandage and pulling up that sleeve, he revealed a black and red band similar to the one I had around my arm but written in a different language. "All of this following getting a tattoo I did not want or need because you insisted it was in something called *The Good Brother Handbook*."

"Yeah?" I studied it with interest. "What's it say?"

His eyes narrowed and there wasn't a trace of the dry humor I'd seen once or twice when he wasn't forcing himself to live a lie. "Don't get my brand-new sheets there wedged up between your ninja-ass cheeks," I said, providing all the humor and then some. "I remember what it says. Maybe I'll tell you on Christmas. Don't go researching ancient Aramaic and spoil the surprise trying to read it yourself." I did remember too, and I didn't have a hangover. For someone who didn't drink often, I was still expert at it. A natural talent for fighting off toxins, the fun kind and the spider kind, that was me.

Yesssss. Never weak.

I moved back to my original position, facing the wall. No one was going to need any help reading that. Covering the entire thing was that one word. *Abomination*. My subconscious had a thing for that word when it came to monsters, a real obsession. First, it whispered it in my head and now it spelled it out in reality, covering every inch, every single inch.

Except . . .

Precisely in the middle of the wall were six different words in letters so much smaller than the others that they were barely noticeable. *AbominationAbomination-Where are your brothers and sisters? Give them to me AbominationAbomination.Abomination.* "I gotta say"—I scanned the entire wall—"I'm an industrious worker in my sleep." *Abomination*, I ignored. My subconscious didn't like monsters—or part of it didn't; that was perfectly clear and had been from day one. And from day one when I thought monsters, I'd also thought automatically abomination. But the other thing written on the wall . . .

Where are they? Your brothers and sisters? Give them to me.

Selfish.

Where?

Where?

Where?

It was what she'd wanted in the park. That was what she'd said after demanding I give them to her. My brothers and sisters, and as far as I knew, I had only the one. Ammut, the bitch, making demands I couldn't meet because I didn't understand. I couldn't wait to catch up with her. Goodfellow better have his socialite/cougar trap all but ready.

Wait. When they'd brought me back from South Carolina, that had been scratched in the concrete in front of our place. Where are your brothers and sisters? She'd always wanted that from me, whatever that was, from day one.

I reminded Niko of what was carved out front and said, "Now we know for sure what the 'them' is in the 'give them to me' love note she left yesterday. You're positive we don't have any other brothers or a sister hanging around? Maybe Mommy Dearest sold one in a Walmart parking lot for booze?" I groaned as I massaged my hand and sat down next to Niko on the bed, practically bouncing off the snug, hospital-corner-tight army blanket. "You going to tell me what happened in the park now? Before you sent me on my vacation down South? I told you what I remember. Why don't you tell me?"

He gave up on that particular deceit—liar, liar, pants on fire—and this time told the truth. "I don't know." What came after that sounded true too, but uneasy as if he didn't know, but he'd started guessing and his guessing would be good. He was too smart for it not to be. He had his suspicions, but he wasn't sharing them—a different type of deceit, but deceit all the same. "I don't know what Ammut wants or what that means." He rolled off the bed and stood abruptly, then gave me his back with the next words. "I'm the only brother you have." I wonder if he knew that sounded more like a question than a fact. "And she has no reason to want me. I won't taste any better than any other human."

I didn't call him on it. Niko was so far over the edge in this mess that he was going to have to ride it all the way out. The lying and half-truths were nothing compared to what else he'd done, something completely outside his moral code.

I'd seen that moral code this week or so. He'd walk back three blocks to give back change to someone who hadn't charged him enough for a PowerBar. He was loyal to his friends, devoted to me, possibly pathologically so, loved a vampire—seeing past the outer monster to the core of the true woman beneath, and had given up vamp nookie to babysit me until the amnesia passed. He'd raised me from birth—what person did that if they weren't functional parents? Not even brothers did that, but this one had. The guy had honor in a way that almost eclipsed the word itself.

What he was doing now, not only lying, but *doing*—

he'd be punishing himself so thoroughly on the inside that I didn't need to add to it.

One time had been enough for me to figure it out—one time and a spider in a box. New toothpaste plus memory relapse. That and the constant harping on my dental hygiene. *Brush your teeth, brush your teeth.* He was worse than any dentist. I didn't have to be a genius to know where he was putting the Nepenthe venom. It was only enough to keep me from recovering any further memories. Keeping the status quo, thanks to the box o' spider he'd FedExed to Robin—one of the few memories of that day I'd hung on to.

If anyone would know how to make that ancient nepenthe potion of the pharaohs, or know someone else who did, it would be Goodfellow. He was the one who'd known of its existence in the first place and who knew its effects. He did that for Niko, and he'd given me enough of a clue in the bar for me to make my own decision. Under the cloak of talking about my mother's alcoholism, he'd told me . . . Sometimes, genes or no genes, you simply had to accept who you were.

I didn't know personally if Cal was a good guy or a bad guy, but I did know he was a shadowed one. I also knew what Ishiah had told me, but that wasn't anything I'd repeat. I also knew people reacted to me like a grenade that inexplicably didn't go off. I know Wolves and boggles had lost respect for me, even though I could still kick their asses. I knew body-temple Niko wouldn't have gotten a tattoo for his Cal unless he thought it would help the return of part of that Cal—some of him but not the part that remembered, not that unhappy part. No one who cared for his brother wanted him unhappy.

Niko wasn't the kind to make mistakes often, but with me . . . and with Cal, he had.

I didn't know Cal, that was true, but I knew myself. I

wasn't a murderer. I *was* a killer, but only if I had to be. I wasn't an abusive shit like our mother was said to have been. But most of all, I wasn't a thief. I wasn't stealing Cal's life or Niko's brother. I'd thought it before: Niko Leandros was a born martyr, but now it was time for him to walk away just this once and let someone else take the stoning in his place. Cal wasn't happier this way, because I wasn't Cal; I was only a piece of him.

Whoever Cal was didn't make a difference. I wasn't complete. I wasn't the real deal, but real or not, illusion or the foundation of an actual person, *I* was a good guy. If you could have anything in the world, that was one of the better things to have. Tombstones crack and fall. Fortunes come and go. Legends fade. What you did with your life, no matter how short it was or how real it was, that counted.

That lasted forever.

"Did you fall asleep?" A sharp elbow stung me over my ribs.

I let it all slide out of sight. It was a waiting game now. My memories would come back, but I couldn't pick when. That was out of my hands, although using Niko's vomit-worthy toothpaste instead of the minty-fresh venom-laced one would make sure it did happen and sooner rather than later. Sitting around thinking what a damn heroic guy I was wasn't going to make anything happen on the Ammut front, though. I had to pay that rent.

"Thinking how annoying it would've been to wake up to five or six Nikos instead of just the one. You're damn annoying all on your own. More brothers? No way." I elbowed him back. "Since we don't know anything about what bat-shit-crazy Ammut wants from us, why don't we dangle ourselves in front of her so she can ask us personally? Get Goodfellow to hold whatever rich shits

of New York party he's going to tonight." The puck had
said it would take days to do right and be believable.
But if we put enough bait in the trap, it wouldn't have
to be believable—only too good to pass up. "Have him
invite a crapload of vamps and Wolves and whatever
else crawls out from under the beds along with humans.
Stack the deck. It'll be too juicy a temptation. Ammut
will either try to eat the guests or jump us to ask us
about the brothers-and-sisters thing."

The Peter Pan albino crocodile smiled in my head
and that long grin ... Oh, shit ... It was made of metal.
Every tooth was bared in that horrific grin, shining like a
serial killer's blade. *Here we have left you presents. Here
you have brothers and sisters.*

Or my mind could stop goddamn teasing me and tell
me itself. I waited a second, but there wasn't any more
from the crocodile that seemed to know more about
things than Niko and I combined. Lucky crocodile.
Lucky me, because I didn't want to see it anymore, not
the gleam of one hideous fang.

"You call him," I said as I stood back up. "I'm scared
shitless he might have it set to speakerphone and I'll
hear something that will make me jab my eye out with
the closest sharp object."

"Where are you going?" he demanded—overprotective or on my ass to keep away the lazy. The result was
the same.

"To brush my teeth," I said before he could. I couldn't
save him from the chain of deception, but I could save
him from at least one link in it. It was all in that brother
handbook.

Whatever part of that brother I was.

It was Delilah who led us one step closer to Ammut
and a bigger step to the old me—hours before the party

Goodfellow had managed to set up. She called us with the location of a brownstone with a basement full of bodies. That was a surprise; then again, maybe not. Niko had said she wanted to impress the Kin by killing or saying she'd killed Vukasin, but she'd impress them even more if she killed an Alpha *and* helped bring Ammut down—all while letting us do the heavy lifting.

Ambitious and smart didn't begin to do this chick justice. If I had one chance before this was all over ... Ah, damn, she'd eat me alive. Literally. During the act probably. The real Cal, like me, was a killer, but unlike me, his moral judgment about it had to be more blurry than mine. He could run with the Wolves, while everyone else heard only baaing when I was around. I was nothing but a sheep in their eyes—a very badass sheep, but badass or not, a sheep was a sheep. Kill someone in the middle of sex? I couldn't do that. But I didn't doubt that Delilah would and Cal could. She would for the sheer fun of it. Trying to kill Vukasin and the council before Ammut beat her to it showed she loved her slaughter, and Cal would do it in self-defense. I hoped it would be self-defense.

Niko missed his brother. Yeah, self-defense. That guy loved the hell out of his brother, and a stone cold killer—he wouldn't have raised one of those. He was like frigging Gandhi with a katana and a boot in your ass—ethical but pragmatic. He wouldn't have brought up a human version of a monster.

The laughter in my head was twofold this time, one fold hysterically amused and one fold darkly bitter. What lived in Cal, good, bad, and in-between, made me not particularly sorry I was only part of him, the silhouette of him on the sidewalk fading more every hour as the sun moved across the sky.

I wondered if I'd remain part of him, aware, or if I'd disappear completely.

Now I lay me down to sleep . . .

What of you *would I possibly want to keep?*

Or maybe I'd be a voice in his head. I hope I said better things than I'd had to hear. But better yet, I wouldn't be there at all. Better to sleep, locked in his subconscious, because I had a feeling he wouldn't listen to much of what I had to say.

"What are we doing here?" Goodfellow said as the taxi stopped. When he'd called us to tell us about the party, Niko had said we'd gotten wind of Ammut moments before his call and to grab his sword and pick us up at our place.

"Delilah called," I said as I opened the door and stepped out of the cab. "She said there were some leftovers here for us. Investigation, clues, all that crap."

Once he and Niko were out and the cab was pulling away, he said, "If Ammut shows up at the charity event"—which was what rich people called an excuse to get hammered—"this entire trip will have been a waste of time. I hate wasted time. It interferes with my wickedness and dissolution. Do you think becoming this degenerate comes without practice? I've invested millennia in becoming the magnificence that stands before you. But it takes time and upkeep to maintain these heights. Time not spent in what may well be a putrid pit of spiders and bodies."

I shrugged. "Hey, preaching to the choir, but Niko insisted. Said he'd paddle my ass with a sword if he had to."

"I already have someone to do that. Although once upon a time if Niko had said that to me . . ." Goodfellow didn't finish the sentence. He didn't need to. Niko was already leaving us on the sidewalk as he headed up the brownstone's stairs at a fast pace, quick as legs could move without it actually being labeled running. It was much better being on the other side of the Goodfellow personal-life TMI seizure for once.

"That was fucking great." I grinned. "Do it to him again."

And that request had Niko through the door and inside before Goodfellow had a chance to say or do anything. I knew I could pick a lock from my few days in the Landing. One night I'd forgotten the key to my room. I hadn't felt like waiting for the guy at the motel desk to get out of the bathroom when he was done whacking off and since I could *hear* him whacking off, I hadn't felt like looking around for a master key either. I'd gotten through my door in about three minutes. Niko went through the brownstone door in three seconds. Or so I thought until I reached the top of the stairs myself and saw the lock was busted out with claw marks and the smell of Wolf on the door. Delilah and her pack didn't care about picking locks and bricks might save the Three Little Pigs from them, but it wouldn't save anyone else.

It was a one-residence brownstone. You didn't see many of those anymore. The hallway was dusty enough to tell that no one had lived here for a while, but the path through that dust said someone did use the place now and again. The pictures on the wall were of an older woman and man. Ammut didn't seem the domestic kind of monster, with the life sucking and all, which made it easy to guess this couple had owned the brownstone and Ammut had eaten them. It had most likely been when she'd first come into town before she got settled in a place of her own and started eating things tastier than human sheep.

I heard a faint crackle under my shoe and crouched

down to touch a finger to an all but invisible glitter on the floor. They were scales, the ones I hadn't been able to see at the canal, but not crocodile scales. There was no Peter Pan villain here. These were more like snake scales. Smaller, finer, and they smelled like poison . . . of something rank and rotten—the Nile during a drought with dead fish and creeping putrefaction for miles. "Holy shit." I half gagged and brushed it off my hand quickly. When she'd left the hearts at our place, she must have been in human form, or mostly, because I hadn't caught a whiff of this.

Straightening, I pulled out the Eagle. The smell was getting stronger. Farther down the hall, Niko already had his sword in one hand. With his other he made a gesture. It wasn't the finger, which right now was one of the few gestures that meant anything to me. I had to know signs and be a monster killer too? Was there a merit badge for that at monster killer Scout meetings? Disemboweling revenants in your bathroom and hand signals for something that wanted to do the same to you? Then hot chocolate and cookies. Good time had by all.

I gave Niko an expression that was universally recognized as "What the fuck?" by the memory challenged and nonmemory challenged alike. His sword hand gave a minute twitch that made the katana-paddling threat more genuine, but instead he gave a few more generic motions of his hand. He pointed up and then down. Okay, that I got. How anal-retentive one had to be to have hand signals for up and down that weren't simply up and down, I didn't get, but the rest I did. I was the bloodhound. Where was the hamburger? I took a deeper breath as behind me Goodfellow silently closed the door. After my pretty loud "holy shit" of moments ago, being quiet was most likely behind us, but you never knew.

I tilted my head back, up toward the stairs, and took one more breath. Down—the stench was definitely stronger down. Delilah hadn't been lying when she'd said a basement full of bodies. She hadn't mentioned the maker was down there with them. Ammut couldn't have been here when the Lupa were. The Wolves wouldn't miss that stink and Ammut wouldn't miss a chance at some furry num nums. Suck the life force, bypass hairballs and indigestion later. It was efficient. I had to give her that.

I moved down the hall next to Niko and pointed toward the floor. Decomposition, adrenaline, fear, Wolves, urine, and Ammut; it was all under our feet. Since I also didn't know the sign for "The bitch is right here," I used my free hand to squeeze his wrist hard. He nodded. Monsters in daylight were nothing for him, but to me it was wrong and Ammut was a monster; no some are good and some are bad here. Her invisible trail had unnatural and, yeah, abomination, all but embedded in it. Her, I had no problem killing.

There was a flicker of motion—dark, light, dark—at the door we'd just walked through. Behind Goodfellow appeared white blond hair, amber skin, a tattooed choker of wolf eyes, and a sly smile. Our own Delilah had shown up for the party.

The gun in my hand was aimed and the trigger was on three pounds of pressure and holding before I had a single thought. When that thought finally showed up, it was to forget Ammut. This was the bitch I would *enjoy* killing. What I'd felt for her at the missed massacre of our clients had been a happy, curious mix of dangerous, hot, and damn straight I'd nail that.

That was what it was like to be human. To have violence not be your first instinct. Huh. Who fucking knew?

Well, I'd been happy then when it came to Delilah, but I wasn't happy anymore.

She'd betrayed me, but I was past that. I'd expected that. We were predators. We did what we did best. Kill to live, kill to protect our own and, in Delilah's case, she was her own. Her self-interest was the only thing that mattered to her. And if she played a game or two with someone or something outside Wolves, that was all it was—a game. I'd known that all along, but I'd liked the game and I'd liked her. I'd expected her to go after me eventually. That was part of the game and I knew her rules. But she knew mine too. Going after my family or my friends broke every goddamn one of them. I should've blown her away days ago when I saw her for the very first time since she'd pulled that shit.

It was an easy mistake to fix.

"Not the time." Goodfellow moved next to me, out of the way—no one said his sense of self-interest wasn't finely honed as well—and pushing the Eagle down. "Very much not the time," he hissed, barely audible. "Throw her at Ammut first if you want. She makes good cannon fodder."

True. Then there was shooting her in front of Nik. . . . Wasn't that why I hadn't shot her when she'd stabbed us in the back last year? I hadn't wanted him to see me do the chick I was screwing—do in a way that ended up with a bullet in her head and my Auphe out instead of in. Wasn't that it?

Then a pain hit and hit hard. Jesus, what hurt? What inside me felt ragged and ripped, torn, and trashed?

There it stopped, the flood of cold rage and the memories, the pain—all of it. I blinked and it was gone. I remembered vaguely Delilah about to shoot a healer and a friend sometime in the past. I couldn't remember why I hadn't killed her—whether it was due to Niko or some lingering affection for her wild ways. The wild ways themselves were a blank too. No mental sex shots

for me. Wasn't that the way? Wondering about non-
sense words like Auphe or about being human made
no sense, and I didn't have the time to stand pondering
the philosophical nature of humanity now. What made a
man a man? Who cared? There was a killer in the basement and a killer flanking us, and this place stank worse
than a slaughterhouse. Time to go to work. I'd handled
Ammut's spiders. I'd do the same to her . . . only without
the fork.

I turned my back, depending on Goodfellow to watch
it, and moved past Niko to stand behind the door to the
basement. A rug beneath my feet puffed up dust and
the smell of death as I pushed at the door carefully with
the gun muzzle. Ajar, the heavy wood swung with ease
and no haunted house screech of rusted hinges. Too bad.
That would've given an excuse to flip on the lights, if
the power was still on, and go pounding down the stairs
shooting anything I could see—"see" being the key
word.

Niko's hand on my shoulder stopped me from edging
down the first step. I waited and, as my eyes adjusted,
a small amount of light became visible. A street-level
window was somewhere down there, a small and filthy
one from the amount of light it let in, but when you're
old and have bad hips, you don't come down to your
basement to clean the windows in case someone needs
to come to kill the monster that ate you. They couldn't
have had a housekeeper?

The first foot on the step wasn't mine. No surprise.
Spanking boglets and sending them running back to
mommy kept me from being benched, but lacking my
entire mind didn't make me MVP. I did make sure mine
was the second foot, and Goodfellow and Delilah didn't
fight me for the honor. I couldn't see what color the
stairs were, but I could tell they were painted. Brown,

gray, some color that wasn't impossible to see in the gloom, but neither were they easy.

The body was.

It was . . . I had no idea what it was. It had wings but not feathered, more like that of a bat. It had a child's face, sharp teeth in a small gaping mouth, and large eye sockets. The closest thing I could come up with was a flying monkey from *The Wizard of Oz*. The eyes that had been in those sockets were desiccated to the size of raisins and the wings looked brittle enough to disintegrate with a touch. Dark blue or purple veined every inch of the skin I could see as it had the victims in the scrap metal shed. The rest of it was wrapped in a spiderweb cocoon, which was apt as it looked as if it had been sucked dry—a fly in a spider's web. Ammut had her pet spiders storing food for her here in her emergency freezer. This one hadn't made it all the way down to the pantry. She'd eaten it on her way out.

That last Oreo on the go. It happened to us all.

I edged around it, following Niko's lead, and kept moving down the stairs, one slow, cautious tread at a time, and stayed grateful the body didn't have a vest and fez. That would have been beyond my weirdness threshold, assuming I had a weirdness threshold that didn't involve undead cats and naked pucks. Swiveling my head, I tried to cover both sides of the basement around the stairs until Niko's painless but pointed jab in my gut combined with pointing to the right had me focusing on that. He'd cover the left, I'd cover the right, and nothing would be lost in the seconds it took to watch both on your own.

Killing monsters for a living was not for the loner, not for a long-lived one at any rate. We reached the bottom of the stairs, and I could barely see the paler color of Niko's hair at all. The rest of him bled into the darkness.

The man wore way too much black. As if I could talk, I amended to myself, and checked over my shoulder. Delilah, whose almost-white hair stood out in the gloom, a moth wing pressed against a night's window, was behind me and Goodfellow behind her. It was good planning on the puck's part. With the partial new opinion I had of her—knowing implicitly what she was capable of caused very confused emotions—trusting her to guard all our asses wasn't an option. It didn't matter that I could see how that amused her, a spark of reflected light in amber eyes. She could be amused all she wanted as long as Goodfellow put that sword through her if something looked off or if she breathed wrong.

At the bottom I automatically moved to stand back to back with Niko. I couldn't tell where Ammut was more specifically than the basement. I smelled her everywhere, the pungent odor rolling at me from all sides. I could smell too much and couldn't see enough. I felt something against my foot, a shadowed heap. I used my toe to flip it part of the way over . . . slow, silent, careful. It was a Wolf—male, not a Lupa. It had human features except for the mouth crammed with wolf teeth and tufted ears. It too was mapped with dark veins and cocooned. The veining would be part of whatever process Ammut used to pull the life out of her victims. It wasn't pretty, but it wasn't fresh hearts pooling blood on your countertop either.

As Delilah came to the last step with Goodfellow right behind her, I stepped away from Niko and farther into the deepening shadows to make room for the two. Blind was no way to work, not and stay alive, but Niko took care of that and finding Ammut all in one fell swoop. It wasn't ninja magic. It was good old mundane road flares; one tossed past me and one on his side of Ammut's cookie jar. They lit up the space like two

small bloody suns. There were at least seven bodies I
could see before me. All were cocooned. Here were
some of the missing victims we hadn't been able to track
down, spider-delivered from the parts of the city where
Ammut was too snooty to go herself. Fortunately, the
basement was damp with one pool of moisture by the
heap of bodies. That moisture kept them from burst-
ing into flame as the flare was close enough to touch
them. I scanned the area. Cracked concrete walls that
revealed the old brick beneath, bodies, puddles; that was
it. I even checked above my head. If a spider was going
to jump you . . . If anything was going to jump you, that
was where it would be in this place. Seeing nothing there
or under the stairs, the flare banished shadows there as
well, I turned to take in Niko's half of the space.

More bodies; almost twenty in a pile reached to the
exposed aged beams above us. The basement was bigger
than I'd imagined before Niko played God and lo, there
was light, but it wasn't so big that I could see there was
no sign of Ammut. I smelled her, but I didn't see her.
Either she'd left two seconds before our cab dropped
us off or she was under that mound of bodies. It was big
enough for a monster to burrow beneath.

I was already moving toward it when I discovered
there was a third option that I hadn't considered.

While it was large enough to hide Ammut, it was also
big enough for six spiders to leap out of while Ammut,
on the petite side for a monster, came boiling out from
under the seven bodies behind me. All in one moment, I
saw the thrash of long black jointed legs, cocooned bodies tumbling; Delilah literally ripping off her clothes—I
heard the material shred under her hands—and becoming a large white Wolf that fell to all fours to jump;
Niko's and Goodfellow's swords swinging, and Ammut.

It was one moment of ivory fur, claws, and fangs, sil-

ver slicing quickly enough that the air itself should've
been cut. It was one moment of yellow eyes and dripping venom with legs scrabbling too fast for nature to
have intended—a hideous, inescapable speed.

It was a lot to take in and I didn't bother. I had Ammut
on my ass and that took priority. I was firing as I swiv-
eled. When something is that close to you and moving
that damn fast, equally quick as her spiders, aiming is a
luxury. If you've got a full clip, pull the trigger and keep
firing. You'll hit it, one way or the other—hopefully before it hits you.

I hit Ammut with three hollow points. It gave me
enough breathing room to get a split-second look at
what I was shooting at rather than just a greenish blur.
Mythology sketched on a bar napkin said she was part
lion, part alligator, part hippo, and that would have been
a lie because mythology was always a lie. Deduction told
us she had to look human part of the time. That time
wasn't now. No, now she faced me, a glittering coil of
green and bronze scales, the same coil that had yanked
me into the canal. There were arms, appearing disturb-
ingly boneless, and the face was almost lionlike, a blunt
muzzle only finely scaled. The scales on the sleek head
were almost all copper and bronze compared to mixing with the deep green below. I could see how it might
seem like a lion's mane, a shining cascade of tawny glitter, because her eyes were almost all cat too.

Round and gold but with no discernible pupil, they
were clear and luminous as the moon had been in the
night sky of Nevah's Landing. Despite her death-in-
water stench, despite her being a monster, she wasn't
repugnant. She was ... natural, a creature you'd see in
the jungle or slipping into the waters of the Nile. I hadn't
expected that. The spiders were repulsive, because, let's
face it, spiders suck. They're creepy and nasty even

when small, and they need smashing with your boot, but Ammut didn't give off that feeling. If she'd had wings, she would've been a dragon, and I'd just shot that dragon.

Not that she seemed to care. I'd burned through one clip—three rounds in her and the rest in the wall. She was so quick I'd barely seen her at all, much less how she slithered, diving and striking out of the way of the bullets. Her last move had been the quickest, her tail wrapping around my legs. As I pulled at my Glock in its holster with my other hand, she said softly, "Where are your brothers and sisters?" A human voice—a woman's voice; musical and husky, it was almost sexy.

Softer still. Her face was close enough to mine that I could smell her breath. It smelled of flowers, sweetness overlying the rest of her foul scent. "I will not devour you or your companions. You have only to tell me." Closer. *"Where are you brothers and sisters, half-breed?"*

The last words were uttered in a voice not human in the slightest. It was the voice of the Eden serpent. But it wasn't cajoling Eve into taking a bite; it was flat-out telling her to get her naked ass in gear toward that apple tree before he ripped off a mouthful of her nude flesh and shoved it down her throat. That was the snake on me now, and the hypnotic speed and breath drenching the air with a gallon of overwhelming perfume/pheromones was not distracting anymore. It was a sign I'd screwed up. The weight heavy on my legs was a sign too. The sign of my changing all that was the muzzle of the Glock I jammed in one of those round eyes and the trigger I pulled with it.

I didn't get her, not completely. She was that goddamn fast, but I winged the side of her muzzle, bright gold blood spattering. The coils wrapped around my lower legs tightened until I felt the bone seconds from snapping. That I, somewhere from my past, already knew what that felt like didn't make me any happier. I was about to shoot her again, only this time I was smarter. I shot at the one part of her that wasn't moving—her length crushing my legs. I aimed for the edge of the coil. I'd seen—or not seen actually—that impossible speed in action. The last thing I wanted to do was shoot myself in the leg when her snaky self disappeared. Good thing too, because she did disappear and I hit the floor instead of my foot. That didn't mean I stayed on my feet. She hadn't broken my legs, but she'd bruised them and then some. I fell as they gave out beneath me, but that didn't stop me. Four spiders on a beach, even more in my apartment, a boglet too big for his britches; I'd be damned if an overgrown garter snake was going to get the best of me whether I could walk or not.

She streaked past me, seeing all her spiders but one dead, and decided discretion was the better part of valor against a puck, a Wolf, and two highly pissed-off sheep. Smart move. I nailed her in the tip of her twitchy tail with my combat knife, through the flesh, and into the wood of the bottom stair as she slithered up. Smarter move, I smugly congratulated myself . . . until she ripped off the stair and kept going. Motherfu—

Get ahead of her.

Sure. When I could fly.

You know how. Open the door. Your door. It's easy. Easy-peasy pudding and pie. Stomp the snake and watch her die.

I didn't listen to the crazy. I was getting expert at that now, lots of practice. Not to mention the basement door already was open, which was how she was getting away. Instead, I started after her the only way I did know how. Yeah, I was crawling, but I was crawling with a gun, another knife, and one badass attitude. My time wasn't of the Olympic variety but the never-give-up mind-set was. Already at the top of the stairs, she turned and spit. It wasn't the usual villain spitting in disgust at the feet of his enemies. That would've been B movie over-the-top and disgusting, but not as bad as this. This was a spray of something venomous. It wasn't the Nepenthe poison—as the last spider squealed and died impaled on Goodfellow's sword while Delilah, still in wolf form, was tearing the legs off an already-dead one. This was something else. Niko immediately started vomiting as he'd been lunging after Ammut and me. He managed to vomit all over the back of my nonfunctioning legs. I didn't hold a grudge. He owed me one from the canal incident. Delilah spit a spider leg out of her white muzzle and yakked up something best not thought about. Goodfellow turned green and bent over to gag, but managed to hold it back.

Me? I wiped the mist off my face, over my hair, and said, in perhaps not my kindest moment, "Pussies."

Better parts of me surfaced, and I struggled to turn over and pat Niko gingerly on the back, as he'd done for me at the canal and, unfortunately, he suffered the same result I had. Half of me was glad I wasn't a sympathy puker and the other half was getting worried. Niko *was* my brother, my family. He was all I fucking had. "Hey." I squeezed his upper arm instead of the back thing this time. "You need a doctor. I know you said when the spider clawed you that we don't do hospitals—no spreading the supernatural word, but you and I are human. And right now, that's good for you. A hospital can handle an unknown poison." At least they'd better be able to handle it or some white coats would be damn, *damn* sorry.

Whatever I'd said caused Delilah the Wolf to nearly choke on her next yak, and I wasn't sorry at all on that

one. Goodfellow straightened, the green in his face still
there, but he was upright and that was something. "No,
no hospital needed. Ammut's venom isn't like Nepenthe
venom. It's more a defensive mechanism as opposed to
an offensive one. It's not lethal, not even to humans. It'll
wear off in about fifteen to thirty minutes." And some
creatures were more affected than others. Goodfellow
somewhat, Delilah somewhat more, humans . . . It was
the aftermath of a New Year's Eve party. Puke, breathe,
then puke some more.

I couldn't walk, Niko and Delilah were not in prime
fighting condition, and Goodfellow looked as if he had
a case of the flu. He could've gone after her, but he
wouldn't have caught her. She was too quick and if he
had—one person against Ammut wasn't the best way to
keep your friends alive.

So we sat in the basement while Ammut either ran
out of the house in her human form—buck-ass naked,
I assumed, or maybe she wore scales even in human
form—or sped up to the fourth floor of this place, burst
through a top window, and snaked off across the rooftop. I'd take the rooftop if I were her. One more spider slunk out behind Ammut's seven-victim pile, but it
was small and I took care of it with one round. My legs
slowly regained feeling. I stripped off my jacket, then
my shirt—apathy means never having to . . . eh, fuck the
rest—and sacrificed it to Niko's occasional eruptions of
tofu, health shakes, and faux food that didn't belong in
the body anyway. I held his braid out of the way, very
prom date of me, rested a hand on his back, and trusted
Goodfellow. The expression I shot the puck said if that
trust wasn't earned, I'd be strangling him next with a
fluid-stained snarky T-shirt that wasn't that clean to begin with.

Delilah emptied her stomach only twice. Wolves

were tough. Then in a fluid movement of skin and fur, she was human again, crouching close by—close enough that I had my gun pointed at her. She didn't notice she was nude or didn't care. Didn't care, I'd say. She looked proud—as proud as she had as an enormous white wolf straight out of the Arctic. "You are not." Her eyes were as amber when she was human as when she was wolf, but intriguing with their oval tilt. She could've had Japanese Wolf in her, with those eyes and that same amber skin, but the snow blond hair was a trick. Who could say who she was? No one had that right. And who was I to care? She was unique and stunning, as implacably deadly as the edge of my knife, and I wanted nothing to do with her—nothing good.

"You are not. Yet you are. And you know nothing," she said, her voice almost as husky as Ammut's.

A predator. A murderer. A manipulative liar. A killer through and through. I hated her. I did.

But, goddamn, she had the most amazing breasts ever. She put that little red Wolf at the strip club to shame. With the tattooed choker of wolf eyes and Celtic swirls that circled her neck, the vicious scars across her stomach, she twisted me inside and I couldn't say why.

She smiled, her teeth white and even, human, but they'd worn blood in their time, I knew. "*Baa baa*, little boy lost in the woods. Are you a sheep in killer clothing or a killer in sheep clothing? Find out. Soon. Or I will." She was gone almost as quickly as Ammut, snatching up her clothes and taking the stairs three at a time. And, yes, her ass was as amazing as her breasts.

Sometimes it's either shit or go blind. This was one of those times. Horny and hate—two sides of one coin.

Goodfellow and I continued to wait and, when Niko could finally sit up, my legs were sore but functional, and he was a much lighter green than before. He hadn't puked in at least ten minutes. I gripped his shoulder. "You with us, Nik?" I asked. If I sounded concerned, shit, I was. It would be hard to drag a half-dead brother to a hospital while choking the life out of a puck who'd lied to you.

"Cyrano?" My grip tightened. It hadn't been enjoyable watching him struggle against the poison and it had been less enjoyable not knowing what to do about it. Not knowing what I'd do without him, my family—a family I'd gotten attached to way too soon, but some things you couldn't control. I'd looked over my shoulder in Nevah's Landing often enough to know that someone should be there, standing with me. Now that I knew who that was, he was staying there. I didn't care what I had to do to make that happen.

The truth isn't pretty, but it is what it is. And questioning it is a waste of time.

He'd fed me when the woman who whelped me hadn't. He'd clothed me. He'd made me go to school. . . . Okay, that had doubtless sucked. He searched for me when I was lost. He kept me alive when I was drunk and Wolves wanted to eat me. He gave me a home. He hired metaphorical buses so he could not so metaphorically throw himself under them for me. He did all of that for me.

Brothers—it went both ways.

He slowly wiped his mouth on my shirt, then coughed. Finally, he raised his head and rubbed at his bloodshot eyes. "It was nearly worth it to get rid of this offensive T-shirt of yours." He tossed it over the top of the tofu special on the floor. Tofu did not make for fragrant vomit. "I have had much better days than this." More of a graygreen now, he said, "You called me Nik. Then you called me Cyrano." Uneasy, pleased, and then both emotions vanished under a set expression. "Did she hurt you?"

"Drain a little life out of you?" Goodfellow added, sitting on the stairs above me where he'd moved about fifteen minutes ago out of Niko's immediate range, his voice drifting down from behind. "Although you've more than enough to spare. It might improve your attitude. Mellow you somewhat. That's not necessarily a bad thing."

I reached up and smacked his leg hard as I answered Niko. "No. She choked me with a few gallons of perfume, which slowed me down some. It was strong"—almost impossibly so, close to hypnotic—"and after, it was the same old, same old. 'Where are they? Give them to me. Where are your brothers and sisters?'"

Behind, I heard Goodfellow make a noise, unidentifiable, but when I glanced back, he was smooth faced and innocent as a babe again. Right. I gave my attention back to Niko, who had been looking at Robin as well with what was my best guess of puzzlement and dread, but trying to read emotions under green nausea was difficult. "How about we go home? Because I am done with basements. This one or any future ones." We made it up, neither one too steady, but Goodfellow helped and, despite aching legs on my part and a rebelling stomach on Nik's part, we made it upstairs, down the hall, and out the door. I zipped up my jacket to conceal the missing shirt and to keep from freezing my ass off as Goodfellow flagged down a taxi.

Niko was alive, Goodfellow was alive, I was alive, and Delilah was gone. As things went, that put us on the plus side of the scoreboard. The fact that no one was curious why I hadn't gotten sick wasn't discussed. They also hadn't commented—very cautiously hadn't commented—on my not being curious as to why Ammut's poison hadn't made me all but vomit my stomach then intestines up . . . as it had Niko, as it would a human. I didn't bring it up either. They didn't want to have to answer, and I didn't want to ask. I didn't want to hear Niko have to make up another lie—that her perfume had protected me by canceling out the poison and that being bitten by her spider had inoculated me against other poisons of the Ammut kind. He would've come up with something. No, I didn't want to ask.

Let sleeping dogs lie.

Listen to Wolves such as Delilah who don't always lie.

Stop lying to yourself.

Half-breed, Ammut had whispered. Twice now, she'd said that. *Half-breed*, and that made me important to her, a monster that thought people weren't worth eating. She needed me to find others like me, those half-breed brothers and sisters—whoever they were, wherever they might be. Brothers and sisters Niko, I was positive, knew nothing about. The look he had given Goodfellow had said as much.

Half-breed.

I *was* half human. I was Niko's brother, so I must be. Had to be.

But, Jesus, what was the other half?

was reason enough. I'd already popped some Tylenol for the residual ache in my legs. "But, hey, whatever. Fun, new knowledge . . . about the correct name of where gladiators could put their dicks if they were out of other options."

"In Rome, you always had options." His wicked smile was enough to have me bolting for the door as he started talking on the phone again.

"Cal, I told you I didn't want you going out alone, not when Ammut obviously knows who you are and where to watch for you." Niko stopped his workout. He was still paler than someone with his darker skin should be and the blond hair was almost brown from sweat. He looked sick, better, but still sick, and I kept that in mind.

"It's broad daylight," I protested. I'd showered—for a vegetarian, Niko could vomit with the best of them—and now I was back in fresh jeans and a black T-shirt. Just black. I'd run through all my clean and barely passable as clean T-shirts with nasty sayings that came courtesy of Goodfellow's gift certificate, and had borrowed one of Nik's shirts. Or stolen it, let's be honest.

"And we were only just attacked in broad daylight," he said, extra slowly in case I'd missed that fact.

"Inside. I plan on staying outside where all the world can see. I have a hunch about Ammut I want to check out. You need to get better and you have only hours to do it. I'll be back in no time." From the sweat he ignored running down his face, he wasn't convinced. He squinted his eyes at the flow, like Clint Eastwood . . . damn macho. The sweat did not exist; only me and my idiocy did. "I'll even bring back some Pepto. Have you in the pink in no time." I grinned and was out the door before his poison-weakened body could lay a beat-down on me . . . or a sit-down. That was more likely. He'd tackle me and sit on my back until I came to my senses.

Unfortunately, the senses I was coming to weren't what he wanted, and I slammed the door behind me, sprinting down the block as fast as my sore legs could carry me. Neither he nor Robin came after me. I'd trusted them in the past week, more than I'd have guessed I could trust anyone when I'd woken up in Nevah's Landing. Now it was their turn, and they came through. Without trust, in our world—my world now— you had nothing. It made me feel kind of bad that I'd lied like a dog to them and lied better than Niko had to me since he'd shown up in my lost life. That answered that question. It definitely made him the better brother.

I had no plans on staying outside and I had no hunches, gut feelings, nothing like that about Ammut. I did have them about someone else, which was why I went back to the museum to see the mummy . . . Wahanket? I'd done something to him, something bad, something that kept trying to claw its way out of the pit in my memory that Niko's nepenthe potion had shoved it into. And it wasn't only that, with every new hour I had more and more memories leaking into my brain; dirty dishwater into a sponge. Dirty, because shadowed Cal in that shadowed photo wasn't clean, but that wasn't my judgment call to make. That wasn't my job; being a brother was. Here was hoping Wahanket didn't hold a grudge.

Sangrida—I remembered her name, which was helpful—was equally helpful in walking me past security again and escorting me to the correct basement door. I thought I was done with basements after Ammut, but they weren't done with me. "Why is your brother not with you?" Her blond hair was pulled back into a tight, elaborate braid that looped around her head. She was Princess Leia—with a bleach job and a bucketful of steroids.

"Ammut," I explained. "Nik's okay, but he needs to stick close to the toilet. Hurling issues."

Apparently Goodfellow wasn't the only one with Too Much Information syndrome. She sighed, her massive bosom heaving. On other women it would've been breasts, melons, tits, whatever, but on her, it was bosom. If I forgot that—of all the things I'd forgotten from the last museum memory, this was a thought that still echoed—I was positive a size-eleven Valkyrie boot would end up in my ass. It was a bosom, to be respected, not stared at, and, yeah, maybe I'd go on down the stairs while she was studying me, contemplating God or Odin knew what. I did know that I did not want to end up as Thor's bitch in Valhalla. "Thanks, ma'am," I said hurriedly, and went down the steps faster. A mummy versus a Valkyrie—I'd take the first any day.

There was a basement, then a subbasement, and it was somewhat familiar. Unfortunately, the familiar was of the where-the-fuck-is-he kind. Wahanket liked his privacy and that made finding him difficult; I remembered that—I did, a genuine flash of recalled annoyance. This time I worked on sniffing him out. Although there were quite a few things down there that smelled mummified, the largest one was the one I tracked down. It was a strong scent of mummy and . . . barbecue.

He hadn't moved from last time. I remembered that too—the large space. The computers mixed with Egyptian artifacts. The mummified cats perched on surrounding crates towering high. Salomes wherever you looked. Pooh . . . the koala bear, I meant, was still dead on a metal table. Long dead and no longer undead and that was good. Then I got a look at Wahanket and figured out why he hadn't moved to a new undiscovered location.

He was a torso.

Granted, a torso with a head and one arm, but, basically, a torso.

Yeah, now I remembered. I remembered the axe.

The other arm and two legs were neatly stacked in a pile on the floor and beside that was a large curved needle strung with wire, the same wire that was holding that one arm on with neat stitching at the shoulder. As soon as Wahanket saw me, the arm dragged the body behind an Egyptian bench of some kind and blackened teeth bared as the mummy hissed at me. I'd done a bad thing to him all right. Part of me felt every bit like the monster he was, part of me didn't give a damn, and another part of me felt as if the cats were cheering me on.

And yet another part of me chose to ignore the shadows that grew around me. They were my shadows, and I was done denying or refusing that.

"Hank, it looks like a helluva craft project you've got going on." I pulled up a chair, gold with smooth pieces of inlaid blue, red, and black stone. Sitting, I spread my legs some, took out a knife in one hand—I didn't see a gun doing much good—and patted my knee with the other. In seconds a mummified cat was draped across the denim, making a grinding, grumbling growl of pure bliss. Where Salome was gray and hairless, had lost all her bandages, and was sporting a small gold and ruby hoop earring, this guy—and it was a tomcat with shriveled, mummified balls—was mostly wrapped. But between the yellowed bandages, the skin was paler in spots and almost black in others. It was spotted like a piebald pony.

"How you doing there, Spartacus?" The first to step forward, he got the name—so sayeth the movie. I rubbed between his ears. Goodfellow knew everything and everyone—Captain Cook, Ramses, the Pied Piper, and even Caligula, he'd once said. I couldn't quite hear the echo of that particular memory, but I knew it. Chances were he'd known Spartacus in the day too . . . and had that movie cued up on his DVR and ready to go at all

times. Plus, Salome might be less inclined to bite off my
head if I brought her a friend.

"You did this. You did this to me, you empty vessel.
Worthless and weak." The mouthy mummy remained
pretty crispy too. Niko . . . Niko had set him on fire.
That was what had happened. It wouldn't destroy him,
he'd said. It wouldn't hurt either, only slow him down.
Good informants were hard to find; he'd said that too.
Wahanket would survive it, and he had. Then I'd come
along—me and a convenient fire axe. He'd survived that
as well, but that impression . . . It would be a little more
lasting.

That was the first time I'd seen the shadows and felt
the pain inside. That was the first time my brother had
drugged me. Niko had also said the mummy had once
tried to shoot me and before I'd made with the axe, he
had tried to strangle me as I'd deprived him of something. Wahanket had been clear. I'd had something he'd
wanted, but I'd lost it. But what was that something?
The same thing Ammut wanted? The same quality
the boggles and Wolves thought I was missing? Creep,
creep, came the memories, but not fast enough—not as
fast as Ammut was moving.

Now was the time to find out the why of all those
things. That was why I'd come back to Wahanket. He
knew who I was—what I was—and he was going to tell
me. I wasn't waiting on the Nepenthe venom to wear off
on this. This was something I might not want to know,
but I needed to know. Ammut had proved too dangerous to the others to let things take their natural course.

Wahanket, professional disperser of information, was
going to tell me all those things I didn't want to hear
about Cal, but I needed to, because Cal was far more
likely to be able to handle Ammut than I was. Cal would
be able to protect his family and friend when I might not

be able to. The first night in Nevah's Landing, I'd turned out the light and slept in the darkness, because, while monsters lived in darkness, so did killers.

I'd guessed killer for me. I thought now I'd guessed wrong.

"I don't think I'm as empty as you thought." I sniffed the air. "You smell Extra Crispy. I'd have taken you for an Original Recipe guy, but you never know." Spartacus wrapped his paws around my wrist and proceeded to chew away mouthfuls of the rugged, water-stained black leather jacket and spit them on the floor. "You never goddamn know. Take another look at me, Wahanket, and tell me what I was and what I'm becoming again. Tell me or I'll chop you into pieces so small you won't be able to stitch yourself back together with your teeth, because I'll pound them to dust. And whatever you have that passes for lips, I'll rip off. Your gums . . . hmm. What the fuck. I'll just pop your head in a box and toss it in the East River. See how that affects your sewing project. Home Ec. What a bitch, huh?"

Spartacus agreed by tearing off half my jacket sleeve. Oh yeah, this destructive little shit was going straight to Goodfellow. For all the torment he'd caused me, the puck deserved it. Salome might kill things and people; this guy would kill an apartment—more specifically Goodfellow's penthouse.

Wahanket's marsh-light eyes sharpened as they fixed on me. "You are correct. You are becoming again." The teeth snapped in a satisfied smile . . . or mummy constipation; it was a hard expression to read. "You shall be you again, and if Ammut does not have you, one day I will."

I tickled Spartacus's stomach and the cat opened his mouth to show me a preview of *Jaws 15*, the IMAX version. Luckily, it was a yawn. "Yeah, I'm bored too, buddy.

Now where did I leave that axe?" I didn't ask as a threat. I asked out of genuine curiosity. I *was* bored. I was done playing around with this barbecued son of a bitch. Playing with something that can't run or even crawl—where was the challenge in that? "Who am I, Wahanket? And if you don't cough up something in the next five seconds, you'll have to write down the information I want, because I'm going to cut out your tongue."

Wahanket pulled himself up onto the ancient bench, lying on his chest to watch me. He wasn't bored at all. "Do not worry. I shall tell all you wish to know. The meat tastes sweeter when it knows why it was chosen, flavored with the disbelief that any could bring it down. Despair and disbelief, nothing teases the palate so much as those." Gold flakes had transferred to the bench into the blackened flesh of his hand. I could see the spark of them, a starry night, when he pointed at me. "You . . . You are Auphe."

That was what the boglet had said. I was off, that wasn't news. I was absolutely off. But the word wasn't completely that. It was somewhere in the middle of "Off" and "Ouph-fey." A human tongue couldn't exactly replicate it. But I could see the word in my head, dripping with black bile, smelling of blood, part of me. *In* every part of me.

I was Auphe.

Always had been, always would be. A word made of screams and slaughter, murder and madness, albino pale skin, red eyes, the shine of hypodermic-needle teeth— more needles than a hospital would need in a month. White, red, and metal, like my Peter Pan crocodile.

Here you have brothers and sisters. Baby boy, baby boy.

The shadows grew wider around me, but I didn't stop. I did have a brother. Not one that a crocodile had given

me, but a real one, and he needed the real Cal. And real
or not, Cal or not . . . I kept my promises. I told Niko
I'd be his brother and there was only one way to do
that—by bringing Cal home. "Auphe," I said with a distance so great that I may as well have been on the moon.
"Who are the Auphe?"

"Were. Who were the Auphe?" One of the flakes of
gold fell from his hand to the floor. A speck of the sun
falling to Earth, a soul falling much farther. "They are
all gone now, except for you, half-breed. But once they
were the first."

"The first what?"

"The first of anything. The first of everything. They
were the first to walk this world. They were the first to
kill simply for pleasure. They invented murder, created
torture, conceived terror. This world was theirs for millions of years." The yellow glow softened. "So very long
ago, when Death itself bowed to its masters."

"They set the gold star standard for nightmares like
you. Great. How did I get to be one? Half of one?" Because one of them damn sure hadn't been trolling for a
good time and met up with Sophia. Easy or not, she had
to have some limits.

*The gold is gone, and you're still here, brat. You're still
goddamn here.*

Or not. Sometimes a whore is a whore to feed herself
and her children. Sometimes it's for drugs or rent or because it's her body to do with as she pleases. And sometimes someone like my mother sets a gold star standard
of her own. They'd paid her to make me . . . not to have
me. You have babies; you *make* monsters. I'd been an
experiment; I knew it. I *knew* it. I didn't know why yet,
why the Auphe would want a half-breed, but the hell
with the how and the why of it. That was coming fast and
furious on its own, clawing up through my subconscious.

I'd know, whether I was ready or not, and I didn't need this asshole to tell me that.

"I'm a monster then, like Ammut?"

Wahanket laughed. It sounded as if he were choking on his own mummified organs, if he hadn't removed them. "No, you are not a monster like Ammut. Ammut will be a child in your shadow when you return. Ammut is simply a creature like any other creature, eating to live. Enjoying meals that taste especially finer than others, as you would taste. She kills to survive. You . . . Auphe . . . You are the only monster in the world. We all pale before you." He clacked his teeth together. "Which is why you are a challenge; why your life will taste the most flavorful of all there is."

This piece of shit was sewing himself back together for one reason only—to get his own chance of sucking me dry of Auphe. To make a meal of someone and something he should never have fucked with from day one. Informants are difficult to come by, eh? Then we'd have to try harder. This one had answered his last question, although he had told me what I required. Cal, the real one, could handle Ammut. It was all I needed to know.

I put the mummified cat down and I found that axe.

When I was finished, I didn't need to put his head in a box. A hundred skull fragments weren't going to knit a Christmas sweater or put themselves back together again. I dropped the axe in the midst of a pile of shattered bone, cracked resin, and one very ex-mummy. "The first," I said to the remnants. "I'm one of the First of this world." They invented murder, created torture, conceived terror, he'd said.

"Invent, create, conceive, and you wanted to screw with that. You should've thought about what the First would do to you instead of what you would do to it."

Bone crunched under my boot. "And you, mighty Wa-hanket, were barely worth the fucking time."

When I turned to leave, I felt a weight thud onto my shoulder. Spartacus rubbed his bedraggled, bandaged head against mine with the same death-by-avalanche purr that Salome had. "I'm not leaving you, Kojak. I have a better home for you. In fact . . ." The eyes still glowed on top of the crates. Wahanket had made pets, but he hadn't made any friends. Not one had inter-fered in his destruction. There were what looked like ten mummy cats watching me watching them. "Eh, why not? If Goodfellow is so oversexed that he can't put his damn pants on to answer the door, he deserves what he gets. Come on, guys. Get your wrinkly King Tut tails in gear and let's show a trickster what trickery and revenge are all about."

One of the best things about NYC . . . An ex-but-soon-to-be-again monster can walk down the sidewalk surrounded by a bunch of loping dead cats, catch a cab with an extra fifty thrown in by calling himself a vet stu-dent with some patients in dire need of bandage chang-ing, make an extra stop, and not long after that be back home. I opened the door, sat on the couch, grabbed the remote, and turned on the TV.

Niko was now in the kitchen, showered and mixing something that would not only eradicate any Ammut toxins remaining, but probably anything living at all. "Where did you go?"

"Wouldn't you like to know, Mom?" I changed the channel. "Oh, hey, Robin." He had started talking about tonight's party when I'd left for the museum and he was still on his cell phone, making plans for the catering, talking a mile a minute, when I'd returned. If Ammut ate us, that would be one big, fat wasted catering bill.

"You'd better shut off your phone and get your ass back home. I left you a present."

He brightened, a magpie at the sight of a shiny coin. "A present? I love presents. I can't believe you, especially you, actually got me . . . Oh, *skata*. What am I thinking?" He jammed the phone in his pocket, grabbed his coat, and was out the door before I made it to the next channel.

"What did you do?" Niko demanded, turning off the blender. "What did you get him?"

I held up one arm that was missing three-fourths of what had been a tough, thick leather jacket sleeve and grinned at him. "Eleven dead cats. The doorman thought it was hilarious. I don't think he likes Robin much. And I think the condo board is meeting as we speak to discuss enforcing pet limits with a subcommittee looking into pet aesthetics. Not everyone can be Best in Show or win beauty pageants. Stuck-up asses."

"Buddha save us." From the glance he gave the blender and then me, he was entertaining the thought of throwing the contents at me. "You took Wahanket's mummy cats. Why?"

I shrugged, turned back towards the TV, and changed channels again. "Well, first off, he was a malicious evil shit who killed cats to make mummies out of them. That is beyond sick. They deserved a better home."

"Don't tell me you just said, 'He *was* a malicious evil shit.' "

"That would be reason two." I clicked off the TV. "No one needs an informant like that. I don't care how hard it is to find one. He tried to shoot me, strangle me, wanted to eat me, and he was a cat killer. The first three I could deal with. Cat killer, no." I peeled off the ruined jacket and tossed it over the back of the couch. Twisting again, I could see the kitchen area where Niko was thinking. I could see the quicksilver motion behind his eyes and all but hear the hum. Wheels turning, and it was a few hours too soon for that.

I tried to distract him. "Since you found me, Niko, tried to show me who I was"—and keep me who I wasn't, I thought—"you've been something for me to shoot for. You walk the straight and narrow. You're a good man, best man I've known in my whole week now. But you're a good man in a job where good is a drawback. You've made allowances, excuses, and you've made them, I know, for what you thought were the right reasons. Let a cat killer live; maybe get information to save other lives. But, Nik, when you do wrong, the reason is never right enough." It was a difficult concept to grasp as the shadows wrapped around me, but I did. For now . . . I still did. Cal wouldn't, but I did. Then again, I might be underestimating Cal. For himself, he might never know, but for his brother . . . I thought he did. Niko had his honor, and I would've guessed Cal would do anything to let him hold on to it. Who's to say a monster can't love his brother?

"*You* are lecturing *me*?" Niko sounded as if that would knock him flat before his toxic milk shake would.

"I've seen the T-shirts I bought myself for Christmas. I've seen the way Wolves and others act around me. If there's something to be done, something in the gray area," the dark areas . . . darkest of the dark, "I think that's my half of the partnership." I was proud of that choosy phrasing. "Think," not "know"—and I did know.

If wrong had to be done, I would do it. One of the First, born of the First, and living in the shadow and the murk. As the details of my life grew less and less sketchy, I knew that all of his life Niko had protected me. I'd done the same for him when I was old enough to, and I'd keep doing the same. I would let him be who he was by being who I truly was or had been. I would step into those shadows for the last and final time to let Niko step back into the light where he belonged.

Right now, shadows or not, I was hungry. I got up and made a sandwich, all while Niko continued to watch me, a distinct aura of suspicion overcoming the odor of the sludge in his untouched glass. "You said you'd stay outside. You lied to me."

I raised my eyebrows at the last remark, which took real balls for him to actually say, what with all he was trying to keep from me. I chewed my bite of peanut butter and jelly without comment. It was enough to have Niko drinking his sludge. Ninjas in glass houses . . .

I finished and changed the nonsubject. "Goodfellow said we'd need formal wear for the party. What's formal wear?"

"You are dead to me. No, you are worse than dead. The worst thing I can do to you is let you live to make every minute of every day of the rest of your life an eternal hell."

When he opened his door this time, Goodfellow was dressed—in a way. With wavy hair standing on end and a ratty bandage draped over it, he was wearing an expensive, a given there, tux—James Bond style. I could admit, masculinity intact, that it was pretty sharp, or it had been once. Now it was missing one pant leg from the knee down, one arm at the shoulder, and there was a mummy cat hanging from his shredded tie.

Spartacus showed his garbage-disposal teeth in a grin at me as he swung from the cloth strip that was meant to be knotted in a bow tie around the puck's neck. "Spartacus, hey, pal, are you telling Robin how to dress?"

"You named it. You actually named it, and you named it Spartacus. Zeus, I hate you." He stalked off, Spartacus hanging in there happily. Inside the penthouse, the contour couch was now a scrap pile of leather, stuffing, and wood. The walls were clawed until they formed the optical illusion of the bars of a prison cell. A once highly expensive rug was about a thousand pieces of cloth mixed with strips of frayed bandages scattered about the place, and undead cats lounged everywhere. Salome perched on top of that giant refrigerator with dimly glowing eyes crossed in pleasure—a queen overseeing her domain and her new minions. It was only right. Every power-mad villain merited minions.

Ishiah, his tux in one piece, closed the door behind us. "This wasn't the brightest thing you could have done, Caliban. Robin is one of the best, if not *the* best, tricksters in this world. Are you familiar with the Greek tale of *Oedipus Rex*? It wasn't simply a story. It was truth. There were two prophecies. Robin had nothing to do with the first or the second, but when chariot rage, the original road rage, ended in murder, he did arrange for the rest of the prophecy to come true. Marrying mothers, jabbing out eyes with golden hairpins, suicide. All three members of that royal family were murderers or potential ones. Tricksters don't care for either. That was only a job to him. Justice. This"—he waved an arm at the inside of the penthouse and twenty-four avid yellow eyes followed the movement—"is personal."

I'd felt my own eyes cross the same as Salome's, but mine was in boredom, not pleasure. "Sorry. I missed most of that. Oedipus Rex . . . Was that a dinosaur? Like a *T. rex*?"

"I may as well post the ad for your replacement now." He followed the puck. "Your tuxes are in both bathrooms. If your 'gifts' haven't eaten them."

He flipped me off when I called after him gravely. "Adoption is love. I saw that on the side of a bus, so it's gotta be true."

"That wasn't very angellike," I added as I watched the finger disappear with him.

"Understandable, since he isn't one." Niko went for the first bathroom. "And if Robin does cause you to blind yourself with anything from an antique hairpin to a banana, I will have no sympathy."

All the cats purred louder as I walked through them. At least they were happy to see me. Dogs didn't like me and I'd figured out why now. Nothing could smell a twisted genetic product like a Wolf or a dog . . . but cats didn't have a problem with me. After all, they played with their victims. No rush to judgment there.

I found the other bathroom, only because the door was open. I wasn't opening any closed doors here. Seeing wet feathers in the massive whirlpool tub was enough to have me dressing so quickly, I tucked the shirt into my underwear instead of my pants. The tux was all right, black on black—with no tie of any kind. Goodfellow definitely knew me there, but Miss Terrwyn would've again been shaking her head at my vampire-looking, silly white boy self. Except that vampires existed, and I wasn't white. My skin was pale, but it hadn't come from being some British-Scottish-Irish-German-American mutt. I'd gotten that from the Auphe; otherwise I'd have been a pale brown like Niko . . . or our mother.

Born of the first murderers to walk the earth *and* unable to get a goddamn tan. Welcome to my world.

It was enough to make me wish for the whole amnesia enchilada back and not the half-and-half I had now. But wishes weren't promises, and tainted genes or not, I was keeping that promise to Nik. It didn't matter that he didn't know I'd made it. I knew, and that was enough.

I'd woken up in water, sand, and dead spiders with a deep hatred of monsters. Then I found out I was one. I hadn't seen anything that addressed that on the side

of a bus—only the adoption ad. Adoption and love—
good stuff, but self-worth? You were on your own there.
Ammut thought I had worth anyway and then some.
Here was hoping she'd show up and tell me all about it.
I opened the bathroom door back up to face cold ruth-
less eyes not quite an inch from mine. Ammut's?

Worse.

They were Goodfellow's.

"Do you know there are things . . . No, there are words,
actual, simple *words*—I'm reasonably positive that I could
trim them down to six total—that I could say to you that
would make you unable to function sexually for five
years? Even with yourself?"

Whoa. "You're a witch?" Couldn't be. There was no
magic in the world. Monsters, yes. Magic, no. It was one
of those things I did know instinctually without anyone
telling me.

"No, Caliban. I'm not. I'm merely extremely knowl-
edgeable in the psychosexual fields and I'm also very,
very vindictive."

"Um . . . Niko? You out there?" I backed up a step
and Goodfellow followed, maintaining the exact lack of
distance.

"Remember Alexander the Great? Not that great,
especially when he poisoned my friend. What's good
for the gander is . . . good for the gander." He smiled.
It was the first of his smiles I'd seen that wasn't sly or
wicked. It was goddamn scary. "Then there was Genghis
Khan. He should've paid more attention to the blade I
gave his kidnapped princess and the ingenious place she
was hiding it and less to killing every male child as tall
as his steppe pony's shoulder. The princess was a nice
woman and didn't like child killers any more than I do.
Ah, and who do you think said, 'Release the Kraken'?
That horny rapist named Zeus? Hardly. He was always

trying to steal my thunder." Two more steps in perfect synchronization—me back, him forward.

"And then there's you—you who released the equivalent of the Ten Plagues on my home. Can you imagine what I plan on doing to you?"

"Nik!"

"Yes?" Nik was behind Robin, his hand on the puck's shoulder. "Do we have a problem?"

"I think Goodfellow wants to poison me, stab me with a knife I'd prefer sterilized first, then make me watch a god-awful, bad-special-effects movie from the eighties." I slid past him before he tried to escape Niko's hand. "I could've stabbed you with that fork, you know," I told the puck, "but I didn't. And with the cats, I saved lives . . . unlives . . . whatever, and this is the thanks I get. Bastard."

"You could've left them with Wahanket," Goodfellow snapped.

That flipped a switch in me. Cheerful and dark. From the feel of it on my face, my smile was the mirror of what the puck's had been—goddamn scary. "In spirit maybe. But the only thing useful with Wahanket anymore is a DustBuster and a Ouija board." I put the smile away. It wasn't for them. I was saving it for Ammut. "And you'll be able to find homes for them. Every rich vamp will want his own mummified cat. Except Spartacus. He stays here. He's for Salome."

"And how precisely do you figure that?"

I kept Niko between him and me. "Spartacus likes me. Salome wants to eat me. Okay, she doesn't eat. Kill me. Whatever. If Salome likes Spartacus, I have it made. He's my wingman to peace and not being eaten."

"You are truly pathetic." Goodfellow shook his head, but he lost his bad humor or switched it to a new source when he saw my shoes. "You are not wearing black sneakers with a Brioni tux. I won't allow it. I won't be seen within a mile of you."

"If Ammut is there, I plan on some running. Those shoes you gave me—nice for looking at my reflection, but they suck for running."

"I think it's time for the party. The discussion about history-making vengeance and foot apparel can take place later," Niko interrupted. "I do have a date, and it's not Ammut, waiting for me there."

That date was Promise, the sad vampire. It sounded like a children's book. Promise, the sad velvet vampire—won't you be her friend? I dimly remembered why she was so solemn now. Her kid . . . Her daughter had died. No . . . That wasn't quite it. Think, think. Ah. Her daughter had been killed—by Niko. Yeah, that was right. Her daughter had been a true nightmare of a creature. She'd done things that not only were unforgivable but also not survivable, depending on whom she did them to. She'd done those things to us all, but most particularly to Nik. Promise had raised a monster beyond redemption.

Why was I sure Niko was incapable of doing the same?

Nature versus nurture.

Genes versus a determined big brother, with fish sticks and Scooby Doo cartoons, who'd taken care of you from your first breath.

Which wins?

After we met Promise at her place, then took her chauffeured car to the Tribeca Grand, the first thing I did when we made it past the doormen, all four of whom looked with disdain at my shoes, I pulled her aside. "Can I talk to you for a second?"

She waved Niko back with a small flick of plum-colored oval nails in a motion so minute that I barely saw it. I wished I had him trained half that well, but then again the rewards were vastly different. "What is it, Caliban? Are you doing better? Niko has been not very forthcoming on the subject." That irritated her. I could tell by the rapid touch of her fingers checking her hair. The brown and blond was swept up into some sort of something that probably had a complicated name I didn't have a clue about, but Promise wasn't the nervous, fidgety type. She was the still pond, the unmoving stone, the unchanging mountain—the same as Niko. Like for like.

If she was irritated, it was because she'd been left in the dark, and not the kind vampires cared for either. "You don't know. He didn't tell you." Across the massive foyer, Niko, fidgeting himself, gave a careful smooth to the front of his own tux. Two Zen peas in a Zen pod.

"Tell me what?"

Her eyes, violet before, were now dark purple with concern. They were the same color as the dress she wore that fell to the floor, the flash of the same color reflected in the black pearls wrapped around her neck. Such an . . . I don't know . . . elegant woman. Not for my kind, but for Niko, yes. He deserved her, and I didn't want to hurt her, but I needed to know. If I was wrong, many more people than Promise would get hurt. "You didn't know he started drugging me a few days ago? With the Nepenthe venom? Trying to keep all my old memories gone for good? He's been trying to keep me . . . shit, happy, I guess."

"Without telling you? No. He wouldn't do that," she denied, her head shaking in the negative instantly. "Niko's honesty is . . . insurmountable. Trust me. I lied to him once and that was all but the end of us."

I came close to remembering that too, but it wasn't important, not now. "And what would he tell me, Promise? What reason would he give me for getting me to take the drug voluntarily? What's the truth he doesn't want me to know?"

She looked away for a moment, then back and remained silent. Goodfellow and Ishiah had been willing to give me clues, but she was completely loyal to Niko. I didn't mind. In fact, I preferred it.

"I don't want to ask you this," I continued, "particularly since I only half remember knowing you, but I have to. It's coming back, all of it—mainly because Niko is a shade less smart than he thinks he is at drugging people and because part of me has been breaking through all along, even when drugged. But that's a small part." I took her hand. It was warm and why wouldn't it have been? Vampires were alive, not dead. Born, not made. I remembered. I turned it over and traced the lifeline. It didn't look any different from mine. "Niko has taken care of me my entire life, from diaper one." I quirked my lips. "And I'll always do the same for him, but I can do that better the way I was before." The way I was close to being now. "I know that. But what I need to know is, in the end, is it worth it? Or am I like your daughter was? Am I beyond redemption? If I try to save Nik, will I end up doing . . . things? Bad things? Things he couldn't live with?" Things he couldn't let me live with. "You raised a monster, Promise. You know one when you see one." I looked at Niko again. "Am I a monster worth its life because I can save my brother's? Or am I just a monster—period?"

She took her hand from mine, cupped my cheek, and as Niko had been constantly doing to himself for me, she threw me under the bus for him. It was symmetry. "You do whatever needs to be done to save Niko. You do that, Caliban. You do anything. Do you hear me?"

In a way, it was the answer I'd been looking for, but not the reassurance I'd wanted. That was life. With the good came the bad. It was all about balance.

I knew she loved him, though, which made it better. She loved him more than she loved anything or anyone. Good for him. Good for them both. I held out my arm. "Is this how they do it? I've seen it on TV."

She slid her hand into the crook of my elbow, already having second thoughts. "Cal, I shouldn't have. . . ."

"I won't tell him." If I did, that would indeed be the end of them. It wouldn't be very brotherly, and it wouldn't be right. "What's to tell? With my memory?" I grinned. "You're good for him, Promise. Better than I'll ever be. We were just talking about you adopting a mummy cat. That's all."

"A what? A mummy . . ." Goodfellow walked up in time to hear her confused remark.

"Ah, good. I'll pick out a nice one for you. Two would probably be better. To keep each other company, less bored, less inclined to kill your neighbors. Would you prefer male or female? Not that it matters. Death and mummification are the ultimate spay and neuter program. I'll have someone drop them off at your place tomorrow, should we survive tonight."

Niko took Promise's other arm and led her away from the dead-cat discussion. Since I'd come back, he hadn't had much time with her and I knew why. He'd expected honesty from her. How could he then be with her when he was being anything but honest even to himself?

A conscience . . . More and more they seemed a pain in the ass.

Goodfellow, Ishiah, and I watched them go, dark blond head bent to the brown/blond one. "She looks like a tiger with that hair," I mused.

"And she'll eat you like a tiger if you piss her off one-fifth as much as you've pissed me off," Robin growled.

I gave him a narrow-eyed glance and an equally

narrow smile. "Do you really want to play, puck? I can make the time."

Surprise flashed behind his eyes and as quickly was gone. Pucks were much better than my brother at playing a part, and he didn't want to have to tell Niko the show was over. That he gladly would let me do. "You're back then?"

My smile—only half of what I'd pretended it was, I hoped—widened. "About seventy, seventy-five percent." I hooked an arm around his neck and squeezed, messing up his tie and collar mostly on purpose. "I missed remembering you, you horny bastard. Besides, think about it. Would a 'good' Cal dump eleven dead cats in your apartment? Or turn Wahanket into a dust pile that could double as an ant condo?"

"*Good* Cal tried to stab me with a fork," Robin pointed out as he tried to straighten his tie, but he didn't shake off my arm. Before Nik and I had shown up, and before Ishiah had come around to admit his own stupidity, Robin hadn't had many friends—any friends. There were prejudiced bastards even among the supernatural kind. Tricksters weren't favorites by any means.

"Good Cal thought you were a monster," I reminded him. "Now I know what a monster is."

"Ammut?" Ishiah standing beside us murmured, and although I couldn't see the wings, I heard them rustle.

"Her too." But she wasn't the only one. I let go of Goodfellow and straightened my suit jacket to feel the weight of my weapons in place. I smelled her all right. She was here, and my grin now? I didn't think there was a word for it. Not in these modern days. Not anymore. The first to invent, create, conceive. The first to smile for all the wrong reasons.

"Come on, guys," I said. "Let's go kick some Egyptian ass."

13

The penthouse party was the same as all penthouse parties—this being my second, which made me an expert. It was fancy; everyone was rich and snooty; it had great views of the Manhattan skyline; there was food . . . absolutely fantastic food. I'd taken over a platter of bacon, mushroom, and crab bits I couldn't begin to pronounce but could eat by the bucketful, and I was hoarding the platter for myself.

"Does Niko know you're almost you again?"

"Can you picture the invisible cross he's dragging around on his back," I asked, "hear the splish-splash of Pontius Pilate lathering up with hand sanitizer?"

"Yes."

"That'd be a no then," I snorted.

"Blasphemy," Ishiah muttered under his breath at my exchange with Robin as a feather wafted out of nowhere to land in Goodfellow's wineglass.

"I'm beginning to have serious doubts about this nonangel crap you peris are spouting." Other than that comment, I went back to concentrating on the room. Ammut was here. I had the musty corpse taste of her in the back of my throat, under the bacon, but the entire room reeked of Wolves, vamps, other supers who could pass for human, and humans themselves soaked in perfume or cologne.

That was what Delilah had meant when she'd said I didn't need to wear my cologne. I had that spray Robin had given me last year to cover up my Auphe smell from Wolf noses when I'd meet to hook up with Delilah. I hadn't used it in a long time now. When she'd smelled me in that stairwell at her attempted massacre of our clients, she'd been smelling the mostly human me; the Auphe part of me had been on vacation—gone fishing, buried, or busy.

My best guess was the Auphe in the rest of my genes had become more or less dormant while the ones in the memory portion of my brain—if Niko had been there, he would've provided the medical word for that—had become hyperactive trying to repair the venom damage. All my Auphe channeled its energy to that one area. For a while, I was more human than I'd ever been in my entire life.

Or would ever be again.

The Auphe immune system wasn't like a human one, it was far more efficient and goal-oriented, or there had been many things over my life that I wouldn't have survived. Those were thoughts for other times though. For now, I was sticking with the original problem—Ammut and her arachnid posse.

Above the penthouse was the rooftop terrace, which was essential. Half the guests were human and taking out monsters was a private thing unless we wanted a shitload of humans convinced they'd been slipped some illegal hallucinogenic. Or we'd have a shitload of dead humans because the Wolves and vamps were certain to make sure the humans wouldn't be spreading the news of the supernatural—who were natural and not super at all. Either way, shit was involved and it was far too much trouble. That was why we had the terrace. . . . It was prime cage-fighting territory, minus the cage, with the addition of the possibility of falling to a splattery death on the sidewalk far below.

Eh. Details.

Speaking of Wolves and vamps, we were quickly surrounded by them. One Wolf made a move on my platter of bacon goodies. I growled. He snapped, and I snapped back. He was in completely human form, a high breed—no All Wolf for him—and I looked as human as anyone else, but no matter how human we both looked, snapping at each other like hungry bears over a platter of hors d'oeuvres drew a bit of attention.

"Stop it. Be good. No treats for you tonight," Goodfellow hissed at the two of us. The Wolf had brown hair pulled back into a short ponytail and ice blue eyes. Average, ordinary, if not for the eyes. If you saw past the unusually pale eyes and smelled what lay beneath, then you'd know much more. He was an Alpha, a big and bad one. "We are wolves amidst the sheep, but the sheep rule this world now. Don't forget it," the puck warned.

The vamps, including Promise, who was standing with Niko, looked resigned at the food-aggressive behavior as they gathered around us. Puppies, always piddling on the carpet, always making a mess, always wanting attention. In the spirit of unity, I let the Wolf take a handful off my platter. "Yeah, like you fang manglers never fought over food . . . while it was still kicking and screaming," I said with scorn to the other vamps around us. At least the Wolves were honest about it. You'd think the vamps never ordered their steak rare, much less had eaten a person in the old days. "All the dental bonding and porcelain veneers in the world can't cover up how you used to get your food in the old days."

Niko lost all expression, not that he usually had much

to lose. He knew something was up, which meant he also knew my Nepenthe venom blood levels were down. But there was no chocolate-mint toothpaste here and that meant my brother was up the creek without a toothbrush, a spider, or a hope. I grinned at him, then handed off the platter to my new Wolf friend and opened my Armani-Brioni some kind of hyperexpensive tux jacket to reveal the black T-shirt beneath: IF BEING A DICK IS WRONG . . . I KNOW I'M NOT RIGHT.

The Wolf growled again when he caught sight of it. "Lighten up, Fido," I said. "I gave you some Snausages, so shut your Alpo-hole."

"Ammut is here," Niko added, stepping forward with a look for everyone except me. "We will kill her and you will pay us the other portion of our fee. If you feel this is a problem, take it out of the Lupa's earnings. They're responsible for at least half of this mess." Not that they were, but if they were going to claim to be, then why not make them cough up the price? "If you don't exert some domination soon, they'll be the only ones of you left to make any messes at all."

Promise had those pristine, perfectly manicured violet nails of hers through the tux of what looked like the lead vampire, a small, unassuming bald man with the blackest, most empty eyes I'd seen. I think her nails went through skin and flesh as well, because there was a pained flicker at the corner of his mouth. "We are civilized now," she said in a voice that was silk over titanium. "We cooperate with others. We pay our debts. We are beings of reason, not of bloodlust. Do not make me remind each and every one of you why I was the sole vampire to survive the Black Death without being burned alive. Show the Leandros brothers and their companions the respect they are due and perhaps no more of us need perish." She stepped back, already with a small strip of silver gray cloth to wipe the blood from her nails. She tucked it into the bald vampire's jacket. "I take blood from no one now. Not even the likes of you."

A hand grabbed my arm and yanked me into motion. "Let's do a circuit of the room and see if you're any closer to finding Ammut's scent than while standing about stuffing your face with all the work ethic of a minimum-wage slushie operator," Niko ordered.

"Do you know how hard it is to make the perfect slush—" I didn't get a chance to finish the sentence. It was for the best.

"You're starting to remember, aren't you?" he demanded in an undertone. "What you did to Wahanket. The cats. Resorting to violence over bacon, a bigger giveaway than all the others. It's coming back."

I kept my eyes focused on every woman we passed. Ammut was an Egyptian legend, but with those bronze scales and the myth of a lion's mane, I had her pinned as a blonde. "Yep. Just like you said it would. You said it would wear off and you were right." The grip on my arm tightened. It felt like the grasp of denial at odds with one of hope, and the double-strength grasp was beginning to hurt.

How did I read emotions from a grip, from the clench of bone, and the ripple of muscle? I'd been hit a damn lot in this job. You picked things up. I could close my eyes and tell you what kind of monster had punched me in the face and if it was because he wanted to eat me, kill me for fun, or was showing off for his girlfriend. I'd been educated in the ways. "I know . . . No, I *remember* how much you love being right," I said, but not rubbing it in too much. After all, he was always right—almost. He'd find out soon enough that this "almost" was one goddamn big one he might never live down. "I also know if you don't ease up, I won't be able to use this arm to shoot anything, much less an Egyptian fake goddess. And, most important of all, bacon is worth fighting over."

He released me. "I suppose I didn't expect that it would happen this . . . quickly. I thought that flash with Delilah at the brownstone was a fluke."

"Right now, it doesn't much matter. When I'm all the way back, we'll have a party. Celebrate my homecoming and Ammut's going. Oh shit, there she is." I'd been wrong. She did appear Egyptian and she was a goddess. By one of the long stretches of windows, she stood with a champagne glass in hand. She was alone, a long fall of black hair rippling in waves to the middle of her back. Her skin was dark, but only a shade darker than Niko's, her lips full and painted a dark red-bronze, and her eyes as black as her hair. Her dress was familiar; green-and-gold scales that molded her from a high neck to an inch or so above the floor. She knew it was a trap—anyone with one brain cell would—but she was confident that we would fail and she'd scarf us up the same as those bacon appetizers. I couldn't blame her. We hadn't been much of a challenge earlier, and bacon . . . Damn, it was *bacon.* How could you not risk a little to get a pound of that for breakfast?

She saw us. She could've seen us from the moment we walked in. If it was a trap, it paid to get there first. Saluting us both with the glass, she sipped the champagne and wrinkled a slightly aquiline nose at the bubbles. That quickly the goddess disappeared and something much harder to resist appeared in her place. She took another small swallow and laughed. I could *feel* the sensation of the carbonation tickling my own nose. I wanted to laugh with her. I could now smell her flower-honey-cinnamon scent over the scent of anyone or anything else. She was your cute baby cousin, if you had one, going to her first school dance, and you'd do anything to make her happy.

Get her a limo. Not beat up her loser rocker boyfriend.
Take a hundred pictures like a huge-ass dork.

Tilting her head slightly, she smiled directly at us
both, bent her fingers in the tiniest of waves, and it became ten times worse.

"Okay, is she fucking adorable or is it just me?" And
"adorable"—not a word I'd ever used before, but one
I was aware (just barely) existed—was dead-on. She
was . . . had been hot as hell, gorgeous as they came, but
without the sexual hunger that quality brought out. Be-
loved baby cousin was gone and now we had a kitten, a
soft bunny . . . er . . . rabbit, a puppy with sweet-smelling
milk breath. She was all that, the tactile and emotional
draw of hundreds of them, and you wanted to go pat her
on the head, tickle her tummy, and talk, goddamn truth,
baby talk to her.

How the hell do you fight an adorable goddamn
monster?

Come on, Auphe, kick in. You, the first killers on
Earth, probably wore real, live rabbits on your feet for
bunny slippers. If ever I needed some good old murderous rage, now was the time. And here it came, here it
came, here it . . . Shit.

I had nothing.

I groaned. "We are so dead."

A sex thing, that I could handle. We'd all run across
succubi before. I'd slept with a sexual psychotic. Niko's
girlfriend would be very disappointed in him if he were
susceptible . . . in a way that might lose him his dick al-
together. Goodfellow *was* a sexual predator of sorts. If it
was legal, he would take it down or had in the past. Kink
of the Jungle. There wasn't a creature alive that could
out-sex-vibe him. All of us were inoculated to a certain
degree against that approach. But this one?

Screwed. Screwed, screwed, screwed.

"I didn't know you knew the word 'adorable,'" Niko said as this time I was the one to grab his arm.

"Shut *up*. I want to go rub her stomach and let her chew on my fingers. I want a piece of yarn for her to play with. I want to get her some milk," I said, my grip on him getting tighter with desperation. "Jesus, isn't she getting to you?"

"Some. But I've done all those things before." There was a pause, but I knew it was coming. Sure as shit, I knew it was. "With you. You know, when I changed your diaper and dusted on the baby powder. I didn't want you getting a rash on your tiny little—"

"Say it and I'll shoot you right here, right now." I glared and let go of his arm, but the desire to throw myself into a pile of life-energy-sucking kittens had decreased. "Better yet, let's go shoot her instead." Of course, she was gone by then, but she left a scent trail that had me looking down with every step to make certain I wasn't squashing a puppy. It was headed where we'd wanted her, the rooftop terrace. It was a good choice for her as well. If she was exposed down here, the vampires and Wolves would very easily decide twenty or thirty dead humans were worth killing Ammut, and there were enough of our clients here to do that—to do both. "Should we get the others?"

Niko shook his head. "Goodfellow might be all right, but he does love that murderous bald cat of his. Ishiah? I have no idea. And Promise only just lost her own daughter. I think that opens her up to maternal feelings that could be turned back on us."

We were at the stairwell, locked at our request to keep the civilians out of the combat zone. It wasn't locked any longer. "And you and me?" I asked.

"Do you have a deep, hidden desire to rub my stomach?" he countered with lifted eyebrows.

"Okay. Great job, Nik. Thanks. I'm feeling as pissed off and bloodthirsty as it possibly gets. Let's get this cuddly kitten bitch before I try to beat you to death with a Jersey Costco-sized container of baby powder." I took the stairs two at a time, the Eagle out. He was on my heels, this time with nothing to say about powder, diapers, or baby Cal's diaper-rash-ridden ass.

We reached the roof in seconds and slammed the door behind us, blocking it with a heavy wood lounge chair jammed under the handle. That took care of the civilians, but it wouldn't stop anyone discovering we were missing and wanting to rush up to help.

Civilians. This laugh was nasty and gleeful. *Sheep. Bleating prey. Walking leeches. Foolish tricksters. Pigeons of a powerless god. All are nothing.*

Now you show up, I thought with cranky irritation. Shadow-time is back, got it? We need to get our shit together. All our shit, regardless of how dark. This situation is going to call for it. Or do you want to go out, the last Auphe on the planet, while fetching this bitch a bowl of goddamn milk?

I didn't get an answer. I did get a question, though.

"Where are your brothers and sisters?"

The voice came from everywhere . . . as a goddess's voice would. Gone were the happy and fluffy. She had us where she wanted us and she had friends far more effective than kittens and puppies. She had her spiders. There were fifteen or twenty; they were climbing over the edge of the roof so quickly it was hard to count them all. . . . They were beside us, in front of us, over the top of the stairwell door behind us. I waited until three were on the edge and about to jump when I shot them with three silenced rounds in the midst of their daisy yellow eyes. For all my life, five minutes the way we were going, I'd forever link spiders and daisies—bright, sun-seeking daisies that opened their petals to the light to reveal a poisonous black predator hiding within.

"I'm his brother. If you are that interested, you should be talking to me."

Niko had cut me off before I could ask her what she meant. It was one of the few memories I was still lacking. Niko was my only family, my only brother, and her obsession with me having more was bizarre. It made me wonder . . . Was she in New York by chance and appetite, or was she here for me and everything else was collateral damage? What did she want from me? Besides what Wahanket had wanted?

"You are hardly worth my interest. I want his true family. I want the whispers and the rumors made flesh. Made real. As they must be. If there is this one, how can there not be others?"

Practice makes perfect, baby boy, baby boy.

More spiders swarmed over and landed on the terrace, but I didn't shoot them. My gun was up, finger on the trigger, but . . . fuck . . . she was right. If there was me, how could there not be more? When Wahanket had told me I was half Auphe, I'd known I was an experiment. Felt it in my gut. I was a freak of monster science, but how many brand-new experiments turn out right the very first time? Or the second? Or the twentieth?

None.

Here you have brothers and sisters.

Worthless failures.

Toys for you, baby boy, baby boy.

The saw grass, the moon white crocodile. Nevah's Landing. It hadn't been a sanctuary. It had been an invitation to a fucking family reunion. I could see it—the green, the white, the red . . . the silver flash of metal.

"Nik, there's a crocodile out back." Like in the book . . . like *Peter Pan*.

Alligators you could live with. Other things you couldn't. When I was seven, I'd heard a story about a sanctuary for lost children and then I'd learned there was no such thing. I'd forgotten both, and I couldn't blame that on any spider bite.

"Cal!"

The small patch of Nevah's Landing evaporated from the night and I could see the roof again. I couldn't have been out of it any more than a few seconds, but sometimes only seconds are needed. Now there were at least thirty Nepenthe spiders, black blots of shadow to the casual eye, that had crawled up the side of the building and jumped over the edge of the roof. Advertised as spacious, the terrace wasn't cutting it for that many giant arachnids. Everywhere was a clacking mandible; everywhere was the scuttle of their legs. There was no place you could turn and not see six alien eyes staring back at you. After this experience and *Spider-Man 3*, if I ever saw Tobey Maguire, I was going to punch him in the face.

They were on the chairs, crushing the small tables, spilling over one another and, though I turned to aim at the ones behind me, they ignored me. They all teemed in one direction—toward Niko on the other side of the terrace. I'd seen my brother fight nearly every monster alive, and I'd never failed to be awed. I was a hybrid of a creature that every other creature in history had feared, loathed, lived in terror of, and I could kill easily, too easily, but there wouldn't ever be a day in my life I'd have anything on Nik in sheer skill. But sometimes all the skill in the world wasn't enough. This many of them—Niko was only human. The most skilled human I'd ever seen at fighting, but at the end of the day . . . human. Sometimes you needed something that had less in common with unadulterated ability and more about having a soul you could pack away at a moment's notice.

Souls . . . inconvenient scraps of nothing.

The spiders had Niko backing up, but he was taking down every single one within reach and some that weren't. I lunged forward, shooting them from behind, which wasn't the best location for putting a bullet in a spider. Blowing huge ragged holes in their abdomen to leak out was good, messy, but ineffective in the short term. A fork in the head, my favorite, worked great but shooting from behind while gory wasn't good for killing them. For that I needed a head shot, but not one of the sons of bitches would turn around. Intent on Niko, I could pop them like party balloons and they didn't care.

Fine. I would see exactly how much they didn't care. I waded into them, a Lovecraftian version of a herd of Shetland ponies. All we needed was Cthulhu singing "Rawhide." I moved up beside one spider and blew its brains all over the one next to it, climbed the dead one, and took out its buddy before it had even managed to get the brain goop out of its eyes well enough to see. Those daisy, sunshine eyes. I moved on to the next one. It was beginning to get how things were going and was starting to turn. "It's going to be a bright, bright, bright sunshiny day, Shelob," I said with enthusiastic dark cheer. "Too bad you won't be here to see it." Another round, another spider brain turned to pudding.

Niko was swinging his katana with one hand, his tanto with another, and if the son of a bitch would just let me get a machine gun or carry those convenient grenades to parties full of people, I'd have kicked his ass for not using them. One blade sliced through the head of the spider closest to him, bisecting it neatly. The other shorter blade he used to nail a jumping spider in midair.

The silver, sheened with green-gray slime, exited the top of its head, but the mandibles thrashed on in the death throes and Niko swiftly flung the spider off his weapon. One bite had sent me to la-la land. One bite would kill him.

That was not fucking happening.

I moved to the next poisonous piece of shit, put it down, and was about to do the same to the next, but it was too late. Niko had tried to get around them, to fight back to back. We did that when the attackers were this many, but there wasn't enough time and too many had never been this many. The closest ones to him were rearing on their back four legs to block the most of any escape route that they could—not that there was one. They had a plan and a purpose. Their goddess couldn't kill me and get what she wanted, information I didn't have, not yet. It was coming. Close . . . so close, seconds away, but not yet. And she wanted that more than anything, because what could be better than eating a half-breed Auphe? Having a literal buffet of them. She hadn't tried to kill me in the canal, only take me . . . to where she could ask and I could answer.

Niko continued to take out the spiders right and left, his sword slinging spider blood in all directions as I continued to move toward him, even though we both knew it wouldn't be enough. Plastered in sweat, covered in their blood, he couldn't climb over them when they stood more than seven feet tall, but he could bury his blade in their vulnerable underbelly. It didn't help. As each one fell dead, two more stretched high in its place, upper legs ending in curved claws striking. And when they died, the same happened again. Death meant nothing to them. They had only cared about one direction, one thing—getting him to take two steps backward. Niko knew it and I knew it, the same as he knew to watch his back if I wasn't in a position to do it. He knew when he was being herded, but options could sometimes be limited. Having thirty Great Dane–sized spiders in your face was one of those occasions. It was only two steps, and as many bullets as I fired, as quickly as I tore my way through them, those two steps happened. And they were enough to get him within reach of Ammut.

She'd been behind an arched wooden covering that protected a couch and table with small candles lit in glass bowls. Following that, she was on top of the covering and her tail was wrapped tightly around Niko's upper chest and throat. I'd forgotten her speed from the brownstone. When something can move that fast, you can't remember it, not in accurate detail. How can you remember what you can't see?

Snakes were swift and she was all snake again. She lay sinuously on the wood, her claws scoring it. Bronze and green, copper and gold, with that flower smell so strong it could've come from a hundred funeral homes. It was cloying and thick, never quite covering the ripeness of decay. She was beautiful still, in the way of nature if not woman, but I could smell what she really was. It didn't matter. She could've smelled as beautiful underneath it all as she appeared.

Nothing mattered—not a goddamn thing in the world except that she had my brother.

He swung his katana, only to have it bounce off the scales, not doing any more damage than my bullets in the brownstone basement had. He couldn't turn to strike at her face or eyes as the coils tightened around him, holding him in place. But this was Niko. He didn't need to see his target; he needed only to know where it was. He reversed the grip on each of his blades and jabbed them backward and up. It was useless. I never thought I'd see anything faster than my brother. I was wrong. She avoided every blow with ease, her gold eyes strobing because her head moved so quickly. But Nik kept striking behind at Ammut's face and then finally at those coils around him. Metal bounced off its equal. Ammut *was* copper and bronze, not only the appearance of it. Metal scales met the metal of his sword, and the faintest of sparks was the sole effect.

Niko didn't give up, though. He didn't know how to; he never had. He kept fighting because he was who he was, all the while turning more and more blue in the candlelight that was left from those he hadn't knocked over in his struggle. Too quick, that color blue. She wasn't going to asphyxiate him. She was going to break his neck—my brother's neck. She wasn't going to bother to take the time to suck out his life force. That wasn't what she wanted. She was impatient and tired of waiting for me to give her what she did want. She was going to kill him and there wasn't a goddamn thing I could do about it. I'd shot her before. It didn't work. What the fuck, I tried again. It was the same as Nik's attempt. I couldn't hit her eyes. Her head weaved so fast, I saw only the afterimage of it. After she broke his neck, then broke me only in a different way, she no doubt thought, she'd have more time to pry what she wanted from my lost memories.

Only she didn't know they were lost. Because of that she was going to kill Nik and I couldn't stop her. I couldn't, not with a gun or a knife—not with any weapon I had.

She is nothing. A worm beneath your heel. A sheep with scales instead of wool. She is not like you. There is nothing like you. You need no weapon.

You were born *a weapon.*

Niko's eyes rolled back. One hand let loose of his tanto. His other hand loosened on his katana. To drop his katana, Niko would have to be dead.

My brother . . .

Dead.

I thought I'd lost it, lost consciousness, lost my brother, died myself wrapped in Ammut as it all went black—everything. There wasn't a sole Manhattan light, not a flicker of a candle or the orange sky of nighttime NYC. There was only the dark . . . because I knew now. I was at home. The dark was me. I told myself stories there—every story about myself that I knew. Some were gone forever; only stories of stories, and that was how it had to be. Some stories weren't nice and some were chaotic jumbles of terror and malice. Some were of Niko and me living short lives that seemed long, of the things we'd done—good and bad. I told myself about the killing, when it was necessary, when it wasn't, and how you couldn't always be perfect. Best of all, I spun the tale of why I'd been made . . . what the Auphe had needed . . . what I could do, what they had passed on to me. I told myself about the traveling, how I could slash a hole in the ether of the world anytime I wanted. Gates that were doorways to anywhere.

I liked that.

That was useful.

The first to walk the earth, and the earth would let us do anything, include rip screaming tears in it, if we would only walk through the gates and leave. If the earth hoped, if it prayed, that was what it prayed for—in vain, because we never left for good.

Blackness flickered; the blackbird's wing that had taught me about death fluttered across my vision and then was gone. I could see. I could feel. And I could remember everything. Not the seventy-five percent I'd walked in with, but one hundred percent prime-grade Cal. I could remember me—all of me, human and Auphe. I could remember what I'd told myself in the dark:

The thing I was.

The things I'd done.

The things I might do.

I was okay with that—better than okay. There was pain. I'd expected it. I'd had it after my first encounter with Wahanket, my first coming back, the first of the shadows, then again at the brownstone. It was hot and white—my soul, if I had one, giving up the ghost or sinking down to bide its time, buried in a shallow grave. My human genes bowed down before the Auphe ones as they always had before. I muscled through the burning ache of it and hung on to that moment where everything felt right. Nothing felt more right than this. Sad, in a way, but it was the way things were meant to be. Some would say I was giving up something I might not get a chance at again. I said I was getting something back—me. The real me. All of me.

He slipped away, the Cal I could've been, but never would've been—thanks to memories. Yeah, maybe. But mostly thanks to genes that had been too busy fighting off the spider venom to make themselves known. That was why Delilah hadn't scented Auphe the first time. In body I'd still been part Auphe, but faded—faded to practically nothing because every capable working Auphe gene had been concentrating on feeding its power to those in the part of my brain that could get me back to normal—my normal. During that time, while Auphe genes had been reknitting old memories, I'd been human, as close to human as I ever could be, with human emotions, human decisions, human instincts.

I hadn't known. My entire life—I'd never known how far away from that I was. How far away I'd always been. I hadn't known that human was only a word, and that never had that word been for me.

The time we'd spent looking for Ammut, looking for the monster, I'd been the monster all along.

Me.

What we'd been chasing was nothing compared to what lived inside of me—what *was* me. With every job we did, every case we took on, every mystery we tried to untangle, I'd been the real monster and we'd all pretended we didn't know it. I'd been half right a week ago. A killer had woken up on that South Carolina beach. A killer *and* a monster; that was who I was, and it was never going to change.

So what?

I gave a mental shrug, for once in agreement with that particular inner voice. After all, this voice was me. The other one had been a soul I barely had fighting for an existence in a body that simply wasn't meant to support one. Again . . .

So what?

If you couldn't change it, you used it; otherwise, it wouldn't be long before it used you. That was why I'd had Niko get the Aramaic tattoo—to understand what I did; not to regret what he had done. Brothers before souls. Bros before souls. Although if I said it like that, he'd kick my ass, and so what if it didn't actually rhyme? Close enough. It got the point across. Brothers before souls. I'd made the decision to be the brother Niko truly wanted—even if he could'nt admit to himself that a human Cal and an Auphe Cal couldn't be one and the same. Now I saw as I'd seen before that he needed that same brother, the old Cal—the real one, but not for the reason he thought. Not for a shared past. Not for a lost familiarity.

Not for what I could do.

But for what I *would* do.

Her mistake was letting me so close, because she wanted me. No matter what you wanted, you should never let someone like me get close. No matter what you wanted, you should never let some*thing* like me be on the same fucking planet.

"Let him go," I said, calm and sure. And I was sure . . . of precisely what she wanted. "Let him go and you can have me. Me and my brothers and sisters."

"Yes? You care so much for him? You'd give up yourself and your siblings?" She was suspicious, but she also wanted this, maybe more than anything in her snaky little life. An Auphe. To feed on an Auphe; no one would claim that. To feed on many of them—that would make her the goddess she claimed.

"Cleopatra, I don't give a rat's ass about anything else. Let him go and it's all yours." One of the best things about having an Auphe as a father and a sociopath as a mother was that lying was by far easier than telling the truth. Nik hadn't learned that. He was too damn good, and I wasn't letting that kind of good pass from this world. I'd take down the world first and anything else that got in my way. "I'll even let you have a taste first before I tell you about the rest of the family."

That was too much temptation. Temptation and greed make you stupid, and honestly she hadn't seen me be much of a threat so far, except as an exterminator. And, hard as it was to admit, she was right. Then. Now was a different story. The coils around Niko's chest and neck loosened. His neck wasn't broken, and I could hear the ragged breath he pulled in. He fell to his knees, barely conscious, but he still had that sword in his hand. An entire army of samurai was nothing compared to him.

Ammut slithered down from the protective wooden covering and balanced in front of me. One hand rested on top of Niko's bowed head as he struggled to breathe.

"I do not have to break his neck to take his life. I can do the second as easily and just as swiftly."

"I'll behave," I promised. I wanted to grin. Goddamn, I wanted to, but I was good and lived by the lessons both my parents had taught me—human and monster. Lie, steal, slaughter, and never let them see it coming . . . until it's too late.

I dropped the Eagle. Why did I think I needed a gun? As I'd told myself, I was a weapon—one more effective than any automatic. I put my hand against her chest, the scales a razor-sharp scrape under my palm. "Let him go," I repeated. "Him for me. That's the only way you're going to get what you want. What you've wanted since you came here, Auphe to devour. Vampires and Wolves, they have to get boring after a while, centuries of fur and fang. But me . . . and my brothers and sisters. There's nothing like us. You know that. You came here for that, didn't you? Not all the others, but for me—for me and my brothers and sisters?" I knew it. Everywhere we'd gone, she'd left messages for me I hadn't understood . . . until now.

Give them to me. Where are your brothers and sisters? Givegivegive.

And I was. I was going to give her what she wanted. It was her bad luck that she didn't know I was more poisonous than any Nepenthe spider.

"I can tell you where they are, the rest of us half-breeds, and me? I'm right here." I felt the strange suction where my flesh touched hers as she drew a little of me . . . of my life out. It was barely a mouthful and I had a lot of life to give. She was welcome to it. "I know you can feel me. I know you can taste the Auphe in me, can't you?"

"Yes." The gold eyes, wild and striking in their way, closed. Ecstatic yet almost hesitant. That answered that question. She'd never sampled an Auphe in the flesh, not before me. She was intoxicated instantly. Some couldn't handle their liquor; some couldn't handle their life force. Too bad for her. Someone's eyes were bigger than their stomach. "Dark," she murmured. "Infinite in its rage, hate, hunger, and other desires. Desires the same as my own."

Not hardly. Her desires were a Santa wish list compared to mine.

"I'm glad you like it. Consider that one taste a freebie." I opened a gate around my hand, tarnished gray and silver, and shoved it through her chest. Her scaled flesh melted away, gone forever, beneath my fingers until I touched what passed for her heart. I could feel the serpent-slow beat of it against my skin. She couldn't feed through a gate. Nothing could breach a gate unless I wanted it to. The gates, the doors, they belonged to me and only me.

"Can you still feel me?" I tightened my fingers. "How about now? Can you feel me now, *Goddess*? You murdering bitch." The eyes were open again and they weren't so beautiful any longer. "Let Niko go or we'll see how you manage to tie on the lobster bib and chow down on anything in the future without your fucking heart."

Ishiah had told the truth in the bar when I'd asked the question.

I *was* a bad guy, when I needed to be, which made me the right guy for the job.

The fury behind those eyes, in the fast and ominous chittering of all the spiders that surrounded us, didn't matter. That the bronze and green coils unwrapped themselves from around Niko's neck, setting him free, was the only thing that did. He dropped to the concrete on his side, unmoving. In the yellow illumination of the rooftop lights I could see the gray touch, the ashes of mortality in the color of his skin. It would fade as his breathing returned to normal. His color would come back; it was coming back. He was all right. Safe. That was the only way it could be.

A good guy or a bad one, a monster or a man, which-ever, I fucking loved my brother.

A soul I could do without. I couldn't do without Niko. When it came to options, there I had none. I didn't want any. And when someone messed with him, hurt him, es-pecially because of me . . . goddamn what a big mistake they'd made—one they would regret as long as they lived.

Yeah . . . That wouldn't be too fucking long, now would it?

"Release me." Her heart was beating faster beneath my fingers now. She was a predator, but all predators had someone higher than them on the food chain. Something bigger. Something badder. They all had to answer to someone. Today her someone was me. "I did as you said. Release me. *Now!*" The goddess voice was back. Ammut, Eater of Hearts, Devourer of Souls. Hear my voice and obey. Bow and *obey*. The hypnotic flower aroma was back too, everywhere, thicker than ever as it soaked every molecule of air, but it wasn't helping her now. Fool me once. . . .

There was no second part to that saying in the life I lived.

I cocked my head, as if considering the request. "Why? I didn't say I would. I only said what I'd do if you didn't do what I told you. And in any case, whatever I said, it wouldn't make a difference. Unlike you, I *am* a monster. I was born to lie and kill. You, pathetic fucking monster wannabe, you were born to die." I ripped out her heart, black and gold, and threw it down. Ammut, Eater of Hearts. We would see how she did without one of her own and a huge, gaping hole in her chest. Then, with the gate still glowing gray around my hand, I took her brain. Sometimes the heart wasn't enough. The heart and the brain together always were.

"Wannabe to never was. So long, Queen of the Nile," I said flatly.

She fell, a snake whose back was broken on a country road by a careless driver. As she fell, so did the spiders. I hadn't planned on that. I was about to grab Niko and go through a larger gate. To where? Who cared? Out of here was the important thing. But it wasn't necessary. The remainder of the thirty or so spiders shivered, legs flailing, before they flipped onto their backs into full-blown convulsions and finally collapsed—turning gray and still. They were now the husks Ammut had made of her victims. She'd shared her stolen life force to keep them alive . . . likely from the days of pyramids and pharaohs when Nepenthe spiders were common in the desert. Now they were nothing but long-dead bugs ready to be swept off the windshield.

That was the way some days went—a bitch of one if you were a spider.

A cold February wind blew by and the spiders disintegrated into heaps of gray dust—bad day for spiders; fantastic fucking day for me and the janitors. Ammut was slowly dissolving into an oil slick of gold and black. Profound age made for a great cleanup. The gold mixing with the night color—it was the sun being swallowed by a permanent eclipse. It was beautiful, it was a cataclysm, and then it was only a memory.

I had many of those now.

The irony of the entire thing was that she hadn't been much of a monster at all; we'd faced much worse. Not to mention the only reason she'd come here was for me. I hope the replacement council never found out about that. If I'd been at full capacity—had been myself—we'd have gotten her at the brownstone and been at home watching TV, eating pizza, and not wearing uncomfortable James Bond cast-off tuxes. I crouched next to Niko and smacked his face lightly, then more firmly. He was nearly back to his normal olive color, although the bruising around his neck was going to be nasty. "That stings," he grumbled, his voice hoarse and his eyes still shut.

"Yeah, I'm crying for you on the inside. I swear. Open up those baby grays, Cyrano. I did all the work. At least you could live through it."

He did live. He opened his eyes too, rolling slowly and carefully onto his back. "That's the second time you've called me Cyrano." His gaze shifted to the ash mound of what had been the spiders and to the puddle of Ammut. "You killed them. You killed all of them." I couldn't take credit for the spiders, but, then again, why not? It had been a weird week. I'd take all the credit I could get.

I reached down under Niko's neck and back to pull his braid free, laid it on his chest, and gave it a pat. "No need to cut your hair. I'm back. All of me. I've been on my way back for a while." I shook my head and snorted. "Nepenthe venom in the toothpaste, Nik? Really? As if I wouldn't notice that and you becoming Hans the Hygiene King?" I slid a hand behind his back and eased him up to a more or less sitting position. "It wouldn't have made a difference anyway. Not in the end. My Auphe immune system would've fought off the full dose of venom the Nepenthe spider gave me in Central Park." Not Goodfellow's lie about a half dose. Before I gated to Nevah's Landing, I'd gotten a full dose of venom all right. No doubt. But an Auphe immune system had no peer. Had I been full Auphe, the bite might not have affected me at all.

"It would've eventually fought off your minty-fresh

version too. Humans build up a tolerance to drugs. Auphe ride over them hell-bent-for-leather." I tugged his braid, for the first time since I'd disappeared. I didn't know if he missed that, but I'd missed doing it. I'd been doing it as long as he'd had one. "I was coming back, sooner or later, and no one, not even you, could stop that."

"You were happy," he said. He was ashamed for drugging me behind my back, but stubborn too. He wasn't backing down an inch on doing something he'd thought he didn't have in him. Deception aimed at his brother. "Cal, damn it, you were happy." He didn't bring up whether he had been or not. Knowing him, he didn't even think about it. Committing a level of deceit that went against everything he was, that had been *for* me, not for him.

But my Auphe genes had made all that trickery unnecessary. They'd fixed me up, making me right again. Despite what Niko thought about my happiness or what a sliver of my own subconscious tried to tell me about monsters, it was only a matter of perspective. Happiness was an emotion invented by a greeting card company to sell pink bears and shiny balloons. But duty and family had existed since the dawn of time—human time at least.

To thine own self be true. Someone old, smart, and wordy had said that . . . and, yes, I knew who. It was time I started listening to the smart and wordy of the world. I was who I was, and labels such as normal and right and good, like everything, were open to interpretation. It was long past time for me to be my own interpreter.

"You lied to me, you know." I stabilized him as he regained his balance enough to sit without falling over.

"I did." He was obstinate through and through, and what he thought of as his dishonor, no matter if with the best of intentions, he hid out of sight. And he did think that to the depths of his soul—that he had thrown away every shred of honor in him.

"You drugged me," I reminded him, bracing him with a hand on his back.

"I did." Now he sounded empty. No embarrassment, no determination. He'd broken every rule he'd ever made for himself and, while he'd done it for me, how does the most honorable of men deal with that? Losing your brother and losing yourself all in one.

I punched his shoulder lightly and grinned. "How's it feel to be the black sheep of the family for once?" I gave him a moment to think about that before adding, "Not that it counts, since it was for what you thought was my own good and not for your good at all. Only you could turn lying into something noble and pure." I finished up with annoyance and affection mixed. "Always a martyr."

He thought I'd blame him for what he'd done. That I'd hate him. As if I had that in me. I had many things in me some would say I'd be better off without, but hating Niko wasn't one of them. He'd only done what I'd asked for, not especially indirectly either. I wanted to serve up waffles, ignore the reality of monsters, and get a gut from diner food, because that was what ordinary people did. I'd been content—I'd thought. I'd been normal—I'd thought. I'd made it clear at the beginning that I wanted to stay that way and not be the dark reflection in that Halloween picture.

He'd been willing to give it up for me, all of it—our memories, our history. Knowing someone better than one knew oneself. All that he'd done for me throughout my life . . . to keep me sane and keep me alive. All the things I did to do the same for him. Sometimes it was the smallest things that did that, the sanity part—the nicknames, the purposeful aggravation, the pokes, and elbows in the ribs. Sometimes it was the biggest things, such as surviving Sophia together.

But he'd tried to do it, to let all that go. He did his best to carry that entire burden alone. To accept a new Cal when it must have felt like the old Cal had died, his real brother had died, and all because he thought I was happier that way, being human. That was Niko. For me, he'd lose me and he'd do his damnedest to never show how it felt. That was my brother, the one I remembered from the first memory I'd ever had.

I'd been about three when we hid in the closet as Sophia trashed the house in a drunken rage. Three years old and the glass breaking and the chairs hitting the wall, scary noises, but someone's arm was tightly around me. Someone was there to keep me safe. I'd heard his voice, whispering reassuring words, although I didn't remember those words. I did remember what I felt . . . not alone. I wasn't alone.

I couldn't leave Nik alone either. He'd stayed with me then, and I was staying with him now. After what we'd lived through, Sophia and the Auphe, no one should have to carry that past by themselves. He needed the brother he'd always had—not a Stepford version, not a Boy Scout.

Not one who would hesitate to tear out the heart of what, at times, had been a beautiful woman. The best predators were always beautiful. It made them good at what they did. My Auphe made me good at what I did—protecting my brother. The other Cal—he wasn't equipped. I'd told Niko before if there were gray areas in what we did, that was why I was there. Those places weren't for him. It didn't stop there. If there were those pitch-black places to go, unimaginable lines to be crossed, that was for me as well—not him.

Someone's heart ... quivering in my hand ... It was the very least of what I would do for my brother.

Don't ask what the most would be.

Sitting beside him, I leaned against him so he could pretend he wasn't leaning against me. He always had to be the strong one. Who was I to take that away, even once? "I was going to work at the bar when she and her spiders jumped me in the park." I ran there on occasion. Boggles made great incentive on improving your running time. "She kept asking me where my brothers and sisters were. I had no idea what she was talking about. It was her and about forty spiders. If I could've seen her, I could've taken care of her then, but I couldn't. She was hiding in the trees and her scent was everywhere. And forty spiders?"

I shrugged. "I'm good, but no one's that good. One bit me and my memories began to disappear, erasing backward. It was strange how I could feel that. Like those old VHS tapes when you'd rewind them. So I traveled. I built a gate and went through, but the venom was so damn fast, it hit my memories of being seven and in South Carolina at the same time that I hit the gate. By the time I went through and ended up on the beach, it was all gone. But I remember now. I remember being seven at that glorified shed we stayed in. I remember you telling me the Peter Pan story. And I remember the Auphe that talked to me when I was playing out back, the one I thought was the crocodile from the book. White with red eyes and metal teeth—no wonder I thought that story was scary as shit." The third voice in my head wasn't a voice at all. It was only the echo of what wasn't even a memory, unless you counted repressed ones.

"The alligator you told me you saw." I had forgotten everything; Niko had remembered it all.

I looked up at the sky. No stars. There never were

here. "Can't blame a spider for that one. I forgot all on my own there. The Auphe told me I had brothers and sisters. Rejects. Failures. Toys for me to play with when I grew up to be a big-boy Auphe. Ammut must have heard the rumors. Who knows from where. Other life suckers. Or tricksters—they never let a piece of juicy dirt go by." I looked back down and picked at the sole of my black sneaker. "Don't you hate it when someone knows more about your life than you ever did? Gossipy ass-holes." Had Robin known all this time that there might be more of me out there? Could be. But good friends don't always tell you the truth. Good friends know that sometimes a lie is better. I shifted my shoulders. I was turning into a regular emo shrugging machine. "Anyway, that memory disappeared too, and I was in the middle of the one where you were going on about Neverland. Tree houses. Flying. A safe place. That was why I went there, the seven-year-old me falling through a gate, before there was nothing left but amnesia. I was a scared kid looking for sanctuary. I definitely wasn't looking for a killer Auphe crocodile or a freak show family."

Niko exhaled and traced his fingers over the grip of his katana. We all have our security blankets, some more lethal than others, and his and mine hadn't changed an iota over the years. "I'd wondered before," he started cautiously, then more resolutely, "how many times did the Auphe try before you? How many failures were there before you were born? I've wondered that since I was old enough to take my first biology class in school. What they were trying to do . . . Whom they were trying to make. Human genes crossed with Auphe genes would never work with only one attempt. I can't imagine how many it would take." He'd wondered, huh? He'd wondered; Robin had very well known of the possibility. I should have thought about it too, but I hadn't wanted to. I was the very best at not doing or thinking things I didn't want to. Cowardice or self-survival or both; at those I excelled.

The Auphe hadn't been keeping an eye on just me in those days, but on multiple mes. For some reason the others hadn't been allowed to "be human" for a time while being observed. The Auphe needed two things from their breeding program: the ability to travel—to build gates and move hundreds of miles in a second—and the capacity to still be human enough to host a parasitic creature called a Darkling that could channel a power enormous enough to cross millions of years instead of only miles. Humans were the only creatures the Darkling could possess, and it had accidentally blown up a few Auphe while proving that. That the creature slid in and out of mirrors, more slippery than any reflection and no less homicidal than the Auphe, had been the beginning of my mirror phobia. That it had taken my mind and slid in and out of it as easily wasn't something I wanted to think about.

It would've taken a while to find out if the rest of the Auphe-human half-breeds were defective, or maybe they'd been defective from the day they were born. I didn't know which would be worse—being defective or being the success, the goddamn golden boy of Auphe genetics. I was about to find out, though. The ones that were alive were in Nevah's Landing—as the albino crocodile with the smile of metal had told me. Waiting . . . They were waiting for me.

I hadn't gone there for them at the beginning of all of this; I hadn't known they'd existed, but I was going for them now.

"Let's get Promise and Goodfellow out here to help you," I said, standing. "I have something to do." Something that should've been done before I was born. But the Auphe, in their infinite ability to be sons of bitches, hadn't done what I would have guessed. They hadn't killed the failures. That would have been too easy for them and for me.

Niko shook his head. "No. Do not even think about it. You are not going to Nevah's Landing to take out a nest of half Auphe by yourself—if they need taking out at all. Think, Cal. They might be like you. Only without the power to build gates. They could be the same as you."

That was funny. Goddamn hilarious. They might be like me. Of anyone in this city, only Niko would think that made it better. God, I did love my brother, no way around it.

"No, I'll go. This is mine." I helped him stand and, within seconds, he was good—stable and capable of taking care of himself as I called Goodfellow on the cell to get his ass out here. I wished he'd taken better care of himself in the past week and less care of what had only been a reflection of me—the best reflection.

"They're not your responsibility, Nik," I said. On this I had no give. "They're not your family." Thank God they weren't. He didn't deserve that. "They're mine. I don't want you to see that." I met his eyes quickly before looking away. He wasn't the only one ashamed. We'd both have to learn to get over it. "I don't want you to see them in me, all right? I don't. I'm not sure that's something I could live with, knowing what you might see."

And there was no way I wanted him to see what I might have to do.

"I'll check them out. See if they're salvageable. I'll call if I need help. There come Promise and Robin now." The chair was kicked aside as the door to the roof opened. "They missed the real thing, but they can take you to the after-party." I gave his braid one last yank, tossed it over his shoulder, and said, "Ask Ishiah what your tattoo means. I'll be back in time for you to kick my ass over it. Swear."

He sheathed his sword, jaw tightening before he exhaled. "You're the most goddamn stubborn man I know. Goddamn it, I missed you, you asshole." Three curse words in two sentences—that was more big-time emotion for Nik. He wrapped one arm around me and that brotherly man hug I'd tried to avoid in Nevah's Landing came back to bite me in the ass. The one arm made it brotherly. That my ribs nearly gave way and my spleen pretty much did too made it manly. That I returned it just as hard was, hell, just manners.

I was always about manners.

Epilogue

(The Alpha and the Omega)

Nevah's Landing smelled the same as it had when I'd left. Salt, a touch of swamp, water, and saw grass brown and crisp for the winter. People, the metal tang of cars, of old asphalt parking lots that might never see the fresh tarry black of it. Spanish moss . . . I liked that smell. If a plant could smell like air, Spanish moss would be the one.

Air and nothing else. No blood. No decay. Only air. That was provided you didn't count the hole in reality hanging there, gray, silver, black, and swirling with a hunger to gobble up the world. I shut the gate down with that mental twist I'd learned at the age of nineteen. It went . . . sulky and snarling in my mind. It could sulk as much as it wanted. It knew who held its leash.

I was behind the motel where I'd lived that so-called normal life for four whole days. I didn't want to slice open a tear in the world and walk through to see two people screwing on a mattress that lay on top of my guns. My babies. Most of the asses in the Landing, thanks to the diner food, weren't small. They were big and wide as a barn door, as they say. I could just imagine them moving back and forth in stretch-marked thrusts. . . . I did not want to see that. No one wanted to see that.

I wiped the blood pouring from my nose, fought the skull-crushing headache, and let the sweat pour down my neck and face, soaking my hair. Once I'd made gates as I'd pleased, as Auphe did, and as often as I'd pleased. Rafferty, our long-gone healer that Delilah had tried and failed to kill, thanks to my gun muzzle behind her pretty ear, had "fixed" me. Limit the gates, everyone thought, and limit the Auphe genetic influence on me, because there hadn't been a doubt that the more I "traveled," the more Auphe I felt. Rafferty had done some chemical rewiring on my brain, though only a little, because he couldn't break me down genetically and remove the Auphe half. That would leave half a human, and that, well, I guess that would be an unpleasant puddle of gore on the ground.

He'd found a way around that. He'd given me something called serotonin syndrome. One gate, bad. It would trigger an uncontrollable flood of serotonin in my brain, which would cause my blood pressure and body temperature to go up radically. Gate two, worse—the same as what was behind door one, but doubled. Gate three would probably mean death from a burst aneurysm in my brain. Since the two I'd used on Ammut for her brain and heart had really been only one—in theory, this was technically number two. If Rafferty was right, I'd survive it.

I guess I'd wait and see. It took me two days or so to "reset" the gates, which meant I'd be driving back to New York—again, thanks to Rafferty.

He was a great healer, the best in the world as far as I knew, and he'd even said it himself—Auphe genes always won. Limit the gates, limit the gene's effect on my mind and my control. He'd said it; I remembered every word, but I don't think he got it, actually got it. Auphe genes *always* won. Maybe a hyped-up superhealer could slow them down by short-circuiting my traveling, but it wasn't only gates and traveling that made an Auphe. We all wanted to forget that. We wanted to forget the truth. Traveling made an Auphe in the same way as walking made a human. It didn't work that way. The truth never did.

But I had better things to do than think about the truth—better things to worry about than whether I was a pretty good guy fighting bad genes or a very bad guy resisting good genes, or whether I was a human with a little monster in him or a monster with a little human. I'd thought it through back in New York and I was done with the subject. It all depended on your point of view and the specimen didn't get to make that call.

That was me . . . a specimen. Surprisingly, that didn't bother me as much as it once would have.

Holding my arm to my nose, I let the cloth of my shirt soak up the blood while I looked for a car to steal. Even with that thought in my head, I was tempted to go see Miss Terryn, Lew, and the diner to remember what it was like to be that good guy; to be human and only human. I did know; however, that wasn't what they'd see if they saw me again. They'd see the shadows. Everyone, including cameras, did. The shades that lived around me weren't real to the eyes, but something in a person sensed them. That something was a long-lost survival instinct, a soul—if they existed. It was futile to wonder. Besides, those days were over. That was past. No more substantial than a dream, long gone. Dreams like that never stuck around. Those were the memories, unlike others, that didn't last. And that . . . That was just life. In that way, I was the same as everyone else.

I found a car—unlocked. Southerners.

It was while I was at the gas station, one of three in

Nevah's Landing, that I went over another memory. I'd mixed it up for more than sixteen going on seventeen years with the story Nik had told me—flying children, pirate ships, princesses, waterfalls, and an albino crocodile. We'd been squatting in a shack at the Landing, a long-abandoned one, near saw grass that had taken over the water's edge and most of the yard. Niko had been making me lunch out of moldy bread, carefully pinching away what green he could, and bologna when I went outside. Sophia was in town, doing whatever was best for ripping people off that day. I scrabbled around for a rock I could throw in the water. The grass was too tall to see it land, but I would hear the splash.

That was when I'd seen it. Stripes of white showing through the green, the bloodred eye, and a thousand needle-fine metal teeth—teeth no crocodile could ever claim. And though I'd known it wasn't the ghost of the crocodile Niko had read about to me, I'd pretended it was, because if I hadn't— Seven-year-old boys went crazy too, when they saw something like that, so wrong and so close—close enough I'd been able to smell the blood on its breath. It had whispered to me without bending a blade of that grass. It had told me not about Never Land, but about something else.

Caliban, baby boy.

I'd frozen, crouched in the grass with fingers still reaching for that stone.

We told your pathetic human ape-whore of a mother to bring you. We want you to know. Here you have brothers and sisters. Here we have left you presents. Play with them as you wish. When you wish. Destroy them and sharpen your skill on them. They deserve no better. They are worthless failures in an experiment that begins to weary us. There are so many, we grew bored of killing them, but for you, we left some alive.

*Toys for you. Toys for our one success. A present so
that you do not forget where you come from, what you
are. Toys so that you do not forget we can turn* you *into a
toy if we please.*

And someday when you're a big boy and bloodthirsty—
the smile was hideous—*you will come play, will you not?*

*Because you will not forget who you belong to, off-
spring of the Auphe. You will not forget who you are.*

Never.

I had forgotten, though. Instantly. I went back inside,
ate my bologna sandwich, and never thought of it again.
I simply told Niko I saw a crocodile out in the grass. He
automatically corrected it to alligator, and went looking himself. He didn't find anything. No gators. What a
relief.

What a goddamn relief.

And I hadn't remembered any of it until the past
week, thanks to the Nepenthe venom hitting that precise cluster of neurons when I'd gated out from Central
Park, and thanks to Ammut demanding my brothers
and sisters. Where were my brothers and sisters, a string
of lives that could feed her for years? For one split second I'd remembered, before every memory, including
that one, was swallowed by darkness. But even after the
amnesia had taken hold, there had still been whispers.
Ammut hadn't given up and neither had that long-dead
Auphe crocodile. *Where are your brothers and sisters?
Where are they? Where?*

In Nevah's Landing when I'd been there working at
the diner, I'd feel a hand groping inside me, tugging, saying, *Here. We're here.* Every day I'd felt the connection,
but I hadn't known what it meant. I obviously didn't belong there, despite a human Cal wishing he did. I hadn't
known what it meant then, that pulling and presence,
but I knew now.

All Auphe felt one another. I'd learned to travel years before I learned that skill. If an Auphe was around, I'd feel it. I'd know it. That was the biggest reason I hadn't wanted to leave the Landing when Niko came for me. They were calling me, but I couldn't make it out. I didn't know what it was. I wouldn't have thought there were any of them left to feel after Niko and I had destroyed the last, but a white crocodile reared its head, finally, in the back of my brain and told me differently. I'd forgotten a lot about the Auphe in my life, mostly on purpose. If you think seeing one in the grass sucked, try being raised by them for two years. At least I knew that was one memory that wouldn't hop out and say hello. Or if it did, my sanity wouldn't be around to say, *Right back at you, buddy.* I'd be catatonic or I'd be a killing machine with no memory of Cal Leandros at all.

Either way, I wouldn't know about it. Smooth sailing into crazy world.

"Hey, boy, didn't you work in Miss Terrwyn's diner?"

"No." I didn't bother to look at the gas station guy as I continued with my business of pumping gas. Nevah's Landing Cal would've said, *Hey* or *Nice day. Caramel-apple-pie day at the diner.* That Cal was gone, and, to me, this Cal in the here and now, this guy was just an annoyance.

"Ain't that Ralph James's car?" he persisted.

With vocabulary skills worse than mine.

"No," I repeated without interest.

I finished up, paid him, and left. Whether he called the cops or not didn't much matter. He might not. People here were so friendly that when faced with bad manners, and I could fucking dish out bad manners, they struggled over whether you were a dick or took what you said at face value. I'd said I was all about the manners on that building roof with Niko before I'd left; I simply hadn't said what kind. Again, it didn't matter. I wouldn't be here long.

I drove with the lights on, piercing the night, and "felt" for my kind, truly my kind. I was Auphe, but only half, and so were those brothers and sisters I was looking for. It took about forty-five minutes of driving before the feeling grew strong enough to have me bouncing the car down a road that had never been paved and probably never would be. The house revealed in the headlights was nearly hidden by trees drowning in Spanish moss. I stopped the car in front of the place. It was old, two stories. If it had ever been painted, I don't know what color it had been. It was gray now, the gray of termites, mice in the walls, and dead possums at the side of the road.

The porch was still standing with a dim light on, hard to believe, and with a man in a rocker. He looked up when I slammed the car door. He had short ginger-turning-white hair—snow on the mountain as they said here. His skin was dark and spotted from the sun and he had a wide yellow smile. It was the man whom I'd caught a glimpse of when working in the diner. He'd walked past, with pale orange hair and Miss Terrwyn's stamp of wickedness on him. I hadn't known Miss Terrwyn long, but in that time she had always been right. This one proved it. "Well, there you are, Mr. Caliban. They told me to wait for you, but I didn't know it'd be so long." He jerked his head back and forth hurriedly as if they could see him or hear him. He didn't know then . . . about his masters. The Auphe were gone—the true Auphe. . . .

"But I'd have waited. For as long as it took. I'm Jesse, but what few people I see call me Sidle, 'cause I'm so good at sidling out of sight when I have to." He put down the book he was reading, a Bible—no understanding that one unless he probably skipped to the smiting parts. Yeah, I could see that. Mmm. *Got to love me some smiting,* he'd say. Not righteous with the Lord—any Lord—but Keeper of the Flock.

"They're inside. Waiting for you. I kept them all alive. Can't say they're happy, but that wasn't the point, was it? Keep them here, good and miserable, until you came and showed them what misery really is." I saw a spark of red in his eyes flare then, buried behind the I'm-a-good-dog facade. Takes a thief to catch a thief, a killer to catch a killer, an Auphe to watch the Auphe. Here was another failure—an Auphe without teeth. Worse, an obedient, fawning one. They would've despised him even as they used him. "Go on. Go up and see for yourself. Taste that pain, ripe and juicy, and show 'em worse."

Keeper of the Flock. Keeper of the Fucked.

I did. I walked past him, not wasting words on him. What would you say to something like him? Inside, the first floor was empty except for rotting furniture and a kitchen with a huge humming refrigerator stocked to the gills with raw meat. It wouldn't do to let the brothers and sisters starve while they were waiting for me to show up years later. *My toys,* the Auphe had said. *My failed brothers and sisters.* And what do you do with failures? The Auphe had told me that too. You "play."

Even monsters knew, all work and no play . . .

Upstairs was one open area. I flicked on the lights to see a long-ago ballroom with boarded-up windows, boarded then banded with rebar. The room was lined with cages, although one was empty and long so from the lack of blood and the accumulation of dust. Good old Watch-me-Sidle had lied about keeping them all alive. One had apparently not survived his tender loving care. Considering what was up here, a lie was the least of his sins. Eight cages and that was where they were, the failures. The cage bars weren't just vertical, but horizontal too. The guard downstairs didn't trust them to do the job, though; the prisoners also had chains anchoring them to the wall. The manacles had been on their ankles so long that flesh had grown over them in spots. That was why they were failures. They couldn't travel; they couldn't make a gate out of this hell. My traveling was the only reason the Auphe had needed me. I'd been the first one capable of that. I was the first breeding program success—which meant they'd all been here longer than twenty-three years. God knew how long that was. There were seven of them—all naked. Some male, some female, but it wasn't easy to tell. Some were more Auphe in appearance than human. None looked completely human, not close. Hair hung to the floor in a matted mass, some Auphe silver white; some ordinary human brown or black. Some had gnawed their hair off until it hung just long enough to cover their face. The stench was unbelievable, so god-awful that my sense of smell cut out immediately.

"Brother." The one in the closest cage looked up. His eyes were light blue, not far from my own gray, shining through the tangled black hair that hung in his face. He was pale too. He had black hair like me, pale like me, eyes close to mine. And then he grinned. The hundreds of sliver thin metal teeth were brighter than his eyes. And the eyes were no party when you looked into their depths. They were the eyes of something rabid. There was someone home in there, but you didn't want to know who it was, what it was, or what it would do to you given the chance. "You have come. Let us go. All of us. We are family. We will hunt and rip and tear and kill."

We didn't share the same mother and most likely not the same father. There had been hundreds of Auphe when I was young. Plenty of sires to be had. We weren't family . . . but when you were the last of a race, albeit a created perversely, twisted hybrid race, were they that wrong to say we were?

The others echoed him, a murmuring bloody wind. "Hunt, rip, tear, kill." Claws, Auphe black or torn human nails, clutched at the bars. I guess the Auphe hadn't told them that all the hunting and killing was the kind I was supposed to do to them. No, that wouldn't be right. That wasn't the Auphe way. They'd have told them all right—wanting them to suffer, but sometimes you forget what you don't want to know. I had. So had they. All they wanted was freedom—the freedom to kill until they didn't have the energy to kill anymore. Rest and then kill again until they could find nothing left to kill. Then worse—they would breed. The Auphe would live again . . . in a way—distorted and less, but killers all the same.

The Auphe had been wrong. These offspring were far more the success than I was.

Yet more than twenty-three years of living hell. It was hard to blame them. I looked at them all, every face. Red eyes and dark skin. Blue eyes and jagged metal teeth. Silver eyes, silver hair, blackened teeth and nails, and every yearning, murderous face was the same—as Auphe as the Auphe themselves had been; murder given life; homicide given a host.

Some things done can't be undone. Some things made can't be unmade.

Monsters who had been tortured would've been monsters who would have tortured if things had ended up with me the failure behind the bars and them loose on a world full of human sheep. "Kill, brother." The first one wore a crust of dried blood over his mouth. "So tired. We are so tired of dead flesh fed to us. We want the real prey. We want to bury our teeth into the living and tear it away and bathe in the blood. Let us out, brother."

Some things once done can't be undone.

More echoes: "Brother, brother, brother, set us free. Brother, brother, brother, brother."

Some things made can't be unmade.

"Brother, brother . . ."

Shit happens.

"Brother . . ."

"I have only one brother," I said as I shot the first one in the head.

The others were harder. They were thrashing, trying to climb the walls, the ceiling, but in the end they were only fish in a barrel in their tiny cells. There was another good, down-to-earth country saying: shooting fish in a barrel. I was patient, aimed at the spaces between the bars, and in ten minutes they were dead, every last one. I made sure. When they were lying on the floor unmoving, I double-tapped them all. Triple-tapped, I guessed—the first one that had put them down, followed by the two in the head just in case. I ejected the mostly empty clips and filled the Eagle and Glock with fresh ones.

They wanted freedom. Now they were free in the only way they could be. It was the best I could do for them. The only thing I could.

I went back down the stairs, thinking who was the lucky one? The failures or the success? Those upstairs or me? At the moment I didn't have an answer. It could've easily gone the other way. Very easily.

Out on the porch, Warden Sidle was shifting from foot to foot, nervousness showing in the speed of the movement. I didn't see it—the back and forth shuffle, because I didn't bother to look at the worthless shit, but I could hear him. That was fine, because I had no particular desire to see him at all. "That was quick, Mr. Caliban. Did you enjoy yourself? The masters said it was important you enjoy yourself, so I kept them for you. A long time. A real long time. And when they screamed, and they screamed up one helluva commotion, I taught 'em better. Splash of acid. Hot poker through the bars. I kept them safe for you. I kept your playthings safe."

Playthings.

I put a round through his head, still without turning— I have great peripheral vision.

His body fell hard onto the porch. I heard the splatter of brains and blood hitting the weathered wood as I kept walking. He hadn't been worth words before. He wasn't even worth a glance now. At the car I pulled out the full plastic gas cans I'd bought at the gas station—because I'd known how this would turn out. I'd known from the very beginning. I spread the gas around the base of the house. It wasn't long before it was in flames, the entire structure. It was how Vikings had gone out, given up the flame to the gods—usually in a boat, but I didn't have a boat, so a house of nightmares would have to do.

I got back in the car and I watched it burn, lighting up the night. I watched my family burn. Until I heard the sirens, I would stay and continue to watch. Better safe than sorry. I didn't have as much hair to offer now, but I took one of my knives and sawed through a four-inch-long lock. When friends die . . . when family dies, you cut your hair and you mourn. So I'd been told and so I now remembered. I held the dark strands outside the window to be swept away in a bonfire-heated drift of air, my hand soon empty.

My hand—the hand of something new and something old and something unlike anything on this earth.

That was what the healer who'd tried to fix me had said I was. I never forgot that. Who would? In a fog of amnesia, I'd thought all monsters were an abomination, because there was some part of me that thought *I* was an abomination. I'd been called that more times than I could count—by the supernatural, by my mother. Why should there not be a piece of me that thought the same?

But I was wrong.

I'd always been wrong about that. It was time to retire that word, because I wasn't an abomination. I was the Wolf I'd killed my second day back in New York. She'd evolved to be what she was. She had choices, but some of those choices were defined and limited by her genes. It was the same for me. I was what I was. That little boy who'd learned about death by grieving for a dead blackbird was long gone; he'd evolved. And the Cal from the past week ...

The Cal that could've been, should've been, but never was—he was gone as well. It was as if he'd never existed, and in actuality he never had. He hadn't been a reality, only a possibility—more like an impossibility, a dream. A good dream, but only a dream ... as genuine as he'd felt, as real and right as the choices he had made—for Nik and me. You can fight the world, but you can't fight yourself. You can't deny yourself. Not forever. It didn't stop me from cutting another lock of hair to let fly, for him this time—for the better Cal, the one who couldn't exist for more than a moment in our world.

He'd been more than the good guy he'd obsessed about. He'd been a hero. He was worth mourning. That was something I couldn't say about myself, but I could say this:

I was Caliban Leandros of the Clan Vayash.

I was Caliban, Auphe.

I was something new and something old and something unlike anything on this earth. I was the only one. I sat in the car as the house burned eight others like me to less than blackened bone.

The only one ...

Now.

I heard a voice again, tickling at the base of my brain. It wasn't the one that had warned me about monsters and abominations, the one that had warned me most of all about myself. This one was still me, though, but it was the other half of me . . . or more than half. Souls . . . How to divide them up? Who knew? Listening, I heard the voice whisper sly and satisfied as I watched the fire rage on:

So much for the competition.

ABOUT THE AUTHOR

Rob Thurman lives in Indiana, land of cows, corn, and ravenous wild turkeys. Rob is the author of the Cal Leandros Novels: *Nightlife*, *Moonshine*, *Madhouse*, *Deathwish*, and *Roadkill*; the Trickster Novels: *Trick of the Light* and *The Grimrose Path*; and the novel *Chimera* and its sequel (to be released later in 2011), *Basilisk*.

Besides wild, ravenous turkeys, Rob has three rescue dogs (If you don't have a dog, how do you live?)—one of which is a Great Dane–Lab mix who barks at strangers like Cujo times ten, then runs to hide under the kitchen table and pee on herself. Robbers tend to find this a mixed message. However, the other two dogs are more invested in keeping their food source alive. All were adopted from the pound (one on his last day on death row). They were all fully grown, already housetrained, and grateful as hell. Think about it the next time you're looking for a Rover or a Fluffy.

For updates, teasers, music videos, deleted scenes, social networking (the time-suck of an author's life), and various other extras, visit the author at www.robthurman.net.

Read on for an exciting excerpt from
Rob Thurman's new science fiction thriller,

BASILISK

Coming in August 2011 from Roc.

On the day a ten-year-old girl killed Stefan, he didn't see his life flash before his eyes.

It's what they say you'll see, but not him. Clichés, who needed them?

That this was the second time in his life that he'd thought the same exact thing would've been worth mentioning ... if it wasn't for the actual process of dying. That tended to be distracting from pithy observations. He was aware that he was lacking in the last thoughts, much less last words department. He knew ... but what could a guy do?

Life is like that. Sooner or later, it boils down to, What the hell can you do?

His brother, Michael, had once told him that when he had no hope, he dreamed of sun, wind, and horses. It was part of his past—in a way—the best part. Every night he dreamed of them. Sun, wind, and horses. When Stefan had no hope, because dying doesn't leave a person much, he saw the same.

Sun, wind, and horses.

Stefan felt his heart stutter and skip. He wouldn't have thought that one or two missed beats would hurt that much, but they did. Invisible fingers of agony fastened around that beating hunk of muscle and squeezed once, twice as his lungs staggered in sync—then red, as scarlet as a field of poppies, bloomed behind his eyes, and he was on the beach. There was pale sand, pounding waves, and a sky so blue it couldn't be real. It was a child's painting, carefully covering every bit of the paper. Blue and dense enough that you could probably scrape a thick peeling of color away with a thumbnail. He could smell the salt that stung his nose, feel the water that soaked his legs and the warmth of the horse beneath them, the coarse mane he hung on to as he galloped through the surf. There was a wind in his face that made him feel that he could fly. It was one of those moments no one forgets. The exhilaration, the sensation of wind, water, and sun branded forever in the mind of the fourteen-year-old kid.

He couldn't see his brother, but he could hear him laughing. Behind Stefan, he was on his own horse, sharing the adventure. It was a great memory, there, then—before the blood. Before the red coated the rock and sand, it was better than great, it was the perfect memory. The strippers in his old Mafiya haunts didn't beat that. Even the first time he fell in love didn't beat that. Didn't come close.

The next flash was when he'd saved his brother ten years after his abduction on that same beach. Stefan didn't see him through his own eyes this time. He wasn't Stefan anymore. He *was* his brother. He saw himself from his brother's point of view—a stranger all in black standing in the doorway of his prison, then pulling him out of a place of horror. He felt his confusion, his lack of trust, but years of brainwashed obedience had him allowing the grip on his arm and the tug and run to freedom. The gravel and glass under his bare feet, the pain of the cuts, the ear-ripping explosions of firing guns, and the stars, Stefan felt and saw it all. Pain, blood, and flying bullets, he'd thought that would be what would stick with the kid—Michael—but it was the stars he remembered the most. The students . . . the prisoners . . . of the facility weren't allowed to wander the ground at night and they didn't have windows in the small cell-like rooms. Death behind him, and, for all he knew, death in front of him, but it was the stars that he saw. Far from any city, deep in the Everglades, the sky might be the color of a Reaper's cloak, but Death's robe made the ideal background for a hundred stars.

Brilliant light that shone down on you and could almost make you believe in miracles.

A light that could almost make you believe escape could be real and life was more than being trained to kill, turned into a weapon with no will of your own.

A light that was worth dying to see.

Only Michael had it in him to think that, which was unbelievable, too. A wonder. He was a good kid. A damn good kid. The best. Even dying, Stefan knew that as well as he knew anything in the goddamn world.

Michael left the bullets and the stars behind. The next was a string of emotions: fear, confusion, exasperation, more confusion, bewilderment, denial, annoyance, finally a reluctant acceptance and a sense of belonging. All those emotions had been caused by Stefan, and while he wished the ones at the beginning could've been avoided, he was damn proud of the ones he felt . . . that his brother felt at the end.

Aside from emotions, there was also life in the world outside a concrete/razor-wire wall. Movies, TV, books, people that weren't instructors or torturers, restaurants, pizza, girls, a smelly ferret, making his own decisions—a life. A real life, something he'd thought impossible. And family, something he thought a fairy tale. Michael had been stunned by that. Amazed. He had family, a concept that even a genius like him could barely comprehend and never have imagined applied to him. Someone cared about him. Someone told him he belonged. Someone would give up everything for him. Someone would give up *their* life for him. He wasn't alone.

He had his brother. He had Stefan.

Almost impossible to believe, but it was true.

If someone could like dying, Stefan liked that he was reliving Michael's life and not going through a rerun of his own. This way he didn't have to wonder if he'd done good by the kid, done good by his brother, he knew. He absolutely *knew* he'd done good. No doubts. Not a one.

The kid could've done better than him, he thought in disjointed chunks as he faded further into the darkness, but it was something, it was . . . what Michael thought so fiercely as that Reaper's cloak wrapped tighter around Stefan. Family. Brother. You always watched out for your brother, even if he was the older one. You held on to your family because having one was a luxury no one . . . *no one* could afford to take for granted. You didn't let your family down and you didn't let you brother down, no matter how many times he called you a kid.

How did Stefan know that? How did he know what his brother had experienced thought by thought years ago? What he was thinking now? How did he know Michael felt that way—even down to his annoyance at being called a kid? How did he get that last gift?

That's easy.

Because on the day Stefan died, that kid proved what his brother had known all along.

That damn kid . . . he was a miracle.

"Hey, kid. I'll take a black coffee, large. I need something to keep me awake in this boring-ass town."

I didn't bother to look up from my book resting on the counter. "I'm not a kid." I repeated that every day to my brother, not that he listened. I turned a page. My name was actually Michael, but I couldn't tell the customer that, couldn't tell anyone that. "And it's already waiting for you at the end of the counter. That will be three fifty." I'd seen him come in, a flash in the corner of my eye and heard his loud voice from the sidewalk long before he'd entered. If he were a regular, I'd have given him my immediate attention and the service-friendly smile that exactly echoed the one of the former employee of the month, whose picture was framed on the wall. It was the right kind of smile . . . friendly but not too stalker-friendly. It said, "I make minimum wage, but it's a nice day, and you seem like a nice person. How can I help you?" It was natural, nonnoteworthy, and appropriate for the job. It took me two tries in the bathroom mirror to copy it, and I'd used it for every patron since the day the coffee shop had hired me. It was the expected smile—the normal smile.

It was important to be normal.

Very important.

This tourist was my first exception. He'd come in every day for a week, ordering the same thing, tipping the same amount—nothing, and saying the same insult: boring-ass town. Cascade Falls was not a boring-ass town. It was a nice town. It was small and inconspicuous and no one had tried to kill me or my brother here yet. That made it the perfect town really, and I wished that this guy's new wife—it had to be a new wife, he wasn't the camping type—had planned their honeymoon elsewhere, because I was tired of hearing him carp every morning. I was tired of him period.

Also, only my brother could get away with calling me kid.

The man, five foot ten, about forty to forty-three, mildly thinning blond hair greasy with the sheen of Rogaine, hazel eyes that blinked with astigmatism or too much alcohol the night before, twenty-two to twenty-five pounds overweight, and with a small crease in his earlobe that indicated possible heart problems due to his body's inability to cope with his diet, glared at me over the top of sunglasses he hardly needed on a typical Oregon day in the Falls and tossed down three dollar bills and two carefully fished for quarters. He snorted and flicked the tip jar with a finger. "Like you caffeine pushers do anything worth a tip."

He made his way down to a cardboard cup of coffee, still steaming, that was waiting for him, grabbed it and headed for the door. I could do something worth a tip, quite a few somethings, if that was his complaint, but I doubted he wanted to experience any of them. Although, making him impotent on his honeymoon would be a poetic punishment. . . .

I shook my head, clearing it. Simply because I could do certain things didn't mean it was right. I knew right from wrong. My brother Stefan had commented on it once—that I knew right from wrong better than anyone raised in a family of Peace Corps pacifists descended from the bloodlines of Gandhi and Mother Teresa. Considering how I'd actually been raised, he said that made him proud as hell of me. Proud. I ducked my head down to study my book again, but I didn't see the words, only smears of black ink. Stefan was proud of me and not for what I could do, but for what I refused to do. It was a good feeling, and while it might have been almost three years since he'd first said it, I remembered how it felt then—and all the other times he'd said it since. It was a feeling worth holding on to.

Stefan also said that despite his former career he

knew right from wrong too, but before he found me he was beginning to lose his tolerance for it. It was a lie—or maybe a wish that he could actually do away with his conscience. He was different. He'd worked for the Russian Mafiya. He'd done bad things to . . . well, probably equally bad or corrupt people, but the weak too. The weak always get in over their heads in dark waters. What Stefan had done, he didn't want to tell me and I didn't push, but I did my research. You didn't work as a bodyguard in the Russian mob like Stefan had and still not do some serious damage to people who may or may not deserve it.

Regardless of that and regardless of the things that Stefan had done for me, under that ruthlessness to protect, and the willingness to kill if that's what it took to keep me safe, there was a part of him that wanted to believe in a world that was fair. He wanted to believe that a concept like right and wrong could be viable. Despite all he'd done and had been forced to do, he wanted to believe. Stefan had heart and he didn't even know it. Why else would he search for a kidnapped brother for ten years when his . . . our . . . own father had given up?

Older brothers, especially ex-mobsters, weren't supposed to be more naïve than their younger ones, but Stefan . . . sometimes I thought that he was.

If he hadn't spent almost half of his life looking for me and doing what was necessary to finance that search, I wasn't sure what Stefan would've been. Not what he was, I did know that. When I had been taken—such a simple word—it had ruined lives, and when it came to Stefan, when I had been abducted it had done more than ruin. It had done things I wasn't sure there were words for. And when it had happened, it had changed my brother as much as it had me—which wasn't either right or fair. But true as that was, we were both alive and free now, and that was a thousand times more than I'd ever expected or dreamed. Where I had spent most of my life, freedom wasn't even a concept, only a meaningless word to be looked up in a dictionary.

My brother had made it mean something. Cascade Falls was part of that, which only made me wish I had made that tourist pay for his contempt. And that was a slippery slope. I concentrated on my book and the words swam into focus. I was close, very close to what I was searching for . . . it was only a matter of months or maybe weeks, I hoped. Seven years of a normal life before I'd been kidnapped—although I couldn't remember them, ten years of captivity—which I remembered with stark, vivid clarity, and nearly three years of freedom, freedom to do research and now the time was almost right. I was almost there. All the more reason to learn more and do it faster.

"Parker, you're always studying. If you're not going to college, why bother?"

Parker wasn't my real name, but Serafynna didn't know that. Then again, Serafynna didn't know how to spell her own name and that made me doubt she cared that my name was actually Michael. Or Mykyl. When it came to Serafynna, I wasn't too sure that wasn't how the letters popped up in her brain. I wasn't sure Serafynna had a brain at all without an MRI to back that up. All that Sera, the nickname was much simpler and it didn't make my mind twitch, knew was how to put whipped cream on top of the lattes and how to flirt. To "mack," or hit on guys. Since I didn't know who Mack was, I went with the other one. Hit. That was more modern than flirt . . . hit on guys. Whatever.

Saving brain cells for important information outweighed saving them for teenage slang.

In three years I'd learned about flirting and sex, but

now . . . nineteen closing in on twenty, I liked intelligence in girls or women. Sera was entertaining and let me know my hormones were working at top capacity because she was gorgeous . . . hot, I meant. Hot is what someone my age should say, but she didn't have it all. I'd come to find out that I needed smart too and Sera had everything except that. She had sunshine bright blond hair—fake, big, turquoise eyes—fake, and she bounced wherever she went. That meant certain things, also fake, on her bounced with her as she went and rarely stopped bouncing. The first time Stefan had met her, he waited until I got off work that night and took me to the drugstore for a box of condoms.

I told him I didn't need them, and he told me I was an idiot if I didn't want to play in that sandbox. I was nineteen, he said with a grin, and that's what nineteen is all about. Knock yourself out.

But I didn't. I saw her fake colored contacts and thought about the one I wore that turned my one blue eye mossy green to match the other one—two fakes don't make a reality—thought about her lack upstairs of anything but whipped cream, and it seemed like a waste. We'd lived two years in Bolivia before we came to Cascade Falls. I'd played in sandboxes there, whatever Stefan said. It wasn't like I was a virgin. But I'd had the experience . . . experiences. I'd been seventeen before I'd gotten to make my own choices, even a single one. Now that I had three years of making decisions for myself, I wanted to be sure that each one I made now was the best one I could make.

Sera did bounce in a very intriguing way though.

"I might go to college someday," I said, turning another page. What I didn't tell her was that I was going to the equivalent of college and then some. I had the knowledge base for a medical degree with a specialty in biogenetics with an emphasis on polymorphism and pseudogenes, and a PhD in biochemistry and neurology.

Theoretically.

Nineteen and a doctor three times over, but it was amazing what you could learn when you can hack into the computer system of any university in the world. Computer hacking had actually been the easiest thing to learn. It was pretty boring.

I'm smart, I know.

The question was: Was I born that way or *made* that way?

"College sounds like a lot of work." Sera's voice brightened. "Except for the parties. I'll bet frat parties are fun. Maybe I should go. My parents keep bitching at me to since I graduated." She pushed up to sit on the counter, against the rules, but I was reading. Technically I shouldn't notice.

And technically my eyes didn't wander to technically not watch her bouncing . . . lying to yourself can be fun . . . when I saw past her to the television in the break room. What I saw on it made Sera's whipped cream skills and bouncing vanish. The sound was turned down, but I saw him on the small screen. I saw a man I'd never expected to see again. His face with that enigmatic smile that could save your life or far more likely put you in your grave: Stefan's father.

My father.

Anatoly Korsak.

Dead.

I told Sera that I felt sick, and then I went to the bathroom and threw up, nice and loud—no finger needed. Genetic skills, I had them in spades. And you don't tell stories you can't back up. You always do what needs to be done to provide evidence to support your deception. I hadn't learned that from Stefan. I'd learned it at the Institute—the place where Stefan had rescued me. The Institute had thousands of lessons and some still hung around. Lingered—when I was awake, when I was asleep, they most likely would my whole life. When it came to making people think what you wanted, a small amount of those lessons were harmless, the rest considerably less so, but all were efficient.

My trip to the bathroom got me a "Shit, Parker, sweetie. Are you okay?" from Sera and a call to someone else to replace me. Ben Jansen. Ben liked the bouncing even more than I did. Or that Stefan said I should.

Stefan . . . he should know better. He shouldn't have done this. There was protective and overprotective then what Stefan practiced. Now this. Anatoly. It had to stop. Three years free and twice I'd saved his life; it was a two-way street now. He had to trust me with the bad as well as the good. I wasn't a child anymore. I could carry my own weight.

The coffee shop door shut behind me and I started down the sidewalk with my hands in my pockets, heading to my car. It was seven years old, gray and a Toyota. They were virtually invisible. That was Mob and Institute knowledge, oddly coinciding. Low tech meets high tech with the same purpose: clean getaways. Although the Institute expected if you did your job adequately no getaway would be necessary. I guessed we'd fooled them, because Cascade Falls was a clean getaway so far.

In the distance I could see through the trees the silver glint of the Bridge of the Heavens crossing the Columbia River. When we'd picked this place to live, Stefan had quirked his lips. "Bridge of the Heavens," he'd said. "How about that, Misha? That must mean this is Paradise." Sometimes he could be a little thick, my brother. He didn't always get that everywhere I went outside of the Institute was paradise. If there was actually a hell, the Institute would make it seem like paradise too. But while I thought certain people deserved hell, I doubted it was that easy. Life isn't. I didn't think death would be either. But I didn't tell Stefan any of that, because he was right. No matter how many paradises you went to, they weren't the Institute. They were all, in the end, paradise. Maybe Stefan wasn't so thick after all.

"Hey, kid. Smart-ass. You get tired of ripping people off with your high-priced shit?" The words, tainted with bile, came from out of nowhere or nowhere if your attention was off and mine was.

It was the tourist. He was sitting on the wrought-iron bench, always freshly painted sky blue, outside Printz's Bakery. He had a cheese Danish the size of a four-year-old's head in one hand and a smear of buttery cheese on his chin. Nope, no doubt—his body had its work cut out for it taking care of him.

But it wasn't my job to take care of him, unlike his unlucky heart, and I ignored him and kept walking. That was normal too. I was a teenager, and teenagers usually aren't polite to annoying people. Or assholes. Stefan would definitely say he was an asshole. He wouldn't be wrong.

"Smart-ass, I'm *talking* to you." I'd only just passed him when there was a hand grabbing my arm to give me a shake and from the smell he'd put something in the coffee after he'd left the shop. Cheese, alcohol, coffee, and natural halitosis, I'd smelled better things and I'd smelled worse. People smell worse on the inside than the outside.

The Institute had had anatomy classes and enough cadavers to make Harvard Medical School jealous. The Institute taught its students to hurt people, taught them to use what had been stamped on their genes. But I'd never wanted to hurt anyone. I'd never wanted to kill anyone. The thought of killing even in self-defense had made me sick ... once. That didn't mean I wasn't forced to learn.

The Institute also had biology classes. One thing they taught us in biology is that as adolescent males grow, the production of testosterone increases, and so do levels of aggression. The natural kind that gives you the instinct to protect yourself if attacked. Three years ago I wouldn't have hurt this on-my-last-nerve irritating tourist. I wouldn't hurt him now. He wasn't a threat, despite being much bigger than me. But although I wouldn't, it didn't mean I wasn't slightly more tempted now than I would've been when I was younger—that my temper wasn't running hotter now than then.

Slippery slope, I repeated mentally to myself, same as in the coffee shop.

"Alcohol is bad for your liver and not too great for your stomach either," I said as I pulled my arm free. His eyes widened, he dropped the Danish he was still holding in his other hand, and I backed away quickly. I made it in time as he bent over and threw up on the sidewalk. I'd done the same to myself earlier, but not quite so ... explosively. I couldn't say he didn't deserve it. Out of range and unsplattered, I turned my back on him and kept walking towards my car. I heard him vomit one more time, curse, and then vomit again. He would chalk it up to strong coffee, whatever alcohol he'd put in it, and the Danish. After all, what other explanation could there be?

Well....

Other than me?

He was fortunate I wasn't more like my former classmates. If I had been, that one touch of his hand to my arm, that hard shake he'd given me—I could've ripped holes in his brain, torn his heart into pieces, liquefied his intestines. That's what I was. A genetically created killer, lab altered, medically modified child of Frankenstein, trained to do one thing and one thing only.

All with that single touch.

Isn't science fun?

R0008

MADHOUSE

by

Rob Thurman

Half-human Cal Leandros and his brother Niko aren't
exactly prospering with their preternatural detective
agency. Who could have guessed that business could
dry up in New York City, where vampires, trolls, and
other creepy crawlies are all over the place?

But now there's a new arrival in the Big Apple. A
malevolent evil with ancient powers is picking off
humans like sheep, dead-set on making history with an
orgy of blood and murder. And for Cal and Niko,
this is one paycheck they're going to have to earn.

"Stunningly original."
—Green Man Review

Also Available in the Series
Moonshine
Nightlife

**Available wherever books are sold or at
penguin.com**

R0011